the

message

catcher

Praise for The Message Catcher

"With *The Message Catcher*, Darryl McGrath has written a beautiful, nuanced portrait of trauma, grief, and resilience that challenges our culture's tidy linear conceptions of mourning. What it means to love someone, to lose someone, to fumble ahead in the days and years that follow, is all captured in an intimate and gracefully written novel sparked with hope. The hope doesn't negate the pain, which McGrath conveys with breathtaking frankness. But she also conveys the light along with the darkness — the joy that seizes her protagonist, Davie, in fleeting moments on her trek through mountains both literal and figurative. The result is a deeply moving journey."

Amy Biancolli, journalist and author of
Figuring Sh!t Out: Love, Laughter, Suicide, and Survival and
House of Holy Fools: A Family Portrait in Six Cracked Parts

"*The Message Catcher* is a gorgeous piece of writing that explores the rings of grief that encircle the grieving and demand our passage on our journey to a new home. In this, McGrath rightly presents how the magnitude of loss must echo out and be heard before you can bring it in and rebuild. A lovely novel, with great depth, to be read by all."

Marion Roach Smith, author of *The Memoir Project:
A Thoroughly Non-Standardized Text for Writing & Life*

"Deep love and deep loss thrum throughout Darryl McGrath's poignant and heartfelt novel, which reads with the revelatory quality of a memoir. In telling the story of a young wife whose husband dies while saving her life, McGrath takes the reader inside the real world of sudden widowhood with clarity and insight, making its trauma palpable. But its recovery is equally palpable. A must-read for anyone who has loved and lost and learned to live again."

Bridgett M. Davis, author of *Love, Rita* and
The World According to Fannie Davis

"Darryl McGrath's *The Message Catcher* offers an unflinching, unforgettable portrait of a woman who, after confronting unbearable tragedy and loss, learns how to continue living. It's a novel that powerfully explores the challenging, winding paths of recovery, letting us see the ways friendship, love, and the natural world can help lead us toward healing."

Edward Schwarzschild, author of *In Security* and *Responsible Men*

"For Davie, the narrator of *The Message Catcher*, grief is a journey to complete, a puzzle to decipher, a scar to bear, a stone to carry. But none of those metaphors are enough to contain it. In a story both raw and tender, Davie finds grief, at last, to be a teacher, guiding her to embrace a life of meaning and passion not despite a loss, but because of it."

Akum Norder, journalist and author of *The History of Here: A House, the Pine Hills Neighborhood and the City of Albany*

the
message
catcher

a novel

Darryl McGrath

Published by
Darryl McGrath

For information, contact Darryl McGrath
themessagecatcher@aol.com

Library of Congress Control Number: 2024926741

9798218576691 (print)
9798218576707 (epub)

Page iii illustration: Whip-poor-will (Black Oak, or Quercitron. Quercus tinctoria.),
by John James Audubon, published in *The Birds of America, Vol. I,* 1840, accessed from
The New York Public Library, General Research Division, https://digitalcollections.nypl.org

Whip-poor-will cover painting by Mark Joseph Sharer
Text and cover design by Laurie Searl

This book is set in Adobe Garamond and Poor Richard.

For Jim and Ellen,

with love and gratitude

Prologue

By the time the first anniversary of Michael's death came and went, Davie thought she must have told the story of how he died more than one thousand times. She knew it wasn't really that many times, but that was how it felt.

It was a good story, meaning a compelling one; that much she knew. Especially so if you could step back and look at it from the perspective of the people hearing it for the first time. It was guaranteed to keep people on the edge of their seats and then reach for their wallets to pull out their credit cards and make a donation to the host organization. This was why the local United Way asked her to speak at three different fundraising events almost immediately after the first anniversary, apparently having waited that long out of some sense of decorum associated with the first year of mourning, and with apologies for pressing her to do so. Why didn't she tell the United Way to go to hell by Round Three? She knew it was because she was still under the spell of the phase she now thought of as the "Grieving Widow Good Girl."

She felt back then that it was very important to be gracious and magnanimous and patient because she was terrified of people falling away from her, of seeing them pull up short, speechless and aghast, if she let the depth of her anguish and anger show. The recipients of such an outburst at the United Way would surely have reeled back from the intensity of the venom spewing forth as she unloaded her grief and fury at the world and told them they could find someone else to serve as a prop. So, she made the three appearances and kept her remarks to the sanitized version of events. She must have been effective; during the second event, she saw one woman at the back of the audience sitting bolt upright in her chair with her fist pressed against her mouth, an expression of absolute disbelief in her eyes. A sure bet to pull out her wallet and pledge her retirement account to the United Way, Davie thought at the time.

Michael's story, the last great story he never told, the story he never knew the ending to, was the story of how he died saving her life. He came from the Irish, a people renowned for their storytelling, and he was the storyteller extraordinaire, the person who could hold forth at any gathering as he recounted a yarn from his childhood, or an encounter with a politician, or a scene from a favorite book or movie. He could tell these narratives in a shape-shifting rollout of accents as he switched back and forth from one character to another. He was an astonishing mimic; he could nail someone's inflection and accent on the first take.

But one of the countless points over which she darn near killed herself that first year was the unanswerable question of whether he knew for sure that she survived. He might have known that she was stable but still on her way to the hospital, but she would never know if he knew *for sure* that she got there alive. So, she imagined him somewhere else now, reaching the climax of this particular story, and then stopping, looking slightly bewildered, as he realized that something was off, that his audience was somewhere else now and could no longer hear him, and she could see him puzzle over this and then ask, "You mean that's it? I don't get to know if I saved her life?"

No, Michael, you do not get to know, but you did save my life, and now I have to live with that fact, she told herself more than once, and often in a surprisingly savage inner tone of voice. She wasn't angry at Michael; she was angry at fate.

Was it a drowning? She could tell that was what her listener usually wondered when she said that her husband died saving her life on vacation. She used to think that would suffice, but she learned that people wanted to know, even though they would never, ever ask. Apparently, asking how your husband died was an inexplicable taboo, widely regarded as off limits and just plain impolite, and Davie found this baffling in a country where people routinely asked and revealed so much.

So, she got used to volunteering the answer, which got easier with the passage of time. She could have said that her husband died of a heart attack, because that was the medical term people understood—easier than acute coronary syndrome, or even cardiac arrest. But saying that Michael died of a heart attack was a disservice to him, because that was such an incomplete description of what happened. As that first year slowly unfurled, she found that she wanted others to know the full story, whether or not they wanted to hear it. Michael deserved that much, she thought, to have his story be told, a story of heroism, of cool-headed courage in the face of terrifying circumstances. For it was really his story more than hers.

No, it was not a drowning, but a few hours earlier, it might have been. It was a chaotic sequence of events that started out slowly and then accelerated. It was a surreal unraveling that Davie remembered first as a sensation of time drifting almost to a halt, followed by a feeling she later would liken to a terrifying, out-of-control, off-the-road spin, like a car rolling over an edge and down an embankment and flipping again and again as it bounced into a ravine. Emotionally, it was the equivalent of a train derailment. It was all of those sensations in one package, a wreckage of her life so jarring and so complete that for a long time, she wished she didn't survive the crash. She genuinely wished she and Michael had died together in the car on that back road on the Cape; the paramedics and the cops would have figured out what happened.

Instead, she survived, and Michael died, when she was the one who originally was dying. It was an impossible story to imagine. The second of three grief counselors she consulted in the first year, an otherwise inept therapist who clearly found it difficult to talk about death—despite the fact that she was supposed to be an expert on the topic—told Davie that the story of how Michael died was what counselors called a "catastrophic loss." That was the only thing that woman said that resonated with Davie. She couldn't have put it better herself.

She did not remember parts of that night at all; there were blank spaces she could never recover. What she did remember was a waking nightmare that played out in the gloaming of one of the most beautiful summer days Davie ever saw, two traumatic and horrible hours which left her feeling gutted, and which also left her—at age 43 and after ten years of marriage—widowed.

The First Year

chapter 1

Later, when Davie looked back at that September day, she would remember several of the people she encountered at different times through what would have been, under any other circumstances, just another gorgeous day on vacation. Had the day ended as it began, in the cottage she and Michael rented just off Route 6 in Truro, it would have been indistinguishable from countless other days they spent on the wild, rural far end of Cape Cod, a landscape of dunes and scrub pines and an unobstructed horizon that melded into the distant edge of the ocean. She probably would not have remembered the day at all.

Instead, the fifteen hours that marked the last day of Michael's life started with Michael getting up that morning and calling to her from the bedroom, "Hey, it's high tide. Let's go to the beach," and ended with Davie standing over his body in a room of the emergency department of Cape Cod Hospital. Afterward, it was impossible not to go back over every mundane activity, every conversation, every brief encounter of that day, except for the parts she could not remember and did not think she ever would. This went on for many months.

She never again saw any of the people who crossed paths with her that day: the couple on the beach who could barely conceal their amusement at the spectacle of Michael directing her to pick up the blanket one more time and put it down exactly perpendicular to the dunes as he endlessly adjusted its alignment. The girl at the counter of the seafood takeout place on the Wellfleet wharf who, at Davie's insistence, showed Davie the box of gloves used by the kitchen staff so that Davie would know for sure they were not latex, because Davie was allergic to latex. The attending physician who stepped out of the cubicle during the resuscitation effort so that he could explain to Davie why it was time to stop trying to bring Michael back. The nurse who came down the hall of the emergency room toward her, a terrible expression on her face, when fifteen minutes earlier she was calm and reassuring about Michael's failure to appear, even though Michael was following the ambulance in his car and there was no logical explanation for why he never showed up at the hospital.

The memories of those exchanges and encounters spaced throughout the day took on an exaggerated and poignant significance, driven by Davie's determination to fill in the gaps, the parts she lost. Davie imagined herself tracking the people down months later and asking them, *Remember me?* The doctor and the nurse would have total recall. So would the snickering couple on the beach. Was there some hint that Davie missed that early in the day, back on the beach? Was there some aura radiating from Michael and her that would have made someone look a second time at them, as though sensing that one of these two people would be dead twelve hours later? The girl at the window of the takeout place, who almost certainly was back in her home country in Europe a few days after Michael's death during the Labor Day week, would have stared at Davie and shaken her head, frowning. No, how could she be expected to remember a thirty-second exchange at the window of a takeout clam shack with a line fifteen feet long, at dusk? She'd probably never even seen Davie's face clearly in the glaring lights under the awning. But she did show Davie the box of gloves, and Davie did read, "Latex-free 100% vinyl gloves." Of that, Davie was very sure.

Such microscopic mental reconstructions were, Davie later learned, a common experience for people who survived a traumatic incident. Those reconstructions were part of the desire to keep replaying the *before* and *after*, wondering how you could not have seen what was coming at you. The concertgoers or the dancers in a club before someone let loose with a gun. The fire in a high rise when some got out and some did not. The juncture in the mountain road with a cluster of vehicles carrying frantic neighbors trying to outdrive a wildfire, and life or death depended on whether you turned left or right. Davie replayed the night endlessly, looking for some clue, something she could have done differently, always stopping at the point where she realized that maybe there was something she could have done differently. She never got past that point in the mental video; she just hit rewind. She knew rationally that there was no reason to blame herself, but the blame always came back anyhow.

They went to the beach that morning, a bay beach that Michael especially loved. They were four days into their week on the Cape. It was

Wednesday, two days after Labor Day. They never planned anything for their Cape vacation; they never raced around to historic sites or museums or special restaurants. They cooked at the cottage most nights, after a day on their bikes or on the beach, and they usually picked up seafood at the market down on the wharf. They took long walks at twilight on the beach, sometimes on the ocean side and often on the bay side. One night every year during their week on the Cape they went down to a bay beach late at night and skinny-dipped in the moonlight.

They had had their late-night nude swim three nights earlier. Now, in bright sunlight on the same beach, they stretched out on the blanket after they got out of the water. Michael brought some work from his job to read, even on vacation. He was forty-six years old, the executive director of a well-known social-services nonprofit organization in Albany, New York. That was the Evening Star Agency, and it advocated for the homeless, for low-income people in the region and for better affordable housing. The agency ran a youth services division and an adult shelter for homeless men and was trying to start one for women—against opposition from the city, neighbors and businesses that did not want to see more services for homeless people concentrated in one area.

Michael was well known in Albany and reporters frequently sought him out for comments. He was a steady presence during public hearings before city, county and state legislators; and he also regularly contributed commentaries on the local public radio station, in the state capital newspaper and occasionally the *New York Times* or the *Wall Street Journal*.

He was unsparing in his testimony and public comments; he often told elected officials where to get off, in an acerbic tone and a beautiful style of speaking and writing. He could evoke obscure economic theories in a flash, summarize a complex situation at a moment's notice, do mathematical calculations in his head, pull up a salient literary reference and quote the late Senator Daniel Patrick Moynihan and the late Speaker of the House, Tip O'Neill, both of whom he admired. He was an unabashed socialist in his approach to public funding, and he was respected but not always liked by the people with whom he clashed.

He came from a blue-collar part of Boston, a cul-de-sac of triple-decker houses in an old neighborhood that was very much an emblem of the city at that time, a mix of every second- or third-generation immigrant culture that ever landed in Boston. Saint Elizabeth's Hospital, where Michael was born into a mid-sized Irish Catholic family, was a few blocks from his childhood home. His father was a union carpenter who worked on the construction of some of the modern landmark buildings in Boston in the 1960s. His mother continued as a floor nurse at Saint Elizabeth's even after the four children were grown, until she and Michael's father died in a car accident on Storrow Drive in a snowstorm when Michael was in college. That was the coincidence that Michael and Davie discovered on their first date: in young adulthood they both had lost their parents in an accident. Davie's parents died when they went down in their Cessna over the southern Berkshires on a flight to the Adirondacks. Davie's father was at the controls. Davie was twenty-eight at the time, an only child.

Michael came of age in Boston during the busing crisis sparked by a court-ordered school desegregation plan that J. Anthony Lukas chronicled in his Pulitzer Prize-winning book *Common Ground*. Michael never saw the violence that played out in South Boston, however, when people threw bricks at buses carrying black children, because he graduated from the Boston Latin School. Boston Latin was one of a handful of high schools in Boston that required an admissions test, and it was already integrated because its student body came from all over the city. A head-fucking factory, Michael later called it, where he sat as a scared and silent eleven-year-old in the auditorium on his first day and heard the head of school actually tell the assembled incoming students to look to their left and then to their right, because one of them in that set of three new students would not graduate. Both students sitting on either side of Michael graduated, as did Michael, and they all became good friends.

A photo of Michael with a group of his Boston Latin classmates roaming around Brighton on a Saturday afternoon during their senior year of high school hung in Michael and Davie's home. Davie called it the "Junior Goodfellas Photo," because everyone in the photo wore the cocky faces of young hoods getting ready for trouble. In truth, they were just harmlessly rambling around one Saturday afternoon on their way to a soccer game, even though they looked like they were about to jack up some cars and take the tires.

Davie knew these stories well, because she and Michael traveled to Boston at least once a year and he always drove her around his neighborhood in Brighton and took her to all his old haunts, inevitably running into someone he knew. She got used to seeing a barely concealed double-take on the faces of these people—friends of his long-dead parents, former teachers, high school friends who never left Brighton—because Michael was a wild party boy in high school, the last guy you would have expected would get married at all, or even leave Brighton. And Davie was so obviously a good girl in the stylishly classic way she dressed, her manner of speaking, her careful decorum—the type of woman these acquaintances could never have imagined Michael introducing as his wife—that she could sense Michael's hidden delight at the additional surprise that introduction elicited.

Davie majored in mathematics in college, got her MBA a few years later, then started a career in finance, but not initially in the money-making end of finance. She was at the Community Loan Foundation for a long time before starting a new position with a private financial services firm. She was good with numbers, but her real skill lay in translating complex technical material into readable material.

Michael joked that one of them needed to make a living wage at last, now that they realized they couldn't much longer postpone the work they needed to do on their ramshackle old house in the city's historic district. That really was a joke; his salary as executive director at the Evening Star Agency was quite decent, but Davie's new position promoted her into a six-figure salary for the first time in her career and guaranteed that they quickly could pay off any loans that financed renovations. Of the two of them, Davie was much more temperamentally suited to handle the job she landed. As with her work at the Community Loan Foundation, she was part of a team that oversaw several client accounts. Unlike the Community Loan Foundation, the clients at the new job were all small rich companies, some with shareholders and some still privately held. Davie's employer went by the name of its three founding partners, Levellewyn, Grenoble and Carl, P.C., and it provided a wide range of hand-holding tasks for the clients, from working up long-range investment projections, to doing all the preparation for shareholder meetings, to writing marketing strategies or white papers for their products.

Davie met Michael twelve years earlier on a hot July night at a party in the apartment of a friend of Davie's, Jay Baldwin, whom she knew in high school in New York City. Davie and Jay ended up in Albany after graduate school—an MBA with a concentration in economics and finance for her; a master's degree in conservation biology for him—and they reconnected there. Jay worked for an environmental agency that did data analyses and field work for clients, including the U.S. Fish and Wildlife Service. Jay and Davie ran around together a lot in their single years, when each sometimes dated someone else and both often needed a sympathetic listener and advisor after breakups.

Davie got to the party a bit late. She went directly there from a rare late Friday at her office, so she was still in the skirt suit and dressy flats she'd put on that morning. As she walked to the front stoop, she saw a tall, burly man standing on the sidewalk in profile to her, deep in conversation with another man. He wore a small backpack slung over one shoulder, with a stance suggesting he was settled in for a long conversation. She could hear his baritone voice and see him gesturing, but she couldn't pick up exactly what he was saying as she went up the stoop. She figured he was either coming or going. The party spilled onto the back deck and the fire escape to escape the stifling heat in Jay's third-floor apartment. The man Davie saw on the sidewalk stepped onto the fire escape, looked around, spotted her, and without further ado walked over and introduced himself as Michael Devlin.

Later, when they were a couple, Davie asked him what made him seek her out that night. He spotted her coming down the sidewalk in a quick sideways glance, he said, and he noticed two things about her: the suit, and her purposeful, confident stride. He thought she might be on her way to Jay's party, even though she was dressed for a board meeting. He saw with another nonchalant glance that she turned up the stoop of Jay's building. He knew everyone else who would be at the party, so he went inside, threw his backpack on the couch—he carried it to and from work, instead of a briefcase with a strap like the men in Davie's office—pulled Jay aside in the living room, described Davie, and asked if she was there and where he could find her in the crowd. Jay pointed him to the back bedroom, which led to the deck and the fire escape.

"How did you know what I looked like?" Davie asked him. "You only saw me for a second when I was going in. You must have eyes in the back of your head."

"I sure did that night," he said.

They left the beach at noon, after one more long swim and a walk toward the jetty so that Michael could practice skipping stones. He spent a whole college summer perfecting his stone-skipping skill when he worked as the assistant to a shellfish warden in a South Shore town, while he waited for the shellfish warden to come back from his four-beer lunches at the local tavern. That was also the summer Michael learned to skipper the warden's boat, because letting the warden do that most afternoons after lunch would have been suicidal.

Michael and Davie went back to the cottage, showered, put the bikes on the car, ate leftovers for lunch and drove to Provincetown. They parked at the entrance to town in the first open parking space they saw at the bottom of Commercial Street, pedaled as far as the wharf, locked the bikes and went their separate ways. Michael would walk down the wharf and spend a long time looking at the boats, watching the horizon and breathing in the salt-marsh scent that he loved. Davie would buy an ice-cream cone and work her way down the rows of boutiques and art galleries. She was buying a book in a shop way up Commercial Street when someone rapped on the window from outside and she looked up and saw Michael. She gestured, *Give me a minute*, paid for the book and met him outside, where he stood with his hands in his pockets, looking up and down the street with an expression of great serenity. For all that he loved his job, he often found it stressful, and even now, on his week away, he put in some time every day on work from the office. He answered emails at the town library—he refused to bring his computer on vacation, and the internet connection at the cottage was very spotty—so she was glad to see him look so relaxed.

"Ready to head back?" he asked. "I thought we could just drive down to the wharf and maybe get a snack down there later and skip cooking tonight." He loved to wander around at the far end of the wharf and watch the fisherman loading their boats and tinkering with tools as they prepared for their next trip.

"That sounds good." They were standing close to each other, about to unlock their bikes, when Michael opened his arms wide apart, his signal that he wanted a hug, and Davie moved to him and felt him wrap himself around her.

"You make me very happy," he said. "Marrying you was the best thing I ever did in my life."

She pulled back, still in his arms, and looked up at him.

"Wow," she said. "We ought to go on bike rides more often." She tucked back into his embrace. "Are you OK about how last month turned out?" she asked with her head turned to one side against his windbreaker. She briefly thought earlier in the summer that she might be pregnant just before her forty-third birthday, frantically thinking *Dear God, please no*, when she counted and realized that she was more than a week late with her period. Two tests were negative, and her doctor told her that a bad cold that ran on for several days, coupled with worry over a looming project at her job and the fact that she missed two days in the office because of the cold, could have thrown off her schedule. Michael chuckled.

"Oh, more than OK," he said. "Forty-six is a bit late to be contemplating how I'll teach a kid to play soccer with these knees." He was a varsity soccer player in college and, as he liked to say, he had the knees to prove it.

The wharf in Wellfleet was packed with families with young children, and they circled the big parking lot near the harbor master's building twice before they found a parking space.

"It's after Labor Day. Don't these children go back to school?" Davie asked as they got into the line at the takeout window. "There can't be that many home-schoolers in Massachusetts."

"I think school starts Friday, or Monday . . . apparently not tomorrow," Michael said. "Let's split a lobster roll." They ordered a small order of oysters on the half shell, the lobster roll, and two lemonades.

"Do you use latex gloves in the kitchen?" Davie asked the girl who took their order.

"No, we do not use the latex gloves," the girl replied in careful, slightly accented English. A lot of the businesses on the Cape hired summer help from Europe on special visas; the mostly young summer waitresses and cooks were overwhelmingly from Ireland and the former Soviet republics. "We use only the vinyl gloves."

Davie knew to never take anyone at their word about latex versus vinyl. In this way, she had avoided having a latex reaction for many years. The first reaction occurred in college, a few hours after she and some friends ate dinner at a restaurant in New York City during winter break. Back home, Davie broke out in hives around her mouth, and she felt light headed and congested. Her parents insisted on taking her to the emergency department. A likely allergic reaction, the doctor told them, and she recommended testing with an allergist. Two weeks later, and before Davie underwent the scheduled testing, her hands broke out in itching red blotches when she used a pair of latex gloves while cleaning the bathroom in her new apartment off campus. The allergy testing confirmed a latex reaction and Davie began carrying two EpiPens. Fewer restaurants used latex gloves now, but Davie always asked to see how the box was labeled, following a time when she was told a restaurant used vinyl gloves. An hour later she needed to inject herself with the EpiPen. When she called the restaurant back the next day, posing as a customer about to book a reservation, the staff member told her that yes, they used latex gloves in the kitchen.

"Could you please let me see the box?" Davie asked now, pointing through the window to where the box sat on the counter. She realized that the girl thought Davie didn't trust her English. "I know you said those weren't latex gloves, but I would like to see the box, please . . . thank you," and the girl offered her the box, and Davie read that the gloves were latex-free and one hundred percent vinyl. She nodded, gave a thumbs-up sign to the girl, smiled and thanked her. She and Michael carried the lemonades over to a table near the pick-up window and watched the scene on the wharf. The sunset looked almost artificial, the sky was streaked with orange and pink, long rippled bands of color that started to pull apart even as they watched, and then the late-afternoon cloudless blue began to fade.

"Did you talk to Andrea before we left?" Michael asked. Andrea Sorensen was Davie's best friend of many years and the friend who stood up for Davie at their wedding. They met when they worked at the Community Loan Foundation, and Andrea still worked there. She and Davie talked or emailed each other several times a week.

"No," Davie said, frowning. "You know, I was thinking about that earlier today. I think the last time I heard from her was . . . last Tuesday or Wednesday, maybe? I meant to call her, but I just got so busy trying to get out of work."

"Was she even around last week?" Michael asked. Andrea was a serious long-distance backpacker who disappeared for at least two weeks every summer in her quest to hike the Appalachian Trail in sections. She had started this project years earlier, and she was more than halfway finished. Davie understood very little about Andrea's quest, but she did understand that Andrea was hiking from Maine to Georgia, instead of the more usual Georgia-to-Maine effort.

"Oh, she was around," Davie said. "She did her big hike for the summer back in late June. She just probably got busy with something at work. I'll check in with her sometime this week."

"How much did she do this year?" Michael asked. He liked Andrea very much. Davie had only two close friends in Albany now who predated her marriage to Michael: Andrea and Jay, and Michael, of course, knew Jay before he knew Davie. The other friends from Davie's single years at the Community Loan Foundation either lived somewhere else now or drifted out of Davie's life when they got married and started to have children. With her own marriage, Davie became part of Michael's group of friends, most of them couples. Her present job was not one in which she expected to make many friends; the atmosphere of the place squelched the kind of socializing or casual conversation that led to office friendships.

"She hiked one-hundred and eighty miles in fourteen days, of which twelve days involved actual hiking," Davie said. "She hiked an average of fifteen miles a day. She took two days off in those two weeks."

"Jesus!" Michael said. "How the hell does she do that?"

"She says it's the Viking in her ancestry, only she's going by land, not by sea," Davie said. She turned and looked at the flaming sun over the bay.

"It's going to be gorgeous tomorrow," she said. "What would you like to do?"

Before Michael could answer, he felt his phone vibrate in his pocket, pulled it out and muttered a few swear words when he saw who was calling. He got up to walk down the wharf, away from the noise, talking and gesturing with his free hand as he spoke. Someone from work, Davie thought as she watched him striding around some fifty yards down the wharf—he never stood still—and she thought she could have picked him out in a crowd anywhere. He was tall and imposing, bearded, with hair long enough to pull back in a pony tail, but he only did that for public hearings. If you didn't know what job he held, you could have just as easily placed him hitchhiking on a back road in Vermont. Michael cared less about appearances, less about trying to impress people, than anyone she ever knew.

He was sometimes difficult to live with; he was so passionate about his work and cared so much about situations he knew he probably could not change, that just listening to him go on about them at home sometimes got to her. But that passion radiated from him in other ways; it extended to his momentary acts of kindness to people whom everyone else just swept by without noticing. He often said the janitor in his building at work, a man named Reuben Diaz, should be placed on the board of directors at the Evening Star Agency, because he possessed better life experience and greater insight on the toils of working-class people than anyone else serving on that body, and Michael included himself in the "anyone else."

"Let's go for a walk on the beach," Michael said when he got back to the table. Davie put her paper cup and plate on the tray and looked at the sky once more.

"Ocean or bay side?"

"Ocean."

"Do we have a flashlight in the car?" she asked as they walked across the parking lot.

"Under your seat," Michael said. "I saw it there yesterday when I was looking for a strap for the bikes." The bikes were still on the car. Michael stopped before he unlocked the car, and he again held his arms wide and wrapped them around her when she turned to him.

"You know what that sky looked like back there?" he asked. "That's what seeing you for the first time was like. It was like seeing the ocean and the sky together, for the first time."

He always surprised her like that, offering a comment out of the blue that conveyed his passion far more than, "I love you." He often told her they would have been great friends as little kids, and he reinforced that sentiment by never using a conventional term of endearment for her, such as "darling" or "sweetheart." Instead, he referred to her as "buddy," and he rarely used her name unless he really wanted to get her attention or was referring to her in a conversation with someone else. She was never as expressive, although she felt every bit the same about Michael as he did about her. She stood for several moments, feeling his arms around her and smelling the salt-marsh scent of the parking lot stirred by the breeze coming across the bay. Then they got into the car, drove out of town and crossed Route 6. They went a short distance toward Provincetown and then turned onto a road that wrangled down to the ocean beach. Michael turned the radio on to the Red Sox game.

They were well down the road when Davie felt an itchy sensation in her throat. She started to clear her throat, but she couldn't get rid of the sensation, and then she couldn't even really clear her throat; she felt something thick and viscous and concentrated in her throat but she couldn't swallow it and she couldn't cough it up.

"Hey, are you OK?" Michael shot her a quick look. The road was very narrow, with high sandy banks on both sides, and it was dusk, so he was driving slowly.

She shook her head. "I don't know," she said hoarsely, finally beginning to cough. "Something doesn't feel right."

"They didn't use latex gloves, right? You saw the box?"

Davie nodded, because talking was suddenly very difficult. She fumbled in her tote bag; she kept some over-the-counter allergy medication in a little cosmetic bag along with two EpiPens, which she hoped were not somewhere else with all the switching back and forth that week from the cottage to the beach to the bikes.

"I think I must have breathed something . . . some pollen or something," she said, her voice rasping. Michael reached over and snapped off the game.

"You're having an allergic reaction to something," he said. "We need to go back, right? Just in case you have to get to a doctor. Do you have an EpiPen with you?" Davie nodded again, even though she wasn't sure, and pointed behind them and circled her finger in a pantomime of turning the car around. Yes, she wanted him to go back the way they just came. Whatever was happening, she did not want it to play out on this isolated road at dusk, where cell reception was so poor.

Suddenly, a sensation like nothing she could never before remember feeling came over her as it seemed a floodgate opened in her throat and fluid poured into her airway faster than she could swallow it. She felt like she was drowning; she couldn't draw a full breath. Her chest was as stiff as a wooden box, she could not pull in enough air, and she began to panic. But she did not want to panic Michael. She fumbled in the tote bag for the cosmetic bag, thinking, *Please don't tell me I left it in the cottage* . . . no, there it was. She unzipped it, felt the EpiPen in her hand . . . she thought she'd carried two, but she only could find this one . . . where was the other? Well, she only needed one. She pulled it out, but it was difficult to remember what to do. She hadn't done this in a long time, and her brain wasn't working at its normal speed. She needed to tell Michael to pull over so that she could get out and stand up, but she realized he was trying to turn the car around on that narrow road.

He couldn't; there wasn't enough room, and there was no shoulder, just the steeply banked sides, thick with underbrush. Instead, he stepped on the gas and kept going down the road toward the beach, faster than he would ever have driven even during the day. The surface of the roads that close to the water were always difficult to drive on, half dirt, half sand and a lot of potholes on the ones that were paved. She could feel the bikes bounce up and down on the rack. And then, just before full darkness fell on the road, he saw a driveway that he could pull into, a driveway that led to a house barely visible through the trees. It didn't look like anyone was home, and it was unlikely that anyone would be there; it looked like a summer home, closed up already for the winter.

Before he backed out to swing the car around, Davie put a hand on his arm and held up the EpiPen and opened the door. She had the cap flipped up, she spilled the EpiPen from the tube and got out of the car, leaning against the doorframe. She never even stood up all the way. She heard Michael ask her something. He was about to get out and come around to her, but she gestured for him to stay where he was, because he couldn't do anything to help her, and she wanted them to get up the road as soon as she finished. She pulled off the blue safety cap that prevented the pen from firing off prematurely, dropped the cap on the ground and swung the pen as hard as she could into her thigh, through her denim shorts.

She was supposed to hear a clicking sound that meant she had gotten a hit, that the needle had come out of the pressure-triggered tip and injected the medicine . . . did she hear it? It had either worked or it didn't; there was nothing she could do about it now. She fell back into the car, nodded to Michael and he pulled out, skidding on the road, and throwing the car forward. The EpiPen in her hand felt the way it should have after a discharge—the needle would automatically be covered by a blunt plastic tip released by the spring action—but it was so difficult to see in the dark interior of the car. Whether she got any of the medication into her system, she could not tell. She didn't feel any better. The EpiPen fell out of her hand; she no longer cared if she had gotten a hit or not, and it didn't matter, because once she had discharged it, she had no way to inject it a second time. Benadryl … maybe Benadryl would help … she thought she had some in her bag but she knew she would never get the little plastic bubble open. It had been so long since she had crossed paths with latex that she had stopped being vigilant every day, to make sure she was ready. Now she could hardly breathe.

"Michael," she said, very slowly. Her voice was very shallow and sounded distant. He jerked his head toward her and then back straight ahead, and reached for her hand as he followed the twisting, hilly road in the dark. "I know where we're going to go," he said, far more calmly than she felt. "Davie, we're almost there. Just hold on, please hold on, buddy."

"The police station up the road … go there," she said. She meant the Truro police station, and she knew it was miles away, but they were in an area with very few public services. You saw a cop car maybe once or twice a week at this end of the Cape. She didn't think he heard her. "Michael … go up to the police station up the road," she said again, but she could hardly hear herself. They did not have time to sit and wait for an ambulance, that much she knew. *I'm not going to survive this*, she thought with an astonished sense of watching the scene unfolding from somewhere else. Breathe in … breathe out … she tried to focus on just that, on just breathing, she wanted to take in a deep breath, fill her lungs, but she couldn't, and her field of vision was narrowing. She was dying, she realized with a dispassionate sense of calm. So this was what it was like … and then the car swung hard to the left; Michael was pulling in somewhere. Where were they? She could see a building, and lights, but the building was too far away, they would never get there in time.

Michael braked, flung open his door, he didn't even cut the engine, he just threw the car into park, and then Davie had her hand on the latch of her door, even before Michael could get to her, and she spilled out of the car, half fell, lurched forward, almost fell again … she could see the building now right in front of her, it must not have been as far away as she thought, but everything looked watery and blurred, like she was trying to see through a window streaked with heavy rain. She slumped up against the glass of the front door and tried to pound the glass with her hand, but she had no coordination; she just slapped her hand on the glass and dragged it down as she began to collapse. Then Michael was beside her, holding her up, and she saw a wavering figure moving to the door. A cluster of people gathered around her, she could hear them talking, asking questions, and she tried to answer but their faces were blurred and she heard Michael talking. That was the last thing she remembered, until she realized they were outside, and she could still hear voices around her, and she was on her back, under the glare of lights . . . she had no idea what just happened. She was trying to talk, but she couldn't form any words. Something was over her face, and she wanted to push it away, but she couldn't move her arms. Michael . . . where was he?

Michael gripped her shoulder. "You're going to be OK," he said, and that was the only thing she heard clearly. "You're going to be OK!" Davie was barely there, she couldn't feel anything, but suddenly she was surrounded by light and voices and she realized that she was in the back of an ambulance. And the ambulance was moving, turning. But Michael was not there, she knew he was not with her, because she would have heard him if he had been there.

Her head was clearer now; she could sense that the ambulance was moving faster, so she knew they must be going down Route 6 toward Hyannis. She still had the oxygen mask on, and she tugged at the sleeve of the medic bending over the IV line in her arm. When the woman looked up, Davie wrenched her hand free and tapped her wedding ring and held up her right hand, palm up, asking without speaking, *Where's my husband?*

"You husband is following us in his car," the woman said. Davie put her head back and closed her eyes. The headrest was at an angle, which was good, because she could not have breathed easily lying flat. Why didn't Michael come with them? Probably because he wanted to have the car to get her home, she realized. She was thinking in real time now; the sensation of watching herself was gone. She thought Michael would be with her in the ambulance, but he would soon be with her at the hospital. What the hell happened to her? This felt nothing like her three latex reactions of many years earlier.

The attending physician in the emergency department at Cape Cod Hospital couldn't tell her what happened, other than that she'd possibly suffered a severe allergic reaction. She was coherent enough by then to answer his questions; whatever they gave her in the ambulance worked, but she was listening for Michael's arrival as she spoke, and it was difficult to concentrate on the doctor and try to follow the sounds of people coming and going beyond the curtain.

"My husband should be here. I thought he was following the ambulance," Davie said. The nurse looked up from the monitor. "We told the front desk that he might try to call," she said. "People take the wrong turn coming off the rotary all the time. We'll get him to you as soon as he gets here."

The doctor tried to reconstruct what she did just before the reaction started. Davie told him she asked about latex gloves at the window. Well, the doctor said, they might have used latex somewhere else in the kitchen; old boxes mixed up with new ones even after they stopped ordering gloves made with latex. Or she could have crossed paths with something she didn't even know she was allergic to; that happened all the time, he said. Did she ever have a shellfish reaction before? No, never, Davie said. Did she get stung by an insect outside at the wharf? She shook her head; not that she remembered. Was she on any prescription medications? No. Did she take any over-the-counter medication, take any drugs, mix anything with alcohol? No, she kept saying, wishing Michael was there to field the questions. The doctor was trying to help her, she knew, but she couldn't offer anything other than the possibility that she crossed paths with the one thing she knew she was allergic to: latex. But this didn't feel like a latex reaction.

"It was so *fast*," she said. "The only times I had a latex reaction, it just wasn't like this. It . . . it snuck up on me. This just . . . I never felt anything like this."

"You may never know what it was," the doctor said. "You can become allergic to something at any time, even if you were never allergic to it before. You may have developed an allergy to shellfish. I would strongly recommend that you avoid shellfish for the rest of your vacation, and you should see an allergist when you get home."

They were going to give her something now to reduce the possibility that the reaction would recur—a rebound reaction, the doctor called it. He was going to write a prescription for something he wanted her to pick up in the morning as a further buffer against a rebound. He would also write a prescription for a pack of EpiPens. Davie tried to think what her insurance would cover . . . she thought she could get the EpiPen, because it was at least a year since her last refill. Then the nurse and the doctor left and told her to try to get some rest.

Davie nodded and lay back. She was exhausted, but she knew she would never fall asleep. She wanted Michael there. She debated calling him, and thought, no, he would call the hospital if he got lost, and if she called him, he would have to pull over to answer the phone and that would just delay him. He'd be here any minute. Besides, she realized, she didn't have her phone; she didn't have her tote bag or anything from the car. But it seemed that Michael should have been there by now.

It was astonishing how fast everything unfolded. A glance at the clock on the wall told her it was maybe an hour ago that the allergic reaction started. Davie kept thinking, should she call Michael? and she wondered if they would let her use an outside line. The nurse came back in then to change her IV bag.

"My husband should have gotten here by now," Davie said. "I think he must have gotten really lost. Or pulled over for speeding." She could imagine that, and she could also imagine Michael bursting through the double doors into the emergency room, a local cop following him, with Michael yelling, "You *see*, you asshole? I *told* you my wife was here. So you still want to give me that fucking ticket?"

"He'll be here very soon, I'm sure," the nurse said. She was an older woman who looked like she had been telling that to out-of-town vacationers who landed in the ER for more years than she could count. "OK, you are all set for a little while now. We'll send your husband right in when he gets here. I have to go help the doctor now."

Davie was too restless to lie down anymore. She sat on the edge of her cot, attached to the IV, and she thought again, this was ridiculous, Michael really should have been here by now. Maybe he'd gotten a flat, maybe he'd been pulled over—highly likely—or he overshot the entrance to the hospital and was trying to figure out how to circle back and get to the parking lot, in a town he didn't know at all, in the dark . . . it was easy to end up back on Route 6, heading back to Provincetown; she did that herself once, trying to meet a friend in one of the towns she didn't know as well at this end of the Cape. But this was way past the point of a reasonable delay. She was going to find the nurse and ask for an outside line. She didn't want to be told one more time that Michael would get there any minute now.

Davie got off the cot, pulled open the curtain, rolled the IV stand with her, and then stopped before she stepped out, struck by a sensation so pronounced, so disturbing, that she thought the allergic reaction had returned. Later, she would remember the moment almost as a physical awareness, the kind of invisible, instinctive warning that would make an animal jerk up its head and then run for its life. It was a profoundly oppressive feeling of despair, or fear; a certainty that something was terribly wrong. *Michael,* she thought, frozen in place. She just suddenly knew that something awful was wrong. A car accident . . . something. She needed to find the nurse. She stepped out of the room and saw the nurse walking down the hall, a look of appalled, grim determination on her face. Davie watched her approach, and she knew the nurse was coming for her.

"I need to talk to you," the nurse said. She took Davie's arm and steered her back into the room.

"Your husband is here," the nurse said without preamble. "He had a heart attack on his way here and he came in by ambulance. He is down the hall, and I'm taking you to him now."

Davie's knees buckled. The nurse caught her with surprising strength and held her steady.

"Come with me now," she said.

Michael was in a room three doors down, the door was open and the nurse brought her inside, to a scene Davie knew she would never get out of her mind. *Jesus,* she thought, *how long had he been here too?* Wires, tubes, monitors lit up everywhere in the midst of what struck her as oddly silent frenzy, because no one was talking. Everyone was intently doing something, but no one was saying anything. No one looked up when she entered, their concentration appeared to block out everything but the resuscitation effort. A nurse bent over Michael, pumping his chest like she was operating a pile-driver. They had cut Michael's clothes off, his legs were splayed and his arms hung down on each side, limp. The thought flicked through Davie's brain, *He would hate this*—meaning, he would hate to be undressed in front of all these strangers—and she moved forward, afraid to speak. The doctor—the same one who had treated her—was at the other end of the gurney.

"Can I take his hand?" she said. She was in such a state of shock that she sounded almost normal.

"Yes," the doctor said, without looking at her. Davie reached for Michael's hand, and then she knew. He was already gone, he had been dead for some time, his hand was already cool, it felt like there was no life in it, the skin was no longer pliable. The doctor would not have to tell her he was dead, she thought wildly, looking at Michael's still, peaceful face, the only peaceful sight in the midst of the silent frantic scene playing out all around him. And then she looked at the monitor behind him, and the line was flat, just a straight line across the screen.

Another nurse led her out and sat down with her in the chairs in the hallway. Davie could hear them shocking Michael, she heard someone call out, "Clear!" and then she heard them doing it again, and she realized that they did not want her to see that. Then the doctor came out of the room. Davie stood up and said nothing. The doctor looked as though no matter how many times he did this in his job, each time was like the first.

"He has been without oxygen for a long time," he told her. "We've been working on him for a half hour and we haven't gotten even a flicker of a heartbeat, and we don't know how long he was without oxygen at the scene." *What* scene, Davie thought. She stared at the doctor, having trouble believing what he just said, even though it was exactly what she expected to hear.

"What are you trying to say?"

"I need to tell you that even if we get his heart started, he's going to have brain damage. He's past the point where he's going to be the person you remember."

So Davie let them stop trying to bring Michael back, and someone led her back down the hall to the room where she was treated earlier. Later, she would wish she had gone into the room while they shut down the code and undid all the wires, the monitors, the tubes. She couldn't think, she could barely walk, and so she let herself be led away from Michael's room. She did not remember when her IV was disconnected, but it was no longer in her arm. The nurse who came to tell her about Michael said she was going to stay with her until the doctor could come back and talk to her. Davie didn't hear anything the nurse said to her, nor did she even realize that the nurse was with her. It was as if nothing could get past the shock of the last two hours.

<h1 style="text-align:center">chapter 2</h1>

A police officer showed up in the ER as Davie waited for the doctor, and Davie stood in the hallway outside of her room and listened as he explained that a passing driver saw Michael bent over outside of his car, hanging onto the open car door in a small commercial parking lot five minutes from the hospital. The person who saw him pulled into the parking lot because he thought Michael needed help. Michael collapsed before the police got there. The Good Samaritan was a volunteer firefighter, and he called 911 and did cardiopulmonary resuscitation while he waited for an ambulance. Michael never responded, the officer told her. They tried using the automatic external defibrillator while he was on the ground in the parking lot before the ambulance arrived, and they never got a heartbeat.

"Is there someone we can call for you?" the officer asked. Davie shook her head. She realized the officer found her silence unnerving. No, she told him, finding her voice. She couldn't remember what else he said, but later, she found his card in her pocket. He must have handed the bag with Michael's wallet and phone in it to someone; Davie later could not remember how it ended up with her.

"I want to go back in and sit with him," she told the nurse. "Can I go back to him now?"

"The doctor is going to come down and talk to you, and then I'll take you back to him," the nurse said. Even by the standards of what they must see every summer in that particular ER—drownings, the occasional shark attack, parasailing accidents, surfers hit by boat propellers—the nurse looked rattled, Davie thought.

Sudden cardiac arrest, the doctor told her. Acute coronary syndrome, which started with Michael's lungs filling with fluid, then progressed to a wild, erratic, quivering heartbeat and ended with his heart stopping when he collapsed outside of his car. How long? Davie asked. How long did all this take to play out? Because there was not even the slightest hint that something was about to go so horribly wrong during their time in the car; she was the one who was stricken. The doctor shook his head; he could not know. Did Michael complain of feeling ill? he asked. Did she remember him saying anything at the fire station? No, Davie hardly remembered what happened at the fire station. He might have had asymptomatic heart failure, the doctor said. People didn't always get any warning signs, or if they did, they dismissed them, never thinking it was something with their heart. Was he ever treated for any heart problems? No, Davie kept saying, her eyes dry and fixed on the doctor's face. She thought the doctor also expected her to fall over screaming and crying and pounding the floor. She was so calm that she thought he was evaluating her as he spoke, taking stock of her lack of visible reaction.

Did he have any history of heart failure in his family? Not in any of his brothers, she said, and his parents died some twenty-five years earlier. She never heard Michael say anything about his father having a heart condition. Michael never complained of fatigue, or shortness of breath, or anything that might have been a signal. Biting her lip, Davie told the doctor about making love with Michael that morning. Could that have brought this on? No, the doctor told her, highly unlikely. This was, tragically, the day that this was going to happen, and it could have happened earlier in the day, or later, with no certain connection to anything they had done or not done.

Except, Davie said to herself, he thought I was going to die in the car. If that wasn't enough to send his heart into overdrive, nothing was. The point was so obvious to her that she didn't even raise it.

"I'm so sorry," the doctor said. "We didn't know it was your husband until the police called the hospital after they ran your plate. He came in without any way to identify him." Davie still just stared at him. The situation was incomprehensible.

Why didn't the ER staff have Michael's wallet? Why did it take so long to figure out that her husband, whom everyone kept telling her would be right along, was down the hall from her for . . . how long? Even as she thought this, she realized the chance that the man without identification was Michael was so remote, so impossibly remote, that she couldn't blame anyone. The ER staff didn't care who he was; they cared about trying to get his heart started.

"Are you here by yourself?" the doctor asked. "Do you have any family here with you on the Cape?" Davie nodded her head yes to the first question and shook it no to the second. She could not begin to fathom how she would get home from the Cape under these circumstances. Nor did she want anyone there with her; she was too stunned to talk, too dazed to think.

"We'd like you to stay here tonight," the doctor said. "We don't think you should leave tonight." No, she told him, suddenly coming to; there was no way they were going to keep her there. She wanted to go back to their cottage. Where was the car? The police towed it to their headquarters, the nurse told her, and they could get a cab to take her there, but the nurse agreed with the doctor—she thought Davie should not leave.

"Will I be leaving against medical advice? I am well enough to leave? You will sign me out?" Davie asked them. She detected a quick, silent exchange between them, an acknowledgement that they would not be able to persuade her, then the doctor told her he would write out the prescriptions he wanted her to fill the next day. Was there someone they could call for her? No, Davie told him. She would call Michael's family in the morning. She wanted to leave. Did she want a chaplain to see her? No, she didn't want anyone else in the room with her and Michael.

So, they told her they would call a cab when she was ready, and then they took her back to the room where Michael now lay with a sheet drawn up almost to his face, his hands folded out of sight, a terrible abrasion down the center of his forehead, his eyes not quite closed. The nurse who led her in left and closed the door. Davie was sure the nurses would have tried to fully close Michael's eyes, and that made her realize more than anything the doctor said, more than the feeling of Michael's hand when she held it, that he was dead when he got to the hospital. He had been dead a long time, his heart stopped too long to bring him back, and the proof of that was in the fact that it was evidently impossible now to fully close his eyes, because she was sure the nurses would have done that for her if they could have.

Their wedding ceremony had taken ten minutes. In that same amount of time, Davie now stood by Michael's body, taking in every detail of his face, wondering what he hit when he collapsed to make that raw, wide scrape down his forehead, all with a sense of disbelief that she was looking at him for the last time. What in the name of God happened? She wondered if she would ever know. He never complained of feeling that anything was wrong, he never had any heart issues, he never smoked. Everything unfolded so fast that all she could fixate on now was the scene in the car, so frantically terrifying even as it was so preternaturally calm—the panic was all inside, and if Michael felt it also, as he surely must have, he never betrayed that . . . even in telling her to hold on, he was calm. What was it that he said? *I know where I'm going to go.* He must have remembered the fire station was at the top of the road, she realized. It was one of those anonymous buildings you drove past without usually noticing, but Michael remembered it was there. He took a chance that someone would be there, that the crew was not out on a call, that it was not a volunteer station, where everyone would have to converge from separate directions . . . he bet correctly, and he saved her life. *For what?* Davie thought. What good was it to her that she was alive, if he was dead?

Davie felt unsteady now, not ill, but just exhausted and ready to leave. It was too difficult to stay in the room any longer. This was the part of getting married that no one thought about, she realized with a sickening jolt. You could end up standing over your husband's body decades before his time and know you were never going to see him again. This day could crash upon you without warning, like a piece of marble siding falling off a building from ten stories up at the exact moment you were walking by, that sudden death from a medical event you never even *heard* of could just happen, *just like that.* Davie always thought they might have forty or more years together, and she never, ever imagined that their marriage would end like this, after ten years.

She bent to kiss Michael's forehead, above the abrasion, just at the edge of his curling, waving hair, and his hair still carried his scent. She thought if she kissed his lips and they felt like his hand felt, she would start screaming and she would never stop. She opened the door of the room, she turned and looked at Michael one last time, then she pulled the door closed. That sound of the door closing also seemed to close down any reaction in her mind; she needed that blank interior so she could get out of the hospital. The nurse waited outside the door to take her back to her room down the hall. Davie didn't even see her standing there.

The nurse who came for her originally, the older woman—whose expression was now an odd combination of compassion, tightly controlled distress and professional neutrality—gave her a voucher for a cab and led her to the front entrance of the hospital. Did Davie have another EpiPen? the nurse asked. Davie didn't know if she did. She never thought about where the second one was after Michael got her to the fire station. The nurse reminded her of the prescription for two more EpiPens the doctor wrote, and said Davie should fill them as soon as she could in the morning.

Did she have Benadryl? Yes, Davie said. The nurse told Davie to call 911 if she felt the allergic reaction starting up again; that could happen, the nurse said, but it probably would not be as severe on the rebound. She told Davie if she felt any symptoms return, she should take two Benadryl tablets while she waited for the ambulance. Davie thought, I hope it does start up again, because this time, I'll just sit there and do fucking nothing. That internal comment did not show on her face, and to the nurse, she nodded her thanks.

The cab waited at the front entrance to the ER. The driver took her to the police station, five minutes away, Davie handed him the voucher and then realized she didn't have money for a tip. She didn't know where her tote bag was, and the tote bag held the keys to the cottage and her wallet. She assumed everything was in the car.

"I'm sorry. I don't have anything with me," she said to the driver. "My husband just died at the hospital. I'm picking up our car, and I don't have my wallet with me. I don't know where it is." She said the words with a sense of disbelief. *My husband just died.*

The cabbie shook his head. "Don't worry about it, miss. You just get yourself back home safely. I figured something pretty bad happened."

Inside the station, a young police officer handed Davie a plastic bag that contained her tote, her wallet, her keys, the keys to the cottage . . . everything was indeed in their car. The officer handed Davie a second bag with Michael's keys and a few other items Davie didn't bother to look at while the officer spoke to her. She couldn't figure out why Michael's possessions were divided into two bags: the one the other officer gave her at the ER, and the one this officer now handed her, but she figured it had something to do with towing the car, needing his keys and then going through the car more thoroughly after it got to the police station. This officer at the station explained they went through Michael's pockets to look for identification, that they kept the wallet so they could call the hospital, and that was why the hospital didn't immediately know Michael's name. The officer asked if Davie felt well enough to drive. Yes, Davie told her. The officer told her how to get back to Route 6, and watched as Davie pulled Michael's Subaru out of the space in the lot behind the station where the tow truck left it. She found the signs for Route 6, toward Provincetown, and started the drive back to the cottage on the nearly empty road. It was almost one o'clock in the morning.

Somewhere after the Orleans Rotary, Davie let out a cry that was neither a scream nor a sob. The anguish, the shock, came from deep inside, and she pulled it up again and again for the remaining miles of the drive, until she turned off Route 6 and parked in front of the little white cottage with red trim in a grove of pine trees. By then, her throat was strained and raw. She sat there at the wheel, dizzy even though she was no longer moving, reluctant to open the car door. Before they'd left for Provincetown, she'd switched on the front light, anticipating they'd be coming back in the dark. Now a cloud of insects clustered around the glow. She needed to go inside, she realized; she could not sit there for the rest of the night. She couldn't remember if they left the cottage locked—they often did not, as there was nothing in it worth stealing—but the knob turned without the key and she slowly stepped inside, switched on the light in the tiny living room and looked around as though she expected to see Michael.

He was everywhere. His coffee mug and the book he was reading were on the table in front of the couch. His green duffle bag was unzipped in the back bedroom, his clothes spilled over onto the bed from when he rummaged through his bag that morning for his corduroy shirt. The *Boston Globe* from two days ago was folded on the table on the screen porch. His jeans were bunched over the towel rack in the bathroom. Davie walked through each room, in a state of shock at how her life had unraveled in just a few hours.

She walked into their bedroom. Had it just been yesterday morning— no longer this morning—that she'd sat up, about to get out of bed, when Michael had reached out to her? She'd felt Michael's hand reach over and slide down her naked rear, his touch surprisingly gentle, as it always was, but unexpected for such a strapping big man who was often so full of bombast. She thought very few people ever saw the tender side of him that he showed her from the beginning. She remembered how she turned at his invitation and got back into bed for fifteen minutes of snuggling and fooling around like a couple of kids on prom night—although, as Michael pointed out, that was a dated reference, because probably no high school kids in the United States were still virgins on prom night—and they both laughed as they felt each other's warm skin and began exchanging lustful kisses, hands reaching everywhere. A high school quickie, Michael called it, dated references notwithstanding; all that they lacked were the bucket seats of the '67 Plymouth Barracuda his father owned, he said. They both cracked up laughing again, falling back on the bed as they finally contemplated starting the day. Then Davie got ready to run out to buy the newspapers, as she did every morning on the Cape.

Now, she picked up the pillow on Michael's side and inhaled its scent. She buried her face into the pillow. How could everything be so normal and then turn so catastrophic? No warning. No possible way to know what was coming at them both.

She walked back through the cottage, back out onto the porch, and then, when she re-entered the living room—and after a few moments of looking around for something she could break—she instead hit the knotty pine-paneled wall with the flat of her hand so hard she almost lost her balance. Again. Again. Now she was finally screaming, real screams, long, drawn-out rattling cries of anguish at the top of her lungs, as she repeatedly hit the wall with both hands. She didn't know if anyone was in any of the other cottages, and she didn't care. She screamed until she couldn't get out any more sound, her vocal cords seemed to stop working, and her hands were numb.

No one came to the door to see what was going on, no headlights from a cop's car ever showed up in the front yard because someone called to report a disturbance. The secluded location of the cottage at least gave her that much privacy, which she would never have gotten in the hospital. They would never have let her do this there; they probably would have urged her to take a sedative. She slumped up against the wall and slid down until she was on her knees, her face pressed to the paneling. She wished with all her heart that if Michael had to die, that he'd never made it to the fire station. She wished they'd both died in the car. Probably no one would have found the car until the next day, so far down that isolated road, she thought. By then, she and Michael would be together, long past those terrible last few minutes of their lives.

❧

Davie and Michael married on a Friday in June ten years earlier. They sort of eloped, in that they both scheduled vacation days for Thursday and Friday, without telling anyone the reason except for the three people who met them at City Hall to be their witnesses: Davie's college friend Jay Baldwin, who was also a friend of Michael's before Michael and Davie met at Jay's party; Jay's girlfriend Alanna Smythe; and Davie's best friend, Andrea Sorensen the Appalachian Trail backpacker. Andrea had gone through a bitter divorce years earlier; her family was rich, and the division of the assets was nasty. The fact that Andrea really loved her husband, who fell for a woman fifteen years younger than he was, made it all the worse. The fact that he sought alimony, as he was allowed to do under New York law, because he earned less than Andrea and possessed far fewer assets—even though he was the one to leave the marriage—just cemented the anger, the vitriol, the prolonged court fight. Andrea tried to fight the alimony, to no avail.

Davie barely knew Andrea's husband, who did not seem to be in the picture much by the time Davie and Andrea became friends. But the divorce left its mark on Andrea, and she asked Davie if Davie really wanted such damaged goods as a witness to her wedding vows. Davie could not believe that Andrea used that term—damaged goods—and she thought she must have never realized how difficult that time was for Andrea. How would Davie have known? Such reactions were impossible to imagine, until Davie too planned to marry someone she really loved.

Davie wore a mid-calf-length silk skirt, taupe with a pattern of large abstract flowers with edges that bled one into the next, and looked like they had been painted onto the fabric by Georgia O'Keefe in the throes of a hangover. The skirt was her mother's, and Davie wanted something of her mother with her that day. She added an ivory silk tank top and an ivory-colored Dupioni silk jacket with three-quarter sleeves, both of which she also already owned. She and Michael by then were the owners of a very old house that needed a great deal of work, and this was a wedding on a budget. Davie wore mocha-colored vintage suede pumps with low heels that she also already owned. Michael loved those shoes, but she rarely wore them because she was never comfortable in heels of any height. Michael wore new khaki slacks, a blue linen shirt, a navy tropical-weight wool blazer and a pink tie, bought by Davie and decorated with a pattern of small periwinkle-blue flowers. Davie carried a cluster of peonies, made up for her as a special order by the flower shop on Lark Street. She didn't own a blow dryer and she let her wavy brown hair, now with a lot of gray threaded through it, dry on its own. She fastened a seed-pearl comb in her hair on one side.

They picked out a thick gold wedding ring for Davie with a vintage 70s feel to the design, angled planes all the way around the band. Davie wanted Michael to wear a ring, but she knew he would not. During their courtship, when they were far enough along that she thought she could buy him a significant birthday gift, she picked out a small emerald in a jewelry store and had it set in a gold stud earring, because Michael once expressed a desire to wear an earring. He put the box into his backpack after he opened it over dinner in her apartment, and then lost it. He never knew what he'd done with it; it probably fell out when he'd unzipped his backpack to look for something, somewhere in his travels around Albany. That was how Davie knew she really loved him; to any other past boyfriend, she would have delivered a patient, well-thought-out lecture about the importance of treating such a gift with consideration. With Michael, she realized, he really was the least materialistic person she had ever met, and she felt that he valued her greatly, so she never said a word about the lost emerald earring. She knew better than to ask him if she could buy him a wedding ring, but she asked anyhow.

"Do I need one?" Michael looked doubtful.

"Well, no, you don't need one as part of the ceremony. I just thought it would be nice to buy you one. I mean, you bought me such a great ring."

"I could borrow one from somebody at work and just have it for the ceremony," Michael said. He meant it.

"You are seriously not going to do that," Davie said. They never discussed a wedding ring again.

Their wedding day was a clear, mild, early June day. The bridal party converged on the steps of City Hall at eleven o'clock in the morning. Davie and Michael introduced the maid of honor to the best man, and they went up to the city clerk's office. He was finishing a telephone call at the front counter, so they waited for a little while, as Michael and Davie nervously smiled and nodded thanks to the congratulations and good-luck wishes of strangers coming and going in the office. Davie suddenly handed Andrea her bouquet and her little beaded bag and told Michael, "Don't start without me." She then ran for the bathroom on the other side of the great open stairwell that let you look down each floor of the nineteenth-century building into the beautiful old lobby. She had to pee, despite the fact that she had hardly eaten or drunk anything that day. She was full of excited jitters, that was the problem. In the bathroom, she looked at herself as she washed her hands, and thought she could not ever remember feeling so beautiful. She was not beautiful, she was unconventionally attractive, but at that moment she felt beautiful.

The clerk finished his call soon after she returned, he showed them into his private back office, richly paneled and with a window overlooking Academy Park, and ten minutes later he pronounced Davie and Michael wife and husband. Feeling starstruck and dazed, the newlyweds went outside in the noon sunshine, trailed by their attendants. A couple of teenagers, probably skipping school one last time in their senior year, walked by and Davie called to them from the steps.

"Catch!" she cried as she tossed her nosegay of peonies with an underhand pitch. The girl caught it and looked stunned.

"Oh, man, you two just got married? That's so cool!" She turned to her companion. "I caught the bouquet! You know what that means?"

"Yeah, it means my meter is about to run out," the boy said. "Let's get going." To Davie, he turned and yelled, "Thanks, lady! I'll never hear the end of this." They all laughed.

Davie and Michael and Andrea got into one car; Jay and Alanna into another. They drove to the Miss Albany Diner for their wedding reception, which consisted of them piling into a corner booth and recounting the City Hall ceremony in raucous joy. They ordered eggs Benedict, coffee and juice. For wedding cake, they all ate large slices of cheesecake with gummy, solidified fluorescent-red cherry topping, cut from the cheesecake in the case by the cash register. Davie asked for whipped cream on her cheesecake, because her nerves finally vanished and her appetite, which had disappeared two days ago, suddenly returned. The waitress grabbed a can of Reddi-wip in a fire hose grip and sprayed it all over Davie's portion. The manager of the lunch shift produced a liquor bottle from under the counter, poured five small measures into juice glasses, and brought the tray and the bottle over to their table.

Davie took a sip after Jay stood up to make a toast. She had trouble catching her breath because whatever the guy had poured, it was strong; the fumes filled the back of her throat. As she put her glass down, she again looked at her left hand. She loved the feeling of her wedding ring; it had heft and presence. She kept holding out her left hand and admiring it.

"Holy gee whiz," Davie said when she could talk. "I think this is single-malt scotch."

"It is," Michael told her. He knew a thing or two about single malt.

"Well, if I drink any more of this, you're not going to get much of a wedding night out of me," Davie said.

Michael put his arm around her and gave her a one-sided hug in the cramped booth.

"It's only one o'clock," he said. "You have time to catch a second wind. And I really don't give a damn about our wedding night. I'm so happy right now that really, I don't care. The hell with the wedding night. We're going to have a wedding life."

Standing now on the screen porch of the cottage, watching the day breaking and remembering Michael sitting there less than twenty-four hours earlier, reading the *Boston Globe* and drinking his coffee, Davie came to the end of reliving their sweet wedding day of a decade earlier. Her hands throbbed; when she turned them over, she saw immense spreading bruises covering her swollen palms, and she also saw that the skin around her wedding ring was puffy. She must have hit the wall harder and longer than she realized. She was surprised she had not cracked the ring. Flickering gilt light came through the pine trees around the cottage as the sun rose; it was going to be another beautiful day of September sky, high and clear and vaulted over the ocean.

She had not sat down all night, but she needed to sit down now, or she was going to collapse. She needed to start making phone calls. She felt that she was about to enter a period of her life so unimaginably bleak and desperate, that for one crazed moment she thought about just never telling anyone right away that Michael had died last night, and finishing out the rest of the week at the cottage so that she could delay dealing with all that she knew was about to befall her. The calls to Michael's family, the call to the Evening Star Agency, to Andrea and Jay and some other friends, and then her office, the funeral home. And because she consented to let Michael be a bone and tissue donor—which meant she also would forgo an autopsy—she expected a call from someone at the regional organ bank later that day. After that, she needed to start packing to get ready to leave the cottage. Then the long drive back to Albany. The obituary. The memorial service.

Everything she faced seemed too much to contemplate; she had been awake for twenty-four hours and had nearly died the previous night, something she somehow forgot until now. She felt like she was in the slow-motion version of trying to get out of a burning building, having realized that the only way out was in, the only way to escape was to try to run through the flames, because in this situation, there was no back door.

She could not believe that she would never see Michael again, that someone with his force of personality, his presence, his booming voice and his sudden declarations of passionate feelings for her could be dead. She stood on the porch and wondered if she was actually in the grip of a nightmare, and that she would wake up in bed next to Michael on the real Wednesday, not the dream Wednesday when he died, and that she would roll over, hold his warm naked body against hers and feel the horrible events of her nightmare slowly dissipate, with an overwhelming sensation of relief.

No, Davie thought, she was really awake, Michael was really dead, and she was alone in their cottage, about to start a day she knew would be second only to the one that preceded it for sheer unadulterated horror. Michael's words during their wedding toast came back to her.

"We're going to have a wedding life," she said to the sunrise, as though repeating that promise could make the previous night vanish. Then she turned and went inside.

chapter 3

Davie slept a total of twelve hours in the ten days between Michael's death and the memorial service. She thought this was about what you would expect for a new young widow whose husband died saving her life, and she was stunned at the number of people who offered her their own prescription sleeping medications, herbal supplements, pot, bourbon . . . she kept telling them no. She was infuriated that she felt pressured to defend herself for how little she was sleeping; it was no one's business. She also thought it was dangerous for people to hand out prescription medications, especially when she still didn't know the cause of her nearly fatal allergic reaction. But she kept her mouth shut and the offers kept coming, in phone calls and emails and even in a note tucked into a little gift bag left at her front door, with a plastic jar of something she was supposed to chew or smoke or brew like a tea. She tossed the bag and its contents. She didn't get any of these offers in person, because she allowed no one in the house until the morning of the memorial service, when Michael's family arrived from Boston.

An outpouring of responses would be coming at her once word of Michael's death spread; of that, Davie was very sure. She called Jay from the Cape the morning she drove home and asked him to post a note on the front door of the house that thanked friends and neighbors for their concern, but also explained that she was unable to receive any callers before the memorial service. She asked Jay to add that the date, time, and location of the service would be announced in the local paper in the next few days. In response to the note, people started to just leave at the door what they would have brought for a condolence call: unlit candles in glass votives, cards, small bags of chocolate, and even five boxes of macaroni and cheese mix. Davie went in and out of the house through the door under the front stoop, so as to avoid running into neighbors and having conversations she didn't feel like having yet. So she didn't immediately notice the growing collection of offerings, which looked like a sidewalk memorial after a death by violence. She cleared everything away the morning her in-laws were to arrive.

She decided she would not allow the house to fill up with callers, like a weeklong wake. She carried a bitter memory of her parents' huge New York City condo being taken over in the week after their deaths by family, neighbors and friends from her parents' workplace, none of whom ever asked Davie if she minded that her childhood home on Riverside Drive was now Central Mourning Headquarters. Her parents were partners in a law firm in Manhattan, they served on numerous charitable boards, and their deaths were a news story in the Metro section of the *New York Times*, so people kept coming and going. She also remembered that the funeral director deferred to her other family members about the arrangements; he talked to everyone else as though Davie was not even in the room.

Maybe they all thought she was too shocked and grief-stricken at being orphaned in one fell swoop to make decisions, but Davie thought they more likely viewed her as an adolescent still, especially the family members seeing her for the first time in several years. She was twenty-eight years old. She finally stood up during a discussion about how to handle the double funeral and told the gathering of lawyers from her parents' firm, her aunts and uncles and the scattering of older cousins—along with the two representatives of the funeral home—that she was making the decisions, not them. She then said everyone better start talking to her, instead of around her, or she would skip the funeral at the Episcopal church on Park Avenue, have her parents cremated and would privately scatter their ashes in Central Park on her own schedule. She actually said that, and a stunned silence followed, but after that the men from the funeral home directed their remarks to her.

That incident created a rift with her family that never healed and was one of the reasons she was glad Michael never wanted a formal wedding. Davie's side of the church would have been pretty sparsely populated. Michael's family found him sometimes baffling, and even annoying, but you had to hand it to the Irish: they demonstrated clan loyalty and they would have turned out in force for a church wedding. On the other hand, they seemed to have no problem with the semi-elopement to City Hall, and they responded with equanimity and sincere congratulations when

Michael finally got around to calling them a week later to tell them he and Davie were married.

Davie found the Devlins all remarkably easy to deal with, for all that she didn't know any of them very well. She realized they accepted Michael as the free spirit in the family, who drew on his blue-collar upbringing for inspiration when the rest of his family never considered their roots. Michael was the author of two books, one of them a carefully researched examination of the decline of America's middle class, and one a coming-of-age novel, a story so clearly based on his own upbringing in a working-class household that Davie sometimes wondered how his far more genteel, discreet siblings viewed that book. They never mentioned it. The novel contained a scene of a late-night bachelor party in an autobody shop where the younger brother of one of the guests lost his virginity to the stripper the guys hired for the night. Davie knew the story was based on a real incident Michael knew about from high school, although, as he always hastened to add, he was not *at* the bachelor party.

In the countdown to Michael's memorial service, Davie's phone filled up every day with calls, many of them from casual acquaintances who left long messages she didn't even try to listen to all the way to the end. Davie realized these people could not possibly know that fielding their five-minute one-way condolence conversations was far beyond her. She not only was barely sleeping, she was hardly eating. The logistics of planning a memorial service that might have six hundred people attending consumed any of her remaining energy, even with the help of Jay and Andrea. She arranged for a month's leave from her job, and she already wondered if that would be enough for her to ever get some sleep.

Jay secured the use of a renovated historic building on North Pearl Street with one entire wide floor set up as a space for large events. It was the former ballroom from when the building was a private home in the early twentieth century. A friend of Jay's managed the place, and he told Jay that Davie could use it for a nominal cost to just cover the staff needed to get the doors open, the lights turned on and the chairs and benches arranged. The funeral home staff would handle the rest, and the catering company setting up the reception in an adjacent room could use a small kitchen on the same floor of the building. Davie found it astonishing that such a large event could be pulled together in a week.

Davie also realized that her initial impulse to have a very small private service with just their closest friends and Michael's family was already way behind her. The decision to have such a large memorial service—something she thought Michael would have loved, however she felt about it—was more or less made for her by the fact that it seemed Michael knew everyone in Albany. He left a legacy, he did work that mattered, he made a mark on social policies in the city, the county and the state. Laws had been either amended or enacted because of his public testimony and his behind-the-scenes negotiations with members of the Legislature. Their congressional representative spoke about Michael on the floor of the House of Representatives the day after his death, so those remarks would be recorded in the Congressional Record. His death was a news story that also went out on the Associated Press wire—minus, Davie noted with gratitude, the specific awful detail that she had been the one expected to die, not Michael.

She was sure that the omission of the full story from the news coverage was simply because the reporters did not know about it, because they got their information from a statement released by Michael's employer. The president of the board of directors at the Evening Star Agency spoke to Davie before releasing the statement, which described Michael's death as an immeasurable loss to the city and the state. Davie did not volunteer anything about the chain of events; she just confirmed that Michael died of sudden cardiac arrest. But then she realized that word might get out, that someone might overhear something, that the story might be scrambled in the retelling. So in the obituary she wrote after she returned from the Cape, she included the information that Michael died of sudden cardiac arrest after helping his wife reach emergency medical care for treatment of a severe allergic reaction, and that his wife was treated and released.

Everything Davie did in those first few days, every decision, felt like she was in the grip of a sleepwalking episode. If only she *could* sleep, she thought. She wasn't sleeping; she was napping. She could not remember much of each preceding day. She found it difficult to follow conversations or think through simple tasks. She was an inveterate list maker, someone who recorded every appointment in her leather-bound date book. Now, she kept making lists and forgetting where she put them, and she couldn't find her date book. She knew it was somewhere in the house, but she didn't much care that she didn't know where it was.

She was aware that she should not be driving because she was in a zombie state of sleep deprivation, but she needed to meet with the funeral director several times, and the only way to get there was to drive. Andrea offered to drive her, but Davie wanted to go alone. She didn't want anyone else at such an awful meeting. Also, she felt that something was off, something was wrong, with Andrea. Not anything to do with her, Davie realized, but something. Whatever it was, Davie could not focus on it, however selfish that reaction might be. The feeling had started with Andrea's first call to Davie on the Cape, before Davie had a chance to call her. Davie called Michael's family early the morning after his death, then the Evening Star Agency, delivering the news calmly because she was so exhausted, and an outburst of emotion required energy. Then word spread with astonishing speed. Someone told someone else, and from there, news of Michael's death took off, even as the president of the board of directors at Michael's job was reading the board's statement to Davie over the phone before he released it.

So Andrea got to Davie first.

"Davie, I could ask Jay to drive out with me, so that one of us could drive home with you," Andrea said.

"No, that's too much for you to do," Davie said. "I'm leaving Saturday morning. I have to wait for the funeral home in Albany to get here and . . ." she paused . . . ". . . get Michael home. I am going to have him cremated. That will be done in Albany."

Andrea talked to her for another few minutes. She had enough money to see her through until she got the life insurance check? Yes, Davie said. Did Davie need Andrea to get to the house first, to do anything for her before she got home? To clear Michael's clothes out of their bedroom, was what she was really asking, Davie realized. No, Davie said. She would take care of everything at home.

Andrea was then silent, and Davie came very close to asking her, "Are you OK? Is everything alright?" Other than the obvious, she meant. Instead, she told Andrea they would talk when she got home.

She'd finally fallen asleep the night before she left. By the time she went to bed Friday night, she realized with some astonishment that she had slept maybe two hours since getting up on Wednesday morning and hearing Michael call from the bedroom, "Hey, it's high tide. Let's go to the beach." The little sleep she got in those two days came upon her as she sat on the couch in the afternoon or late at night, still dressed. She just fell asleep sitting up, and awoke a short time later feeling disoriented and unsure at first what time or even what day it was.

She went into the bedroom she and Michael used in the cottage, burrowed into the covers and fell asleep using Michael's pillow. She had two dreams, both of which she remembered as soon as she woke up at dawn. In the one she remembered as occurring first, she was looking down at Michael collapsed on the ground at the place where he pulled off in his car when he was stricken—a parking lot in front of a small strip of stores, the police officer told her, a place she had never seen in real life. In the dream, she never spoke to Michael or heard him say anything. Since being told what happened the night Michael died, Davie tried not to think of the effort it took Michael to get the car off the road before he lost control of the steering. She knew that someone stopped to help him, but she saw only Michael in her dream. The dream ended there.

Then she dreamed that she was outside of their car, on the road where she was stricken, and she was trying to use her EpiPen. In the dream, the EpiPen didn't work, so she used a second one she carried in her tote bag. That second dream was as brief as the first one, just a momentary scene in her sleep, but both dreams remained with her after she awoke.

In real life, she still didn't know where the second EpiPen was. She didn't find it in her tote bag, or on the floor of the car, or in the duffel bag she packed for the Cape. She thought it must be at home, although she couldn't remember why she might have taken it out of the little zippered case she carried in her tote bag. She realized that the allergic reaction unfolded so fast that even if she had carried the second EpiPen, she might not have been able to use it because she was barely functional. And she knew no one would blame her for how those few minutes in the car unfolded, but she already blamed herself.

She never filled the prescription for the EpiPen pack the doctor in the ER wrote out for her. She thought it was extremely unlikely that she would have another severe allergic reaction while she was on the Cape, and for reasons she could not entirely explain to herself, she didn't want to leave the cottage even to go to the pharmacy. The thought of interacting with other people, even for a mundane transaction at a counter in a drug store, was more than she could bear right now. For all that the cottage was filled with Michael's presence—and maybe for that exact reason—the tiny space seemed like a sanctuary to her before she drove home to what she was sure would be multiple tasks and conversations that would be anything but calming.

At dawn of the morning she left, she was suddenly fully awake, feeling like she had never gotten any sleep, but hoping she was rested enough to get through the drive home. As she packed the car, she found the torn-open paper packets for medical supplies the paramedics left strewn on the floor of the passenger side. She never noticed them the night she drove the car back from Hyannis, and she had no idea why they were in the car, when Michael had collapsed after getting out of the car, but there they were. The used EpiPen was not in the car; the paramedics must have collected it as medical waste. Davie wanted to check it to see if she had at least discharged the needle, as she thought she had. She was surprised at the level of frustration she felt about the medical crew leaving the ripped-open supply packets in the car but so scrupulously discarding the used EpiPen. She threw the packets into the wastebasket in the cottage, left the key on the kitchen table, leaving the door unlocked, and pulled out onto Route 6 to start the long drive back to Albany.

She summoned the last of her energy for the memorial service, which was as close to what she thought Michael would have wanted as was possible to achieve in such a short time. She wore the skirt she wore for their wedding, with a dark-blue silk blouse and the mocha-colored suede pumps Michael always loved. No one would know she was wearing part of her wedding outfit, she decided, and Jay certainly wouldn't remember. Andrea probably wouldn't either, and if she did, she would never say anything. It just seemed right to Davie, to again wear something that reminded her of her mother. The swelling in her hands finally went down; for several days after she got home, she couldn't have removed her wedding ring even if she wanted to. The funeral director—who seemed to understand the extraordinarily horrible circumstances of the whole affair better than anyone else— told her she should wear her wedding ring during the service even if she later decided to remove it. "People will be looking to see if you're wearing it," he told Davie. Davie could not believe anyone would care, but she took him at his word.

Davie had two other indelible memories from that meeting with the funeral director, one of them the kind of experience she thought she would never be able to tell anyone else. Just like she could not tell anyone that the ceiling of their car over the driver's seat was spattered with dark little splotches that Davie realized were bloodstains. When Davie noticed the bloodstains and slowly understood what they were, she gained an even more brutal understanding of the willpower Michael showed in getting the car off the road and into the parking lot when he was stricken, as he started to spew out bloody fluid from his lungs.

That day at the funeral parlor, as they went over the final arrangements for the service, Davie needed to use the bathroom. Maybe it was the fluorescent lights, she thought when she looked at her reflection over the sink, but it was far more likely the result of no sleep for more than a week. Either way, she had never seen herself look so ghastly.

"We do it all wrong in this culture," she told the funeral director when she sat back down with him. "We give the brides-to-be the gift certificates for a spa day. It's the widows who need them. I look like hell." He smiled a professional smile—Davie doubted he would ever share a laugh with a client—but Davie slumped down in her chair and laughed hard, partly out of feeling punch-drunk with exhaustion and partly at the image of gift cards to spas arriving in the mail every day instead of condolence cards. That seemed like a wonderful idea.

There had been a green tote bag on the table, which had a mirror finish to its mahogany surface and, like everything else in the funeral parlor, looked like part of a movie set that was never used in real life. The funeral director brought out the paperwork for her to sign so she could take the box of Michael's ashes home with her, and he explained that the cremated remains were not really ashes, but more like pulverized concrete. If she wanted to scatter any of them on a body of water, they would sink because they were bone, he assured her. The ashes were in a very strong plastic bag inside a heavy cardboard box, in the green tote bag.

"How much came home?" Davie asked. "Is there enough for me to scatter his ashes?"

Michael was a bone and tissue donor, and Davie now knew that the organ bank took everything it could use except the major internal organs. The dead person needed to be on life support to donate the heart, the lungs, the kidneys or the liver, because those organs deteriorated rapidly. The tissues and bones, however, could be taken as a donation within twenty-four hours without life support, even if the donor was already dead upon arrival at the hospital, as Michael was. The body of the bone and tissue donor was held in the hospital morgue until it went to an operating room, where a surgical team removed all that could be used. This was explained to Davie in the hospital.

Yes, the funeral director told her now, pulling her out of the memory of being back in the ER. There would be more than enough for her to scatter.

No one could possibly visualize this part of dealing with your husband's death, Davie thought as she sat at the flawlessly polished table during this conversation. No one could imagine what she was dealing with now, and no one would want to know. Probably most people who even thought about this would expect that a nearly complete body would have come home from the Cape even after a bone and tissue donation. That made no sense, but the human mind was not equipped to visualize what really happened in these situations. Davie wanted an answer, though, even though she realized the funeral director wanted to avoid providing one.

How much came home, Davie asked again.

The funeral director then told her that all he brought back from the Cape in the hearse were a few stray pieces of bone and Michael's skull. Davie was surprised at how heavy the green tote bag was when she left with it a half-hour later. She knew she could never tell anyone how little of Michael's body was actually cremated; it was too awful to think about, even for her.

And then at last the day of the memorial service arrived. The funeral home sent two limousines for Davie and her in-laws, and also Andrea and Jay and Alanna, because Davie insisted that they come to her house first and go to the service with the family. Davie thought Michael would have gotten endless comic mileage out of the idea of limousines for his memorial service, when he and Davie got into his second-hand Subaru, with all its dings and scrapes from years of being parked on Albany streets, to drive to their wedding. As the limousines pulled up near a side entrance for the building where the memorial service would be held, Davie saw a large gathering on the sidewalk in front of the main entrance. Dozens of clusters of people who knew Michael and knew each other were smoking, catching up, even laughing. The scene looked more like a crowd waiting to go into a Springsteen concert than the attendees of a memorial service for someone who died tragically and young, but that was, Davie, realized, exactly how Michael would have wanted this. He really loved a good party.

A small group of formerly homeless men—graduates of the building trades training program at the Evening Star Agency—served as ushers, and one of them delivered a deeply moving eulogy about Michael. Davie did not speak, a decision she wondered if she would later regret, but was the only decision she could make at the time. She knew she could not deliver a coherent eulogy. She could already count a lengthy list of physical symptoms from what she realized were trauma and grief and lack of sleep. She was nauseous and also queasy in a way that was not quite nausea but also not quite normal. She had headaches and lightheadedness, difficulty focusing and a racing heart. She could never have stood and spoken. She was even more relieved later that she stuck to her decision, when she had an experience that she would learn was called "splitting."

She was sitting in the small parlor in back of the ballroom where the memorial service would take place, waiting to walk in with Michael's family after everyone else was seated. She was surrounded by Michael's brothers and sisters and their spouses, nieces and nephews and one new baby, born to a niece, but she knew she radiated a silent but visible order that no one was to engage her in small talk. She was happy to let everyone else cluster together in the room, talking quietly and admiring the baby. She was aware of the occasional glance in her direction but also aware that she would be left alone, which was all she wanted. What she also really wanted was to be anywhere but there. Then she found herself accomplishing just that. She never left her chair, but she felt that she left the room. The conversation around her faded; she slipped into a kind of daydream, or more like a trance, she later thought. She didn't know how long she sat like that, imagining that she had left the room, when one of Michael's nieces came over to her with a look of alarm and asked Davie if she was well. Davie was shaking slightly, but she nodded that she was fine, and she sat up and tried to act more present.

Six hours later, she was home, having bid goodbye to Michael's family. They did not want to come in, and she did not want them to stay any longer. *Wonderful*, Davie thought, *something for everyone.* That was one of Michael's favorite expressions, which he usually delivered as a jocular and irreverent summation of a project or plan that did not turn out the way he expected, leaving him to watch as the victors looted through the broken storefront windows of a great idea. The affordable housing bill that crashed and burned in the Legislature without explanation when promised votes failed to materialize. The state grant application that he worked on late night after late night, writing, editing, researching, rewriting, only to see the grant awarded to a less-deserving nonprofit organization that contributed heavily to the governor's reelection campaign.

Davie stood on the sidewalk in front of the house for the requisite show of good manners after she got out of the limousine. She waited as her in-laws switched seating arrangements in several cars and then pulled away, turned the corner and headed back to Boston, almost certainly very glad to be leaving. She knew they found her completely composed navigation of the day unsettling. They probably thought she was on pretty strong medication; in truth, she was so sleep-deprived that she was beyond the ability to feel exhausted or even grief-stricken. She also knew that at least half the people at the service thought they would be invited back to the house after the reception, for what would have turned into an Irish wake. Davie could never have survived that. She realized they waited in vain for one of Michael's brothers to ask for everyone's attention at the height of the buffet lunch and say that anyone who wanted to drop by Michael and Davie's house afterward would be welcome. Davie didn't care what everyone might have expected. Alcohol and grief didn't mix well, Michael once said, and Davie thought, how right he was. Davie stayed with Michael's family at the reception until the crowd started to thin. Andrea came over to say goodbye and told Davie she would call soon.

"Try to get some sleep," Andrea said. It was a measure of how well she knew Davie that she did not offer to go back to the house with her; she could read all the signs that Davie was at her limit.

Davie went into the house, peeling off the notice that Jay taped to the front door as she entered. She forgot to remove it before her in-laws arrived and she wondered what they made of her polite request to be left alone. She closed the two sets of heavy double front doors and slowly climbed the stairs to the bedroom she had shared with Michael. Their bedroom, now her bedroom, in what used to be their house but was now her house. She undressed, leaving her clothes in a pile on the floor, got into bed and lay there for hours as the room grew dark. She finally fell asleep for a couple of hours around four o'clock in the morning.

Andrea called her early, two days later.

"Feel like getting out of the house?" Andrea asked. They agreed to meet at the coffee shop on Lark Street. Davie dreaded leaving the house, she dreaded running into people she knew, and the coffee shop was one of Michael's haunts when he needed to take a break from his office on Washington Avenue, or he wanted to meet with a reporter. Andrea's call to Davie was the first time Davie had spoken since the day of the memorial service—she made no phone calls, she didn't go anywhere, she didn't utter a word, she did not have any contact with anyone. She didn't think this was a good sign, so she thought she should get out of the house.

The day shift manager at the coffee shop saw Davie come in and he reached across the counter by the cash register.

"Jesus, Davie, I'm sorry. I read the obituary, and I couldn't believe it." Davie did not know if he referred to Michael's death, or the circumstances. Probably both.

"Are you doing OK?" the manager asked her. There was no way to answer that but to smile and nod yes. "It's good to see you, Davie," he said. "God bless."

Andrea sat at a tiny table in the corner by the front window. It was Monday, Davie suddenly realized, and Andrea didn't look like she was on an early lunch break from work. Davie noticed Andrea was wearing a

T-shirt and jeans, when she stood up to pull the table a little farther into the corner. Andrea ordered chamomile tea and Davie ordered a hot chocolate because she didn't think her stomach could handle coffee, plus caffeine was the last thing she needed.

"Are you eating at all?" Andrea asked. Davie shrugged. "Not much," she said. The waitress brought their drinks, and Andrea asked her to please also bring a cinnamon roll for them to share. Andrea cut the roll in half, and because there was no room on the table, she put her half on a napkin and pushed the plate over to Davie.

"I need to tell you something," Andrea said. Davie remembered their phone conversation while she was on the Cape, and her sense then that something was wrong. Because Andrea's words eerily echoed those of the nurse in the ER on Cape Cod, Davie also felt a chill. She recalled briefly thinking again in the days leading to the memorial service that something was going on with Andrea, but Davie never really focused on that in the subsequent sleepless days of exhaustion and planning. She waited, suddenly wide awake.

"I have cancer," Andrea said. "I found out a few days before you and Michael left for the Cape, and I didn't want to tell you until you got home. And, well. . . ." She bit her lower lip and made a gesture with one hand that took in the past two weeks.

"It's ovarian cancer," she continued. "It's been caught pretty early, and as these things go, my prognosis is actually very good. I'm starting chemotherapy this week, and I'll probably have surgery, and then I'm going to do my next section on the AT in June, and I'd like you to go with me. I'm in Virginia now." The juxtaposition of informing her closest friend that she had an extremely serious form of cancer with a discussion of her plans for the next summer had a scatterbrained quality that did not sound like Andrea, Davie thought, or it sounded like Andrea was thinking in overdrive.

Andrea had started backpacking at Williams College with the outdoor club, and after years of hiking the Appalachian Trail in Vermont, Massachusetts and Connecticut, she decided six or seven years ago to hike the whole AT in stages. Section-hiking, it was called. This required an enormous commitment of time and planning, and this was how Andrea took her vacation every summer—by disappearing for two weeks on the Appalachian Trail. In this way, she had gotten as far as Virginia, just north of Shenandoah National Park. Davie felt no interest in backpacking and couldn't have found Shenandoah National Park on a map. She didn't know what states the Appalachian Trail traversed, or what was involved in back-packing, other than it required long stretches of walking in hot weather without the possibility of a shower at the end of the day. She had followed this adventure without really understanding it.

Please don't go anywhere, Davie thought. *How am I going to get through the coming months, years, without Michael, if you're not here?* She knew her first reaction was bizarrely self-centered, but it was at the same time completely normal. It was a measure of how much Andrea meant to her. Davie did not have any siblings, parents or close cousins, and only a distant—albeit cordial—relationship with Michael's family. Andrea was the sister she never had. So Davie took in her friend's face—the beautifully angled bones, the auburn hair falling in loose ringlets and waves, Andrea's impenetrable brown eyes, steady, waiting for her response—and Davie thought, *I cannot bear this.*

"I'm going to be OK," Andrea said when Davie remained silent. "I know this is a shock, especially right now, but this is treatable. It's serious, but it's treatable. I caught it early. You don't usually catch ovarian cancer this early. I'm on leave from work right now, until I get the chemotherapy up and running, because all I've been doing is going from one doctor's appointment to another. But I'll be back at work in a few weeks, and then if I have surgery, I'll be out again just after New Year's, but my goal is to get back to my section hike in June. I would like you to go with me. I could use the company, and I think you would love it."

"Andrea . . . I . . . let's think about backpacking in the spring . . . how are you handling this so calmly? You're not just putting this on for my sake, right now, because . . . ?"

Andrea shook her head and reached across the table and put her hand over Davie's.

"I'm going to be OK," she repeated. She could not possibly know how that phrase evoked the last words Michael said to Davie, and now made Davie inwardly cringe. "Everything I've been told, everything I've read . . . I went down to Sloan Kettering last week to meet with an oncologist there. . . ." Davie realized that trip fell at the height of her planning for the memorial service, so no wonder she didn't really think about the one day when Andrea didn't call her until evening " . . . and he's the same doctor my oncologist up here did his residency under, and everything I'm being told indicates that this has been caught early, and it's treatable."

"I hear you," Davie said. "I believe you. Then we'll help each other, because right now, I am an absolute wreck. So let me know what you need, and I will help you any way I can. Is it OK if I . . ." *tell Michael?* she almost asked, and then stopped. Andrea knew what the rest of the sentence would have been, Davie realized.

"Believe me, I will let you know what I need," Andrea said. "And you do the same. We will indeed help each other. And it's going to be a perfectly fucking awful next year, but we'll get through it."

chapter 4

Davie was halfway through her six-week leave, and she still could not get a whole night's sleep. She was often exhausted but rarely sleepy. She went to bed close to midnight and woke up before dawn. She hoped that even if she could not sleep, she could at least rest. Instead, she spent the time closing Michael's bank and credit card accounts, meeting with the estate attorney, talking to the staff at the customer service center for Michael's life insurance, writing thank-you notes to the people who spoke at the service, removing Michael's name as her beneficiary and sending proof of his death to Social Security, his two investment plans, and the agent for his life insurance policy.

Davie went through these steps with a sense of déjà vu, because the process was remarkably similar to what she did for her parents fifteen years earlier, with the exception that her parents were multi-millionaires who held multiple investments, and Michael's finances were far less complex. She found a good estate attorney through a lawyer acquaintance who served on the board of the Community Loan Foundation. The estate attorney supplied her with numerous copies of Michael's death certificate, signed by the doctor who told Davie in the hallway of the ER that Michael would never be the same, even if they got his heart started. The certificate listed the cause of death as acute coronary syndrome. Davie found it astonishing that in an era of digitalized information, the worst moment of her life could be captured on a single sheet of paper, with the blanks filled in by the doctor's sprawling, rounded backhand.

Davie already knew that settling the estate might take a few months, in part because she was required to wait several weeks to see if any children surfaced to claim their share of Michael's assets. Jay and Alanna went to the attorney's office to sign paperwork attesting that to the best of their knowledge, Michael did not have any children, and then Davie just needed to wait. She never seriously considered that Michael was a secret parent, but her attorney told her this happened more often than people expected.

She now owned two cars, both of them Subarus and either one a good car for her to keep. She could not possibly continue driving Michael's Subaru, in which he was stricken, so she arranged to donate it to a local charity.

She scrubbed out the rust-colored blood splatters above the driver's seat, cleaned the car thoroughly, vacuumed it carefully, checked under the seats, filled out the paperwork and made sure the registration and insurance cards were on the passenger seat when the two graduate student interns from the charity arrived to claim the car. She didn't know if they realized the circumstances of the donation, and she volunteered no information as she signed some forms, using the hood of the car as a desk.

She wanted the car gone, but she couldn't bear to see it go. What if there was something of Michael's somewhere in the car that she missed, something that no one would ever think of returning to her?

"Hold on, please," she said. The young man who was about to get into the car stopped.

"I want to just take one more look, in case I missed something?"

"Sure, take all the time you need." So while the two interns stepped back and looked at their phones, Davie sat in the driver's seat and flipped the sun visor down, got out and pushed the seat back so she could see all the way under, and she reached under it as far back as she could get her hand, even though she had already checked under both seats a couple of days earlier. Then she got into the passenger seat and did the same thing. When she pushed the seat back as far as it would go and stretched her hand underneath, she felt a plastic tube, recognizing it immediately as an EpiPen. She pulled it out from where it was wedged and stared at it, then stood up, flipped open the top of the tube and slid the pen out to read the expiration date. This was not an old EpiPen she lost in the car years ago; this was the second one she thought was in the emergency kit in her tote bag ... how did it end up under the seat? Did it fall out of the case when she fumbled around inside her tote on that dark road, as Michael tried to find a place to turn the car? That was the only explanation. Then the EpiPen must have rolled way back under the seat when the car was towed that night.

"Is everything all right, Mrs. Devlin?" The graduate student looked at her from the other side of the car.

"Yes, everything's fine," Davie said. "You can take the car now."

Probably nothing would have turned out differently, even if she'd not dropped the EpiPen in the car that night. Or would it have? She would never know if having it that night would have made any difference, because she would never know if she would have been capable of using it. That question was just one part of the burden of guilt she carried, a burden she knew would have appalled Michael. How did anyone recover from something like this, she wondered. This was not healing she faced; it was an endless expanse of trauma, remorse, self-recrimination and second-guessing, layered over missing Michael so much that she could not imagine ever feeling better. It was like standing on one of the bluffs of the Cape on the ocean side, envisioning all that lay between the surf at the base of the dunes and the next shoreline across the Atlantic, something you knew was there but you could never see from where you stood. Davie watched as Michael's car disappeared around the corner, then she went back inside and put the EpiPen in her purse.

It was good for another year, and she wondered if she would ever need to use it. More to the point, how would she ever feel safe again if a medical emergency like the one that happened the night Michael died could happen out of the blue? Without Michael there with her, how would she handle something like that on her own, in this new life alone that she faced? She needed to make an appointment with an allergist. In the terrible rush of events when she got home, she never got around to doing that, but she knew she also dreaded making the appointment. It would mean telling the whole awful story again, and Davie was not sure she could face doing that.

In the remaining days of her bereavement leave, she booked a haircut, got notification that she could roll over Michael's retirement account into her own, and removed Michael's clothes from the closet. The days passed in aimless silence, except for when Andrea got in touch with her. Andrea told Davie that she would definitely have surgery after the chemotherapy, and Davie wondered if that was an indication that the cancer was more serious than Andrea was telling her. Davie got onto the National Institutes of Health webpage about ovarian cancer one day, and based on what she read, the need for surgery after chemotherapy meant the cancer was past the earliest and most easily treated stage. She didn't dare ask Andrea, who now maintained an invisible "Do Not Enter" barrier around the topic of the cancer. Davie went back and re-read the NIH page and decided to not press Andrea. She feared that Andrea would back away if Davie persisted.

For all that they were each other's closest friend, Davie knew that Andrea was intensely private, something Davie could relate to, being fairly private herself.

Jay and Alanna asked her to dinner. They rented an old house a couple of blocks away from Davie's home, which Davie could not stop referring to as "our house." She walked to Jay and Alanna's house in the early October dusk. She was able to eat a little, but everything else about the evening was agonizing. Did Jay and Alanna feel the same way? Davie wondered, for all that they made a good show of welcoming her. The tremendous gaping loss they all carefully avoided mentioning sat there in the living room and moved into the dining room with them, making it impossible to feel normal.

It was, Davie quickly realized, going to be very difficult for anything to ever feel normal again around people who knew Michael well. Jay and Michael became friendly years earlier when the environmental agency Jay worked for pushed hard on a bill in the Legislature and sought the backing of the agency where Michael worked at the time. Michael was the policy director at that previous job, and he ran a long and successful campaign against industrial pollution in poor neighborhoods. Out of that shared effort the friendship between Michael and Jay took hold and lasted. Jay confided now, in this first careful, awkward get-together after Michael's death, that he had hoped Michael and Davie would connect at that party where they met more than a dozen years earlier. That was a safe topic, Davie realized; the fun they'd all shared. Alanna was by nature very quiet, so it was Jay who kept the conversation going.

The evening was the longest time Davie had spent with other people in many weeks, and she found it exhausting to follow the conversation, to respond, to sound better than she felt. Michael's absence at the table was like the Missing Man tribute in a flyover at a military funeral, the part where the fighter jet peeled out of the formation to signify the lost member of the group. Davie imagined his place set at the table with the plate turned over, because the memory of all those past dinners and conversations hovered around the three of them. She found the time with Jay and Alanna unbearable, and she left as early as she could. She knew that Jay wanted to ask many questions about what happened the night Michael died, and she also knew he was very hesitant to broach the subject.

Davie's appointment for her haircut was the next morning, at a salon a few blocks from her house where she and Michael were clients for years. It was a weekday morning when Davie walked to the salon, no one else was there, and the stylist who had cut her hair for years was the only employee working that morning. Davie felt her eyes drift closed as she sat in the chair. Normally, she would have chatted with the stylist about work or vacation plans, but she had nothing to say today and she was relieved that he seemed to sense that.

"You know, you're looking very beautiful, for someone who's just been through what you've been through," she heard the stylist say. She opened her eyes and regarded him in the mirror; he was looking down, working on her hair, not looking back at her reflection. Davie let that remark drop unanswered; it struck her as a little odd, but she also thought she might be overreacting. Maybe he was just trying to make her feel better, because she knew that she looked awful right now. So she said nothing.

"I mean, you are really looking beautiful," he continued. This time, he looked at her reflection in the mirror. Hearing this from someone with whom she never had more than casual conversation during five years of haircuts was bizarre and unsettling. He certainly never before commented on her appearance, which Davie knew full well was not beautiful at that particular moment and was none of his business, she thought, even if it was true. *Oh-kay,* she thought, realizing he was hitting on her. *So now I have to put up with this jerk?*

He finished the haircut, and she stood up. Before she could turn around, he said to her, "Wait . . . you have some hair there." She felt his fingers brush the back of her jeans, her rear end, touching her the way Michael had on their last morning, to be precise, and it was not accidental and she knew it was just an excuse for him to touch her. She froze for a moment, furious and stunned, and then she turned. He was standing between her and the door. He was a tall, big man. Davie wished she had picked up a pair of scissors before she turned around, but she hadn't, and now she needed to think fast. Three realizations seized her. Incredulous, she thought she was suddenly in a fair amount of danger—the salon was in the half-basement of an old building, two steps under the stoop, and no one could easily see in past the door. He could do anything he wanted to her. And then she thought that she needed to act as if everything was normal, that her ability to get out of the salon depended on remaining calm. And last, she thought, *Michael would have killed him.* Never had she felt so vulnerable, with this man standing between her and the door. He thought he could touch her, all because Michael was dead.

The stylist watched her, watched her face. Then unexpectedly he stepped away and Davie stepped forward. The desire to get out of the salon, and the overwhelming conviction that her best chance at doing so lay in acting as though nothing was wrong, propelled her to the counter in front of the register. She was genuinely afraid; she thought the situation could go either way, and she envisioned lunging for the door and feeling him catch her and pulling her back. If she didn't let him realize how afraid she was, she could leave. She knew that made no sense, but acting normal seemed the best way to get out the door.

"How much do I owe you?" She handed him her credit card, he ran it through and handed her the receipt. She signed it, then drew a diagonal line through the place where she would have added the tip, folded the payment slip and left it on the counter. She usually made her next appointment before she left, and when she said nothing further, she realized he knew how frightened she was. She saw him unfold the receipt and look down at it, and that seemed to unlock her legs; she turned and walked to the door without another word. She resisted the impulse to look back at him, while she expected to hear him coming up behind her as she reached the door. She was terrified. She hoped he would spend the rest of the day wondering what she was going to do.

That was certainly how *she* spent the rest of the day. He touched her, and she was truly afraid for a few vivid minutes. He was more likely a creep, not a rapist, who acted on an opportunistic impulse because he was a creep, but she didn't know that for sure, and whether he would have acted on a compulsion because he was in fact a rapist was a whole separate question. Whatever went through his head, he paused to consider the consequences of going too far. What little she knew of laws governing assault, she remembered hearing a cop sometime . . . maybe in college? . . . at a talk on campus safety? . . . describing the two main components of a criminal sexual abuse charge. The investigating officer would ask you if the guy put his hand on an intimate part of your body, and if he did so without your consent. Yes and yes, Davie thought.

But she lived alone now, and her stylist knew her address. Davie imagined going to the cops and filing a report. The possible repercussions made her pause. What if he owned a gun? He lived in a rural town outside of Albany. Many people owned a gun in the rural towns in Albany and Rensselaer counties, where it could take a long time for the county sheriff or the state police to show up in response to a 911 call, simply because of the distances they covered, often on dirt roads. What if he was so enraged because he had to explain his behavior to his wife that he didn't care what he did, didn't stop to think about the consequences the next time?

So she did nothing, although she couldn't stop obsessing about the incident for days. But she never mentioned it to anyone, not even Andrea when Davie went to see her the weekend before returning to work.

Andrea was doing chemotherapy now. She was tolerating it well, and she brushed aside any questions about how she felt, Davie noticed. She had just returned to her job at the Community Loan Foundation, and her backpack was in her living room, propped up in a wooden chair, the afternoon that Davie stopped by to see her.

"I'm trying to decide if I want to buy a new pack," she explained. Davie went to the backpack and asking, "May I?" lifted it by the shoulder straps, not by the grab strap at the top of the pack, as she later learned was proper. "What's in here?" she asked.

"That's the stuff I leave in there between trips. My compass, my bear line, my first-aid kit, some of my cooking gear . . . my stove . . . my water pump . . . I have duplicates of some things, so you can borrow my stuff or we can share. We won't need to carry two water-treatment systems, just my pump." Davie had no idea what any of this was.

"I haven't said I'm going backpacking," Davie replied, replacing the pack on the chair seat.

"I'm planning on it," Andrea said. "You're going."

"How much does this weigh when you have it all packed?"

"In the summer, about thirty-two pounds. I never seem to be able to get it down any lighter."

Davie burst out laughing, one of the few times since Michael's death that she laughed at finding something funny instead of finding something ironic. "*Thirty-two pounds?* For how long? And you do climbing and that kind of stuff?" She remembered some of Andrea's descriptions of the Hudson Valley, terms that made no sense to her . . . knife-edge ridges, boulder walls . . . all she knew was that Andrea sometimes climbed up some steeply sloped, rocky places with this thing on her back while carrying two poles in one hand that served as walking sticks, and that she often had nothing to hold onto other than tree roots and the edges of rocks.

"Well, not real rock climbing. You have to free-hand it up some boulder walls. But the area where we are going is mostly level, and it's gorgeous," Andrea said. "We'd just be hiking along the top of one long ridge, overlooking the Shenandoah Valley. You will love it."

≈

Davie's return to work did not go well. She was still barely sleeping, and she refused her doctor's suggestion of sleeping pills. She just did not want to

54

start down that road; she was afraid of never being able to sleep well again if she needed drugs. And now she had a steady feeling of ... queasiness? Nausea? She didn't know what to call it, she just knew she didn't feel right. Chewing fresh ginger helped. Mostly, she was exhausted in a way that was unrelated to her lack of sleep. In this frame of mind, she returned to her job at Levellewyn, Grenoble and Carl.

About two hours into the first day, she wished she was anywhere else, but she could not imagine telling her boss, Irina, that she wanted to go back on leave indefinitely one day into her return. She found Irina difficult to figure out or, for that matter, even engage in simple conversation. Irina insisted on calling Davie by her real name of Davida. Davie never used her own real name, no one ever used it and Davie did not particularly like it. Michael and Davie were a couple for a year before Michael found out her real name, so Irina's persistent use of Davida told Davie all she needed to know about her boss: Irina was unapproachable and formal. After the first month, Davie stopped breezily telling her, "You can just use Davie; I never use Davida." They would never be friendly or even really cordial. Davie did not remember hearing from Irina after Michael's death, nor did she recall seeing her at the memorial service, but she didn't entirely trust her memory right now, so she decided to give Irina the benefit of the doubt.

She also quickly realized she should never have come back this soon. There was no provision for indefinite leave, outside of federal Family and Medical Leave, and that didn't last forever. Davie used two weeks of vacation and two weeks of federal leave, all with pay, to stay home after Michael's death, and she did not want to use any more leave.

Irina called Davie into her office the morning of her return. Earlier, Irina stopped by Davie's office to hand her some papers. Irina stood with barely concealed impatience as Davie nodded to her and held up a finger to indicate: *I will be with you in a moment.* She wanted to let the guy from her workgroup who stopped by finish his conversation. He was at Michael's memorial service, along with a lot of people from the office who attended the service. He stopped to see Davie, welcome her back and tell her how beautiful he thought the service was. Irina showed up partway through this, and while most people catching the drift of the conversation they wanted to interrupt would have waved from the door and said, "I'll be back later," or, "Stop by to see me when you're done," Irina cut into the conversation. "I need to see you now in my office," she said without preamble. Davie thought this was deeply rude. Her colleague gave her a sympathetic look as he left and Davie walked down the hall to Irina's office.

At a nod from Irina, Davie took the chair in front of Irina's desk. Irina had a habit of standing up as soon as a staff member sat down, which was what she did now. She was a petite woman who always wore a designer skirt suit and stiletto heels, and whose too-blue-to-be-real eyes could only have come from tinted contacts. Davie used to wonder if Irina stood up to automatically make herself look taller, until a colleague told Davie that Irina acquired this habit in a management training seminar based on a theme of exerting control over subordinates.

"The client needs you to pull these focus group reports together into one document, turn it into a nice narrative flow and have it ready by Friday," Irina said as she handed over a stack of papers separated into groups with binder clips. "The PDFs are in your email. You know, I didn't realize that you didn't leave an auto-message on your email, and when you didn't return several messages from the client, they contacted George"—George was the head of Davie's team—"and this didn't go over very well."

"Well, I was dealing with a lot, Irina, and composing a cordial email signature in the middle of dealing with Michael's death wasn't the first thing on my mind," Davie said. "Why didn't someone here check to see if I'd put a message into my email, and then ask IT to do it?"

"That's not the point," Irina said. "The point is that one of our clients felt he got less than great service from us."

Davie stood up now. Tit for tat, she thought. There was something awful about the way Irina was standing over her desk, talking down to her, instead of sitting down in the nearby chair away from her desk to take some of the sting out of her words. So now Davie stood. She took a deep breath, but the words came out in a tightly controlled rush despite her effort to seem calm.

"Did the client understand that my husband just died? Did anyone bother to explain that to him? I mean, maybe even the privileged people we deal with every day here might understand that."

"I certainly didn't mention it, and I doubt that anyone else did." Irina was impatient to wrap up the conversation. She had yet to ask Davie how she was doing. "Our personal business is no concern of our clients. Our concern is delivering the service they are paying for, and doing it promptly and professionally." She nodded to indicate she was finished. Davie turned and walked back to her office.

Trembling with tension and anger, Davie shuffled through the papers. She was not interested in dealing with them; she was not interested in anything connected to her job. Three hours into her return to work, she didn't want to be there. She didn't want to be anywhere, she realized. So she went to the personnel office, told the human resources director that she returned to work too soon and that she wanted to go back on leave for another six weeks. She did this with a sense of stunned disbelief that she was seriously about to walk out of her job for another medical leave, coupled with an even more profound disbelief at how her life seemed to be unraveling. Davie was no fool; she knew the HR director's first loyalty was to Levellewyn, Grenoble and Carl, and that much like the funeral director, she would never allow personal feelings to show. Even so, Davie thought that this woman was concerned and even compassionate.

"Davie, we will need a note from your doctor to put you back on Family Medical Leave," the HR director said. "I can print out the paperwork right now, and if you plan to see your doctor in the next few days, you can bring this all with you. If you aren't going to make an appointment in person, then I can mail it to your doctor."

"I'm going to go see my doctor," Davie said. "Do you know the circumstances of my husband's death?"

"Yes," the HR director said.

"It gets worse, if that's possible to imagine," Davie said. "Two weeks after I got home, I learned that my best friend has ovarian cancer. She stood up for me at my wedding."

The HR director turned from collecting the papers she had just printed out and looked steadily at Davie.

"You are dealing with too much right now. I need a note from your doctor to set the leave in motion, but these six weeks will carry you through almost to the end of the year, and then the clock on Family Medical Leave resets. You start over with another twelve weeks if you need them after the new year."

"My God, I sure hope I'm back at work before then," Davie said. "I need to go back to my office to set a few things in order. Should I talk to Irina, or will you?"

"I'll take care of that."

So Davie went back to her office, without speaking to anyone in her department. She closed her door and composed a message as an automatic reply on her email, because she did not want another lecture from Irina six weeks from now. The message read, *I am on an extended emergency personal leave following the sudden death of my husband. I will not be checking or responding to email for the next six weeks. If you have urgent business, please ask the switchboard operator to connect you with my team manager, George Horowitz, or my department manager, Irina Kostya. Thank you.—Davida Devlin."*

She pasted the message into the template for an auto-reply, then opened her email one final time to see what was new that morning and to make sure the auto-reply worked. Right at the top of her inbox was a message from the client who complained about her not leaving an auto-reply the first time she went on leave. Davie opened the email and read: "Ms. Devlin, Irina has told me she is giving you the focus group reports to turn into a draft by Friday. I really hope that you can complete this by Friday, because you have not been very communicative these past weeks. Please let me know that you got this message."

A reckless feeling of rage spread through Davie. She knew she should count to one hundred and do nothing when she felt this way, but she hit reply and wrote: "Good afternoon. This is Davida Devlin. Yes, I received your message. Please know that I have a few bigger issues on my plate right now than your focus group reports. Here is the auto-reply I should have set up in September. Have a good rest of the day." She hit the key for pasting in a message, so that her reply to the client ended with, *"I am on an extended personal leave following the sudden death of my husband. I will not be checking or responding to email for the next six weeks. If you have urgent business, please ask the switchboard operator to connect you with my team manager, George Horowitz, or my department manager, Irina Kostya. Thank you.—Davida Devlin."*

She hit send, then she left, grateful that everyone was out for lunch and wondering if she would have a job to return to in six weeks. She realized she didn't much care either way.

❧

Davie set up an appointment with her doctor. She thought about how she would manage if she did lose her job, which was starting to seem like more than a passing thought. Michael always earned more than she did, but she was not far behind him since starting her current job. Still, she was going to be living with a reduction of more than fifty percent to her household income, and the house needed a ton of work. It was built in 1884, and it was a mess of code violations and spongy old window frames that Davie filled in with Durham's Water Putty, slathered over cotton balls stuffed into some of the gaps where the freezing outdoor air came through in the winter. Davie and Michael delayed doing the work the house needed because up until a year ago, Davie was still at the Community Loan Foundation, where her salary was about what you would expect from a

58

do-gooder nonprofit that preached a message of self-actualization to small startups and charitable organizations.

Davie was excellent with numbers and finance, hardly a surprise given her background in mathematics, but she thought she should do something she so far had avoided, which was to take a hard look at her financial situation as a new widow.

She stumbled upon a support network for young widows on Google Groups and she applied to be admitted. Although she never posted anything to the group, she was now reading more than enough about the financial struggles many widows faced to realize that she was better off than most. She read about houses being lost to the bank because the couple calculated the mortgage payment on two incomes and didn't have life insurance for the survivor to use for the mortgage. Who wouldn't calculate the mortgage on both incomes? Davie found herself wondering. That was what she and Michael did; it was what most couples did, and it was also how the bank calculated the loan. She read about jobs being lost after the husband's death as the widow floundered in shock and grief; about the difficulty of paying property taxes on one income; about unexpected expenses no one could have anticipated, no matter how carefully they planned—furnaces and major appliances breaking down, roofs needing replacement, legal fees beyond the normal costs of settling an estate, grief counseling sessions at $100 an hour that were not covered by insurance . . . it was enough to both scare her and make her grateful that she was able to pay off the mortgage with Michael's life insurance and that her income would let her carry the expenses on the house.

She suspected that some of her friends wondered why she was keeping a house in a borderline neighborhood a few blocks from an elementary school perpetually in state receivership, around the corner from a park that had a gun homicide the previous year. The answer was partly because she could not imagine where else she might want to live, partly because she was incapable of making such major decisions right then, and partly because Michael loved the house and it was a connection to him she could not surrender.

So she spent the first full day of her second medical leave going through her expenses, trying to decide whether she could get a loan to do some of the work on the house when she felt ready to tackle that, while also figuring out the bare minimum she needed to live on if she lost her job without a severance package. It was difficult to realize that she was considering that, but she believed in being prepared. She also realized that she was planning for two completely opposite extremes. Everything in her approach to finance in her career had taught her to review the numbers in all likely scenarios in whatever project she faced.

The widows' group offered other helpful information. Davie read the group's Top Ten list of dumbest things people said to widows, with, "You'll remarry!" leading the list. No one had said that to her yet. The women in the group wrote about clueless doctors, about unhelpful in-laws, about steering young children through their unresolved anger about Daddy's death. Well, Davie thought, at least she didn't have to face that issue. She could not imagine trying to shore up children right now, when she felt like such a mess.

She got the point about the clueless doctors when she went for her appointment with her own primary care physician, to talk to him about her decision to go back on medical leave and to drop off the paperwork she collected on her way out the door at work. He was in his sixties, probably close to retirement, and she always liked his low-key approach to medical issues. He dressed in hiking clothes at his job—pretty common in Upstate New York—he didn't stand on ceremony, and Davie expected nothing more than a perfunctory visit with him. Instead, he lectured her on her decision to go back on medical leave.

"I'll approve this, but this is a serious relapse," he said. Davie sat up straighter in her chair, astonished at his judgmental comment.

"A *relapse?* My husband hasn't been dead six weeks." The doctor did not answer; he was reading through the Family Medical Leave papers. He signed them and handed them back.

"Now, when women in your situation don't turn a corner within a year, that's when I tell them it's time to find some volunteer work in a nursing home, or something to get their minds off their grief," he said. "You will have to get a letter from me before you return to work, and I want to see you doing a lot better. You're young, you're going to eventually remarry, and the best way to get your life back together is to take better care of yourself. I'm going to approve this leave, but you have been resistant to my suggestions on how to deal with this. Your blood pressure is elevated, you aren't sleeping, and you won't seek help." Davie didn't know what he meant by help; probably he meant her refusal to take sleeping medication.

"I am doing what I think is best for me," Davie said. She could feel her heart pounding; she could hardly get the words out without shaking.

"We will re-evaluate your progress in six weeks," the doctor said as if she had not spoken. No, we won't, Davie thought to herself, and you can go to hell.

She went home and spent the rest of the day calling primary care practices in the area until she found one that would take her on as a new patient. This was a crazy way to find a new doctor, she thought, sort of like flipping open the Bible and taking the first passage your finger landed on as a sign from God. How could she know if this new doctor would be any good? She didn't; she just knew that she needed to change doctors fast, and that she could not go back to her longtime doctor and be lectured again about her failure to get over Michael's death as fast as he thought she should. She explained to the staff member doing the intake over the phone that she was changing doctors at the start of a medical leave following the death of her husband, and she realized that switching her doctor mid-stream like this might complicate her leave. The staff member told her they could deal with that, and the woman set up an appointment for Davie for a month later. Davie ended the call and sat with her head in her hands. She wanted to pound a wall or scream, but she knew the last thing she needed was to reinjure her hands or strain her throat again until she couldn't speak.

Should she be speaking to someone? A grief counselor, a therapist, maybe the members of a support group for women in her situation? She could not think how to get started on such a quest, and she also thought her circumstances were so uniquely awful that she might not fit in, even with a group of other widows. She had the feeling that having your husband die saving your life was different from your husband dying from a car accident or cancer. Maybe she was wrong, but she had the feeling she was right. So she did nothing.

With six weeks to herself staring at her, Davie drew up a list of what she wanted to do. She wanted to find out who stopped to help Michael. She didn't know who that person was, but she wanted to talk to him. He was the one who called 911, so she figured his name would be in the police report. She called the police department in Hyannis and filled out an online Freedom of Information request for the incident report about the police response to the parking lot where Michael collapsed. In addition to wanting to know the name of the man who stopped, Davie wanted to read what happened in what she thought of as the "missing ninety minutes" between the time she left the fire station, and the time the nurse came down the hall in the ER to tell her Michael was already at the hospital.

She went to the Evening Star Agency and cleared out Michael's office, put all his mementoes from his desk drawers into boxes, and took down his photographs from the shelves and his bulletin board. She talked to no one in the office as she did this, once the acting executive director led her to Michael's office and closed the door to give her privacy. Davie had called ahead of time to schedule this visit, and she found empty cardboard boxes and a cart to carry them out to her car in the office. No one interrupted her as she worked in silence during the lunch hour, the time she thought she would least likely encounter sympathetic colleagues. She did not think she could hold up through a round of condolences. Michael was a pack rat, and Davie also found old crumpled lunch bags, truly ancient tubes of lip balm and a ticket stub from a ferry on Cape Cod from five years earlier. She worked quickly, in silence, and left without any conversations or encounters.

She still had Michael's clothes, packed in boxes and bags. She kept the wedding tie she bought him. She didn't want to give the clothes to the collection center at the Evening Star Agency, because the idea of the staff learning that their dead executive director's widow had donated his clothes—some of which they might remember seeing him wear—struck her as unimaginable. So she drove to Troy, to the smaller Rensselaer County agency that did equivalent work, and she unloaded the bags and boxes onto a couple of carts brought out by a young staff member. Davie wanted to open one of the boxes and bury her face in Michael's clothing one last time to inhale the scent of his skin, as she did while packing the clothing, but she just could not do that while someone was watching. She wondered if she would be able to pull up that scent in her memory in the future. The young staff member who helped her saw her wedding ring—Davie caught his quick glance at her hand—and it was obvious that she was handing over the contents of her dead husband's closet. At the end, as she handed back his copy of the donation form, he said, "I'm sorry," and he sounded like he really meant it. Irina had yet to say that to Davie.

And then at home, the day before Davie returned to work, she finally went through the plastic bag the police officer gave her at the ER the night Michael died. The bag held some personal effects the paramedics and police collected at the scene: Michael's wallet; his belt, cut in half, because Davie now realized the belt was in the way of the medics; his phone; his reading glasses, which had been in his pocket and shattered when he collapsed; a baseball cap. Davie wished, for the first time since their little city hall marriage ceremony, that Michael had worn a wedding ring. He was so completely unmaterialistic, he owned so few valuable personal possessions, that she wished she could have that one token reminder of him.

Early in their marriage, Michael and Davie established a policy that either could open any piece of mail that came to the house, even if it was addressed to the other. That way, they reasoned, they wouldn't miss anything important. It was only later that Davie learned how unusual this arrangement was for married couples. But even so, she never went through Michael's phone. She knew his password to unlock it, as he knew hers. It felt odd to be doing this now, Davie thought, as she plugged in the phone to charge it. She realized that she was at the stage where a lot of widows probably got some unpleasant surprises, as they went through their husband's bank account, email, desk at work, phone calls. So far, the only surprise for Davie was to learn that Michael's retirement account held $30,000 more than she had thought it did, the result of his making a change a few months earlier in the mix of investments.

A half hour later, she opened the recent calls list on Michael's phone and found that the last call he made was to a number on Cape Cod the night he died. Davie called the number and the woman who answered identified the place as the Wellfleet Fire Station that Michael got her to that night. Davie did not have to go very far into her explanation before the woman recognized her. She was part of the ambulance crew that night, she told Davie, and the person Davie wanted to speak to was Captain Dwyer, who ran that shift and stayed at the station when the ambulance left, she said. He was on his days off, but she promised to give him the message when he returned. With this task checked off her list, Davie faced the realization that she would return to her job the next day, and she dreaded doing so.

When Davie went back on leave, she thought she would use the time to somehow end up feeling ... if not "better," then more ready to return to what parts of her life she could reclaim without Michael. Her job, time with friends, long walks through the downtown park with Andrea. What she quickly realized as this second leave unfolded was that she could never recapture anything of the life she left in Albany when she locked the front door of their house on the day she and Michael drove to the Cape in late August. Her sense of utter desolation was not depression. It was a feeling of despair, coupled with an inability to start moving, physically or emotionally. She knew she should get out of the house each day and at least go for a walk; instead, she ended up sitting still for long periods, lost in contemplation. The scene in the hospital that night, the memory of the nurse leading her into the room during the resuscitation effort, came back to her over and again. She tried not to think about her job and all the work she would have to make up in the coming days. She thought she would have very little support or understanding at her office, but she thought her only choice was to return. In this frame of mind, still not sleeping, still feeling like she could barely move, she went back to work in the bleakest time of the year for the newly bereaved—just before Christmas, when everywhere she turned, she saw reminders of holiday joy.

chapter 5

Davie was in her office maybe ten minutes on the day of her return from the second medical leave when her phone rang. She saw that it was the HR director calling. She doubted that this was a call to welcome her back to work. Maybe they were checking to make sure she was in the office and on time? No, as Davie learned when she answered the phone, the HR director wanted her to come to the personnel office, please, and yes, right now.

Irina was also there. The HR director got right to the point.

"We are taking you back into your position on probationary status, Davie," she said. "We are aware of the note you sent to one of our clients the day you went back out on leave. That was, to put it mildly, inappropriate. You will be on probationary status for six months, and we will periodically review your progress and your performance. You are an employee at will, and we can terminate you at any time. Instead, we are taking this approach, which we feel is better for you under the circumstances."

"Thank you for that," Davie replied. She meant it to be sarcastic; she couldn't help herself, but she immediately realized that Irina and the HR director took it as a statement of humility, an indication that she realized that she was on very thin ice. So much for the glimmer of compassion the HR director showed when Davie went back on leave three hours into her return six weeks earlier. They got to her, Davie thought. Someone told the HR director in no uncertain terms what she was to say and do, as well as the tone she was to adopt during the saying and the doing.

"There will be no more stunts like the one you pulled with our client," Irina said. "I hope you understand that."

"You know, I'm not even sure you should be in this meeting," Davie replied. "I think my conversation here should be private."

"You have no . . ." Irina started to say, but the HR director cut her off with a raised hand.

"Davie, your manager has every right to be in this meeting. I repeat: you are an employee at will. Your behavior has been concerning and erratic. I cannot compel you to seek professional help, but I can strongly advise you to do so, and I can record in your personnel records that you were counseled to seek professional help for your behavior."

"Are we done?" Davie asked.

"Yes," the HR director said. Davie got up without another word and went to her office. She closed her door, opened her email and started to catch up with her work. But she could not concentrate. Hardly a surprise, she thought.

It was the second week of December. Michael had been dead a few days past three months, and to Davie, it felt like more like fifty years of unrelenting trauma and grief. She could not ever remember feeling so vulnerable. The rapid succession of jarring events upended every expectation she ever held about how life was supposed to play out for those who lived carefully and followed the rules. Now, she knew, everything depended on your husband staying alive. She thought of all the married people she knew, friends and co-workers, and now she thought of them as standing on the other side of a great divide, the *before* and *after*. They were the before, she was the after. They could not possibly grasp what a thin margin separated their nice, safe, secure lives from hers.

All it took, Davie thought bitterly, was someone running a red light, someone walking into the corner bodega at exactly the moment the place was being held up at gunpoint, someone starting to quietly choke at the dinner table and stepping out of the room to try to handle it without making a fuss . . . a heart attack; an aneurysm that lay in wait, undetected, inside someone's head until the day it burst . . . no one was safe, she thought; everyone just thought they were safe, until suddenly they were not. That was how she used to think, that she was safe. Any assumption that people would treat her with compassion for the cataclysmic, you-can't-make-this-stuff-up experience she'd suffered—well, that was out the window, too, Davie realized. The hair stylist whom she feared might try to rape her, just because he thought he could. The doctor who scolded her for grieving her husband only weeks after his death. The HR director who knew she was being horrible, who knew she was being inhumane, but who cared far more about keeping her job than she cared about taking a stand on principle.

Davie realized she had no protector, no fallback plan, against the people who now saw her as someone who could be picked out of the herd. What would she do if she lost her job and her six-figure income? If she'd lost her job a year ago, Michael would have told her to not worry, that he would cover her. She should just quit, she thought, but she was afraid that doing so would really mark her as ruined, unreliable, too much of a risk. Albany was a small city. Michael was very well known. Word would quickly spread that his widow had cracked up, lost her cushy job at Levellewyn, Grenoble and Carl, and good luck landing something else.

Irina was gunning for her, that much was clear, and Davie thought she was on borrowed time even if she didn't quit before they could fire her. Irina was related to one of the founding partners of the firm, and if she wanted Davie gone, if she thought that having Davie on her staff would in any way reflect poorly on her own reputation there, she would get Davie out one way or another. Davie decided she'd better view every paycheck as a plus, to ride out this stressful situation for as long as she could while she waited for what she was sure would be the coup de grace. Maybe there would be something else out there for her, she thought, but it was impossible to make a decision when she was so distraught, and the stubborn part of her personality that had carried her this far without breaking into pieces would not let her quit. They would have to fire her.

Three days later, as she pulled into the parking lot, her phone rang. She pulled over, took her phone out of her purse, and saw that it was a number from Cape Cod. She thought she knew who this was.

"Hello, this is Mrs. Devlin," she said. She turned off the engine. Other cars drove by, she was partially blocking the lane, but she didn't care.

"Mrs. Devlin? This is Captain Dwyer from the Wellfleet Fire Department Emergency Services."

"Thank you for calling me back," Davie said. She undid her seat belt.

"Mrs. Devlin, I didn't want to contact you because I wasn't sure you would want to hear from us," he said. "I got your message about why you called. I'm actually glad to have a chance to talk to you. You know, every emergency services group on the Cape knows what happened that night, and everyone knows that your husband acted with real courage. He died a hero. You know that, don't you? Your husband saved your life. I'm surprised you didn't die in the car. You were incoherent when we got you inside the station. We were trying to understand you, and you were hardly able to talk."

Davie swallowed and cleared her throat. This was the part she didn't remember. Her memory of those first minutes at the fire station jumped here and there. She remembered slumping up against the glass door and feeling Michael catching her before she fell, and then feeling an underwater, slow-motion sensation as people tried to talk to her, and finally being outside under the glare of the overhead lights on the roof of the fire station. She barely remembered trying to talk.

"Yes, I know that, sir," she said. "He would have done anything for me." She stopped again and drew in a long, ragged breath. "There were some things I needed to know. I'm sorry to ask you this, but would you have let him ride in the ambulance if he had asked? Would you have allowed him to go with us? I would understand if you didn't allow that."

"We tried to get him to go in the ambulance," the captain replied. "We asked him to ride with us. We told him to hop into the ambulance. We would always have let a family member ride with us in a situation like that. Sometimes there are medical reasons when it's not advisable, if the patient is so badly injured that we need the room to maneuver in the ambulance, or because we're trying to stop major bleeding, which can be terrible to see, but generally, we prefer that the family member not try to follow us in their car when they are so upset. He wouldn't go with us. He said he wanted to have the car to get you home later that night. So when I realized he wasn't going to come with us, and the ambulance was about to pull out, I gave him directions to the hospital. And then they were pulling out, so he left."

"You asked him to ride with us?" Davie repeated. "I don't remember that."

"Mrs. Devlin, you don't remember hearing that because you were barely conscious. You really didn't start to come around until you were well down Route 6."

The phone call, Davie thought. She needed to find out about the call Michael made.

"Could I ask you about a call my husband made to your station? I think it was fifteen or twenty minutes before he died, but I don't know for sure. I finally went through his phone, to see if he'd had any time to call 911. He didn't, but I know someone stopped to help him . . . I'm waiting for the police report from Hyannis . . . I don't even know that person's name, but I thought maybe you could tell me if you talked to my husband when he called?"

"The person who stopped to help your husband was an off-duty volunteer firefighter on the Lower Cape, but I don't know his name, either," the fire captain said. "You should see that in the report when you get it. I can find out for you if you would like me to ask."

"I think I'm going to get it soon," Davie said. "Why did my husband call you? Did he pull over for some reason? Did he get lost?"

"I think he was at a red light on Route 6," the captain said. "I never knew exactly where he was, because the connection was so bad. The call kept breaking up, and he didn't want to take a lot of time. I did understand that the ambulance was ahead of him, and he'd lost it. Your husband was trying to find out your condition. He might have been somewhere just before the Orleans rotary, based on what time he called me. And you know it's difficult to pull off the road in some stretches along that section of Route 6, especially at night. There's really not much of a shoulder. It's just a very difficult place to pull over there. The ambulance got ahead because they were using lights and sirens." She didn't remember that, either, Davie thought. "I told him you were stable as far as I knew, but I don't know if he heard me," the captain continued. "He said he was having a very hard time understanding me, he asked me to repeat what I'd said, and I don't think he wanted to call back. I heard him say he couldn't hear me. I think the light must have changed then, and I think he must have hung up. I didn't want to call him back because I thought it would just slow him down more."

Davie started to shake.

"My God, so he never knew . . . He never knew for sure that I was OK?"

"Mrs. Devlin, I am so sorry. He did not call back, and I don't believe he could hear what I was saying. The call was really breaking up very badly. He just wanted to get to you as fast as he could."

The man could have lied to her, Davie realized, and told her that Michael got the message that she was fine. Maybe he understood that she needed to know the truth. Maybe he would never lie about something like this, because he knew that lies eventually caught up with people, or because this call would end up as a report in his records and he wouldn't lie even if he wanted to. Whatever the reason, what he was telling her made perfect sense to Davie. Cell reception was often terrible on the Cape. The area around the Orleans rotary was congested, it *was* difficult to pull over there and she envisioned Michael calculating how much time it would take to try and make the call, even as he was frantic to get to the hospital.

"You don't know exactly where he was when he called? Did he say anything about not feeling well?" Davie knew this kind man found the conversation very distressing; he could tell how upset she was, but she couldn't think about him. She was trying to figure out how much more time remained to Michael when he made that call. Did he feel even then that something was going wrong inside?

"I am sorry, Mrs. Devlin. I don't know exactly where he was, but he never said anything about feeling ill, from what I heard. If I'd heard that, I would have told him to pull over anywhere, the first place he could, and wait until I could get someone to him. People sometimes get a feeling that something is wrong, the doctors call it a feeling of imminent doom, and that can happen in a situation like this, but if he felt anything, he didn't tell me. The little I was able to understand, I know he was frantic about you. I'm just deeply, deeply sorry. I wish I could tell you more. I wish I could have done something then, persuaded him to go in the ambulance, but I tried, and he wanted to have his car at the hospital."

"Thank you," Davie said. She was about to lose control so badly she thought she should get off the phone. She was sitting in her car, looking at the parking lot fringed by a row of trees alongside the sleek suburban building where she worked, and then, very suddenly, she no longer saw any of her surroundings. She had followed the conversation, and somewhere along the way she started to imagine herself standing on the bluff overlooking Longnook Beach in Truro. That was one of her favorite places on the Cape. And then the imagining became what she saw. She felt a profound sensation of being in two places at the same time, as if a part of her was no longer in the car. She knew that she was still sitting in her car, but everything had slowed around her and she knew that she was also standing on the bluff, by herself... where was Michael? He loved that overlook; they drove there almost every day when they were on the Cape. She could imagine following the gray horizon of the ocean, just drifting so far out that no one would know where she had gone. She thought she could just... let go, and *leave.* She felt herself pulling away from the present, beginning to really let go ... somewhere else, she didn't know where, and she didn't care.

"Mrs. Devlin?" The captain's voice came out of the phone that lay on her lap. "Mrs. Devlin? Are you still there?"

Davie felt a shiver go up and down her back. She picked up the phone.

"Yes ... yes, I'm sorry ... it's just ... this is so painful to hear. But I wanted to know, and I am so grateful you called me back. And I know this has been difficult for you to tell."

"We are all thinking about you," he said. "Everyone here at the station was just in shock when we found out what happened. None of us has ever seen a situation like this. I've been doing this for thirty years, and this was the worst call I ever supervised. Your husband adored you; I could tell that from just the couple minutes I talked to him. I hope you remember that."

"Thank you," she said again, very quietly.

"If there is anything else we can help you with, please call and ask for me. I hope you re . . ." With some astonishment, Davie realized he was about to say, *"I hope you recover from this."*

"I hope you take care of yourself, please," he said instead.

"Yes," Davie said. "I will." The call ended.

Then Davie bent her head over the steering wheel and started to cry harder than she had ever cried in her life. She had not cried since Michael's death, but now she rocked back and forth in the seat, clutching the steering wheel and sobbing so hard that Michael's Irish ancestors would have called the sound she was making keening. She pulled her sobs up from a place so deep inside that she didn't know it was possible to reach that far into raw, unmanageable anguish, like digging out a rotting spot in huge, gut-wrenching scoops.

Someone rapped on the car window. She didn't even look up, she just furiously waved whomever it was away, and then when she sensed that the person was gone, she sat up and tried to breathe more slowly. No one was near the car; the person who rapped on the window must have hastily headed into the building. Dear God, she needed to go into the office, at least to tell them she was going home. She felt like she was breaking apart, just cracking, or cracking up. She tilted the sun visor down and flipped up the cover on the mirror and looked at her swollen eyes and mottled skin, with awful smudges of her eye makeup on her cheekbones. She pulled out a little mirror from her purse and examined herself from a different angle and better light from the window, but she still looked and felt awful. She had no way to fix her makeup, but if she was going home, it didn't matter. She tried wiping the worst of the mess from her face with a handkerchief that she dampened from a half-filled water bottle—she actually carried old-fashioned linen handkerchiefs in her purse—but she still looked terrible. She turned the car back on, pulled into a parking space and slowly walked into the building.

Her department assistant rushed over as soon as she saw Davie. She looked frantic, and then frantically relieved that Davie was there.

"Davie," she whispered. "I need to talk to you." They walked into Davie's office, and the assistant turned and closed the door, which she ordinarily never would have done without Davie asking her to do so.

"Irina is looking for you. You missed your conference call with a client . . ."

"What time is it?" Davie asked.

"It's nine forty-five."

Davie had pulled into the parking lot at a quarter to nine. She had been in her car out there for almost an hour. She never realized that she sat there that long.

"So I missed a call … " ". . . she shook her head. "I don't even remember that call being scheduled."

The assistant grimaced. "I think you'd better go see Irina," she said. "But Davie, you look ill. You look … you don't look well at all. Did something just happen?"

Davie passed a hand over her face, rubbing at her eyes.

"Yeah, you could say that. Where's Irina? Is she in her office?"

The assistant nodded and opened the door. Davie walked up the hall and stood in the doorway of Irina's corner office.

"You needed to see me?"

Irina did not ask her to step in, sit down, or close the door. Instead, Irina stood up behind her desk.

"You blew off a conference call with a client. I don't know where you have been, or what you were doing, but you have probably just cost us an account. So do you have anything to say about what you've just done?"

"Yes," Davie said, holding onto the door frame with one hand to steady herself. "You can tell the client to go fuck himself. And while you're at it, you can do the same."

Michael had taught her the value of the judicious use of profanity in the workplace. You needed a sense of timing, he said. He once told a panel of state lawmakers that their proposal for an affordable housing plan, designed to look good while protecting the governor's bloc of richest donors on Long Island, was bullshit—his exact word, delivered on live stream. The other thing Michael told her was that you needed to be prepared to be fired every day of your career, so that you would go forth fearlessly and never sell your soul. Well, then, Davie thought, her husband would be proud of her and her soul was in good order. Because she was suddenly at her limit with her job, and she was not only prepared to be fired, but she expected to be fired within minutes.

She turned and walked down the hall to her office and started packing her possessions into a couple of tote bags. Her photographs of Michael, and one of her parents standing in front of the plane in which they would die; the little brass dish that held paper clips and was her mother's, picked up decades ago on a trip to India; and then all of the pens and notepads, because she thought those would just be tossed and she might as well take them.

In the hushed, old-world atmosphere of Levellewyn, Grenoble and Carl, the shock value of her language alone was enough to get her fired. No one in the firm ever used profanity; everyone talked as though their richest client was always standing just to one side, invisibly and silently listening. In one of his many irreverent observations about the place, Michael had likened that particular detail to the apostles telling early converts to Christianity to live as though Jesus was always in the room with them. Staff rarely used personal names in referring to clients or the higher-ups in the office; they spoke of "the client," the "founding partner" and "the president of the board of directors." It was a third-person world, discreet and very monied. Gossip, the occasional off-color joke or the sound of someone emphatically slamming the paper-tray drawer on a recalcitrant photocopy machine simply did not happen.

She figured it would be fifteen minutes before someone came to escort her from the building. It was more like ten. The HR director showed up, closed the door to Davie's office and told Davie she was being terminated and needed to be off the property within a half hour. The HR director held out a sheaf of papers. Davie would get one month of severance pay, no unemployment and she needed to remember that she had signed a nondisclosure agreement. The HR director could give her a copy, in case she didn't have the original handy from when she was hired eighteen months ago.

Davie listened, standing on her side of the desk, with all the drawers she was emptying still pulled out around her like a knee-high cattle chute, and she thought, there was no way they got all of this ready in a few minutes, there was no way that the HR director single-handedly decided on a month of severance and no unemployment in the time it took Davie to start clearing her office. Not even LGC, as the firm was known in private conversations in the office—but never in front of a client—could move this fast. They planned this, and it would have happened very soon anyhow; her scene with Irina was just the first excuse that came along to get rid of her.

All Davie felt was a sense of satisfaction at beating them to the punch. The HR director told Davie to sign a document acknowledging the terms of the severance payment, which would be deposited into her bank account the next day. Davie knew that as an employee at will, she could be fired for any reason, or no reason at all. If she didn't sign the severance agreement, if she tried to negotiate more, she would not get anything at all, so she signed the form. The HR director told her she would remain in Davie's office while Davie finished packing. It was two weeks before Christmas.

⚌

Davie went into her house through the front door at the top of the stoop, not the door underneath the stoop, where nobody could see her coming and going, because she figured the neighbors would soon realize she was out of work no matter which door she used. Why did she care so much about that? she asked herself as she hung up her coat. Because it was bred into her, she realized, to keep up appearances. She married the world's most irreverent, outspoken, blunt-talking man, and she was born and bred to conduct herself properly. The curriculum at her private day school in Manhattan included instruction in etiquette and civil discourse. She got through her parents' deaths and the accompanying shock and mourning with a stoicism that came naturally to her. That was how her parents would have behaved and it was how she behaved. The scene at Irina's office that morning was so out of character that Davie could hardly believe she had experienced it.

She walked aimlessly upstairs into the room she and Michael used as a living room. The house was ridiculously oversized for one person; just twenty feet wide, with four floors connected by one staircase that kept winding upward until it reached their bedroom; it was a bit like living in a chimney. She and Michael used the third floor as their main living space, where there was an open floor plan and a modern kitchen. The next floor down was a long, open room with an arched doorway at the back that led to a butler's pantry, and they called that room the ballroom. She and Michael hosted a huge open house on New Year's Day in the ballroom every year, a custom they started in their first year in the house a decade earlier. They bought the house in December and married in June, and they thought they would live there together for the rest of their lives.

Davie sat down on what they called the "sort of couch," which Michael abbreviated as "the SOC." The SOC was a real Japanese futon on a twin-sized steel platform bed frame, with pillows piled up against the wall behind it. They both hated traditional sofas; this alternative seating had a modern, streamlined look; and Michael wanted something where he could stretch out and read with the excellent natural light that poured through the tall windows. Davie started calling this piece of furniture the SOC also, because she thought all couples should have a shared private language. So now she sat down on the SOC and tried to figure out her next move. She was still in her work clothing: a black knee-length

74

designer-label wool and alpaca skirt, a white silk-cotton blouse and a silk-wool jacket in a blue and green tweed. A lot of good her closet of designer names was going to do her now, she thought. The house was cold; she forgot to set the heat up when she came upstairs, but she didn't feel like moving, so she just sat there.

It was her nature to plan, to crunch numbers and calculate the best or most likely scenario. Davie could not imagine a best-case scenario right now, and she hoped the most likely one that she could imagine would not come to pass—that being a long slide into financial ruin. Barely three and half months earlier, she had left for Cape Cod with Michael, on vacation from a job that paid her a salary of $135,000 a year. Their combined household income had been $285,000, and with their newfound financial bliss, they discussed a loan to finally start the work the house needed. Davie earned $50,000 a year at the end of her time with the Community Loan Foundation, and far less when they had bought the house. Michael was director of policy and planning at another social services agency a decade ago, also earning a lot less than he ended up with at the Evening Star Agency. So although they did exceptionally well in the second half of home ownership, they had remarkably little set aside for retirement. Even that was not a huge worry, because Davie's parents left her with a sizeable trust fund. She could not access that trust until she was sixty-two years old, however; her parents meant it as her retirement fund, so that she would be free to do what she wanted in her career without worrying about whether she could afford to save for retirement.

A good idea, Davie thought, but not one that would help her right now. Her parents clearly never considered a world in which healthy, careful nonsmokers did not live to see retirement when they established that trust. They would die at age fifty-eight, Michael was barely forty-six when he died, and Davie, who outlived them all, was forty-three. The ferocity, the vengeance, with which fate or the gods or whatever the hell it was had come for her was stunning. So, this was how it happened, she thought, recalling the stories on the widows' group website that recounted lost jobs, lost houses, lost lives. The women writing those accounts meant the last category literally; the site contained a long section on recognizing suicidal feelings and dealing with grief so desperate that you would do anything if you thought it would reunite you with your husband.

Well, Davie said to herself, she had just lost the job, and she hoped the house wouldn't be next. She certainly wished that she had died in the car with Michael, and she didn't know if that counted as suicidal ideation, but that imaginary ending still played through her mind more often than she would ever have admitted to anyone, including Andrea. She missed Michael so much, she so yearned to see him, and she still found it so difficult to accept that he would never come through that front door downstairs again that she wished that God, in whom she had not believed in years, had just settled the matter that night. Because Michael, like her parents, could never have imagined this outcome: she was alive and alone and out of work, and likely to remain so—all three situations—for some time to come. She hoped that the cruel treatment heaped upon her at her now-former job would come back to haunt the higher-ups at Levellewyn, Grenoble and Carl, but she held no more faith in bad deeds coming around to settle scores with their perpetrators than she held in the existence of God.

She'd recently paid off the mortgage, using Michael's life insurance, of which ten thousand dollars remained. There were another fifteen months of car payments and a student loan. She punched up the calculator on her phone and multiplied her after-tax direct deposit salary by two, and came up with six thousand and change. If she was about to start a job search at the worst time of her life, she wanted that nearly seventeen thousand dollars to last as long as possible before she needed to pull anything out of her investment account.

She figured she could last six months—no, five, because a school tax payment would soon be due. Actually, she might have only three or four months in which to find a new job, she realized, because nothing went faster than money when you were out of work. What would a woman do if she found herself widowed with three kids and a job at Walmart? A few days ago, Davie thought of the very thin line between devastating grief and everyday married life that separated married women from widows. Now, she realized, she faced the next great divider in this horrible new life she was living: the equally thin line between financial security and financial desperation. The thought of looking for a job right now was more than she could handle, when all she wanted to do was crawl under her down quilt in her dark bedroom upstairs.

She did not call Andrea to tell her she was fired; Andrea would know soon enough and Davie did not want to sound as drop-dead awful as she felt right now when she told her. But before she went upstairs, she did send an email to her sister-in-law Moira in Boston, the one who organized family gatherings. Davie kept the tone light and friendly, and wrote that she wanted Michael's family to know that she would spend Christmas with friends in Albany and she hoped she would see them soon in the new year—which of course she knew would never happen.

Nor had the aforementioned invitation from friends in Albany happened. Andrea faced cancer surgery; Jay and Alanna were flying to California to spend the holidays skiing and visiting Alanna's family. Davie added to the note to Moira that she was back at work, omitting any mention of the events of the day, and she wrote that for now, she planned to stay in the house. It was all an act, she realized; if she wrote an honest account of her life, she would scare her sister-in-law. Moira had not contacted her about any family plans for Christmas, so Davie wondered if her own note would be perceived as a bit in-your-face, but she didn't care. She really didn't mean it to be confrontational. She strongly suspected there might be a family discussion going on in the Devlin clan about whether to invite Michael's widow to spend Christmas in Boston, when none of the Devlins really knew her well. Davie did not want to be anyone's responsibility or obligation.

Then Davie did go upstairs and crawl under the covers. She was completely, utterly drained. What a day she had just endured. In the span of ninety minutes, she learned that her husband died without knowing he saved her life, and she had been fired. That was pretty difficult to believe, especially when you considered that it all played out before most people took a coffee break. She was the one who had just lived through this godawful day, and even she found it difficult to believe. But as bad as the day was, it did not begin to top the day only three and a half months earlier when she nearly died, but it was her husband who died instead. And then there was Andrea, who probably needed more support than Davie could give her right now, and who probably wanted to give Davie more support than she could, either.

Who out there in the universe was responsible for these things? Davie thought about all that happened since Michael's death. She never even considered the possibility that Michael would die so young. Now, for the first time, she seriously wondered if she was strong enough to handle this avalanche of grief and horror, and for the first time she also thought: maybe she was not. She didn't let that idea go past, "maybe she was not," but nor did she rid her mind of the thought; she just let it drop for now.

She lay on her side, looking at the sky out of the window at the back of the house, her arms folded up against her chest, as she waited for the bed to feel warmer. She knew why she could not sleep: the absence of Michael in bed, the loss of his solidly reassuring warmth next to her, the memory of him turning without waking up and throwing an arm around her as he often did, haunted her. She would never get used to this. She was still sleeping at most five hours a night, sometimes less, and this had been going on since the night Michael died. She often could not fall asleep until midnight, and she almost always woke up before dawn.

Yet that night she did fall asleep, only about a half-hour after she got into her bed. Sometime later, she woke up, instantly, fully, not with a feeling that anything was wrong—she did not detect any faint smell of smoke or the sound of a window breaking downstairs—but something jarred her awake. She felt a strong sense of Michael, she realized, a strong awareness of him. It was not a dream; she felt that he was in the room.

"Are you there?" Davie called out into her dark bedroom after she jolted awake. She did not expect an answer, of course, but she sat up, the covers pulled around her, and listened. The house was utterly still. The vivid sense of her dead husband, the feeling that he was there, faded. The sensation had been strong enough to have awakened her. *Are you there?* An odd turn of a phrase, she thought, instead of, *Are you here?* Meaning, in the room, or in her mind, as in a dream she did not remember.

She did not believe in messages from the dead. She did not believe in visions, premonitions or the sense that people in the Middle Ages would have called the Sight. Nor did she believe that Michael was in heaven. She would never see Michael again, neither here nor after she died. She knew that he died saving her life; he died not knowing that he had. It was bitterly unfair.

※

Jay called her late the next morning.

"I hear that you had a spectacular exit from LGC," he said.

"How did you . . ." Davie started to ask, and then stopped. "Oh, of course." She forgot that she worked with a friend of Jay's, or, more correctly, she forgot that she used to work with a friend of Jay's.

"Can you talk? Are you on your way somewhere?" Jay asked.

"I have no place I have to be today, which is about the only advantage so far that unemployment seems to offer. I would say that I plan to catch up on my sleep, but I know how that's going to go. I think my main plan for the day is to make sure that my four weeks of severance pay show up in my checking account."

"Really? That's all they gave you?"

"Considering that I told my boss to go fuck herself, I'm surprised I got that much."

Jay laughed.

"I heard about that, too," he said. "You were standing well within earshot of a lot of people when you did that. Apparently, you have a lot of admirers there for doing that . . ." *Yes*, Davie thought, *but none who came to ask me if I was OK after they overheard that awful scene at Irina's door . . .* and then she had an unexpected insight: although Jay found the story funny and admirable, he also seemed completely unaware of how angry and humiliated and desperate Davie must have felt in the last hour of her job. He couldn't know about the call with the fire captain that preceded her firing, but even so, his jocular comments seemed to lack the ability to read the situation. He did not ask if something triggered her firing, nor did he ask how she was doing; he just seemed to find it funny. He could not possibly think that she just walked into her office and told her boss to go fuck herself on a whim.

Davie was not surprised that none of her colleagues stopped by her office to comfort her or offer help as she had packed her belongings; they were afraid of being seen doing that, and she understood that she already was marked as prey and was being separated from the herd. It was human nature to avoid someone marked as prey, but Jay, her friend of many years, should have seen this situation as something more than stand-up material, even though his breezy tone suggested just that. Was she expecting too much? Davie wondered. This was a side of Jay's personality, this disconnect in reading a situation astutely, that she always sort of knew was there, but which she also never needed to consider beyond recognizing it. That aspect of Jay was, she realized now, one of the reasons she never considered him as anything but a friend. Michael—for all his sardonic take on situations, his irreverent sense of humor and his slightly jaded view of the world— Michael always, instantly, honed in on her moods and her unspoken worries like a laser, and he always switched from comic to serious the second he sensed she needed that from him.

"But enough of that," Jay was saying now. "I didn't call to congratulate you on telling Irina what to do with herself. I called to tell you that I have a job offer for you."

Davie said nothing. She was extremely surprised.

"I'm glad my good news made you jump for joy," Jay said, but she could tell he was smiling and that he realized she was momentarily without a response.

"A job? How?"

"We were going to do a search, but honestly, Davie, if you want this, it's yours."

"What would I be doing? I'd be useless to you as a wildlife biologist. You're not going to try to make me go hiking, are you?"

"I promise I will never try to make you go hiking. We need someone who can work with data. You know we do a lot of work for the feds and the state?"

"Yes."

"Well, we could use someone who could work up projections and do different models on our field data and also the data that's been collected by the agencies we have contracts with. They do their own field work, and turn it over to us. We analyze it, run different scenarios, and unfortunately all too often tell them the bird they are trying to save is in worse shape than they thought. We can do this stuff, but not as fast as we should because we can't free up someone full time on that. And your additional skill at writing reports that someone would actually want to read would be a bonus."

"Jay, this sounds fascinating, but I don't know a thing about birds or animals. Nothing."

"You have an undergraduate degree in mathematics, if I recall correctly, and an MBA with a concentration in economics and finance from Columbia Business School? And you've spent most of the last twenty years doing financial projections for impoverished startups, until you started helping rich people learn how to get richer? Well, think of this as financial planning for birds. It's the same idea, but birds are nicer clients than millionaires, and they need more help."

Davie was silent.

"You'd be earning a little less than half of what you earned at LGC. Can you handle that?" asked Jay, who correctly interpreted her pause.

Sixty-five thousand dollars. Well, that was quite a pay cut. On the other hand, Davie knew people who managed quite well on that amount, and she managed on less than that for years at the Community Loan Foundation, when she lived alone and rented a gorgeous apartment overlooking Washington Park. It was only in the last eighteen months that she earned a salary that passed for royal living in Upstate New York.

"What would you want me to do? Come in for some interviews?"

"Yes, but not until after the holidays. This place is already starting to empty out. You could come in and talk to the management folks the first week of January. But if I could tell them that you are at least interested, I'd love to do that before I head out the door myself."

"Yes, please tell them I would like to talk to them," Davie said.

"Great. I'll call you the day I get back to work, which will be January second. I'm thinking they'll bring you in the following week, the first full week of January. Could you keep that week open?"

"Yes. Gosh, Jay, this is good of you to think of me."

"I would never have asked you about this if you were still at LGC," Jay said. "You would have laughed at me if I'd tried to lure you away for half of what you were making there, even if it meant leaving behind Irina. I'd be really glad if we could hire you. So, we'll talk when I get back? Great. What are you doing for Christmas? Are you going to spend it with Michael's family?"

"I'm thinking about it," Davie said. She was thinking about it; Jay didn't have to know that this was as far as the trip to Boston was likely to go. *Good answer*, she could imagine Michael saying. He was an avid poker player in college, where he was also a varsity soccer player who managed nonetheless to consistently pull off a grade-point average that hovered around 3.8. He was fond of saying that he learned more about life from playing poker than from any of his college courses, and the number-one lesson he learned was to never seem desperate.

"I hope you go see them," Jay said. "They probably miss Michael, too. Alanna and I have been thinking about you a lot. We'll have you over again after the new year starts." He paused. "It sucks, Davie. I miss Michael so much that it hurts, and I can't imagine what it's been like for you."

No, he could not, Davie thought; no one could.

"I am just trying not to look too far ahead, Jay. It's been a lot of upheaval, and I think in some ways I've never really taken the time to think about Michael being gone. I know that doesn't make sense, but that's how I feel. Do the people you work with know that I'm newly widowed?"

"They knew what happened, even before I mentioned it."

"I'm not surprised. Michael got a lot of attention, all of it deserved. Do they know I was fired?"

"No, and they never will, if I have anything to do about it. They know that the job was not the right fit for you, and that became more evident with everything you're dealing with right now. I think they see your time at LGC as an interlude. They were very interested in your time at the Community Loan Foundation. That kind of work is more in keeping with the philosophy here."

"Well, then, I will talk to you after New Year's," Davie said. "But yes, I am very interested. I have a resume in pretty good shape because it was only less than two years ago that I left Community Loan. Thanks, Jay."

She called Andrea next.

"I want to tell you that I got fired yesterday, but I may already have a job lined up."

"Do tell!" Andrea said. "I hope you got fired because you told Irina to go fuck herself. And, I was about to call you. Come for Christmas dinner at my brother's house."

"I thought you were getting ready for surgery and wanted to just be with your family."

"I am, and I was, but I have decided that there are better gains to be had by being surrounded by as many nice people as possible. Come for dinner. And now tell me what led up to your telling Irina to go fuck herself?"

"How did you know? That is exactly what I told her. They had me out the door forty-five minutes later."

"I didn't know, but I have been fervently hoping for the last year that you would do that, or something equivalent. She is really an awful person. Did something prompt this?"

Touché, Davie thought. Trust Andrea to figure that out fast.

"I missed a conference call with a client. I just forgot I had it scheduled, and I missed it. I was running late, and Irina asked me if I had anything to say to account for my actions. I guess I did."

"You're amazing," Andrea said. "I am not glad you just lost your job and the salary, but you've only been back to work a total of four days since Michael died, and that woman has treated you like dirt every one of those four days. Has she ever even asked how you are doing?"

"No."

"Davie, let me tell you something. Irina is such a small part of your life that in a few months, you will have trouble remembering her name. Sometimes you have to take a stand. Michael would have told you the same. May I ask, did something cause you to miss the conference call?"

Ahhh, Davie thought. She both wanted Andrea to ask that, and she didn't want to answer. Andrea did not know that Davie was trying to piece together that missing time. It would just cause her worry.

"I just kind of zoned out in the parking lot. I was a little tired, and I just was sitting in the car, and I . . . didn't go into the building right away. I lost track of time."

A few seconds of silence. Then Andrea spoke, and what she said was the single kindest remark anyone had yet made to Davie since Michael's death.

"Davie? My heart breaks for you. Michael was a special light on this Earth, and an astonishing gift to you. This is going to take a long time. It is very important that you do, as far as you can, things to help yourself get through each day. If that means leaving the wrong job, so be it. Where would the new job be?"

Davie explained, and said she was probably going to have an interview in early January.

"Make sure you tell them you need two weeks off in late June to go backpacking with me. We're going to the Shenandoah National Park in Virginia."

"Andrea, the little that I do know about birds and what biologists do with them, I have the feeling that June is going to be a difficult month for me to schedule a vacation."

"Not so," Andrea said. "They're collecting the data from May to July, and then you'll be analyzing it once they have it. They'd rather have you on vacation in June than August or September."

"How do you know all of this?"

"I read, and I used to date a guy who was kind of a bird nut. So remember: you need two weeks off in late June. Tell them it was already scheduled, and that you have nonrefundable reservations. And if you feel like driving to my brother's house, pick me up around noon on Christmas day."

"What am I going to do with all my clothes?" Davie mused. "I've got a wardrobe of silk blouses and dressy jackets. Hell of a lot of good that's going to do me. The people in Jay's office dress in hiking clothes. Although maybe I should see how long I last at this job. I might need the investment banker look again come spring."

"Do you even own a pair of jeans?" Andrea asked.

"Of course I do. You see me wearing jeans on the weekends."

"Oh, that's right," Andrea said. "Your everyday attire at that hell hole of a stress factory LGC kind of blinded me to your more casual side. Well, wear the jeans on the bottom and the silk blouses and dressy jackets on the top and you'll look fine. Hiking boots, not those Cole Hahn flats you love so much, or at least some chukka boots. And you might want to buy a pair of hiking pants, because you're going to need them soon. We'll talk about that after the holidays. I am going to give you a list of what to buy for your first backpacking trip, and then you and I are going gear shopping."

Davie was glad she decided not to detail the circumstances that led to her parting conversation with Irina. The memory of her conversation with the fire captain was too upsetting, and she was, if not precisely guarded about how much she disclosed, at least inclined to think about how such details would affect people who also cared about Michael. The bone and tissue donation and what came home from the Cape; the terrible abrasion on Michael's forehead—which conjured up such a heartbreaking image that she could not imagine telling anyone else—and now this revelation, that Michael never even knew for sure that she got to the hospital alive. These were details she realized would make people uncomfortable. The scene in the hospital, when she went into the room to see Michael's body, was too upsetting to share, the ultimate example of too much information.

And yet, because she could not talk about such memories, she also could not stop thinking about them. She had a recurring memory that seemed to play out in her mind three or four times a day. She called it "the endless loop tape," and it started with the moment she looked down the hall and saw the nurse coming toward her. It progressed to her reaching for Michael's hand and realizing his skin was already hardened, and it ended with her sitting in the hallway outside of the room where the code played out, in full earshot of the last two times the nurses and the doctor tried to shock Michael's heart back to life. She could still hear the nurse calling, "Clear!" and then again, and then the steady, flat whining sound of the monitor, but no sound of a heartbeat. She found the memory so haunting, so sad, so poignant, that she wondered how it would ever recede from her everyday awareness.

She went for her first visit with her new doctor. The doctor was young, female and compassionate; she listened steadily to Davie's halting account of Michael's death. Davie learned on that visit that her blood pressure was still quite a bit higher than usual—she was a textbook one-twenty over sixty when she wasn't in a state of shock—but the doctor thought that was stress, grief and lack of sleep, and that it did not require medication. She asked Davie if she wanted a referral to a grief counselor, which Davie declined. But now Davie called the practice, got one of the nurses on the phone, and said she wanted the referral after all.

The doctor gave Davie the name of a clinical psychologist who practiced in Columbia County, almost an hour from Davie's home. She said he was very good, she used him herself a few years earlier, after her five-year-old daughter died when a drunk driver's car ran into the family's front yard.

Davie wondered how she would manage subsequent appointments with a new job, if she even wanted to see this guy again after the first appointment? The drive out to rural Columbia County might also be very difficult in bad weather. Then Davie thought, maybe these people she was about to start working for would be reasonable. She was newly widowed. Maybe she could work this out. If she had an appointment on a day when the roads were bad, she could reschedule. Working the appointments into her schedule might be a lot easier than she anticipated. Maybe she should just try it first, before she made a decision.

She got an appointment for December twenty-third. The therapist spent some time talking to her over the phone, a kind of intake, Davie reasoned. She told him a bare-bones version of what happened, she told him she held no religious beliefs at all and she told him she wished she had died in the car with Michael. He could make of that what he wanted, she figured. She might as well not have worried, Davie later thought, because the appointment was a disaster.

The therapist told her he had a home office, which gave her pause, but she drove out for the appointment. His house was on an isolated road—hardly a surprise in Columbia County—and he used a living room off the kitchen for his sessions; there was no separation from the rest of the house. His daughter was also a psychologist, he mentioned, and she also used the space for her clients. Davie had seen the daughter in the kitchen when they walked through on their way to the living room, but she wondered, would there be someone else in the house every time she went there? The whole setup struck her as strange.

She found it difficult to believe that her doctor advised her to try this therapist, and then she realized, her doctor probably thought the therapist still had an office and a secretary. The therapist explained that he only worked a couple days a week now. Davie thought of just turning around and leaving, but it had been a long drive—too long, she now knew, to be practical—and so she sat down and gave it a try. After a few preliminaries, the therapist asked her if she believed in angels. No, Davie replied, she already told him she didn't have any religious beliefs. Didn't he remember that? Was he listening during the intake by phone? she asked. Then she stood up and left without waiting for an answer. The therapist did not charge her for the visit.

She could not get out of the house fast enough. He might have been the nicest, most professional psychologist in the world, but she would never have felt safe or comfortable there. The question about angels grated on her and seemed a portent of his approach to grief. The experience also gave her an inkling of how difficult it would be to find someone who would be a good match. She didn't have the energy to take on the search for a therapist and start a new job, she decided. The memories, the scene in the hospital, the fact that she never dreamed of Michael again after those first two night-mares on the Cape—she just mentally packed everything that bothered her so much into a box in her mind and tried to forget about it all. If she could have handed this box over to someone the way she had handed over the boxes of Michael's clothes, she would have. But if she didn't land the job Jay lined up for her, if she didn't find a new job, all the grief counseling in the world wasn't going to do her much good.

chapter 6

She went for an interview at Jay's organization the first week of January. The office sprawled over the second floor of an old building on Broadway; she could walk to work if she got the job. The interview with the executive director and the senior managers went well. A staff member brought Davie to the executive director's office and told her he would be right along. He showed up a few minutes later and got straight to the point: they wanted to hire her, he made an offer, she accepted it. The starting salary was sixty-two thousand dollars. She was glad for Jay's forewarning on this, so that nothing changed in her expression when she learned she would start at even less than Jay thought she would. Instead, she nodded and thanked the executive director.

Mentally, she clicked through her budget, wondering how she would make up that three-thousand-dollar gap, then realized that if she could manage for three months while she paid down and closed her credit card, she could pull this off just fine. She had always been able to do calculations in her head even while carrying on a conversation, and the executive director appeared to notice nothing awry in her demeanor. She could begin the middle of next week; they needed to clear out an office for her that presently held field gear they used for surveying birds. She explained she had a vacation already scheduled for early June, that it involved plans with a friend who was going to travel with her, and she wanted to keep those plans, if possible. No problem, the executive director told her; everyone was out in the field most days in June. Andrea was right, Davie thought. For all the years of her friendship with Andrea, she never realized Andrea knew anything about wildlife biology.

The executive director handed her a heavy hardcover book, with a dust jacket illustration of a bird Davie could not have identified if threatened

87

with torture, and he offered to show her around the office. She could keep
the book, he said. She might find it a helpful reference. They were going
to be working on some of the data for the next edition, which would not
come out for more than a dozen years, but was already in the early planning stage. Davie read the title: *The Atlas of Breeding Birds in New York
State*. She suspected there was a purpose behind the book, that she should
make time to look through it before she started next week. The executive
director joked that the book was a gift to soften the news about the starting
salary, and then very seriously added that he realized the offer was a huge
reduction for her. He also realized that she knew nothing about birds or
wildlife, and like Jay, he told her that didn't matter; what mattered was her
ability to turn raw data into analyses and projections and reports. He said
they all felt lucky to have her join the staff. He asked if she felt like seeing
the rest of the office and told her to leave the book; she could get it later.

She found the atmosphere of the organization relaxed and she found
the charts and posters and photographs everywhere on the walls fascinating.
Birds, mostly, but also snakes and turtles and butterflies. She didn't know
the names of any of them. The executive director took her to her office; it
was filled with what looked like rolled-up badminton nets, leaning in bun-
dles against the walls and stacked on the desk. Mist nets, he told her. She
had no idea what mist nets were. The office was on the side of the building
overlooking North Pearl Street, and Davie could see the Hudson River.

"You'll find that this place is pretty casual, even if the work is serious," he said. He wore a wool flannel shirt, hiking pants in some high-
tech fabric, and hiking boots. Davie wore a black skirt—she owned three
for work, and one for dressy evening functions—a light-blue silk blouse, a
blue wool-cashmere jacket and black suede boots with low heels instead of
pumps because it was so cold that day. She realized he was telling her she
could dress down quite a bit more. She smiled inwardly at his comment; at
about this point in her interview at LGC, the HR director handed her the
internal policy manual and suggested she pay especial attention to the dress
code because a professional appearance mattered to their clients.

Davie asked if she would ever be allowed to go out in the field with the
biologists and get an idea of what their work was like out of the office? Of
course, her new boss told her. They would be going out on a couple of projects in the spring. Whip-poor-wills and the something-or-other thrush, the
name of which went right by her. Davie had heard of whip-poor-wills. She
thought it would be cool to see one, because it was possibly the only bird
other than a loon that she could have identified by sound. She nodded and

said it would be good to see what the staff did. She didn't want to handle their data without ever understanding their part of a project.

On her way out, she stopped to see Jay, and he handed her another book, the *Sibley Guide to Birds*. Davie realized there was a pattern here; they wanted her to read these books. Jay told her that he and Alanna wanted to get together soon. Maybe at her home, Davie said, surprising herself. No one had been in the house since the morning of Michael's memorial service.

All of this made her feel better than she expected, considering that she felt like hell last week, and it also made her feel like she had taken a huge step toward what she already knew would be a gradual departure from her life with Michael. Davie was cautious: she realized her optimistic mood might be fleeting, given the wild swings of the past week, from being fired to being hired. When she thought about rebuilding her life, she always saw a mental image of standing on the deck of the Staten Island Ferry, which was one of her favorite things to do in graduate school when she needed a day to herself. In this image, she always saw Michael standing on the loading area as the boat pulled away from the dock. This was not a dream, it was an imaginary summation of how she felt about the changes in her life, and she said to herself, if she was going to think in cliches, couldn't she come up with a better one? She could also almost hear Michael saying that, but the image kept coming back to her.

When Davie got home, she sat down at her kitchen table and worked up a revised budget for her new salary. She suspected she would get a raise very quickly, but things would be tight the first year. OK, she thought, she would make it work. She could cover all her expenses; she just wouldn't be taking any vacations for a while. Or saving very much. For years, she fantasized about living without a credit card, ever since a seminar on personal finance and bankruptcy in graduate school taught her about the racket otherwise known as the credit card industry.

Then she took a legal pad and started a list. She labeled it "The Top Ten Things I Want To Do With The Rest Of My Life," but then she thought better of that. Maybe she needed to scale back everything, and see how she managed in the next year, before she started making life lists. Besides, she had no idea how she would feel the next day, much less next year. Her normally steady moods were like a swing on a playground these days. Today was a good day, but tomorrow she might find herself toying with the darker thoughts that started with Michael's death. Better not aim too high, she thought.

She tore off the page, started a new list, headlined it "The Top Five Things I Want To Do In The Next Year," and wrote:

1: Honor Michael's life by the way that I live.
2: Replace the windows on the third floor.
3: Get the trim on the house painted.
4: See a whip-poor-will.
5: Start hiking the Appalachian Trail.

She taped the list to her refrigerator door so that she would look at it often.

When Davie got her mail that afternoon, she found an envelope from the Hyannis Police Department in between two thick, square envelopes she recognized as condolence cards. She set those aside and opened the envelope that contained the police report on Michael's death, the one she requested through the Freedom of Information Law. She was glad this had not come just before her job interview, because if she had read it ahead of time, she would have blown the interview, and if she hadn't read it, she still would have blown the interview from distraction.

She sat down on the SOC, slit the envelope open and pulled out two stapled pages of a report form. She thought most people very reasonably would have poured a little bourbon to accompany this task. She did still have the remnants of a bottle of bourbon in the house left over from Michael, but she also was very aware of how often she thought about doing that, and not just when she was about to read the police report describing how her husband died. So, she remained sitting on the edge of the SOC, unfolded the pages and started reading.

Michael died about five minutes from Cape Cod Hospital. He pulled his car off into the parking lot of a small strip of stores, all of them closed for the day, and got out of the car. By then, it was fully dark. Even so, a man driving by noticed him in the empty parking lot, saw that Michael was supporting himself against the open car door, realized he was in distress. Davie wondered how many others drove by and never noticed Michael, or saw him and thought nothing of it. This man was an off-duty volunteer firefighter, and he pulled into the parking lot and asked Michael if he needed help. Yes, Michael said, he couldn't breathe. He needed to get to the hospital. Michael was holding his phone; he must have been about to call 911; he would not have had the phone number of the hospital with him. Then he collapsed.

The man who stopped to help him called for an ambulance and started CPR. The police got there first, they tried to use an AED, then the ambulance arrived. They never got Michael's heart started at the scene, and, as Davie knew already, the emergency department team never got a heartbeat, either. The report gave the name of the man who stopped to help Michael.

Davie set the report down and mulled over what she had just read. She wanted to talk to the man who stopped to help Michael, and now she knew how to reach him, because in addition to his name, the report listed the address and phone number of an autobody shop he owned. She thought she should write to him instead of calling him. Around the practical details, she found the report heartbreaking. A little more than an hour before the scene described in the two pages, Michael was striding around the wharf, taking the call that interrupted their dinner, and the biggest decision they faced was whether to go for a walk on an ocean beach or a bay beach.

Davie thought it was entirely possible that the police report omitted some of the details she craved, that it was a sketch of Michael's last minutes but not a complete account. Did he say anything else? How did he get that terrible abrasion on his forehead? Did anyone know what number he wanted to dial? Was he trying to call her, instead of 911? If he was struggling to breathe, he certainly wouldn't have remembered that her own phone was in her canvas tote bag on the passenger floor of the car. She would probably never know what number he was trying to dial, but she now knew he felt desperate and panicked. Michael's death certificate stated that he suffered pulmonary edema as part of his overriding cause of death, acute coronary syndrome. She had already looked up what pulmonary edema meant. It meant that Michael felt like he was drowning. It meant that fluid poured into his lungs. Davie knew how it felt to realize you couldn't breathe; she knew how it felt when fluid poured into your throat so fast you couldn't pull in any air. She remembered the thick fluid clogging her own throat until she couldn't clear her airway in the car that night, and she remembered that at the very end, all she could focus on was telling herself to breathe in and breathe out . . . just try to keep breathing. That was how Michael died, feeling that way. Dear Jesus, she thought.

She remembered reading the report by the National Transportation Safety Board on the investigation into her parents' fatal flight. The report took nearly two years to complete, and it was inconclusive. The investigators could not find any cause for the crash. The plane had undergone a maintenance check the week before the flight. Her parents' flight instructor and people at the airport said Davie's parents went over the plane with almost obsessive thoroughness before each takeoff. Her father, who was at the controls, did not have any medical problems that could have caused him to lose consciousness, and nothing turned up in the autopsy. There were no isolated summer storms in the area, no microbursts of wind. She knew that the NTSB even considered whether the crash was deliberate—a murder-suicide, with or without her mother being in on the plan. That was also discounted after extensive interviews with Davie, with her parents' colleagues, with their financial advisors and their doctors. There were no hidden problems, no undisclosed dire medical diagnoses, no money troubles, no extra-marital affair, no secret double life by one of them. The plane plummeted into the forest, and no one would ever know why.

Davie's parents had just crossed the northwestern Connecticut state line and were flying above Massachusetts when the plane crashed into a region so inaccessible that Davie could only be thankful it was summer. At least the rescuers were not hiking to the scene in three feet of snow and single-digit temperatures, which she learned were common in that area in the winter. There were no roads near the crash site, and Davie vividly remembered waiting at the state troopers' command post for two days in Salisbury, Connecticut, until the rescuers could get her parents' bodies to the nearest hospital for autopsies. She knew that the difficulty of reaching the crash did not make any difference in her parents' survival; they died instantly, as the medical examiner determined, a finding made easier by the fact that the little plane did not burn. There was simply no explanation for the crash, and that happened in a small number of such investigations, as Davie learned.

Davie had loved and admired her parents, who met at Yale Law School and shared a deep commitment to living responsible lives with a strong bent toward social justice. They were privileged, and they felt they should give back to society in some way because of that privilege. That explained their membership on numerous boards of charitable organizations and nonprofits that sought to make a difference in the world. They were good people; their worldview was genuinely based on service. Davie was twenty-eight years old when they died, fully independent, a year out of her MBA program at Columbia and newly settled in Albany. She was stricken, shocked and distraught by their deaths, but she accepted the NTSB's report, and she never considered setting off on a quest of her own to uncover any more details of the fatal flight.

She very much wanted to do that about Michael's death, and she knew why: because Michael's death was inextricably, forever tied to her nearly fatal allergic reaction. She could not uncouple one from the other, and she felt she could never entirely get past either trauma unless she could tell herself with absolute certainty that she did everything that night she possibly could have done in the best way possible, even under the worst imaginable circumstances. She thought that otherwise, she would never be able to alleviate her guilt. And because she could not remember significant parts of the event, she had very little with which to work. She needed as much information as she could gather. She felt that she faced an impossible situation, and she doubted that anyone around her could have guessed at her inner torment.

She had tried so hard not to panic Michael, not because she thought it would trigger cardiac arrest, but because she loved him and she would never willingly have done anything to cause him to panic. He hadn't needed her to tell him she was in acute distress; he realized that in seconds. She often found herself going over everything she could remember; this kept her awake at night, long after she went to bed. She wondered if she had used the EpiPen sooner, maybe she never would have been so near to blacking out in the car. But everything happened so fast, she reminded herself. She wondered if she tried to call Michael when she first realized he was terribly late, would she have realized he was in distress? The hospital would have let her use an outside line. Then she thought no, if she had done that and he answered the phone before he was stricken, she'd be sitting on the SOC right now thinking that she caused his death because she delayed him with that call, kept him from getting to the hospital sooner. And if he'd gotten to the hospital sooner, he might have been at the hospital when he went into cardiac arrest.

So here she was, widowed, sitting in the house where she and Michael made their life, stuck in the worst imaginable aftermath—a situation no one could have thought up if you'd paid them—and she saw no way out of it.

She also knew her widowhood was far more complicated than trying to recover from the death of a husband in a car accident, or a husband diagnosed with inoperable cancer or a husband who died in any of the myriad other ways in which people died before their time. She was in a uniquely terrible category. About the time she got this far in her thoughts, she also started to think about what she internally called her "backup plan." She couldn't talk to anyone about that, either, because she knew full well how scared the people around her who cared for her would be if she told them how often she flirted with the idea of suicide. Even she was a bit shocked at how often she thought about it. She wondered if that very act of allowing herself to think about it might keep her just where she was—thinking about it, but never acting on the thoughts. She was afraid of losing control of her life if anyone else realized her mental turmoil. Who *wouldn't* be in her state of mind after all that she survived, Davie asked herself. She knew she didn't want to be dead, but she very much wanted to shut down the endless loop tape in her head, the several-times-a-day replay of the scene in the hospital.

Suicide was, Davie realized, an unspeakably rigid taboo, one which no one wanted to touch. Had a close friend asked her if she felt suicidal, she might have talked about it, but of the only two people she could imagine discussing this with, one was about to have cancer surgery and the other was about to become a co-worker. Neither ever asked her that question. Davie could not imagine opening the topic with Andrea or Jay, not now, probably not ever. After the experience with her former doctor, she was reluctant to speak to her new doctor, however young and hip she seemed. She was, after all, the person who sent Davie to the therapist in Columbia County.

Davie was quite astonished at her ability to feel this way, to walk around with such dire internal strife so carefully concealed, and still be able to function. On the surface she was, she sensed, just about where people expected her to be—nowhere near recovered from Michael's death, but making a little progress each day. This was how she presented herself to the merchants she knew on Lark Street; the nice guy in the coffee shop; her sisters-in-law in Boston, who did check in every several weeks. This was also how she presented herself to Andrea and Jay and Alanna. She got up every day, she dressed carefully, she fixed her hair and put on some makeup.

No one would have guessed that one night she went into the bathroom at home and rummaged around in the vanity drawer for the bottle of over-the-counter medication she strongly suspected would be a career-ending overdose if consumed in its entirety. She melted the pills in a small amount of boiling water in a Pyrex bowl and quickly poured the liquid into the trash can in the kitchen, then she tied the bag closed and dropped it into her garbage can under the stoop. She thought about that bottle of medication too often and she wanted it out of the house. She knew she could perform at her new job; it was the silent house at night, which all but shimmered with memories of Michael's presence, that haunted her. How would she ever get better? Michael would have been horrified at what his death was doing to her, but she knew he would have felt the same if she died that night, as she thought she would, and it was Michael instead who drove home from the Cape a widower.

It was in this frame of mind that she composed a letter to the young man who stopped to help Michael. She wrote it that afternoon, but she decided to re-read it the next day before she mailed it on her way to an appointment with one of the top allergists in the region. This seemed to be her week to face residual trauma, she thought, and better this week than next week, when she was to start her new job.

She introduced herself in the opening line and added that she realized he might not recognize her name. It was her husband whom he stopped to help, she explained, and she just received the police report and learned he was the person who stopped to help Michael. She wanted to speak with him, both to thank him and because she wanted to learn as much as possible about what happened after Michael got her to the fire station in Wellfleet.

Davie paused there and wondered how much this man might know. He might not have been told that Michael was trying to get to her at the hospital. He probably had very little detail about the whole complicated story. Then again, the fire captain told her that the story of Michael's actions became known throughout the emergency services up and down the Cape, and the man she was writing was a volunteer firefighter. In the end, she explained as simply as possible that she suffered a severe allergic reaction, that Michael got her to the fire station and was following the ambulance when he was stricken. That was the best she could do. She read the letter, and then added, "Please know that I simply want to speak with you. It is very important to me, for my own peace of mind, that I be able to fill in this gap, after my husband got me to the fire station. His actions saved my life, and I know how hard you tried to save his life. Please understand that I feel nothing but gratitude to you because you stopped to help Michael. Because of you, my husband died believing he would get to me in the hospital." Then, she surprised herself by adding, "I bless you for stopping to help Michael. I will be grateful to you forever for stopping. I hope that I can speak with you. Thank you."

I bless you for stopping to help Michael. Davie held no religious beliefs, but she was reaching for something that would convey the sincerity and honesty of her motives. The fire captain talked to her, and she hoped this man would, too. Davie provided her phone number, but she left open the question of whether she expected him to call her or she would try to call him. Most people receiving such a letter would interpret it as an invitation to call the person who sent it, she thought.

She mailed the letter the next morning on her way to her appointment with the allergist. She scheduled the appointment before she knew she would have a job interview that same week, but with the interview behind her, and several days before she started work, she wanted to go. She spent the rest of the day meeting first with the allergist, then with two nurses as they asked her many questions, asked her to reconstruct the hours leading to the onset of the allergic reaction, and tested her for numerous substances known to be common triggers for allergies. They could not find anything she was allergic to, other than her known latex allergy. When she met with the allergist again at the end of the day, he told her it was possible she suffered a severe latex reaction, but it could just as easily have been something she never before encountered. Allergies could start at any time, he explained; something could become potentially deadly without warning, even if you previously used it, ingested it, handled it, your entire life.

In other words, for the second time in her life, Davie would never know the cause of a catastrophic event. One of the reasons she so loved mathematics was that there was always an answer. It might take hundreds of years to reveal itself, but there was always an answer. Now, she detected the allergist's diminished interest in her case because he could not find a solution; it was a subtle shift, but it was obvious he found a patient whose allergy he could not identify a lot less professionally satisfying. He offered no suggestions, other than to tell her to keep two EpiPens on hand. He seemed to give no consideration to the aftereffects of the event; to him, it was a clinical case, not a tragedy. As Davie headed out, one of the nurses caught up with her.

"I'm sorry," the nurse said. Davie nodded her thanks and left.

It must have been their sixth or seventh wedding anniversary that they found that kettle pond hidden way down a fire road in Truro, Davie thought that night as she lay in bed, waiting for sleep she knew would not come for several more hours. She went to bed because the house was cold and she was dispirited by the trip to the allergist, and it was a very long time—months now, since Michael's death—that she had read anything for pleasure. She didn't feel like picking up a book tonight. So, with no interest in trying to fill up a couple more hours, she went upstairs and tried to fall asleep. She found herself thinking about that evening in June, when they spent their wedding anniversary rambling around remote back roads on the Outer Cape. They usually went to the Cape in June, during their anniversary week; they were there in September when Michael died only because a conference he wanted to attend was in June.

But the week that Davie found herself remembering now, on a bitterly cold night in mid-January, stayed in her memory as special. The weather was terrible for the first several days of their precious week away, and although being trapped in a small beach cottage in a summer gale as their vacation ticked by would have driven most couples to the point of considering divorce, it was an unexpected gift to Davie and Michael. They both brought books they wanted to read, instead of work from their jobs that they needed to read. They were capable of spending hours together without talking, each absorbed in a project. Davie bought a half-gallon of vanilla ice cream and made some bittersweet chocolate sauce and ate ice cream sundaes every day until the half-gallon was finished. Michael only liked one ice cream flavor, mint chocolate chip, so Davie methodically worked her way through the half gallon the way a chain smoker would have gone through a carton of cigarettes.

Every morning for the first four days of that stormy week, Michael turned on the community radio station in Provincetown, where you never knew if you were going to hear vintage jazz broadcast from scratchy records on a studio turntable, or a program host reading the history of an obscure agrarian movement in the Midwest during the Great Depression. On the morning of the fourth day of the gale, they listened to the first-hand account of a North Truro resident who found an old shipwreck uncovered by an especially rough surf at high tide during the storm, and they learned that the wreck would disappear again as the beach shifted in the gale. They ventured out to the site, but the shipwreck was already covered when they got out there that same afternoon, and the wind was too strong to even walk on the beach.

The cottage also included an outdoor shower, and the place was so secluded that they stopped wearing anything to go out for a shower. This led to a rediscovery of their sex life, which after nearly a decade of their living together was probably at about the same stage it would have been for any couple: terrific at home when they were not too tired from their demanding jobs—which they were much of the time—and even better after coming in from a steaming hot shower they had just taken together outdoors, despite the fact that it was pouring rain and quite cold.

Then, on Wednesday, the weather cleared and the days became dry and warm. That day also happened to be their wedding anniversary, and after a morning of rambling all over the Outer Cape, they began driving around on the hidden back roads of the ocean side. Many of these were fire roads used for reaching brush fires, covered in soft sand and requiring slow going. *Let's turn down this road and see where it goes,* Michael used to say. He loved discovering the unknown, the unexplored. Davie loved knowing there would be a solution to the equation. *We won't get stuck down here, do you think?* she asked as they started down one such road so slowly that the speedometer needle didn't move. No hell, no way, Michael said. They didn't know where they would end up, but fire roads always connected at both ends to a road used by everyday traffic, so they kept going. That was how they found the kettle pond.

Michael pulled the car over as far as he could, got out and walked to the edge of the water—oblivious to the mosquitoes that swarmed in the cool, damp dim of the wooded back road—thoughtful, assessing, then he turned and called back to Davie. *Hey, let's go for a swim.*

He later told Davie he was astonished at the alacrity with which she got out and stripped to her panties and bra. She felt the need to keep something on that resembled a bathing suit, because she knew there were a few houses dotted here and there in these hidden parts of the woods, and she was reluctant to be caught swimming completely naked. She also felt the elemental pull of the pond, which a retreating glacier dug at the end of the last ice age. Michael, who thought the chance of someone driving by was extremely remote, stripped off his T-shirt and khaki shorts, under which he wore nothing. They waded into the water, feeling the sandy bottom that was characteristic of kettle ponds, and they were so entranced by the solitude, the fading light and the beauty of this hidden place that they felt lost in suspended time. They could hear dusk sounds trilling around them, it was growing dark as they held each other and kissed, and Davie thought it was the best wedding anniversary they'd ever had. The summer night began to settle around them as they walked out of the water. After they got back to the car, they silently dressed, and they hardly said a word as they drove to their cottage.

Lying in her bed, warm at last but no more ready for sleep than when she first crawled under the covers, Davie wondered if she held enough memories of Michael to get her through the rest of her life. She also wondered if she would ever want to go to the Cape again.

❧

She started her new job the following week and quickly realized that mid-January was the ideal time. Starting at this place in the spring would have been more hectic; starting it in the early fall, when the summer data started coming in, would have been like starting at Levellewyn, Grenoble and Carl on April fourteenth. The winter slow season gave her time to become acquainted with the types of projects the biologists did, and she worked up a few low-level analyses and tweaked them as she began learning the preferences of the field people. The executive director announced her hiring in a note to the staff *". . . Davie earned her undergraduate degree in mathematics at Princeton University and her MBA at Columbia University. She worked for 15 years at the Community Loan Foundation, where she oversaw the work with small startups. She comes to us from Levellewyn, Grenoble and Carl, where she was part of the team that worked with privately held firms. She claims that she can't tell an American Robin from a Peregrine Falcon. Cut her some slack; it's not yet nesting season."*

Neatly done, Davie thought. No one would have known that her husband had just died, her life had just been upended and she had been fired and was taking a seventy-three-thousand dollar pay cut. She wore her wedding ring, put a photograph of Michael in her office, volunteered very little about her personal life and focused on her new job. She assumed that most of her new co-workers knew about her; Michael's death was widely publicized, and while she didn't try to hide her past, she noticed that no one mentioned Michael and no one asked about the photograph on her desk. That was fine; Davie realized that people didn't know what to say most of the time.

The winter weeks ticked by, a period of relative calm for Davie. She started to sleep a little better. She noticed that she did not hear from the man who stopped to help Michael, nor was the letter returned as undeliverable. She knew the garage was open Saturdays until one o'clock in the afternoon. She was hesitant to call and have another scene, even at home, like that time in her car in the parking lot at her former job the day the Wellfleet fire captain called her. She didn't want anything to impede her job. So she waited, uncertain of how to proceed.

She invited Jay and Alanna for dinner. The evening went well, even though she once turned in the kitchen while opening a bottle of wine and saw Jay standing in front of the shelf where she kept her photographs of Michael. Surprisingly, perhaps, there were no wedding photographs, because in the haste of their little ceremony, somehow no one thought of taking any pictures. Hiring a professional photographer seemed off-kilter with the concept of a semi-elopement. She possessed photos aplenty of other times in her life with Michael. Now, she turned and looked past Alanna, who was setting the table, and saw Jay standing in front of the photos, deeply absorbed. Davie pretended she never noticed Jay.

Andrea underwent her surgery the second week of February. She said it went great, and Davie did not ask for any more information. Davie went to see her on her way home from work one day. Andrea lived in an Arts and Crafts bungalow in an old Albany neighborhood, with a backyard that was on the city's garden tour for years. It was a pollinator garden, designed to attract butterflies and bees and hummingbirds to the wild tangle of stalks and seed heads and raspberry canes. The garden contained two water sources for pollinators: a birdbath and a bee bath. The two were on opposite sides of the yard, with the bee bath much closer to the ground and near the raspberry canes. Davie realized that Andrea was far better prepared for Davie's new job than she, Davie, had been, at least in terms of understanding the work. Now, in February, the garden was covered with snow, and last summer's raspberry canes leaned away from the fence, unrecognizable as the thicket they would become by June.

"This is for you," Andrea said, handing Davie a thick envelope. She got through chemotherapy with remarkably few side effects, minimal hair loss and little fatigue. The only indication that she was recovering from surgery was the fact that she was stretched out on her couch with her feet up, wide awake but quite content to rest. "Open it. I want to show it to you."

The envelope contained folded maps and thick little booklets for the Appalachian Trail. One set was for Massachusetts and Connecticut; the other set was for Shenandoah National Park in Virginia.

"So we're really doing this," Davie asked, thumbing through the booklets. She was not asking a question; she was acknowledging defeat.

"Yes, we are," Andrea said. "I've got next week off. I've got some follow-up appointments, and I'd like to take it easy for another few days, but I would like to go with you when you get your backpack. So, a week from Saturday, before I go back to work? And I'll draw up a list of what you should consider buying, and you could poke around on some of the gear sites to get an idea of what's out there. Now, you can get some of this stuff on the resale sites of some of these companies, but the backpack and the boots you need to buy new. Those are your two most important pieces of gear. I've got a tent I don't use anymore, and you can use that. I've got extras of a lot of the stuff you'll need, like water bottles. I'll send you the list."

"I find it difficult to believe that I am going to do this," Davie said.

"But before we do this trip, we're going to do a little overnight training hike in May. Memorial Day weekend, OK?"

"And where are we doing that?"

"In Massachusetts," Andrea said. "It's a good practice hike. We'll talk about that later. Let's get you geared up first."

That was on a Thursday evening. That Saturday, Davie called the garage on the Cape and asked to speak with the owner.

"He's not here today," said the man who answered the phone. The call was filtered against the sound of someone tightening lug nuts on a tire; Davie could hear the staccato bursts of a drill buzzing, and she realized the man probably answered a landline installed in the work space of the garage. She spoke more loudly.

"I don't know if he got a letter I sent a few weeks ago," she said. *Keep it simple*, she reminded herself. "He stopped to help my husband last September, just after Labor Day, when my husband collapsed outside of his car. I just wanted to talk to him."

"Well, he won't be back until Monday. Can I take your name?"

Davie spelled out her name and gave her phone number.

"Sir?" she said then. "It's really important to me that he get this message. You will make sure he gets it? I very much want to talk to him. I already wrote this to him, but would you please tell him that I'm just trying to get some answers? I'm very grateful that he stopped to help my husband."

She spoke slowly and clearly, to make sure her words got through against the background noise and the probability that this man could not possibly understand how important this was to her.

"Please tell him that all I want to do is ask him if my husband said anything," Davie added. "I read the police report, but it didn't give me a lot of detail. I'm just trying to find some answers. Please tell him that. Please tell him this will not be a bad conversation."

"I'll let him know, Miss. That's all I can do."

"Thank you," Davie said. "Goodbye." She found it difficult to read the man's responses. He gave no indication that he even knew what she was talking about, and from his polite but casual tone, Davie felt she might as well have been leaving a message telling him she wanted to thank his boss for stopping to help her husband fix a flat.

She wasn't quite sure what to make of the brief call, but, she thought, just be patient. Give it a few days. She could not help but think that if the owner of the garage wanted to talk to her, he would already have called her. For all she knew, he was at the garage during her conversation with his employee.

chapter 7

"You are serious about this?" Davie asked Andrea. They stood in a gear store in Albany, with kayaks dangling from the ceiling, backpacks dangling from the walls and shelves stacked with objects Davie could not identify.

"Yup, I'm serious," Andrea said. She pushed past Davie and headed to the wall of backpacks. "I think you should get at least a fifty-five-liter pack, and maybe a sixty liter."

"You aren't worried that I will slow you down?" Davie asked. Andrea didn't answer; she was already in deep discussion with a guy who worked there.

Davie clutched a list of gear Andrea said she would need. A backpack and boots and hiking poles—the three most essential items, according to Andrea. The boots and the backpack needed to be fitted at the store, Andrea said. If Davie decided she hated backpacking and never wanted to go again, she could sell everything on eBay or on a gear company's consignment site, but she needed to have her own backpack and boots for this one trip. This seemed like a huge outlay of cash to Davie, but Andrea explained that the boots would probably last two or three years, the backpack might last ten and the hiking poles could last forever if she got good ones.

The list also included hiking pants, something called a base layer, something else called a mid-layer, and then an outer layer. Also a rain jacket that could double as an extra warm outer layer if the weather turned cool, Andrea said. Davie thought she would do well to never hear the word "layer" again. Wool socks, maybe a pair of sock liners. Davie realized she was about to spend one thousand dollars for the opportunity to wear herself out in Virginia in late June. She thought the June weather would be sweltering in Virginia, but Andrea kept talking about how cool it could get at night up on a ridge, and how a day of rain would leave you damp and chilled when you stopped moving and set up your camp.

Andrea went over the list with Davie before they went shopping, and she explained that a viscose-wool-blend T-shirt she knew Davie already owned could be her base layer. The fact that it was from Eileen Fisher was irrelevant; wool-blend was wool-blend, Andrea said. Davie learned that she would wear this T-shirt every day for nine or ten days, a fact that she kind of already knew about backpacking but one she never seriously considered until now. She found it remarkable, that you could go a week or more without a shower. Davie already owned a fleece pullover and a beloved but slightly past-its-prime merino wool sweater she wore only on weekends, and Andrea told her she could also use those for backpacking. Andrea added that anything that went on this trip would come home pretty well shot—stained, maybe torn, just permanently consigned to backpacking. Davie would want a jacket of down or polyester fiber-fill at night. She would need a cap during the day, and a warmer hat if it got cool at night. Andrea described a stretchy merino wool tube that could be worn as a neck gaiter or could be tied at one end, turned inside out and worn as a warm stocking cap.

Davie felt her head spinning. She thought backpacking was supposed to be relaxing and absorbing, but this was a lot of planning.

"What are sock liners?" she asked Andrea, after she bought her boots, a half-size up from what she normally wore, because Andrea said she would need the room. Davie crossed off most of the items on the list as she read it to see what remained.

"They help prevent blisters."

"Do you mean to seriously tell me that my new hiking boots, for which I am about to pay one hundred and forty-eight dollars, are going to give me blisters?" Davie asked. "You know this for a fact, before I have ever used them?"

"It's possible," Andrea said. "Better to assume and be prepared. Let me see that list."

She studied it a moment.

"I left something off. Wait a minute," Andrea said. Davie wandered over to the counter to look at her purchases by the register. She liked the deep blue color of the backpack and she was fascinated by the design, the array of small inner and outer pockets. The sales guy had fit it to her, adjusting some hidden part to lengthen the internal frame so that it better matched her height of five feet, eight inches. She held the box of boots and watched as Andrea summoned the same guy who helped them with the backpack, took him to a glass case, pointed, examined something, handed it back, pointed again. She came back to Davie and held out a pocket knife in a small box with a clear plastic top.

"This will be very useful," she said. "Keep it with you. This is a gift; I wanted to give you something. This is not a multi-tool. I find that they have too much clutter. This is a simple pocketknife, a little larger than normal, one blade, easy to open, and the edge is slightly serrated. You could cut wood with that blade. Your hiking pants have a zippered front pocket on the leg, above your knee, that's reinforced for carrying something like this. Your pack's hip belt will make it difficult to get something out of the regular pockets of your pants, and you want this within easy reach, so use the pocket down on your pants leg. Or, you can keep it in your backpack's hip-belt pocket. But don't attach it to the pack."

"Why not?" Davie asked. "And thank you, Andrea. That is very nice of you."

"Because you want to have it in your hand fast if you need it. It's useless if you have to detach it from a loop on your pack."

"Why would I need it fast?" Davie asked.

"You probably never will," said Andrea, who was very good at answering a question without really answering it. "It's just a good thing to have handy, and you don't want to fumble for it when you need it."

Andrea planned to take her on a first overnight backpacking trip Memorial Day weekend. They were going to some location in Massachusetts called the October Mountain Shelter. Davie's wedding anniversary would fall in the first week of June, right after the backpacking trip. Davie would be at work on her anniversary, and Michael's birthday followed on the Saturday right after that, in the first full weekend in June. Davie would spend the weekend of Michael's birthday on the Cape, her first trip back there since Michael's death. Her supervisor readily agreed to let her take Friday off because it was a long drive, but she would have only one full day, that Saturday of Michael's birthday, once she got out there. After several phone calls, Davie found an affordable room for just two nights at a bed-and-breakfast on a side street in Provincetown.

Davie was going to the Cape to scatter Michael's ashes at two locations: Longnook Beach, with the overlook Michael loved so much; and then at the kettle pond where they went for a swim at dusk on their wedding anniversary the week of the summer gale, years earlier. Every time she thought of this plan, she remembered the funeral director telling her that the ashes would sink in water, because they were bone. She put great thought into where she wanted to scatter the ashes.

She didn't want to go to the bay beach where they spent their last morning, because although Michael loved that beach, it was . . . well, it was a bay beach, and for some reason, Davie thought it did not have the special sense of place she wanted. That beach was encircled by the nearby harbor and the fishing boats, and it lacked the limitless horizon that she thought was essential for such a deeply personal task. Nothing about that beach felt right to Davie. It was a lovely place to swim, but it was also where the scallop fisherman left a midden of shells along the water's edge at one end of the parking lot, because they stopped there to shuck their catch on their way back to the wharf so they could get the scallops to the market as fast as possible.

Longnook Beach had the wild feeling she craved; it was a place where she could stand at the bluff above the water's edge and imagine she was looking out to a destination so remote, so far away, that she could completely lose track of time as she watched the waves and saw the seals poke their heads up just beyond the surf. It was the place she visualized the day she had sat in her car and learned that Michael may very well have never known she survived. Michael valued ritual; she was sure he would have understood and appreciated her painstaking deliberations. Because Davie told no one what she planned to do on her weekend at the Cape, she didn't have to explain herself to anyone else. She also thought, a bit grimly and with some irony, that she was spending more time deciding where to scatter her husband's ashes than they spent planning their city hall wedding ceremony.

In the week after she returned from the Cape, she planned to go out one night with a crew of biologists to watch as they captured and banded whip-poor-wills. The biologists explained to Davie that they had to do this on or around a full moon, and because the full moon was a Friday that week, they were going to do it on Wednesday, so close to a full moon it would not make much difference in their prospects. The whip-poor-wills were especially active around a full moon, apparently, when it was easier for them to catch the moths they fed their newly hatched babies. In late June, she and Andrea would go to Virginia to hike in Shenandoah National Park.

This was the most activity Davie faced in nearly nine months. She found it odd to feel so busy, and she also felt a little anxious about so many plans.

The first anniversary of Michael's death would be in early September, and Davie held that as a goal, an aspiration, because she both dreaded the anniversary and she yearned for it. For reasons she could not quite explain to herself, the first anniversary seemed to hold the promise of feeling . . . she wasn't even sure what word to use. Better? Davie didn't think it was possible to feel better about anything connected with Michael's death. Or would she feel like she was looking ahead, more than looking back at her married life? She still felt married, and that was difficult to understand, let alone try to explain to anyone else.

She supposed she was in a situation some people might long for: she was completely independent, she was not accountable to anyone, she could do whatever she wanted, whenever she wanted. That total detachment from the everyday responsibilities so many people her age had—shuttling kids to sports practice and after-school activities, dealing with in-laws, making plans with couples in their social circle—the lack of all those ordinary activities made Davie feel unmoored. Some people envied her unfettered life, Davie realized; she could just sense that. Of course, no one would have expressed that envy to her—and they might not even have recognized it as such—because there was no way to tell someone that you thought it would be great to have such an unstructured schedule when the reason for that unstructured schedule was the sudden, catastrophic death of the husband.

Davie found herself pulling away from her other friends, at the same time she worried about leaning too much on the friends with whom she wanted to spend time. She wondered if she had become too sensitive, too easily put off, but she also now realized that people said truly dumb things to new widows. The website she found soon after Michael's death was correct on that.

She tried to reconnect with friends from her social life with Michael, and this was generally a failure. The husband in one couple told her, when Davie met him and his wife for breakfast, that he thought she should try to sound less angry. Davie never asked him what he meant by that. She knew she often sounded impatient, exasperated and exhausted. If she was angry at anyone, it was herself—for not having the second EpiPen within reach, for not speaking up sooner when Michael failed to arrive at the hospital. After that breakfast, she was angry at the husband for saying something that served no purpose except to make her feel worse than she already did. She never contacted them again, and she never heard from them again.

A neighbor told her he was sorry he missed the memorial service, but he thought it was the Saturday after Michael died, not the Saturday that fell ten days after Michael died. Davie wondered what prompted him to tell her this. She wanted to ask him if he knew how stupid he sounded. How he could have possibly thought that she could have pulled together a memorial service for six hundred attendees less than three days after her husband's death completely passed her.

She got a lift from another friend who saw her walking along Madison Avenue one day—Davie was on her way to her garage to pick up her car—and that woman told Davie in a chipper tone that everything would be better soon; she just needed to get through the first year. Davie listened with astonishing patience and a neutral expression on her face as more than one person told her they could relate to her grief because one of their parents recently died. Davie knew that if she said to these people, sorry, but you expect your parents to die before you do, and by the way, hers died when she was twenty-eight, they would have been aghast at her confrontational tone. They thought they offered empathy.

When a casual acquaintance invoked the death of his dog in trying to relate to her loss—a man Davie knew from neighborhood association parties—Davie did finally snap. She told him roundly and sharply that what he just said to her was inappropriate and just plain dumb. She meant to sound harsh, and she did not wait to let him respond. She turned and walked away without saying she was sorry his dog died, thinking it didn't matter what she said to him; she'd probably never see him again. She also realized that the cumulative effect of these encounters meant quite a few people in Albany would start avoiding her. She didn't care, because she could feel herself pulling away from these people anyhow. She felt very much the single, widowed person in any get-together that included couples. It was so long since she had gone to a party or a dinner out in a restaurant with friends as a single person, as she was trying to do now, that she wondered if everything was this difficult years ago before she was married. No, she thought one night as she walked home from work; this was different. She was a young widow trying to fit into a group of married people, and it felt very difficult because it was. She ached with missing Michael. She was deeply bothered that she never dreamed of him. She yearned to; she wanted to see him even if only in her head, but she never did. It was as though she had shut down something in her mind, and Michael could not get through to her.

She was astonished at how vulnerable she still felt. The online widows' group warned about what she had already realized: men would come onto her, they would see her as easy pickings, and she grew very leery. She soon realized that years of friendship, surface trustworthiness, a seemingly happy marriage to a woman Davie considered a friend—none of it mattered for several of the men she knew through her neighborhood and social circle. She was unprepared for how many men seemed to think that she would be receptive to their come-on hints, their emails or texts on the sly that contained an exploratory tone. One night she got a phone call from the very drunk husband in a couple she and Michael knew; she cut off his babbling about how he'd always thought Michael was so lucky, and then blocked his number and his wife's number, shaking with anger and deeply disturbed. She also wondered about the fact that none of these men seemed to worry she might tip off their wives.

Her hairstylist was not an outlier; she realized; she only thought he was because she socialized so rarely in her first six months alone. Now, she thought he might represent the norm. These men were married friends of Michael's, they were people who attended Davie and Michael's parties, they saw each other at backyard summer gatherings. Davie did not think she and Michael made poor judgments in developing these friendships, but something about her widowed state tapped a very rarely discussed behavior in some men—a primitive assumption that she could be used because she was unprotected. If Michael had not died, this behavior would not have surfaced. She thought an anthropologist would have a field day with this one, an aspect of human nature she had never seen explored any place but the widows' group.

She invited a couple over for dinner one night in April. She and Michael socialized with them off and on for years. Davie always found the wife a bit remote, and it was the husband who got in touch with her, asked how she was doing and suggested they get together. She was in the house early on the afternoon of their dinner, trying to clean, debating whether to run to the grocery store and pick up some beer or let the wine she had on hand suffice, when she heard the door knocker downstairs at the front door. Usually, she would look out the bay window from the second floor, to get a clear view of the stoop and see who was there. This time, she was distracted and rushed and so she ran downstairs, opened the inner door to the vestibule, closed that door behind her and called, before she opened the main door, "Who's there?"

"Davie, it's Andrew. Andrew Petersen."

Davie opened the door, completely baffled. Andrew Petersen was a long-ago friend of Michael's who moved out of Albany a generous six or eight years earlier, when his wife landed a very good job somewhere down south. Michael kept in touch with him. Davie didn't know if they came back to Albany for the memorial service; she did not remember seeing them.

"Andrew? What are you doing here?" *And why didn't you call or text me first,* she thought, *instead of just showing up out of the blue?* She was fairly sure he knew how to reach her, or at least his wife did. Or, he could have gotten hold of her phone number or email address; she wasn't difficult to find. She stepped out onto the stoop and kept the main door behind her open. He stepped back a bit down the stoop when she went outside, so she looked down at him.

"Olivia and I were in town to visit her brother and his wife. I had a little spare time. I was in the bookstore around the corner and thought I would stop to see how you're doing. I wanted to talk to you about Michael," he said. There was something slightly off about his demeanor. Book store, hell, Davie thought; he probably just came from a bar. She was still standing on the stoop. She crossed her arms.

"Is Olivia with you? Is she sitting out in the car?"

"No, she's at her brother's house."

A small warning signal flashed in Davie's mind. There was something really strange about this man turning up out of nowhere, when she had not seen him or heard from him in years. Unlike the day in her hair salon, she did not think she was in danger now—the guy was standing outside, he was doing nothing threatening—but she absolutely did not want to let him into the house. She would not have let him in even if she was not rushing to get ready for company.

"Well, Andrew, you don't just show up like this out of nowhere," she said, astonished at her ability to not sound nice. "I'm getting ready to have people over, and I don't have the time for you to come in and take up my afternoon talking about Michael. Goodbye." She stepped back up into the vestibule, facing him, and closed and locked the door before he could respond.

When she went back upstairs and looked out the bay window, he was gone. She strongly suspected his wife did not know he was there, never would know. Maybe it was a harmless impulse that he came to the house, fueled by a couple of shots of scotch, but the fact that he did not contact her first, nor asked if he and Olivia could both come to pay a condolence call, made her think that her instinct to not let him into her house was correct.

The couple she'd invited came for dinner, and Davie realized after they left that the evening was a tentative effort at finding out if there was a continued friendship there. She decided there was not. Michael was the connection to many of their social contacts. Davie was part of a large network of people in Albany and beyond because she was in Michael's world as his wife, and without Michael, she now knew, many of those connections were proving fragile. These people collectively turned out by the hundreds for Michael's memorial service, but that was history now, and soon, so would be their link to her. Had she relied too much on being Michael's wife, she wondered? Did she somehow stop thinking about developing friendships of her own? She felt no deep connection to people like this, she thought, as she said a final goodbye to her dinner guests and closed the door with relief. They were not part of her day-to-day life, they didn't know how she was struggling, and the conversation was cordial but superficial. She was exhausted when they left, all from just trying to appear better than she felt.

Later at work, when she told Jay about Andrew Petersen showing up on her stoop, he said, "You were smart not to let him in. That's how women get raped." The whole situation seemed surreal to Davie, that she could even be having a conversation with Jay about having possibly averted potential danger from one of her husband's long-ago friends, but she also thought Jay was correct.

Davie could not figure out how to get her backpack down the front stoop without putting it on, and she needed to get it onto a table so she could back into it. For this first trip with Andrea, she packed in her first-floor dining room, and she really didn't want to hoist the backpack onto her parents' antique mahogany dining room table. She might never go backpacking again, but she'd almost certainly end up with a deep scratch in the table's beautifully unmarred surface to remind her of this one half-comical, half-questionable effort to hike part of the Appalachian Trail. So she dragged the pack into her front entrance hallway, through the vestibule and then down the steps of the stoop. It was on the bottom step by the time Andrea pulled up in front, and for that Davie was glad. Given the many times Andrea told her to pack as lightly as possible, she expected Andrea to lift the backpack to check the weight, and Andrea couldn't do that if the pack was on Davie. So Davie took a deep breath, swung the pack over one shoulder—and yes, she remembered how many times Andrea told her that put too much strain on the shoulder strap, that the straps were meant to evenly distribute the weight—and she made her way out to Andrea's car. There, she let the pack slide to the street. Andrea hopped out, opened the back door to reveal her own pack on the seat, and started to reach for Davie's pack.

"I've got it," Davie said, and she made a tremendous effort to lift the pack without revealing how difficult this was, then nudged it into the back seat. "Oh, wait, I left my hiking poles in the vestibule. I'll be right back." She ran up the stoop, unlocked the main door, grabbed her poles and returned to the car.

"How much does that weigh?" Andrea said, looking at the pack as though she could judge the weight down to the ounce on sight. She probably could, Davie thought.

"Thirty-eight pounds, on my bathroom scale," Davie said.

"What have you got in there that weighs so much?" Andrea asked. Davie hated this; it was like being asked by her parents at age seven how she zipped through her allowance so fast with a week to go before she was entitled to the next installment.

"Food. Extra water. A book," Davie said, feeling defensive.

"How much extra water?"

"I bought an extra liter bottle and I have that in the pack, filled," Davie said.

"Well, I'm not going to argue about food, because everyone has different nutritional needs and you should consume a few thousand calories every day when you're backpacking. But the water? That's probably two and a half pounds right there, including the weight of the bottle," Andrea said. "You don't need that. Where is it?" She unbuckled the straps on the lid of the pack and reached in, feeling around for the bottle.

"You know, Andrea, this is a bit much. If I want to carry extra water, I think that is my decision."

Andrea stopped rummaging around in the pack and turned her steady, impenetrable gaze on Davie.

"There is a ton of water in this section of the trail. You can fill your bottles along the way if you need more water. Ounces turn into pounds. You agreed to go with me, and I am trying to make sure that this first trip is a good experience. You should knock five pounds out of this pack."

"You *compelled* me to go with you," Davie reminded her. She was still not entirely sure how she felt about drinking even filtered water from a stream in the middle of nowhere, where animals had put their feet into it, lapped from it and done God knew what else in the water . . . she knew now from her job that a mountain stream was a veritable laboratory of invisible life, teeming with water insects and their larvae, and bacteria and little microscopic critters . . . stuff that looked like it came out of a science fiction movie . . . *ugghh,* she thought; it made her squeamish. And she didn't want to tell Andrea that this was why she packed the extra water. But even Davie now understood how heavy water was; she had looked up what a liter of water weighed: 2.2 pounds, not counting the weight of the water bottle. She already knew she would need to very quickly get used to the idea of drinking water she obtained on the trail. She would just have to try to forget everything she was just thinking . . . no matter that Andrea assured her that the high-quality water pump they were going to use caught everything except viruses in the filter. It was knowing that all that stuff was in the stream in the first place that turned Davie's stomach.

"I tried to point out that I wasn't sure I was cut out for this," Davie said, when Andrea did not respond and continued reaching down into Davie's pack. "And while we're standing here discussing this, we're going to make ourselves late. Aren't we meeting your friend at eight?"

"Yes, and we have plenty of time," Andrea said, pulling out the book. She had already found the water bottle. "I want you to leave the extra water bottle and the book. That gets you down to about thirty-four pounds."

Davie gave up, went back and unlocked her front door again, put the book and the water bottle inside and then got into the passenger seat while Andrea buckled her backpack closed. Sitting there, Davie ran the thumb and middle finger of her right hand over her ring finger on her left hand, a habitual gesture that she did without thinking. She should have felt her wedding ring on that left hand. Instead, her wedding ring was in a little box in the jewelry tray in Davie's bureau in her bedroom. Andrea strongly urged her not to wear her ring on the trail, where it would be subjected to more wear and tear than Davie might feel comfortable about, and where it could cause a problem if Davie injured a hand and her fingers swelled. This made sense to Davie, but she hated being without her ring. She never considered taking it off permanently or moving it to her right hand, which she considered a useless gesture. There was no way to feel half widowed.

"Don't be upset with me," Andrea said. "I am really glad you are coming with me."

Davie mentally ran through everything the two of them had endured in the last eight months—death, widowhood, cancer, job loss—then let out a sigh, and smiled.

"I'm glad I'm going, too, and I will probably end up thanking you for making me unload that extra weight."

They were meeting a friend of Andrea's, a guy named Ethan Van Meter, a classmate of hers at Williams College. He lived in northeastern Rensselaer County, very close to Massachusetts and Vermont, and he drove backpackers from where they parked their cars at the end point of their hike to wherever they began a hike on the Appalachian Trail. Usually, Davie now knew, both the beginning and end of such a hike was in a fairly remote area where the trail crossed a back road. Davie assumed this guy did something else for a living, but that was all she knew about him. She now understood, after carefully studying the map Andrea bought for her, that the Appalachian Trail ran along a ridge above Williamstown, Massachusetts, on its way to the Vermont border a few miles north of Williamstown. That was how Andrea got hooked on backpacking more than twenty years ago, by hiking up and down that section of the trail and on numerous side trails with the college hiking club.

They were meeting this man at a location outside of Dalton, Massachusetts, where they would leave Andrea's car and be driven to their starting point in the town of Lee, Massachusetts. Then they would hike north back to Andrea's car, with the overnight stay at the shelter awaiting them at the end of their first day. The shelter was a three-sided wood structure, like a cabin without a front wall, and this one had bunk beds built on each side wall and a sleeping loft, Andrea explained. Shelters or tent-camping areas were regularly spaced along the Appalachian Trail, usually every eight to twelve miles. Andrea planned the hike so that the first day would be the more strenuous effort—a little more than seven miles—and the hike out the following morning would be a much easier two miles on more level terrain. Davie had never walked seven miles in her life, much less while wearing a loaded backpack, and she was very worried she would not be able to hike at Andrea's pace. Andrea gave no sign of the chemotherapy last fall and the cancer surgery in February.

They drove east on Route 20, passed a sign welcoming them to Massachusetts, wended their way through Pittsfield's downtown and hit a succession of traffic lights as they drove by what seemed to be every major chain store in the United States. Davie could not imagine how they would end up on the fabled Appalachian Trail that same morning, given the suburban sprawl all around them. Then Andrea turned down a road in Dalton and within minutes they left suburbia behind as they drove up a long, gradual ascent with forest on both sides. Several miles later, Andrea slowed and turned into a parking area marked by a large wooden sign on posts, declaring this to be the Appalachian Trail. Georgia was in one direction, indicated by an arrow pointing south; Maine was the other way.

For all Davie's years in Albany, this was her first view of the trail, and she was not impressed. There were woods behind her and woods across the road, and nothing she could discern to explain the fascination that back-packing, and especially backpacking on the Appalachian Trail, held for so many people. Even so, she was glad they were here, glad she was out of her house for part of the weekend.

A few cars were parked in the turnoff, including an old white Volvo station wagon with a man leaning against the driver's side door. He was not looking at a phone; his hands were in the pockets of his windbreaker and he was looking up at the sky.

"A whole flock of bluebirds was just here," he said when Andrea and Davie got out of the car. Davie assumed he was their ride to their starting point, a shuttle driver, as she had learned such a person was called. Then the man straightened up and walked over to Andrea's car just as Andrea came around to the passenger side.

"Hello!" he said, holding out his arms and wrapping them around Andrea in a hug. He straightened up and turned to Davie.

"You must be Davie," he said. "Hello."

"And you are? And by the way, you seem very confident about my iden-tity. I might be someone Andrea just picked up hitchhiking in Pittsfield." From the side, Davie saw Andrea shoot a quick glance at her, which she didn't bother to return.

Davie couldn't explain to herself why she just said that; it was entirely out of character for her. But she was out of Albany for the first time since Michael's death almost nine months earlier and she was about to undertake an adventure. She was giddy and a little apprehensive, but she looked forward to this, and it was a very long time since she looked forward to anything.

The last nine months had held nothing but anguish, sleep deprivation, shock and mistreatment, unless she counted the new job, and that was so closely connected to her firing that she still could not view it as a settled aspect of her life. A part of her half expected that the new job would also implode, when everything else seemed to be doing that, even though Davie realized this was an irrational fear. She was doing very well at work, she got nothing but good responses from the staff, and her immediate boss seemed stunned by their good fortune in hiring her. All of this passed through her mind in a split second, and she smiled at the man to take any edge off her words.

"Oh, I am sorry," the man said, very courteously. "I should have intro-duced myself. I'm Ethan Van Meter. I'm your shuttle driver. I hope you didn't think I was just hanging around here at the trail head waiting for women to show up just so that I could hug them."

"It's been known to happen," Andrea said, going back around to the driver's side to get her pack out of the car. "Hey, Ethan, you wouldn't happen to have an extra water bottle lying around in your car, would you?"

"Well, actually, I do," Ethan said. He opened the driver's side door, felt around under the front seat and pulled out a wide-mouthed liter bottle with a screw top attached to the neck by a plastic strip. This was called a Nalgene bottle, named for the company that made it, and it was the same kind of leak-proof bottle Andrea lent Davie for this trip, the kind many backpackers carried. It was also the same kind of bottle Davie had filled and hidden in her backpack—which Andrea then found and made her leave back in Albany. Davie didn't dare argue; she sensed that Andrea meant her to really get rid of it, and not just bring it along in case Andrea relented. On stuff like this, Andrea could be extremely stubborn.

Ethan started to toss the empty water bottle to Andrea over the car, but Andrea shook her head and pointed to Davie. Davie took the water bottle when Ethan pivoted and handed it to her.

"What's this all about?" Davie asked.

"I think I was a bit hard on you," Andrea said from the other side of her car. "I had water insecurity, too, when I started backpacking. Just take it and put it in your pack, so you'll have it if you want it. It weighs next to nothing empty."

"OK, thanks," Davie said, surprised. Andrea was such a tough taskmaster that Davie was amazed she softened up about the extra water. Davie turned to Ethan.

"Thank you. I can mail it back to you when we're done with our hike."

"Oh, don't worry about it," he said. "I've got quite a few at home. OK. Are you two ready?"

Andrea got into the front seat, and Davie got in behind her, next to their two backpacks. She only knew that Andrea and Ethan were long-ago classmates, but they seemed to have maintained a friendship, based on their easy banter during the drive. Davie didn't really try to follow the conversation. Looking out the window, lost in thought, she realized it was more than three months since she had called the garage on the Cape and left a message for the man who stopped to help Michael. That unresolved quest was always just below the surface for Davie. The man didn't want to talk to her, that much was clear. She had tried twice now; he surely must have gotten her letter and the message she asked his employee to convey. And she realized that even if she somehow got him on the phone, he would probably not tell her anything—say, for example, if she called, and he answered before he knew who was calling. She didn't know what to do.

She was going to the Cape in a week, but she thought she shouldn't just show up unannounced at his business. Why wouldn't he talk to her? The effervescent feeling she'd had when she and Andrea pulled into the parking area faded. That, too, was part of her life now, she realized—wildly up-and-down moods. She couldn't remember what it was like to feel equilibrium. She wondered if she ever would again.

Ethan was asking her a question, she realized. She leaned forward around her backpack.

"I'm sorry . . . what did you say? Were you asking me something?"

"Yes. Andrea tells me this is your first backpacking trip."

"She talked me into it," Davie said. "She wouldn't take no for an answer. I have no idea what I'm doing."

"Oh, you will love it," he said. "OK, here you go . . . this is your starting point." He turned his car into a long parking area, with another large wooden Appalachian Trail sign, fronting a road backed by steeply rising forest across from the parking lot.

Andrea handed Ethan some folded bills, making Davie realize this ride was not a favor from Andrea's friend, that he did this for money. She was embarrassed that she had nothing with her; her debit card was tucked into a hidden pocket in her backpack, but that was no help here.

"Don't worry about it; I've got this, Davie," Andrea said, seeing her watching from the back seat. "Thanks, Ethan, for getting us here."

"Well, let me at least help you get your packs out." He clambered out of his car—he was tall and lanky and serious-looking, dark-haired and not flashy, Davie saw, studying him for the first time—then he slid Andrea's pack out and reached for hers. Davie was curious about how this worked . . . they were friends, this guy and Andrea, but Andrea paid him for what Davie had thought up to now was just him helping them get to their starting point. She wondered if he refused payment when Andrea set up the ride, and Andrea insisted. Davie knew this man could not possibly earn a living from doing this, and she had no idea what he did for a job. Davie reached into the car for her backpack at the same time he did.

"I've got it, thanks," she said from the other side of the car. She didn't want him to comment on the weight.

"OK, then. Andrea, it was very nice to see you. If you need another shuttle, let me know."

"I'm not sure when I'm going out next, Ethan. But yes, I'll let you know." He hugged Andrea and held his hand on her back for a moment before he stepped away from her.

"It's good to see you," he said.

Ethan turned to Davie.

"If you love this, and you want to go out again, maybe on your own, and I'm around, I'll shuttle you," he said. Davie nodded, struggling to hoist her pack onto her shoulders from its resting place on the car seat. She looked up at him.

"Thank you. Right now, I'll be doing well to get this one behind me." Ethan and Andrea both laughed, then Davie realized her hiking poles were in Ethan's car. Once she had them in hand, she tugged the two straps on her pack's belt a little tighter, shrugging the pack to a higher resting place on her hips, and finally she adjusted the tilt of the water-resistant baseball-style cap she bought on her gear-shopping day.

"Ok, I'm ready," she said. Andrea smiled, picked up her own hiking poles from their resting place against the back bumper of Ethan's Volvo, waved to Ethan, and they started off across the road. A small white sign, like a triangle with rounded edges and imprinted with the Appalachian Trail logo, marked the path up into the woods. Ethan pulled out, blew the horn a couple of times in farewell and drove away.

"He seems like kind of an unusual person," Davie said to Andrea after they hiked in silence for several minutes. The road was already out of sight, and they were climbing, slowly and steadily, but so far the pace seemed manageable to Davie. At least she was not winded.

"He is, and he's very nice, but he can be a lot of work," Andrea said. She did not elaborate. Davie remembered Andrea saying she dated a bird nut a long time ago, and she thought about Ethan's opening remark to them about the bluebirds. She detected, now that she thought about it, a subtle familiarity between Ethan and Andrea that seemed a bit more than the friendship of former college classmates. Andrea was very private, far more so even than Davie, and Davie learned early in their friendship that Andrea revealed personal information the same way she handled an application at the Community Loan Foundation: slowly, thoughtfully and in carefully planned stages.

❧

Davie discovered that she loved backpacking.

She would never forget this first day, she thought as they kept climbing. To her surprise, they did not see any other backpackers. Andrea told her this was not unusual; she could remember hikes when she went two or three days without seeing other people. She explained they were a little early yet for the largest group of people trying to hike the entire Appalachian Trail in one season to have gotten this far north. There would probably be other people at the shelter, she said. A few miles up the trail, they crossed a wide stream, picking their way to the other side by slowly stepping from one rock to another. Davie followed Andrea, watching how she considered where to put her feet, how she balanced on her hiking poles.

"You just need to do this slowly," Andrea said. "There's a stream crossing in Connecticut that's a lot wider than this, and I've done that one in early March. That was tricky. Just assume the rocks are always going to be slippery. You just take your time. Do you want to stop now for a few minutes? Drink some water?" Davie did. She estimated she would go through one whole bottle of water and only about half of her second bottle by the time they got to the shelter, but she was still glad she had that extra empty bottle.

"Your friend didn't seem too concerned about getting his bottle back," she said as they stood up to resume their hike. In just those few minutes, Davie had started to stiffen, and getting on her feet was an effort.

"He's probably got a dozen of those at his place from people forgetting to take them when they get out of his car," Andrea said. Davie realized she had no idea if the bottle Ethan gave her was used by a stranger without first being washed, or how long it sat in Ethan's car.

"So what's this guy do for a living?" Davie asked as they started moving again.

"He makes furniture," Andrea said. "Very expensive furniture. As in, tables that sell for twenty-five thousand dollars. The chairs to go with the table go for eight grand a pop. His stuff is in museums and private collections all over the country."

"You're joking," Davie said. "He went to Williams College to become a furniture-maker? And he runs people up and down the Appalachian Trail on the side?"

Andrea shrugged, as much as it was possible to shrug in a backpack; Davie was behind her and she discerned the gesture by the way Andrea threw her hiking poles out to each side.

"He was a physics major in college. He has thru-hiked the AT," she said. "He still does a lot of backpacking. I think he does shuttle-driving as a diversion. God knows he does not need the money; he's got a two-year waiting list for commissions, and he does all his work on his own. He doesn't have an apprentice or assistant. He's got his workshop on his property. So low overhead. That old Volvo he picked us up in is just his shuttle car; he's got a pickup truck for hauling stuff for the furniture business, and I believe he sources a lot of the wood he uses from his own property. He's got...oh, I don't know...fifty acres, maybe, in northeastern Rensselaer County, right next to the Vermont state line."

"So, let me ask, he's your friend, but you paid him for this ride. Did he offer to do this as a favor, and you insisted on paying him?"

Davie had no trouble imagining the look on Andrea's face, although Davie was still just behind her.

"No, it's the other way around. I have never used him as a shuttle driver before this, because he wasn't doing shuttles when I was doing this section of the trail, and I thought he would just give us a ride. He went to some pains to tell me how he calculated the fee."

"No kidding." Davie shook her head. "That seems a little...single-minded. I mean, you've known him for what, twenty-five years?"

"Yes, since we were freshmen," Andrea said. "He was like that in college, too. As you say, single-minded."

They got to the shelter just before six o'clock. No one else was there, after all, although Andrea said other people might come in later. Davie did a rapid calculation in her head. They started at eight-thirty that morning, they stopped three times to rest—she suspected that was more than Andrea would have stopped on her own—and round it up to six o'clock...seven miles and two-tenths...nine and a half hours...they hiked at a pace of a mile and a third an hour, give or take, which seemed very slow to her. Andrea never complained; she in fact complimented Davie on how well Davie did. As a result of the long day, however, they had little time to talk once they got to the shelter, a three-sided cabin with an overhanging roof and no front wall, just as Davie expected.

"Do you want to sleep in the loft?" Andrea asked. "You don't have to put up your tent."

"No, I want to try the tent," Davie said. She also could not bear the thought of climbing the ladder to the loft; she thought her arms and legs would give out if she tried. They picked a sleeping spot in a clearing behind the shelter and put up their tents about twenty feet apart. Because Davie practiced this at home, she found it easier than she expected. She was also very sore, and she could hardly stand after she knelt to put the tent poles together.

"Oh, my God, Andrea...I'll never get out of here tomorrow," she said. "Am I this out of shape?"

"Don't be too hard on yourself," Andrea said. "You did really well. I've got some ibuprofen. Backpackers call it 'vitamin I.' Take some after dinner, and drink about a half-liter of water before you go to sleep. You might get some leg cramps when you lie down, but the water will help."

They picked their way down to the water source for the shelter, a stream at the bottom of a short slope. Davie did end up taking the extra water bottle that Ethan gave her to fill it. She wanted extra water in her tent, and she was so tired, so sore, so thirsty and so ready to go to sleep that she no longer cared who last drank from it.

Andrea looked up and down the stream before she sat on a rock to open her water pump and connect the long rubber tube to the intake valve.

"I once plunked myself down to discover a bear having a drink on the other side of the stream about fifteen feet from me," she said, smiling, as she saw Davie's curious expression. "Not here; way up in Vermont. I'll never know how it did not hear me, but it seemed as surprised as I was. We just stared at each other."'

"What the hell happened?"

"Oh, it took off right away," Andrea said. "It just turned and galloped off into the woods. They are very shy creatures. But in case you are wondering, I packed up pretty fast and got out of there." She shot another sideways smile at Davie. "I'm not as brave as I come across, let me tell you."

Listening to this, Davie realized that as well as she knew Andrea, this was a part of Andrea's life she didn't know at all. Davie found everything about the day fascinating. Sitting on a rock by the stream, holding the water bottle steady as Andrea filled it from a plastic tube connected to the pump, she thought, this was something that she could do again, and she could do it on her own. She did not find the thought of backpacking by herself frightening; she found it thrilling to contemplate. She was hooked.

Lying in her tent that night and reflecting on the day, she heard a sound that even she recognized as a great horned owl. Her introduction to backpacking was filled with discovery, and it lifted her out of her grief for hours at a stretch. She completed the first and most difficult phase of the hike; she did not whine, complain or consider telling Andrea that they would need to turn back because she was at her limit. She did not quit, and now she was in this cozy, private little space of her own, where she could fully stretch out her legs even though her backpack was near the tent door, pushed to one side. Everything seemed to fit in this well-designed interior.

Her sole barrier against the night forest was two thin layers of nylon, no barrier at all, but she felt extremely secure. She unfolded the pocket knife Andrea gave her and set it against the tent wall so that she could reach it in the dark. She set her headlamp by the knife. She never thought she would be capable of using an empty water bottle in which to pee, but that was exactly what she did—making sure that she screwed the lid back on really well afterward before she set the bottle upright in one of her boots.

That solution seemed far preferable to unzipping her tent, crawling out into the pitch-black of the clearing and trying to stand when she was so sore that she could hardly reach around in the dark to pull up her sleeping bag. The owl was the last sound she heard before she fell asleep, and despite her stiff muscles, despite her craving for a hot bath, despite the fact that the only cushion between her extremely sore body and the ground was a half-inch-thick foam pad, she slept well—really well—for the first time in almost nine months. Her final thought as she felt herself drifting was that Michael would not have been at all surprised at what she did today. He always thought she could do anything.

chapter 8

"So how was it?" Jay stopped by her office door Tuesday morning, when they returned to work after the Memorial Day weekend.

"I loved it," Davie said. "I think I'm going to go again."

"I'll be darned," Jay said. "Don't take this the wrong way, but I didn't exactly have you pegged as a convert to backpacking."

"Nice to surprise people," Davie said.

"How's your friend Andrea doing? Is she OK now?"

"She sure seems to be," Davie said. "The cancer didn't spread, they caught it pretty early and she definitely hiked well, at least to my inexpert eyes. She certainly didn't seem like someone who's had chemotherapy and cancer surgery in the past year."

"That's great," Jay said. "Hey, listen, the whip-poor-will group is going to try to meet tomorrow at the DEC." That was the state Department of Environmental Conservation. "Would you like to come with me? You still want to go out with us next week?"

"Yes and yes."

"Good. Why don't we just walk over to the DEC tomorrow? We'll head over around one o'clock." Jay straightened up from leaning against the door frame and Davie saw him look at the photo of Michael and her on the desk.

"Your, ah, your wedding anniversary is coming up, isn't it?

"It's next week," Davie said. "Tuesday."

"And you're not taking any time off, to . . . you know, just have that day to yourself?" Davie wondered how much time Jay thought she could take off with a new job, when she already had two weeks of vacation lined up later in the month. She wished she could get him to drop his persistent questions; she hated explaining her plans, although she didn't know why she felt that way. Maybe because it seemed he expected her to react a certain way to her first wedding anniversary on her own.

"I'll be here through Thursday, Jay. I'm taking Friday off. Michael's birthday is Saturday. But no, I'll be here all next week." The second she mentioned Michael's birthday, Davie wished she'd kept her mouth shut. It just slipped out, probably because it was on her mind.

"Are you doing anything to, you know, get out of the house?" Jay asked. "Michael's birthday, your anniversary . . . it just seems like a lot coming at you."

"I'm going away for the weekend," Davie said. She did not volunteer that she was going to the Cape to scatter Michael's ashes; she sensed that would elicit more questions, more concern.

"Would you feel like coming over tomorrow or Thursday for a glass of wine or something?" Jay asked. "Or we could go out for a drink. It would be nice to toast the day in advance."

"Jay, thank you, but I'm really fine," Davie said. She had no idea if she was—her mood barometer seemed to automatically reset every morning, and she never knew which way the needle was going to swing—but she also felt that she relied on Jay quite a bit since Michael's death, and by extension, Alanna. Jay never said or indicated anything to suggest that her needs affected his relationship with Alanna, but Davie felt self-conscious.

"I have some stuff to do at home, and I'm still in recovery from backpacking," Davie added. "I feel like I could use a whole new skeletal system."

Jay's mood lightened at that; he laughed and headed down the hall.

The whip-poor-will group consisted of four people from the state Department of Environmental Conservation, including the biologist planning the survey project, and two people from Davie's office, with Davie as a guest observer. Jay introduced her as the expert mathematician and data analyst they were fortunate enough to steal from the private financial sector. That smooth detour around the recent events of her life worked beautifully, and it seemed to explain to the DEC people why she was wearing new hiking pants that had obviously never seen a day in the field, very polished chukka boots, a quilted silk jacket and pearl earrings. Davie was working out her own look for her job, a distinctive style that identified her as office staff, not office and field staff, but at least she was getting some continued good out of the upper half of her wardrobe from LGC. She had quite a supply of silk blouses and corporate jackets in beautiful fabrics and weaves.

"Davie's going to go out in the field with us next week to see what we do," Jay said to the group.

"Not dressed like this," Davie said without missing a beat. Everyone laughed. She saw one of the DEC biologists at the far end of the table look at her a little more closely and then automatically glance at her left hand, where she again wore her wedding ring.

On Friday morning, she got up very early and left for the Cape. Andrea knew where she was going—Davie thought someone should at least know that much—but not even Andrea knew that Davie intended to scatter Michael's ashes there. If Andrea wondered, she never asked, nor did she express any concern about Davie doing the trip alone back to the place where Michael died. Davie appreciated that; to her, it signaled that Andrea had faith in her ability to handle her life on her own. Michael's obituary stated that burial would be private, and no one ever asked her where the cemetery was or whether she ever visited the grave. Michael's family never inquired about her plans for Michael's burial, but she at least told them that she arranged for a cremation. She didn't offer to give them any of Michael's ashes, and they didn't ask for any, and she also did not even think about including them in her weekend now. They were good people, she was sure she would see them again, but they didn't know Michael very well; he was the youngest in his family by some years, and she doubted they would want to be part of this.

It took her almost six hours to get to Provincetown. She knew she would be retracing her route to the hospital from nine months earlier in reverse, and she also knew she would drive by the fire station on a corner of Route 6 in Wellfleet. She did both without wavering. She turned on the playlist of her phone, and then, when she thought she was close enough to pick up the community radio station in Provincetown, she turned the radio dial until she found it. It was the Indie Hour at WOMR, and that was exactly what she needed right then. She finished out the drive singing to the Yeah Yeah Yeahs and Patti Smith.

The night before she left, she divided Michael's ashes into two plastic jars with screw tops. This was the first time she opened the box she carried out of the funeral parlor that afternoon soon after she returned from the Cape. She set the box on the marble counter in the kitchen and undid the twist-tie on the heavy plastic bag with a feeling of disbelief. For a moment, she thought she would split, just mentally remove herself from the kitchen, the house and the sight of the remains of her husband inside the bag. The last time she felt like that was the morning she sat in the parking lot and talked to the fire captain just before her firing. His voice coming through the phone snapped the spell that morning. Now, six months later, she gripped the edge of the counter and shook her head a few times until the moment passed with a sensation of coming to after fainting. Davie reached for a serving spoon from the stoneware pitcher of utensils on the counter and began scooping up the ashes and putting them into evenly divided portions in the two jars. She put the lids on the jars, crumpled the plastic bag into the bottom of the box and packed the jars on top of the bag. She threw the spoon into the trash.

She had a certificate from the funeral home to verify that she was carrying her husband's cremated remains, although she could not imagine a scenario in which she would be pulled over by a cop and have her car searched. But just in case, she put the certificate inside the box and put the box back into the green tote bag she carried out of the funeral home on a day that now seemed from a different lifetime.

Provincetown was less crowded than Davie expected. The summer visitors wouldn't arrive for another couple of weeks, the manager of her bed-and-breakfast told her as she showed her to her room. Davie looked out the window at the quiet side street and felt at loose ends. She didn't have any particular plan for how to scatter Michael's ashes, other than that she wanted to do so in privacy. That meant getting up very early to go to Longnook Beach, but getting up early was never a problem for her. She thought she would go to the kettle pond in the afternoon. She did not want to get caught down that fire road after dark. She hoped she could find the place; she had been there only that once, years earlier, and she didn't know if it had a name or was even on a map. She was going to do this Saturday, the next day, no matter what the weather—she could not bear the thought of driving home with this plan unfinished—but the forecast for Saturday was good.

With nothing else to do, Davie took a long walk to the far end of Commercial Street that afternoon, then went back to her room and read one of the bird books she brought with her. She fell asleep at a normal hour, easier to do with the passage of time, and she awoke before daybreak. She very quietly made a cup of coffee in the parlor of the bed-and-breakfast, mindful that no one else was awake. Then she slipped out the front door, got into her car, and headed down Bradford Street out of town.

Davie always loved Longnook Beach, which made her feel as if she was standing on the edge of the earth. She completely understood how mariners hundreds of years ago thought they might drop over that edge when they were confronted with a horizon like this one, the horizon she envisioned the day she sat in her car and learned that Michael never knew for sure that she survived. Now, she picked her way down the steep path in the dunes and looked up and down the beach. It was still so early, just newly daybreak, that she had the place to herself, as she had thought she would. No other cars were in the narrow parking lot on the bluff.

This would be the first time she touched the ashes. In transferring the contents of the sturdy plastic bag into the two containers the night before she left for the Cape, she never actually touched the remains. Now, she sat down on the sand, took off her sneakers and rolled up the legs of her chinos. She very carefully set the jar down, unscrewed the lid and put it in her jacket pocket. Then she picked up the jar and walked closer to the water— she never could tell if the tide was going out or in; that was Michael's specialty—but it didn't matter to Davie. She knelt just ahead of the curled edge in the sand, the mark of the last push of the ocean.

"I'm sorry," she said aloud, as though Michael was there. "I'm sorry." The apology took in everything that still tormented her nine months into her widowhood: her failure to use her one EpiPen sooner, dropping the second one without realizing it; the fact that she was alive and Michael was dead; and her overwhelming guilt that she was not with him when he died. She could not stop blaming herself for his death, although she knew he would never have wanted her to feel that way. She looked up at the sky— it was more gray than blue at this early hour—and she wondered where Michael was, and whether he could possibly be aware of her. She did not believe so; she felt alone at that moment.

She was careful to not walk too far into the surf, which she knew to be strong even just a couple of feet into the water. She could imagine the headline: "Widow drowns scattering husband's ashes into ocean." That was the kind of darkly Irish take on life that would have cracked Michael up laughing, and even Davie smiled at the turn her thoughts had taken. Well, that was better than crying, and it indicated that at least on this morning, she did not want to be dead if she was reminding herself to be careful, she thought. She reached into the jar and ran her fingers through the contents, which did feel like pulverized concrete, just as the funeral director told her, with a dusty residue that stuck to the inside of the plastic jar. Then she tipped the jar into the next wave that lapped around her legs and watched the contents disappear into the churning water as it folded in over itself. She rinsed her hands off and she let some water run into the jar and she swirled that around to clean the jar, then she poured that water back into the surf. The water was very cold; she could not stand in it any longer, so she walked back to pick up her sneakers and then she made her way up the path to the top of the bluff.

Provincetown was starting to stir for the weekend when she turned onto Commercial Street. Davie badly wanted a drink, she realized with some astonishment. Hardly surprising, she thought, and she supposed there was a way to procure alcohol even at this early hour in this town, but it was a fleeting impulse that she dismissed as quickly as she recognized it. Coffee, she thought. That's what she needed—coffee and something to eat. She found a little breakfast place that had just opened. She must have been the day's first customer. She was staring at the ice cream case under the front counter, thinking about Longnook Beach and the way Michael's ashes just disappeared into the water, became part of the ocean, in a second. He would have been forty-seven years old today, that was all that was physically left of him on this Earth, and now it was gone, or it would be by the day's end. She did not immediately realize that the woman standing behind the counter was asking her for what sounded like the second time what she wanted.

"Sorry," Davie said, giving herself a little shake and giving the woman an apologetic smile, and then she ordered coffee and a muffin. She didn't know how she looked, but perhaps she wore a more faraway expression than she realized, because the woman handed her the coffee and a little bag with the muffin and asked, "Is everything all right, miss?"

Oh, fuck it, Davie thought. She was starting to think she was marked for life, that she would always have a bit of an otherworldly look. She often still felt that she was half here, in this life, and halfway . . . there . . . somewhere else . . . she didn't know how to describe it, nor did she know where she meant. This was the feeling that had come over her many times now, including in the waiting room before the memorial service, and in her car the day she was fired, and other times, too numerous now to recount, and not always around significant events like the terrible conversation with the fire captain or the memorial service. She just tried very hard to not let other people see when it was happening, which was difficult, because she didn't really even know *what* was happening. And these episodes were wildly erratic; they just kind of snuck up on her, so she also never knew when she looked like she was no longer present.

"Well, everything is about as good as it's going to get today," Davie said. "Thank you. I just scattered my husband's ashes on Longnook Beach and I think I'm still there, kind of, you know . . . mentally . . . on the beach. And this was just the first installment. I have the second jar back in my room to do at a different location this afternoon. Ahhh . . . would it be possible to get an ice-cream cone at this hour?"

"You can have anything you want, miss, and I am really sorry for your loss," the woman said. "You look way too young to have lost your husband. What would you like?"

Davie got a double scoop of mint-chocolate chip, which was Michael's favorite flavor, and she got chocolate sprinkles on it because she loved chocolate sprinkles.

"Everything's on us, honey," the woman said when she handed Davie the cone. Davie thanked her, dropped a ten into the tip jar, put the bag with the muffin in her jacket pocket and then picked up the coffee with her free hand. She opened the door with her elbow, and stepped carefully out sideways into the morning—which was now bright and clear, promising a lovely mid-June day—and went back across Commercial Street to her car. Instead of returning to her room at the bed and breakfast, she left the coffee and the bag in the car, and she slowly walked up Commercial Street as she ate the cone. She could feel the ice cream hitting her stomach and filling a hole, a need, that normal food at that hour could not have touched. Better than having a drink, she thought. Definitely better.

If the trip to Longnook Beach had been haunting, the trip to the kettle pond that afternoon was peaceful. Davie thought the difference probably had to do with the respective scale of two very different places. Longnook was majestic, sweeping and vast. The kettle pond was partly screened by the trees along the fire road and it was contained, a size you could easily grasp once you got out of your car—it was more intimate—a chapel or a grotto instead of a cathedral. Davie gave herself more time than she was sure she would need to get there, or, as she thought when she got into her car in Provincetown, if she couldn't find the pond with this long lead, then maybe she was imagining her time there with Michael. Why not? she thought to herself; everything else in her perception and memory was out of whack these days.

She found the pond easily, somewhat to her surprise, and it looked exactly as she remembered it. She took out the plastic jar, set it on the ground and looked around. The place was completely, utterly still. She remembered the trilling of the dusk insects from her swim with Michael, but in this afternoon warmth, everything was quiet—no birdsong, no buzzing—just silence. No one was paddling a kayak way out, there were no other cars along the turnoff, no voices carrying from the woods around the pond and not even any sign in the soft dirt of any footprints or tire tracks. It was not yet mid-June; she might be the first person down this road since last season. On that insight, Davie walked to the edge of the pond and removed her clothes, neatly folded them into a small pile, and walked into the chilly but not ocean-cold water, carrying the opened jar of the last of Michael's ashes. She remembered Michael walking into the pond undressed, the feel of their wet bodies against each other as dusk started to drop around them that day, their wedding anniversary day. As she had at Longnook, she spoke out loud.

"Michael, my love, thank you. Wait for me." She had no idea why she said that; she did not intend to say anything, other than possibly, "I love you." Then she tilted the container of ashes into the pond. This time she saw them fan out in the clear, still water beneath the surface and hang there for a moment, suspended the way that a huge burst of fireworks sits in the sky, evoking indrawn breath and murmurs of appreciation from the audience. And then, like a fireworks shell that has sent its streamers out all around the central burst and stayed that way, perfectly still, for just those few moments, the ashes dissipated and disappeared as she watched.

Davie looked back up and gazed around at the pond. She felt right about this place, because Michael found the pond for them, whereas Longnook was a place they gave each other. Tears filled her eyes as she took one final look around the pond, because she did not know when, if ever, she would come back here.

Davie didn't even consider trying to go to the auto body shop in Hyannis owned by the man she was trying to reach, the man who had stopped to help Michael. The logistics of doing so were prohibitive; she couldn't scatter Michael's ashes on her one full day on the Cape and get to the garage before it closed in the early afternoon Saturday. She never allowed herself to consider stopping the day before, on her way past Hyannis. She didn't know what to do about this quandary. Of course, she realized by now that this man was blowing her off, but what she could not understand was why. Everything in her approach to him had been measured, calm, reassuring. He couldn't possibly think that she was going to have a tearful scene on the phone with him, castigating him for not saving Michael's life. Nor could he think that she was going to sue him, and while Davie realized that people worried all the time about lawsuits in such situations, she could not imagine on what grounds this man might fear legal action. Even if she was going to try to pull such a stunt, she thought, he must know that by now he would have gotten some communication from a lawyer. He owned a business, so maybe he was especially wary. Around the time that Davie got to this point in her musings, she realized she was at an impasse, that she could not figure out what she should do or whether she should do anything more.

On her way off the Cape Sunday, however, she did do something she hadn't planned: she impulsively turned down the road at the fire station in Wellfleet to retrace the route she and Michael took the night he died. There was, Davie realized, one question that was entirely within her control to answer.

It was late morning when she did this, not dusk, but it wasn't difficult for her to remember how the road looked at the day's end. She drove slowly, remembering the baseball game was on the radio, and she and Michael were not talking; they were each lost in their separate thoughts as the car moved down the shadow-dappled road. The road was paved; she didn't remember that, but that didn't make any difference in how Michael drove. The sand and salt and winter storms eroded everything here quickly, including black-top, and the town didn't spend a lot of time on maintenance of these back roads. More than once, a winter storm pounding in from the ocean had torn apart the parking lot at the top of the bluff overlooking Longnook Beach, even as high and as far set back as the parking lot was.

Davie remembered that Michael was driving very slowly, maybe only ten or fifteen miles an hour, to avoid the previous winter's potholes. She didn't remember any physical landmark to help her place when she first felt that itchy sensation in her throat, but she estimated the timing as best she could, and she kept driving, until she found what she believed was the driveway Michael turned into so that he could reverse the car. This was where Davie gestured to him to wait, so that she could open the door and use her EpiPen. She was sure of that now, as she looked ahead through the trees that edged the driveway and saw the house. She remembered how fast everything happened. By the time Michael turned into that driveway, she was so out of it that she didn't realize the second EpiPen was on the floor, where it would roll or be pushed under the seat and lie out of sight and reach.

In her memory of that night, the fire station that Michael drove her to was a small building, far off the road. Now, a year later, in the daylight of late morning, almost noon, it was a large building. Large enough to house a fire truck and an ambulance and work space for the shifts, just a short distance off the road. As Davie knew by now, her perception of everything was skewed that night. But instead of turning into the driveway of the fire station, as Michael did, she cleared the trip mileage on the car, continued to the end of the road and turned right onto Route 6, heading back toward Provincetown.

The police station in Truro was almost ten miles further up the road. She didn't bother to note how long it took her, because she knew that Michael would have been driving much faster—but she also knew that he would have been hampered by looking for the police station at night, watching for the sign, not remembering quite where it was, no matter how many times they drove past it over the years. She pulled into the parking lot when she got there, and sat in the car, remembering how she felt that night, remembering how she realized she was dying. She felt like her vision was starting to close in from both sides; she remembered telling herself to keep breathing. Had Michael tried to drive her here—as she asked him to, in the last words she spoke to him—she believed now that she would have died on the way here. As it was, she nearly did die getting to the much closer fire station; the fire captain told her as much.

Michael took a chance. He must have realized she would not survive the extra time it would have taken to get her to the police station, and besides, he didn't know if there was any medical staff there. If the fire station had been staffed by volunteers, with no one on site, she would have died there. She might have died if the only person there had been the crew chief, the man she spoke to, with everyone else out on an ambulance call. Michael faced a terrible choice, one she never really understood until now. He made a split-second decision, the best that he could, and he bluffed his way to a winning hand without ever letting her sense his indecision and his own panic. Because he guessed correctly, he saved her life. He didn't know that, but he at least knew he got her help.

Davie thought back to what she said as she let the last of Michael's ashes into the kettle pond. *Thank you.* She never thought of Michael's actions that night without a mixed feeling of profound gratitude and equally profound guilt. Even so, she didn't even know why she said those words, *Thank you,* in the pond when she could have said so many other things to Michael, or Michael's spirit, or however someone wanted to think you spoke to the dead. It was as though she was meant to do this drive this morning, even though she didn't plan it. Had no one been at the fire station, and she died and Michael lived, he might have forever tormented himself over the precious minutes he wasted turning in there, at the fire station, when he should have gunned it up Route 6 to a place where he at least knew there would be a cop. He would be living out all the terrible conflict, the second guessing she lived with now and had lived with for going on a year.

There was no way to understand why fate handed them this unimaginable ending to their life together, so that one would be dead, and the other would be alive and sometimes wishing she was not. Davie supposed that this greater insight into Michael's calm courage, his decision-making under the worst possible circumstances, should have made her at least feel less guilty, because Michael made the decision he thought best. She was glad she understood this better now, but all she felt was despair. She and Michael never spent much money on gifts for each other; for years, they poured everything into their savings and the house. She could understand the irony that Michael's most expensive gift to her was her life, but what she could not understand was why this happened to them at all.

Davie could not imagine how to feel better. All she had done since Michael's death was plunge from one difficult situation to another, from one heartbreaking discovery to the next. She never stopped to ask herself, as she was beginning to do now: when would this get better? How could she stop feeling this way? Maybe, she thought as she sat there in the car, the reason she never asked herself those questions was because she knew she didn't have the answers, and she doubted that anyone else did, either.

A couple of days later, Davie was in her office when she looked up and saw the biologist from the DEC meeting, the one who was part of the whip-poor-will group and who noticed her in that meeting. She didn't know his name.

"Hi," he said. "I had to come by to go over some things with Jay, and I wanted to tell you that we're still on board for tomorrow night. But the forecast isn't great. We're going to go, but it might be cloudy. It's kind of borderline. I don't want you to be disappointed if we don't catch one. They're pretty difficult to catch, even when conditions are perfect. My name is Steve, by the way."

"Thank you, Steve. I guess you know I'm Davie." She didn't know if he expected her to ask him to come in and sit down. He was still hanging by the door.

"Well, you are driving out with Jay, right?"

"Yes."

"We're all going to meet in your parking lot because Jay has more of our gear than we do. He's got the mist nets from the last time we went out in May. We never got them back."

Mist nets, Davie thought. Those were the nets rolled up in her office when her office was used for gear storage.

"If we don't capture any tomorrow, we'll have to wait until next year," he said. "We won't get another shot at this in July; it will be too late in the nesting season and the parents won't be as active."

"Well, then, I'll hope for the best," Davie said. She smiled, but she was very busy and she really didn't want to ask him in because she didn't want him to keep talking.

"Depending on how tomorrow night goes, we might decide to try Thursday night," he said. "You'd be welcome to come back out with us Thursday."

"That's very nice of you, but I'm leaving for two weeks of vacation on Saturday and I'm going to be pretty busy getting ready to go." The second she spoke, she wanted to kick herself under the desk with one of her own beautifully polished chukka boots. She was trying to move this along, and now he would ask where she was going on vacation.

"Where are you going for vacation?"

Oh, hell, Davie thought. She was tempted to say, *My husband and I are going to Paris*, but he probably knew there was no Mr. Devlin, because there could be no other reason he was trying to prolong this doorway chat. Then she thought, he was only trying to be nice, and this was what people did when they were trying to find out more about someone: they talked and asked questions. But she was completely uninterested in talking or answering questions.

"I'm going backpacking in Shenandoah National Park," Davie said. "With a friend," she added, because she could see the next question forming in his expression.

"You backpack?" He sounded like he thought maybe she was joking.

"Yes. Do you find that so difficult to believe?" She wanted to add, *Why, don't I look the type?* but she realized she didn't look like someone who backpacked. Today was cool and overcast, so she wore a gray cashmere turtleneck sweater, a raspberry-colored pashmina shawl, black hiking pants and a pair of white-gold earrings—Michael's gift to her for her first birthday after their marriage. Her nail polish was the same color as the shawl.

"No, not really . . ." he trailed off, as Jay showed up in the doorway.

"Well, hi, Steve. Davie, I was just going to tell you that we're still going tomorrow night, even though the forecast is a little iffy, but I guess Steve beat me to it."

"He did," Davie said. "So, if I'm going to finish up what I'm doing here before tomorrow, so that I can go with you guys, I'd better get back to work."

She did not see a whip-poor-will the next night but she heard one. The weather was better than the forecast, not windy or even breezy, and the moon brightened the slightly sloped meadow dotted with trees in southern Albany County where they set up the nets. Davie thought it looked like an old abandoned orchard where many of the trees had died of age and neglect. The moon looked completely full to Davie but she learned that

Friday would be the actual full moon. Steve only asked if she was having fun, because everyone was too busy for long conversations—to Davie's relief, as far as he was concerned. Davie learned that they tried to talk as little as possible so as to not spook the birds. She was glad that she wore her hiking boots, because they trekked up from the cars without headlamps and her boots helped her on the uneven terrain. She was equally glad she wore her thin down jacket from the October Mountain trip, because the late-spring night air was far cooler in this remote meadow than in downtown Albany.

The biologists unfurled two nets and set them up like badminton nets, while Jay readied the banding box. He also carried three GPS tracking devices, so if they caught a whip-poor-will, they would attach one to the bird and follow its movements around its territory in the coming weeks.

They never caught one. Jay told her that this was the story of bird work—a lot of preparation, time and effort, with success often measured in small increments with many setbacks. He told her she could go out again next season if she was bent on seeing a whip-poor-will. The biologists could see one darting around the sky—Davie could not figure out how they spotted it; she never did—but it never went into the net, even though they played a recorded whip-poor-will song near the net to lure it closer.

She did hear one singing when they first got to the site, and that was the first time she ever heard one in real life. A few months earlier, she didn't know that whip-poor-wills even nested in the area. Now she heard the song, faint but unmistakable. Davie at least knew what the sound was, and she found it enthralling. Jay told her that whip-poor-wills had been nesting around here for a long time, probably many thousands of years. Davie thought the song was haunting, but that it also sounded . . . she didn't know what word to use. Hopeful, she decided. The three-note song pitched up at the end, as if the bird had asked a question, and was eagerly awaiting the answer. She expressed this thought to one of the other biologists, and the biologist laughed, not because she was laughing at Davie's lack of scientific expression, but because she thought Davie's point was on the mark.

"I guess that's one good way to put it," the biologist said. "He is asking a question . . . he's asking if anyone else is around, because he is claiming this territory, and he's asking if there's any ladies out there who might want to hook up with him."

Hopeful, Davie thought. She would never forget this night, this experience, standing in a moonlit remote meadow in the spring, after such a difficult winter, listening to a bird expressing hope that it would find a mate.

chapter 9

Just getting to Shenandoah National Park was a project. Davie was largely oblivious to the planning that went into each day's portion of what would be nine days on the Appalachian Trail, but she did at least understand that the trip to their starting point was complicated. As she watched each phase of their journey to Virginia unfold, Davie began to understand the challenges Andrea faced for years in her quest to section-hike the trail.

Jay offered to get them to the train station in Rensselaer, the small city just east of Albany on the other side of the Hudson River, so they would not have an exorbitant parking fee at the train station. Andrea had a garage, so she could get her car off the street. Davie picked up Andrea a little before seven o'clock in the morning. They drove to the house Jay and Alanna rented a couple blocks from Davie's home, pulled Davie's car into the off-street parking space alongside Jay's house, and piled their backpacks and themselves into Jay's car. A half-hour later, as Davie and Andrea hoisted their backpacks onto the rack above their seat on the train, Davie saw two men sitting nearby watching them. One of them started to get out of his seat to help them before he realized they already had their packs stowed. Davie smiled to herself; she felt like she was faking it, or playing backpacker for this trip, but she realized she didn't begin to know what lay ahead on such a long hike.

They waited for ninety minutes at Penn Station, got onto their train for Washington, D.C., and Andrea's cousin met them outside of Union Station to drive them to Harper's Ferry, West Virginia. The national office of the Appalachian Trail Conservancy, the organization that managed the trail for the National Park Service, was in Harper's Ferry, and Davie wished they had an extra day there to explore the little town and go to the conservancy offices. Neither their stay in the town now nor their return stay would allow for that, because they would get to Harper's Ferry too late in the day both times. They would spend one night in Harper's Ferry at a backpacker's hostel, sleeping in bunk beds in a dormitory-style room, then a shuttle driver Andrea hired would take them to the entrance of Shenandoah National Park the following morning. They would reverse this process on the way home, ten days later, using a second shuttle driver to fetch them at a crossroads deep in the park.

Andrea was newly promoted to associate director at the Community Loan Foundation, and was earning more money than Davie—a nice reversal of fortune, Davie very sincerely thought. Davie was juggling bills and extending some payments, including her utility bill, as far as she dared on her new salary, but she loved her job and she was managing. Even so, Andrea insisted on covering Davie's Amtrak fare to D.C. for the first leg of the journey to their destination. She also told Davie she would cover the cost of the shuttle drivers to and from the park, the two overnight stays in Harper's Ferry and the Amtrak fare home. She made it clear she would not listen to any protests about this, so Davie accepted the generosity. They got to the park the next morning, filled out permits to backpack there, and started their hike.

As well as Davie knew Andrea, their time together now gave Davie an understanding of Andrea's life and her determination in attempting the huge project of section-hiking the trail. Davie knew Andrea in the context of their friendship in Albany and their years together at the Community Loan Foundation, and she'd gotten a glimpse of the backpacking part of Andrea's life on the simple overnight trip to the October Mountain Forest. Now she saw Andrea's depth of knowledge about backpacking, about making decisions during their hike, a knowledge that remained largely hidden in their time together in Albany.

Andrea's only sibling—her brother, Bern Sorensen—was fifteen years older than Andrea, which meant he was almost sixty now to Andrea's forty-four. Andrea's mother and father were thirty-two and thirty-seven years old, respectively, when Andrea's brother was born, and then to the surprise of everyone in her family, Andrea was been born fifteen years later. A change-of-life baby, Andrea called herself, noting that if she had stayed married, gee, she would have had endless time to have decided whether or not to have kids. Her parents were now ninety-one and ninety-six years old, living in a retirement community in New Haven, Connecticut, still mentally alert but with some mobility problems that made it difficult for Andrea to bring them to Albany.

Instead, she went to see them just about every month.

Her brother and her sister-in-law, Susan Sorensen, were a retired investment banker and a retired venture capitalist, respectively. They lived in West Stockbridge, in the Berkshires. Andrea started following her brother's path in finance by snagging a highly competitive summer internship in her junior year of college at an old-name Wall Street investment firm. That firm hired her into its training program after she graduated. After a couple of years, Andrea found the cutthroat pace exhausting, and she began to question the endless weekends in the office just to make sure she worked a little bit harder than any of the other trainees in her class. So, she moved to Albany and joined the small firm that handled mostly old-family wealth, where her brother was a partner.

She got along very well with her brother and carved out her own name for herself in that job, but she possessed a quality her brother did not: a yearning to use money to make a difference in society. She wanted to strike out on her own and do something daring, and she next went to the Community Loan Foundation. That opened up a whole new phase of her life, when she earned a lot less and made her ill-fated marriage, but when she also rediscovered her personal life and formed a lasting friendship with Davie. Those were the years when she bought and fixed up her house, developed her garden in a backyard originally filled with rubble, and started backpacking. A career in an investment firm in New York City would never have allowed for such opportunities. She would have been hard-pressed to have made the time as an aspiring manager, and not even her job at her brother's firm would have given her such freedom. Andrea wryly observed that someone in the family needed to have a social conscience instead of a retirement account, and it might as well be her—an observation that Michael would later echo, in reverse, when Davie left the Community Loan Foundation and joined Levellewyn, Grenoble and Carl.

Now, on the hike through Shenandoah National Park, Andrea was completely at ease in this unlikely place as a backpacker who exuded confidence and competence. She had already overcome the toughest challenges the Appalachian Trail could hand anyone, in the high-altitude parts of the trail in New Hampshire and Maine. Davie thought about this as they hiked and clambered up to astonishing overlooks, and she wondered if backpacking was the reason Andrea responded to her cancer with such determination and calm. *Fearlessly* was not the word. *Boldly* was more like it, Davie thought. Andrea responded boldly, and now here she was, back-packing again. Davie wondered if backpacking might impart some of the same strength to her for whatever might lie ahead in her fraught life as a young widow.

The days slowly blended one into another. Davie lost track of what day of the week it was. That lapse was easier to handle than she would have expected, and she found herself doing what Andrea had urged her to do: she just gave herself up to the idea that on this trip, on this trail, time meant a lot less than it did in the everyday work world. She also found herself enjoying the brief encounters with other backpackers when they stopped for a few minutes to chat, as they often did. Andrea and Davie were head-ing south, but almost everyone they encountered was heading north. These were often people trying to hike the entire trail in one season—thru-hikers, as they were called—and the most common way to thru-hike was to start in Georgia and head to Maine.

Davie had already learned that the Appalachian Trail Conservancy, which kept a log of thru-hikers, would grant the coveted thru-hiker status to anyone who completed their hike of the entire Appalachian Trail a year from the day they started. This consideration allowed people who suffered an injury or had a personal emergency that required them to leave the trail, for anywhere from a few days to a few months, to get back to their hike and not have to start over from the beginning the next spring. Or, as Davie thought, this policy more likely helped such people decide to not throw in the towel and simply never try again, because she now realized that the effort required to hike this entire trail was more than most people could ever imagine. And the idea of starting it a second time when you had already done hundreds of miles would have been insurmountable for many people, in terms of time, money and their lives at home. The "finish in one year, even if you got knocked off the trail" policy that allowed someone to be a thru-hiker was wise and also very fair, Davie realized.

She was astonished that the designation as a thru-hiker or a section-hiker—someone who finished the trail in sections, sometimes over the span of years, as Andrea was doing—depended on the honor system. She heard of hikers scrupulously explaining why they missed a few miles here or there—often from injuries or the need to hopscotch around a danger-ous storm system—and their determination to keep heading north, toward Maine. She heard a few people say they would go back to the section they had missed and hike it before they filed their application as a thru-hiker or a section hiker, if it was more than ten miles or so, because they wanted to be ethical about how they did their hike. In a world where so many people rarely played by the rules, Davie found this fascinating.

With this newfound insight, Davie had conversations with people that she knew she would never forget, with none of these encounters lasting more than five minutes. She and Andrea met a couple in their early seventies who were picking their way carefully but very competently along a fairly narrow section of a ridge. The husband and wife explained they were thru-hiking the trail to celebrate their fiftieth wedding anniversary, and that their children thought they had taken leave of their senses. They looked and sounded serenely determined.

"Do you think they will finish?" Davie asked Andrea.

"Yes," Andrea said. "They got this far. They won't quit."

They met a young woman from France who was hiking by herself and who spoke very little English, as they quickly discovered. Davie spoke enough French to have a brief conversation with her, and she was able to tell the woman that the upcoming stretch of trail was nice and fairly easy. That made Davie feel good, that she was now able to assess the trail and offer advice. The idea of doing this trip alone when you were from another country and did not have a sound grasp of the language made a huge impression on Davie.

They met a Baptist preacher who was on a personal quest to forge a better relationship with Christ, and they artfully dodged his inquiry about whether they had been saved but enjoyed talking to him. And then, as they continued on, one day after another, Davie remembered something she had not thought about in years, a story about Michael that was perfect to tell in this setting. She told it to Andrea during a long level stretch of the trail when they didn't encounter other backpackers.

Michael took her to Mount Greylock in North Adams, Massachusetts, a month after they started dating. Davie already knew she was wildly in love with Michael. Now that Davie recalled that day trip, she realized she had in fact been on the Appalachian Trail once before, even if only for a few hours, because the trail went over the summit of Greylock. Michael drove her to the summit and they ambled around for an afternoon. Davie was especially fascinated by the warming hut for skiers, built on the summit decades ago at the top of a famous ski trail. She read with interest that the hut was dedicated to "a promising young skier" who was part of the Army's 10th Mountain Division and died in World War II. The warming hut was never locked, Michael told her, so that backpackers who got caught in severe weather on Greylock in the off season when the lodge was closed would always have a place to shelter.

Then they wandered over to where the trail came up into the parking area, picked their way carefully down about fifty yards, and sat on a couple of slabs of rock in the intermittent sunlight of the late August afternoon. While they sat there talking, they saw a young woman making her way up the trail toward them. Davie immediately noticed she was wearing a dress, the kind of dress you might have seen women wearing at rock festivals decades earlier—mid-calf length, in a gauzy, faded blue fabric, with embroidered flowers around the hem. She wore very broken-in hiking boots with the dress, and her backpack was worn but serviceable, clearly an older pack. The woman stopped and talked to them. That was easy for her to do, for Michael talked to everyone, and he made people feel he was truly interested in them.

The young woman said she was working her way south to her aunt's home in Tennessee, and she planned to keep backpacking until she got there. She was going to see if she could find a place on the summit to put up her tent in an out-of-the-way place. Tent-camping was restricted to designated areas on Mount Greylock, and was not permitted at the summit, but she preferred to sleep in her tent, not a bunk room. She bid them goodbye and continued on toward the parking lot and the lodge, where Davie and Michael planned to join the communal dinner for visitors and backpackers.

Davie did a rapid calculation and thought, it's August, and even if she is hiking south, she has a long way to go. She thought this plan would mean the woman would be hiking through some very remote places as the weather turned. Something about the woman's story did not add up to either of them, but it was Michael who said, as they watched her hike away, "She's homeless. That story about her aunt is probably fiction. I bet she's backpacking because she's just been evicted." That was his training from his work showing through, his training in detecting the carefully constructed ways that people built their cover stories for being on the street. He pulled a twenty out of his wallet and said to Davie, "Just see if she will take this, and ask her if she wants to come in and eat with us as our guest at the lodge. If I go after her to try to offer her money, she will get the wrong message."

Davie took the twenty-dollar bill and scrambled up the last bit of the trail to the parking lot and caught up with the woman, who politely declined the money, saying she had plenty of food in her pack. An hour later, Davie and Michael sat at a long table in the dining room of the lodge, listening to three guys in their fifties who were thru-hikers recount their adventures and describe the desperate measures to which they finally resorted to reduce the weight of their backpacks. They told these stories in high spirits; they were having the time of their lives doing a dream trip and they were thoroughly enjoying the six-month sabbatical from their office jobs.

"You get to the point where you're doing crazy things like cutting labels out of your clothes and sawing your toothbrush handle off to carry less weight," one of them said. At that moment, Davie happened to look up and see the young woman she and Michael tried to help looking through the dining hall window with an expression of heartbreaking longing on her face. The second that she and Davie made eye contact, the woman pulled back from the window. Davie never saw her again when she and Michael left the lodge and headed for Michael's car to drive back to Albany. Davie didn't mention this to Michael until they were on their way home, and she also never forgot Michael's kind gesture and intuition.

"I think that was when I realized I wanted to marry him,'" she said to Andrea as she finished telling this story. They were stopped for a water break on a high curving section of rock that jutted out from a ridge.

Andrea looked around at the valley below and tightened the top on her water bottle.

"I know that this has been much harder for you than you have ever told me," Andrea said, and Davie knew that Andrea wasn't talking about backpacking. "That's pretty obvious. I'm sure there's a lot you have never discussed with me. I strongly suspect you never told me the full story about what happened with your job at LGC, and that it involved more than missing a conference call with a client. But I want you to know that I admire what you have done, in just refusing to buckle. You just keep trying to find a way to get through everything, and that is very impressive to me."

They never discussed Michael again on that trip, because there was, Davie realized, nothing much else she could say after that conversation. Andrea really did get it; she got it in a way that Jay did not, and that just about everyone Davie knew did not grasp.

They also laughed so hard a few times that they paused on the trail, because it was very difficult to laugh really hard when you were also trying to walk with thirty pounds on your back.

Signs of black bears were all through the park, and the bears obviously knew how to cover miles like the humans did, because the bears also used the trail. That made sense, Andrea explained; when you hunted or foraged for everything you ate, you learned to conserve energy. The bears were eating lots of berries this time of year, and they regularly left mounds of berry-loaded scat along the trail. Davie and Andrea were commenting on this, and Davie was thinking that this conversation was one she would never have had anywhere else, when a man coming north stopped to say hello. He was backpacking alone. He gestured with the toe of one hiking boot at a softball-sized mound of bear scat, in which individual berries could be seen.

"Excuse me, but I wanted to ask if you two ladies know whether that is ... "

"Bear shit?" Andrea supplied. "Yes, it is. There are bears all up and down the trail through this park. You see that rock that's flipped over? That's done by a bear, looking for grubs."

The man looked slightly rattled.

"Where are you from?" Davie asked.

"Manhattan. New York City."

"I actually know where Manhattan is," Andrea said. "Well, you probably have black bears in New York City proper. Almost certainly in the Bronx up near the Westchester line, where you get some wooded areas."

"Yeah, but they're not doing *that*"—the man gestured to the mound of scat—"in front of Bloomingdale's. This is a little bit closer than I expected to see wildlife."

"You're in a *national park*," Andrea said. "So how far're you going?"

"I am a thru-hiker," the man said, drawing himself up a bit.

"Well, you know about porcupines, don't you?" Andrea asked.

"No, what about them?"

"Don't leave your boots outside of your tent at night starting in around . . . Pennsylvania, probably. And your hiking poles—make sure you bring them into your tent; don't leave them hanging from a tree or the hooks in the shelter."

"Why not?" The man was genuinely curious.

"They will chew your boots right down to the Vibram soles," Andrea said. "And the handles of your hiking poles. They love salt, and they go for anything that's been soaked with perspiration. Hey, good luck on the rest of your thru-hike."

"So do you think he'll finish the trail?" Davie asked after they went their separate way from the Manhattan thru-hiker. He seemed far less capable than the couple celebrating their fiftieth wedding anniversary.

"If he doesn't see any more bear shit on this trail, he probably will," Andrea said. "That is a little bit closer than he expected to see wildlife. Jesus Christ. Wait till he hears the coyotes up in Vermont. He'll think he's up in the Yukon with the wolf packs."

"And he's in a *national park*," Davie said, mimicking Andrea's inflection. "For a former investment banker, you are a walking field guide to the flora and fauna around here. I'm sticking with you. You know what you're doing. I have no frickin' idea." They both stopped and laughed so hard that Davie thought she was going to lose her balance and just fall over on her backpack. She could not remember the last time she laughed that hard.

"At least he believed me when I told him about the bears and the porcupines," Andrea said. "I have had some amazing conversations with male backpackers. You know, some men think women backpackers can't tell direction. It's like the Appalachian Trail version of men thinking that women can't parallel park. Many years ago in Massachusetts, I stopped to chat with a guy who was hiking south. I was heading north. He was completely mixed up, and that came out when he asked me how far I planned to hike that day. I never tell a guy what shelter I'm aiming for, so I think I just said, well, I was going to keep going north as far as I could get that day, and that I was out for another few days. He said, no, *I* couldn't be hiking north, because *he* was hiking north. Which of course he was not. Well, we went back and forth, and I finally said to him, 'Sir, I know north from south. I am hiking north. If you want to be hiking north, you are heading in the wrong direction.' So, he *still* didn't believe me, so he pulled out his compass—which begs the question of why he hadn't done this earlier—you name it, I've seen it on these hikes, all under the general heading of 'incompetent'—and he said, 'You're *right*. *Damn*. I'm hiking south.'"

Davie started laughing again.

"So, what'd he do? Turn around?"

"Oh, yeah, and he had hiked so many miles in the wrong direction that he never got farther that day than my destination, which was the next shelter north, and I guess he had planned to get a lot farther along. So, we both end up at the same shelter, and I knew better than to ask how he was doing. He was very annoyed with himself, that much was clear. He didn't say a word to me. To be honest, about four miles north from where I met him, I figured out where he made his mistake, because I almost did the same thing, the trail took a real sharp turn, almost like a U-turn, and it was very easy to see how he got turned around. What I could not understand was how he didn't realize he'd already passed some of landmarks twice. I'm always looking for stuff on the trail that can be a reference point."

These stories intrigued Davie, who was beginning to imagine herself going out alone on the Appalachian Trail. Attempting such a challenge sounded like the antidote to ten months of anguish, bereavement and confusion. Davie listened closely to Andrea's accounts of how she hiked, details like noticing landmarks, and mentally stowed these recommendations. Could she manage on her own on a hike, so soon after backpacking for the first time, she wondered. She thought she could, but when would she do it, and where, and how would she arrange to get from her car to her starting point . . . Ethan, she thought. Andrea's friend who shuttled them on their Memorial Day weekend hike. She'd hardly thought about him, really, since that hike, but he said he would help her. She could ask Andrea how to get in touch with him.

He was a bit eccentric, she remembered, but he also seemed kind of interesting. Davie mulled that thought over as she and Andrea hiked for a while in one of the occasional long silences into which they lapsed. If she contacted Ethan, maybe he could suggest a hike to her, because he knew the area around Massachusetts and Vermont so well . . . or she could ask Andrea for a good hike to do in a few days' time . . . and then an idea dawned for Davie. She would hike over Mount Greylock to mark the first anniversary of Michael's death, a day she absolutely did not want to spend at work or in her house. She wanted to be somewhere else, and Mount Greylock felt so right for such a hike, especially in light of the story she told Andrea about Michael wanting to help the woman they had encountered there.

With the destination and the date selected, Davie thought again about Ethan, who certainly seemed . . . aloof was not the word; he was very friendly and conversational, but he certainly was a little obsessive about being paid for that shuttle, based on what Andrea said. Introverted wasn't the word she was looking for . . . it was more that he conveyed a sense that he knew how he wanted something done, and he took it as a matter of course that it would be done just that way, plus he saw his way as the correct way.

Davie shook her head; she was giving this way too much thought, and she didn't know why. She knew nothing about him, including whether he had ever been married. She remembered Andrea mentioning his remote living situation on fifty acres of forest way out on the Rensselaer Plateau. She also remembered her distinct impression that Andrea and Ethan had possibly once dated, but she didn't want to ask Andrea about that, and besides, if Andrea wanted to mention that, she already could have done so. Davie decided to ask Andrea later how to reach Ethan, but whether he could help her or not, she felt she had just solved one issue that she didn't even realize was bothering her, that being how she would mark the first anniversary of Michael's death on September 4. She would get out of the house and summit Mount Greylock on the Appalachian Trail. Labor Day was Monday, September 1, Davie knew. She wondered if she could get the rest of the week off, so that she would not be in the house on September 4, watching emails and text messages flow in from people she had not heard from or seen in a year, telling her how much they were thinking about her.

Andrea had already mentioned that she wanted to do a December hike in the White Mountains, up to one of the backpackers' huts which was open all year, and she wanted to know if Davie would like to go with her. Davie wondered if she would be able to deal with the cold, but she told Andrea that yes, she would like to consider that. It sounded thrilling, and a little dangerous, but she knew that Andrea had done this before and that Andrea was also very, very careful in assessing the conditions for an off-season hike.

Andrea planned their Shenandoah hike quite conservatively, with nine days on the trail and low mileages each day, in deference to Davie's inexperience. They would complete sixty-two miles by the ninth day. "I want you to like this, and not want to bail on me after twenty-four hours," Andrea explained. "I'll finish this next year, and I hope you will want to finish it with me."

Davie knew that if Andrea was hiking on her own, she could have hiked the whole 101 miles of the Appalachian Trail through Shenandoah National Park in only a little more time than they would take to do their sixty-two miles. Andrea showed no indication that she had been treated for cancer the previous winter, and seemed tireless. She was also very patient with Davie. The longest day they hiked was nine miles. Davie realized that Andrea routinely hiked twelve to fifteen miles a day when she was by herself, and Andrea told Davie that many backpackers surpassed that daily pace by many miles.

Andrea preferred to enjoy what she saw and stop when she felt like stopping, instead of pushing to just clock miles. Of course, she noted, thru-hikers needed to clock miles, because most of them intended to finish the trail in one long push, and they needed to get to one end or the other before it got too late in the season. If they were hiking north, they needed to get to Maine and the northern end of the Appalachian Trail on the summit of Mount Katahdin before that section of the trail closed in October—usually around the middle of the month. If thru-hikers instead headed south from Katahdin, they wanted to get to the southern end of the trail in Georgia before snow started in the mountains of North Carolina.

The Appalachian Trail went in a fairly straight line through Shenandoah National Park, but there were ways to get off the trail deep inside the park at certain places because the park also contained roads. Some of those roads either crossed the trail or came very close to it. A shuttle driver would meet them on the morning of their ninth day at a road crossing that fell at the sixty-two-mile mark. The driver would take them back to Harper's Ferry in West Virginia, to spend one night at a hiker's hostel with showers and bunk beds. Davie was beginning to obsess on the idea of hot running water. Andrea's cousin agreed to meet them the next morning in Harper's Ferry at the hostel, and she would get them back to D.C., where they would get on a train to Albany and get home late that same night. It seemed impossible to Davie that they could leave all of this behind on one day, and pile their backpacks into a cab outside of the train station across the Hudson River from Albany the next day, or more correctly, late the next night. She thought she might have a bit of an adjustment back home the first day or two, like someone coming off of crossing several time zones on a long flight.

They stayed at a shelter and tent site on a slight knoll above a stream on their last night on the trail. Beyond the stream was a meadow dotted with what Davie thought were apple or cherry trees, as if this was farmland long ago. Sometimes there were only a few other backpackers at a shelter, but on this night, people kept coming up the trail and putting down their packs, signaling that they were done for the day. The shelter quickly filled, and tents went up all around the campsite.

As darkness fell, and Davie was lying in her tent wondering if she would ever feel clean again, whip-poor-wills started to sing. The wild, haunting three-note sound echoed through the tent site and pulled up for Davie a sudden yearning to tell Michael about this moment. She wanted to share this experience with him, even as she realized that if Michael was alive, she would almost certainly not be having this experience. If Michael was alive, he and Davie would be out for dinner on a Friday evening in June in Albany, or they would be sitting on the deck of a friend's home, looking at the garden, talking and laughing and having a beer. Or, they would be on the Cape. Davie would be anywhere but here if Michael had not died, but even knowing that didn't make her longing any less poignant. So she lay very still, trying to imprint the sound in her memory. It seemed that an indeterminate number of the males were singing, because the sounds came from several places in the meadow and clearly involved several birds overlapping each other. Some of the whip-poor-wills were so close that they were very loud.

"I wish someone could shut those damned birds up," a backpacker called from a tent on the other side of the clearing, dispelling Davie's reflective, bittersweet mood in a split second. "They're driving me crazy."

A few minutes later, another male voice came from closer to Davie's tent.

"Jeeez . . . I can't get to sleep. How long are they going to go on like that?"

OK, Davie thought. She'd had enough. She reached for her headlamp, unzipped her tent, ducked out, stood up, put on her headlamp, and switched on the light.

"Listen up, everyone," she said very loudly. She sensed she had the immediate attention of the occupant of every tent within earshot. "They are going to sing all night. Those are Eastern whip-poor-wills. They've been around for thousands of years. They are very beneficial birds, they eat a ton of insects, but they are declining, thanks to us human beings, who just keep messing up their world. So I think we should all be glad we are hearing them."

Stunned silence followed, as everyone seemed to digest the one-minute nature lesson. Davie turned off her headlamp and was getting ready to get back into her tent when someone called, "What are you, some kind of bird expert?"

"Yes."

Another voice drifted out of a nearby tent.

"Thank you, ma'am. I have not heard that many whip-poor-wills in many years. And she's right, fellows. They are very special birds. I could listen to them all night."

"I think you're going to," one of the original complainants said. Laughter drifted out from several tents, and then applause.

Davie's phone screen lit up with a text message. It was from Andrea, whose tent was several sites away. Davie read, "Bird expert, huh? Good for you. That shut 'em up."

Three miles farther down the trail the next morning, the shuttle driver pulled over on a dirt road the trail crossed in the middle of nowhere. Davie and Andrea sat on a log, their packs next to them and their bandanas soaked with water from their bottles and draped around their necks in the sauna-like heat. Davie had taken off her baseball cap because it was so soaked with sweat. She was sure she smelled terrible, but she assumed the shuttle driver was used to hot, grubby, sweaty backpackers getting into her car who looked and smelled like they had not showered or washed their hair in going on ten days.

"How do you feel? Any blisters?" Andrea asked as Davie lifted her pack into the back of the woman's Honda and then pushed her tangled, matted hair out of her face. Davie was sure that if she hadn't done this lift on the first try, she would never have gotten the pack over the edge of the wayback. Whether it was from sitting for a half-hour while they waited for the shuttle driver, or the psychological effect of knowing that she was heading home, she was beginning to feel very stiff and extremely sore.

"I feel great. No blisters. How'd I do?"

Andrea shoved her backpack next to Davie's in the hatch and then turned and gave Davie a serious, appraising nod followed by a genuine, wide-open smile.

"You did fabulously," she said. "Now you're a backpacker."

chapter 10

Late on the afternoon of Davie's first day back at work, her phone rang in her office.

"Hello, this is Steve."

Steve who? Davie asked herself.

"Steve from the DEC. You know, from the whip-poor-will team," he said, as if reading her mind.

"Oh! Sure. Steve from the DEC. Hi. How can I help you?" Then Davie immediately realized with his next words that this was not a work call.

"How was your vacation?"

"My vacation . . . oh, it was very nice. But I've come back to a ton of work here."

"OK, well, I was wondering . . . I wondered if you'd like to go out for dinner?"

Sitting at her desk, Davie looked out the window at the Hudson River and then back at her desk, where a framed photo of Michael and her taken the weekend Michael proposed stood on one corner.

"Steve, I've really got a lot of work to catch up on here . . ."

"Well, you're not going to be working all weekend, I hope. I was thinking about Saturday night."

"Saturday night . . ." Oh, what the hell, Davie thought, she would have agreed to go on a cruise to the Bahamas with him if it meant she could get him off the phone right now. "Yeah, that would be fine. What time were you thinking?"

She gave him her address and her cell phone number, hung up and wondered why she had just agreed to go on a date—if in fact that was what this was, and having a sinking feeling that yes, this was a date—with someone she did not find interesting and felt no desire to sit in a restaurant with for ninety minutes. Why? She didn't have a clue. She was not looking forward to a date with this guy, but she also hadn't been out for dinner in a very long time. She actually thought that going out with him once would make it easier to let him know she really didn't want to get together again. At least he would realize she gave it a try.

Saturday night arrived, and Davie was putting on her lipstick in front of the mirror by the kitchen door when she saw her phone screen light up. Her dinner date was due to arrive in fifteen minutes. When she picked up her phone, she saw a text message from him that read, "I'm on my way. Also, I wanted to make sure you knew that this was going to be Dutch." She nearly dropped her phone. You have got to be joking, she thought. She in fact planned to offer to split the bill, not being sure how much biologists at cash-strapped state agencies earned. Even so, she was at a loss for words that he hijacked her good intentions by telling her that he expected her to pay for her dinner.

"Oh, for crying out loud," Davie said, as though she had a sympathetic listener to whom she could start swearing. What was she supposed to do now? She was about as interested in this dinner date as she would have been if someone had called to ask if she felt like helping them clean their garage that night. Was this guy for real?

As Davie thought through all of this, she heard the door knocker on the front stoop. She was reluctant to go outside clearly dressed for a date and send him on his way because it was July and a lot of her neighbors sat on their stoops on nice summer evenings. The family two doors over would be outside with their dog and their three little boys, with the parents supervising the execution of an art exhibition in sidewalk chalk. She just did not want to have this conversation on her front stoop within earshot of people she knew, people who would notice she was going on a date. Davie fully realized that she should examine why she cared so much about what her neighbors saw and thought, but right now was not the moment to delve into profound questions that probably had something to do with her childhood. Nor did she want to call him; the idea of conversing with her date by text or cell phone while she was upstairs in her house and he was on the front stoop seemed ridiculous. She would feel like she was barricaded in her own home for a hostage negotiation. She picked up her shoulder bag and went downstairs.

For some reason, the evening reminded her of her one visit to the grief counselor in Columbia County, the man who worked out of his home. Davie figured out the connection as they drove to the restaurant: she immediately wanted out of the appointment with the clueless counselor the moment she walked into his home. She also wanted out of her enforced time right now, tonight, with this man whom she found ill-mannered or probably just so socially inexperienced that he didn't realize how he came across to her. To boot, he struck her as boring. How could someone who did his work with wildlife be boring? Even so, that was how he seemed to Davie.

She considered ordering the most expensive item on the menu and just playing dumb about the text message he sent and then serenely telling him that gee, she thought *he* asked *her* out for dinner and she assumed he was paying. She just as quickly dismissed that idea as more effort than it was worth, because she was not good at faking something like that. The rest of the date unraveled so quickly that by the time the check came, she simply wanted to pay up and get out of the restaurant as fast as possible. She thought of telling him she would walk home—it wasn't too far back to her house—but she thought it a bit late to go past a stretch of Lincoln Park that could be a little isolated at night.

The waiter took their order and brought their drinks—Davie stuck with ginger ale—and Steve took a sip of his beer and then said, "You know, I never did know how your husband died."

A thought flashed through Davie's mind that she should add this to the list of unbelievable things people said to widows, the list she saw on the widows' online group site. What an amazing opening line to a dinner date. She thought Michael would completely understand what she did next, which was to spend twenty minutes giving her date a detailed description of everything that happened, right down to her driving home in a car spattered with blood. She explained that the blood was in the fluid from Michael's lungs caused by pulmonary edema.

"You're a biologist, so you must know what pulmonary edema is?" she asked, and then finished her ginger ale. He did not answer; his beer sat untouched once she started speaking, and now he looked like he too wanted a way to get out of the rest of the evening. *Good*, Davie thought. *We're on the same page.* Their dinner arrived, and Davie worked her way through hers in enjoyable silence. She did not order a dessert, and she put two twenties on the table before the check came.

"You can take care of the tip," she said. She was having a better time than she expected with her long-dormant sense of humor starting to come alive, fueled by sheer nastiness that she considered entirely justified.

Michael's sense of humor was based on exaggerated irony; Davie's was based on a sense of harmless but zinging wickedness. As they stood up to leave, she saw Jay and Alanna sitting at the bar, looking her way. She nodded and briefly waved, but she was reasonably confident that her expression warded off any possibility that they would come over and chat. That was the problem with Albany; you were bound to run into someone you knew.

As they pulled up to her house, Davie thought, well, at least he wouldn't expect her to ask him in, nor did she think he was going to try for a good-night kiss. She unbuckled her seat belt and started to open the car door, but he belatedly seemed to realize that good manners dictated that he should walk her up her stoop. She held up her hand when she saw him start to reach for his door handle.

"Don't bother," she said. His head swiveled back around; he seemed startled by the tone of her voice. She was in fact speaking the way she would have talked to a college intern at the Community Loan Foundation who had just screwed up beyond belief.

"I'm going to give you some advice," she said with the car door ajar. "The next time you ask a woman out for dinner, don't tell her while you're on your way to pick her up that you expect her to split the bill. That was just fucking unbelievable. And when your dinner date is a widow, there's a better way to start the evening off than asking her how her husband died. I mean, you really cut to the chase."

"I'm sorry," he said. He sounded genuinely regretful, as though he never considered any of this.

"Don't be sorry," Davie said. "Consider it a favor. I'm so much farther along than you are in life that it's not funny." She got out and walked up to her door without looking back at his car. She heard the car pull away only when she turned the key in the lock.

Jay at least waited until just before lunchtime Monday to stop by her office and ask, "Have a good time Saturday?" The look she gave him could have melted glass.

"Thank you for not bopping over to ask us to join you at the bar," she said. "I was ready to pay the couple at the next table to give me a ride home just to get me out of there."

"Guy's a social klutz. I wish I'd known he asked you out. I had no idea. I would have warned you."

"And you would have saved me forty bucks. Among other bright moments in the evening, he told me just before he picked me up that he expected me to split the bill. This, after he asked me to dinner. But that's

OK. I think I have ensured that he will not be asking me out again. We don't have to get together with the whip-poor-will group again this summer, do we?"

"Nope, you are home free on that one," Jay said. "Maybe by the time next May rolls around, his next dinner date will have arranged for him to be kidnapped and left blindfolded and shoeless somewhere up in the North Country."

Davie thought she should file her dinner with Steve under the category of "First Date as a Widow," and just leave it there. With the experience behind her, she turned to planning her first solo backpacking trip, a trip she would do—as she decided on the Shenandoah hike—to mark the first anniversary of Michael's death.

Davie understood now how to read the Appalachian Trail map that Andrea gave her, and the map made perfect sense to Davie, because she worked with charts, graphs and spread sheets for most of her career. When you opened the map—printed on very durable water-resistant paper—north and south ran to the right and the left, instead of going up and down the page. The overhead view of the region covered most of the unfolded map, and looked like any regular map in an old-fashioned printed road atlas, with rivers and roads and villages clearly marked, and the Appalachian Trail printed in red as it wound its way across the paper.

The elevation part of the map was an inset that ran across the bottom of the page with the miles and vertical gains marked in a grid pattern. The depiction of the trail on this part of the map looked like a sideways view of the mountains after they had been vertically sawed in half. The elevations went up and down, up and down again, then a long stretch of level hiking, and then another climb. Davie carefully studied the elevations, knowing now that what looked like short, easy ascents and descents over the span of a mile might be strewn with rocks that made it impossible to put your foot down flat. Sometimes you couldn't even really walk. You were climbing over boulders too large to step over, too tightly placed to step around, so your only choice was to go hand-over-hand or to sometimes scuttle on the seat of your pants because standing up was so difficult. All while wearing a backpack that might weigh more than thirty pounds. Such sections made for slow, exhausting progress. Backpackers had a name for that kind of terrain, she remembered. Rock-scrambling—that was it. Davie knew that Andrea had a large patch on the rear of her favorite hiking pants where the fabric had worn through because of rock-scrambling.

Davie planned to start her hike Tuesday, September 2. The date of Michael's death was September 4, a Thursday, and Davie planned to be on the last night of her backpacking trip on that date. She asked her boss if she could take the four days off after Labor Day. She did not present the request with any certainty about whether he would give her the time. She didn't explain the reason; she was very reluctant to disclose that, and she didn't want him to think she expected his pity. She was mindful that when she accepted the job, she told him she would need two weeks off in the summer for the Shenandoah trip. On the one hand, she did have the time to use; this place had a generous vacation policy. On the other hand, she was asking for a third week of vacation only eight months into her time there.

Her manager readily granted her request.

"Your husband died last year, didn't he? Around this time a year ago, if I recall?" he asked Davie.

"Yes, September 4. I didn't want to be home on that date. I'm going backpacking," Davie said.

"I hope you don't mind that Jay filled me in a bit on the circumstances," he said. "I mean, I knew you'd had a medical emergency, and that your husband got you to the hospital, but I don't believe I ever knew the full story until very recently. Please accept my condolences for your loss, and yes, take those days. I hope you have a good hike. We are very happy with your work. How are you doing in general now?"

Davie paused, in part because she was stunned that this comparative stranger was offering her condolences when Irina, her boss at LGC, never once mentioned Michael or asked how Davie was holding up after her return to work. Irina also never complimented Davie on her work.

"I'm doing ... I think a little better now. I'm very grateful that I landed this job."

"Well, if you need any more time down the road, let me know. This is a long process, and it can have a lot of ups and downs."

Something clicked for Davie in how he said that. She had a much better grasp now on how many people carried secret and terrible losses, and how rarely those around them in daily life would have ever guessed that. She knew nothing about her boss's personal life, but he wore a wedding ring. Later, Davie learned that his first wife died by suicide ten years earlier, a day after a second opinion at Dana Farber in Boston confirmed a diagnosis of brain cancer that could be treated but not cured, and would kill her within two years at the most. He finished raising their three children on his own and eventually remarried. But as Davie left his office that day, she was simply and profoundly grateful for the compassion and understanding he showed her.

Ethan agreed to shuttle her from Route 8 in the small town of Cheshire, Massachusetts, to a trail parking area in Williamstown. Davie would hike south from the ridge above Williamstown back to Cheshire, a trip she thought she could do in three nights and four days, and which she knew full well that many experienced backpackers would do in just two days, with time left over at the end of Day Two. Davie planned to sleep at designated camping sites on the trail two of the three nights, where she would pitch her tent somewhere near the shelter, and she would stay at the lodge on Mount Greylock for the middle of the three nights.

The shelters on the Appalachian Trail ranged from the size of a tool shed with just enough room for two or three sleeping bags side by side on the floor, to the size of a small cottage that could sleep a dozen or more people. A long overhanging extension of the roof created a place to sit in bad weather and helped keep out the rain. Andrea did not like sleeping in the shelters, because she liked her privacy and she hated when other backpackers hung their food bags from a peg on the shelter wall, in the mistaken belief that a black bear would never enter the shelter to steal food when sleeping humans were there. She long ago gave up trying to convince other backpackers that hanging their food in the shelter was dangerous, and now she always used her tent unless the weather was so bad that she needed a roof. Davie also preferred her tent.

Davie was not sure why she decided to hike south, when it meant that she would have a longer drive home from Cheshire. Andrea was section-hiking the trail from north to south and Davie suspected that influenced her. Her hike would total about twenty-two miles, with a two-mile climb at the very beginning up a side trail just to reach the Appalachian Trail, followed by a long, steady descent to North Adams, Massachusetts. Then, another three-mile climb that looked very steep, with her destination for her first night at the end of that climb. That destination was the Wilbur Clearing Shelter.

No matter where she planned to stay, Davie found herself in a quandary that every backpacker faces—often several times in one trip, as Andrea warned her—and that was whether she could get to her destination each day before dark, or would she find herself still on the trail late in the after-noon, when she should already have been at her shelter setting up her campsite? Because if she ran out of hiking time, she would need to find a level place to camp off the trail in the forest.

This practice was known as "stealth camping," and there were sections on the trail where you were not allowed to do this. The Appalachian Trail was actually a national park, but regional trail clubs governed individual sections of the trail under the auspices of the national governing body, the Appalachian Trail Conservancy. Most of the trail clubs hired seasonal employees known as "Ridge Runners," who hiked sections of the trail in a continual loop, checking the shelters for damage or ill backpackers, checking the trails for downed trees and washed-out footbridges and occasionally assisting in searches for hikers reported missing or injured. Very few people went missing on the Appalachian Trail, and relatively few people suffered serious injuries, but Davie thought it was nice to know someone was out there who might find you if you got into a jam.

The Ridge Runners wore a uniform and were on the trail from spring to the end of the summer. They were sometimes college or graduate students, and sometimes accomplished retirees who still backpacked and knew the trail. They were adept at wilderness first aid and at answering questions, and although they were not law enforcement officers, they could and would tell you to pack up and move if they found you stealth camping in a place where it was forbidden, and they would, if need be, summon park rangers or local law enforcement for a problem they could not handle. Davie had no idea if stealth camping was allowed in Massachusetts. She supposed that information was somewhere in her guidebook or available through the local trail club, but she didn't bother to seek the answer because she wasn't eager to know that she could stealth-camp. She didn't want a backup plan; she wanted to complete the plan she was making now.

She was also jittery about the idea of sleeping in the forest by herself in a random place she picked, even as she realized this would be no different from sleeping at a tent site at a shelter by herself. Sleeping alone in the middle of nowhere in the woods was bound to be spooky no matter where you pitched your tent. Even so, Davie was convinced that being at a shelter, if not in one, would offer at least a psychological sense of security, along with the very real possibility that other people would be there and would lend an additional sense of safety in numbers. The shelters were typically eight to ten miles apart on the trail, and Davie was unsure if she would feel like going any farther than the shelter at the end of the day, especially in a stretch that had some steep climbs.

Adding to her doubt was a realization that dawned on her during the Shenandoah hike: what you saw on the nice, neat elevation part of the map—with each mile marked off by a section of a grid a little more than a half-inch wide—and what you ended up hiking, were entirely different. A section that looked only a little challenging based on the map might contain steep slopes of loose rock or climbs where the boulders were too high to step on and required you to almost crawl over them while still wearing your pack, proceeding hand-over-hand as you slowly made your way to the top. There might be smooth faces of rock on descents that offered very little in the way of toe holds or hand holds, and sometimes left you with no choice but to lower your pack to the next level on a rope or strap and then turn around and back down the face, grabbing whatever you could find, including tree roots.

Any of these situations were possible just about anywhere on the trail, not only in the far northern mountains of New Hampshire or in Maine. By now, Davie knew that the Appalachian Trail guidebooks, two editions of which Andrea bought for her—one just for Shenandoah National Park and one that combined Massachusetts and Connecticut into one volume—were famous for their lack of detail about what actually lay ahead in a particular section. Davie already noticed how many times the guidebook advised a reader that they would "ascend steeply" with no indication of what that meant.

Davie was stunned at how little she ever understood about this tremendous challenge Andrea blithely tackled when Andrea decided to hike the entire Appalachian Trail. Davie remembered how she listened to Andrea talk about it, all the while naively imagining the trail as a smooth, gently undulating path from Georgia to Maine. Sort of like what you saw in a town park, where you could push a stroller or hold a toddler's hand while hiking. Davie didn't know how Andrea's ex-husband responded to Andrea's desire to hike the trail, but Davie knew he was not a backpacker. She doubted that Andrea's annual two-week solo backpacking trips that took her progressively farther south on the trail—while her husband used that time to travel through Europe—caused the break-up of their marriage. There were problems long before the separate vacations began, of that Davie was quite sure. Davie now suspected that the backpacking became a coping mechanism for Andrea.

Well, Davie thought, she would soon find out for herself what this was like.

She kept going through her backpack to make sure she was not leaving an essential piece of gear at home. She tried drawing up a checklist, but found that she kept switching different items in and out of the pack so that the checklist became all but useless. Did she need her very small flashlight if she already had a headlamp? She put the flashlight into the pack and took it out so many times that she finally tossed it into a drawer to get it out of sight, as a way of settling the question. She kept digging through the pack to make sure she had her little collapsible backpacking stove. She was afraid of getting to her campsite and realizing she couldn't cook her dinner because she didn't have the stove, although Andrea assured her this would be manageable if Davie always carried some food that would fill her up and not require cooking—chocolate; cheese; nuts; Snickers Bars; or Andrea's personal favorite, Triscuits. If campfires were allowed, well, it was possible to heat water and cook your box-mix macaroni and cheese over a small fire. A bit tricky, but possible.

Davie found herself thinking she would have done well to have been in the Girl Scouts, which she didn't recall having a strong presence in her private day school in Manhattan, but would have given her some skills she could use now. Andrea once ate cold instant mashed potatoes, rehydrated with water from her Nalgene hiking bottle, for dinner for three days when she forgot her stove and was on the trail in Connecticut, where campfires were not allowed. You do that once, she told Davie, you never do it again.

Finally, on the Saturday of Labor Day weekend, Davie drove all the way out to the trail head parking area in the town of Cheshire to make sure she could find it, so she would not keep Ethan waiting there for her. She was keyed up and a bit anxious.

She thought over her dealings with Ethan as she sorted through her pack and went over her questionably useful checklist. She got his phone number from Andrea, who advised her to text him, as he was more likely to get a text message and the reception for phone calls was sometimes spotty at his home. So she sent him a very brief message, asking if he was available to shuttle her, what his fee would be, and what time would be good for him to meet her? She told him where she would start her hike, adding that she hiked slowly and was concerned about getting to the Wilbur Cross Shelter before dark, so an early start was fine with her. They agreed to meet at seven o'clock in the morning, which meant that Davie would leave her house about five-thirty. His responses were brief, courteous and with an old-fashioned tone to his wording, even in the sparse writing of a text message.

When she got to the parking area twenty minutes early, having allowed way more time than she needed, Ethan's old Volvo station wagon was already there. He got out and offered to help her with her pack, but she pulled it out of her car before he got to her.

"Don't forget your poles," he said.

"Oh, my gosh . . . I almost did," Davie said. "Thank you." She reached in and grabbed them, and then Ethan picked up her pack.

"Let me help you with this. I have every confidence that you can handle everything, but it is always awkward to do this transfer. A backpack is easier when it's on your back." He lifted it with ease and stowed it in the wayback of the Volvo. As they pulled out, Davie found herself enjoying just being in the car with him, on her way to . . . well, on her way to a personal challenge that she hoped would help her get through the looming anniversary and the inevitable recollections of the night that Michael died.

They drove in silence for several minutes, and then Ethan asked her, "The anniversary of your husband's death is this coming week, correct?" He sensed her startled response, that he knew this, and he quickly added, "Andrea told me. I hope you don't mind that she did. She also told me what happened."

"Yes, that's why I am doing this," Davie said. "Maybe I'm wrong, but I just thought it would be better to not be home for the date. I'd rather be somewhere else, and this seemed like a good place to be."

He nodded. "Do you use an old-fashioned map, or are you using an app on your phone?" By that, she knew, he was asking if she planned to use one of the several phone apps that showed you the section you were hiking and could even tell you how far you still needed to hike to get to your destination.

"I am using my map and a guidebook Andrea gave me," Davie said. "You know, I'm a mathematician by training, and I believe in having a physical sense of what I'm doing . . . I don't know if I'm explaining this the right way. I actually know how to use a slide rule, OK? No one uses a slide rule anymore to solve equations. I took a course on it in college. Of course, I use a calculator and a computer in my job now, where I work up projections and analyses of the data that the biologists collect . . . I guess you don't even know what I do for a living, do you?"

"Well, now I know that you work with biologists, so that will suffice for the moment. But I'm more interested in knowing more about why you use a paper map, when so many backpackers depend on their phones. I also use a paper map, by the way. I carry a phone when I backpack, but I have that just for emergencies. I never use it for directions on the trail. Why do you use a map?"

"I'm getting to that," Davie said. "Andrea talked to me about this. She described herself as very old-school; she said a map will never fail you, the battery will never run down, and you're a lot less likely to drop it in a stream and crack it on a rock. I think I just liked the physical sense of the map. I have a compass, but I haven't learned how to do anything with it yet other than set it on a flat surface and get a general idea of which way north and south are."

"You would almost certainly not need a compass for more than that for this trip, and you probably won't even need that much," Ethan said. "OK. We are at your starting point. You know that you follow the Pine Cobble Trail up to the AT, and turn right, which heads you south, and then you are on your way?"

"Yes."

"Well, then, a final question. Do you have someone to catch your message that you are off the trail? That you are back to your car? That's always a good idea, you know. It kind of ensures that you won't be out there with a broken ankle wondering how soon your co-workers will realize you never called in sick on Monday." He smiled, but he also looked serious.

"Andrea is doing that for me," Davie said. "Thank you." She pulled out her cash for him, and got out of the car, as did he. He pushed the wayback door of the station wagon up higher, so that she could use the storage area as a platform for putting on her pack, and then, after she buckled her hip belt and he handed her the hiking poles, he held out his hand to shake hers. Davie belatedly caught the gesture, took his hand and shook it.

"Good luck, Davie," he said.

"Thank you, Ethan."

"If you like this and you wish to do another solo trip, I will probably be able to shuttle you."

"Thank you again." Davie turned to start crossing the road to where the trail started, then turned back and picked up her poles from where they leaned against the car.

"I was about to hand those to you," Ethan said.

"Thank you. I don't know why I keep forgetting them. Well, I guess I am on my way. Thank you. I'm sure I will be back in touch about another hike."

She smiled goodbye and took her first steps, briefly and only a little frantically thinking, well, here was her last chance to bail on this idea, but she kept going toward the trail entrance. She heard the Volvo pull out of the parking lot. Ethan tapped the horn a couple of times, she turned and waved, and then she was alone, just above the road, with no place to go but forward, facing four full days by herself on the Appalachian Trail. She remembered that she was carrying the water bottle Ethan gave her, and she never asked him if he wanted it back. Oh, well, she thought, and turned back toward the trail to start hiking in earnest.

Davie did not pass anyone else for the rest of that day. She wondered: in what other setting could you not see other human beings for an entire day? Not from a window, not from across a field . . . not at all. Perhaps on a long solo sailing trip, or an expedition into some very remote place, like a desert. The forest around her was quite silent. Now that she knew a little more about birds, she knew that this was because it was long past nesting season, and the birds would be more silent, as they were not proclaiming their territories or trying to attract mates. She hiked for an hour and a half in the silence of her thoughts, remembering her time with Michael a year ago, remembering various events of the past year. Her thoughts took her a long way from the trail. And then she started remembering songs she loved, and she started to sing them to herself, aloud, because really, what did it matter? No one could hear her truly terrible singing voice.

She was surprised on checking her map much later in the day, after several water or snack breaks, to realize she would get to her shelter well before dark. When she did arrive a short time later, she decided to do something that she would never have done earlier in the season, when it was more likely that other backpackers would show up: she put up her tent inside the shelter. She knew this was not good backpacking etiquette, but she decided to take a chance that no one else would arrive. She set the tent up on the shelter floor, cooked her box-mix macaroni and cheese dinner, dropped her food bag in the bear box, and crawled into her tent at seven-thirty. She was sound asleep in minutes.

Something woke her up sometime later in the pitch-black of the forest at night. Davie pushed the light button on her watch. It was nine-thirty, so she thought for a moment that another backpacker was coming up the side trail to the shelter, and that she would have to get up and somehow move her tent. She reached for her headlamp on the floor of her tent, in the same place where she always put it so that she could find it in the dark, and as she touched it, she heard a clanging sound. Her hand froze as she realized that she was hearing the chain on the bear-box hasp banging against the metal box, meaning a bear was within easy walking distance of the shelter, trying to get at food it could smell inside the bear box. The box was chained to a tree and locked with a hasp welded to the steel box.

Davie's hand stayed frozen as she realized she was so tired when she crawled into her tent that she didn't set her little pocket knife next to her headlamp. The pocket knife was in her pants, and they were crumpled in the far corner of the tent—not that she thought a pocket knife would be much defense against a bear. She was afraid to switch on her headlamp; she didn't know if it would draw a bear to investigate, or scare it into fleeing. She stayed absolutely still, certain that her fear would radiate through the flimsy walls of her tent and send a signal to the bear that a terrified human was a short distance away, right about where the delicious scent of her dinner still lingered. Now she understood why the safety procedures for avoiding bears advised you to not cook your dinner at the shelter, but everyone did it, and by the time you got to the shelter, you were usually too tired to look for a level place somewhere else. She heard the chain bang one more time, then nothing: the night was silent. She didn't know what kind of sound a bear would make as it walked, but she didn't think they moved with great stealth.

She lay there in her tent, tensed with listening, slowly relaxing as minutes went by and she heard nothing else. Then she fell asleep.

Davie woke up at daybreak, remembering the events of the night . . . gosh, she thought, she never even knew how long the bear was around the campsite before it woke her. She lay restlessly in her sleeping bag, waiting for full daylight, and finally started to dress for her second day, the day she would arrive at Mount Greylock. When she unzipped her tent and emerged into morning light, the day was calm and quiet and reassuring. She saw no tracks on the path to the bear box, but the ground was also rocky and dry and didn't seem like a place where the tracks of even a large animal would easily show. She shrugged and went to get her food bag out of the box. She looked around after she replaced the hasp on the lock, thinking there were probably bears all around out there, but she also didn't think that they were grouped in the forest, watching her every move. The little she knew about bears, her visitor was probably asleep somewhere now.

She took almost an hour to pack up her tent, get her sleeping bag back into the stuff sack, eat breakfast and get ready to leave. She kept looking around, but the morning remained quiet and she didn't expect any more problems. She evaluated her water supply and studied her map on the picnic table at the shelter before she left. She thought a liter of water would get her quite a way, and she only needed to hike three and a half miles to the summit of Mount Greylock. She could get water there, she knew. Of course, the route was three and a half miles of steadily increasing elevation . . . twelve-hundred feet of elevation, Davie calculated, looking at the grid for her day's hike. She figured she would need five or six hours, with stops, to reach her destination.

Davie was under no illusions about her prospective pace, so she decided to get going rather than stand there and contemplate the long day she faced. The date was September 3. She planned to awaken on Mount Greylock on the anniversary of Michael's death, September 4, then continue her hike to the last shelter she would stay at on this trip, the Mark Noepel Shelter on the far side of Greylock—the last shelter before she got back to her car in Cheshire. Davie didn't know who Mark Noepel was, but she figured her guidebook or a plaque in the shelter would tell her. A bunk bed awaited her tonight at the Bascom Lodge on the summit of Mount Greylock, reserved two weeks earlier.

When Davie got to the summit almost five hours later, she changed her mind. She took her backpack off and left it propped against a bench outside of the lodge. She bought an ice cream bar inside the lodge and walked around as she ate it, noting with some surprise that she was less stiff than she expected. She remembered the many times she and Michael spent there, but she especially remembered the day that figured into the story she told Andrea—the day when she and Michael tried to help the young woman who very likely was homeless. Davie wondered what happened to her, and whether she ever got to a safe place.

Davie sat for a few minutes in the field that looked to the west from the summit, lost in thought, and the realization slowly dawned that she did not want to break the spell of her hike. She did not want to sit in the dining hall with tourists and backpackers and answer questions about her solo trip and her life in Albany, even if she never mentioned the real reason for the trip. She wanted solitude, she realized. For all that she had been alone for one day short of a year now, living by herself in the house, what she wanted from this trip was peaceful solitude. What she craved was very different from coming home after work to a house where she would never again hear the front door open and then Michael's booming call of, "Hey, buddy! Where are you?" That was the real meaning of being alone. What she could get here—and take home with her from this hike if she was lucky—was a sense of strength at doing something this challenging for the first time. She thought she would get that not from conversations she didn't really feel like having, but from facing the remainder of her hike without fear of the silence.

With that insight, Davie got up, walked back to the lodge, told the first staff member she found that she changed her mind and would not be staying there that night, and yes, she realized she would not get a refund. She just said she was a little ahead of schedule and decided to keep going.

She bought some treats before she left the lodge—a chocolate bar, a small bag of chocolate-caramel popcorn—stuff she would never have eaten at home. She went around back and filled her water bottles from a spigot. Then she shrugged her backpack on, clipped her hip belt and pulled the straps, and left Bascom Lodge behind, hiking at a brisk, determined pace. She planned to stealth camp. It was almost two o'clock, and she had at least five hours of daylight. She realized she would hike past the side trail for the Mark Noepel Shelter and would keep going. She would camp somewhere off the trail a lot closer to her car than she expected to be. She might only have three or four miles left in the morning. So she would finish this hike in two nights and three days, not the three nights out that she originally planned.

She would get home on the anniversary of Michael's death; she would be in the house for part of the day after all, but she was fine with that. Davie felt that what she was doing more than compensated for ending up in exactly the situation she tried to avoid.

That was how the remainder of her hike unfolded. Davie hiked well past the turnoff for the side trail to the shelter. She found a level spot to camp, and while it was not out of view of the trail, it was far enough off the trail that she didn't think she would be easily spotted. Besides, it was after Labor Day, and the Ridge Runners were mostly finished for the season. The spot she found looked like other people must have used it; there was something about it, a very subtly worn look in the center of the little clearing suggesting that hers was not the first tent to be pitched there. She would have to hang her bear bag over a tree limb, but she knew how to do that from her hike with Andrea in Shenandoah National Park. She fell asleep early, by about eight o'clock, slept through the night, and woke up at daybreak thinking of Michael. She got this far, she thought; she got through the first year. She just needed to keep going.

chapter 11

Davie resolved to move through the second year after Michael's death without the crazed feeling that so often accompanied the corresponding weeks and months of the first year. She wanted to feel better; she sincerely thought Michael would want that for her. She lost so many friendships the first year that she saw this second year as a time of exploring and discovering. The second year was not yet written, she didn't know what lay ahead, but she very much wanted to feel excited about her future. It had been quite a while since she thought of her backup plan, the same recurring fixation on suicide that prompted her to finally discard the bottle of pills in her bathroom drawer. She really wanted to feel better, and she was determined to keep the benefits of her first solo hike in mind.

She did get back to Albany on the anniversary of Michael's death, and she did have cards marking the date in her mail basket, as she expected. She avoided reading the text messages and emails that came into her phone while she was backpacking; she didn't even read them in her car before she headed home. She read them Friday morning, the day after she got home, and most of them were meaningless—although she would never have said this to anyone. She didn't need text messages with heart emojis in them; she needed people to call her and say, "How are you doing? How are you *really* doing? Want to go out for dinner? I'm going up to the farmer's market in Troy Saturday . . . let's go together and get some lunch up there and walk around." But no one did this, probably because it was a lot less effort to compose a line on your phone and hit send than it was to listen to a widow tell you for two hours how difficult her life was now.

Davie realized that word spread, as she knew it would, that she was very angry, very confrontational, very quick to erupt over remarks or incidents other people perceived as nothing. The things that set Davie off did not seem like nothing to her; they ranged from stupidity—the guy who likened her loss to the death of his dog came to mind—to cluelessness. She was very conflicted about the cultural myths and traditions around the first year of widowhood, or mourning in general, which she recalled from a sociology class in college and were deeply rooted in several religions and cultures, not just the white European-based culture in the United States. Echoes of this belief that the first year of grief was the most difficult appeared in a booklet the regional organ donation center mailed to Davie along with a thank-you letter from the director for letting Michael be a bone and tissue donor. To Davie, it seemed that people expected her to start feeling and acting as if everything was better now, and they blamed her for not magically healing in the first year after Michael's death.

Yet Davie knew that she also had also gotten sucked into that tradition, by setting the goal of making the second year after Michael's death a better year than the first—which, she realized, was a very low bar. The second year could hardly be worse than what she had just lived through, she thought. The first year contained traumatic loss; a nearly fatal medical emergency; a firing and the accompanying staggering change in her income; Andrea's cancer; and inappropriate behavior by a number of men, including what she still thought could fairly be called an assault by her former hairstylist— an incident Davie categorized in the "You can't make this one up" column. For good measure, she added to her mental summary of the first year the erosion or outright loss of several friendships. Quite a few, in fact; her social circle was much smaller than a year ago, and then some.

With the one-year anniversary of Michael's death now having come and gone, the United Way and the regional organ donation center contacted Davie to ask if she would be willing to speak a few times about her decision to let Michael be a bone and tissue donor. She found letters from both organizations in her mail basket when she got home from Mount Greylock. Davie realized that the United Way must have been especially itching to contact her, but probably held off on doing so until after the first anniversary of Michael's death—just barely, Davie wryly thought—most likely for the same reasons that Davie saw that date as some personal benchmark. The Evening Star Agency was a United Way organization, as was the organ donation center, and Davie knew that the Evening Star Agency benefited from United Way funding.

Davie realized that in saying yes to both organizations, she was scoring high on what she caustically thought of as the Grieving Widow Good Girl

Bar Chart, doing something that would make people ooh and aah at her courage and her terrible story, but she said yes anyhow. Those talks would come later in the fall. Davie could not guess what Michael would have thought of her decision; he held mixed feelings about the United Way, but he was a pragmatist who realized the donations filled in some gaps at the organization he ran very well with never enough money.

She was thinking about the upcoming talks as she walked to her neighborhood market the day after she got back from the Mount Greylock trip. It was Friday and she was not at work. She had already taken the day off, and no one needed to know that she beat her own hiking expectations and finished early. The market was only a few blocks away and she didn't want to move her car from the parking space in front of her house.

Davie puzzled over how her burst of confidence and optimism during her hike dissipated so quickly, a mere twenty-four hours later, and how now, on her first full day home, the future once again seemed so fraught. Was it the gush of messages and cards, she wondered? Or was this part of a larger pattern she now thought she could trace through the first year, one of pretty steady ups and downs? She could not seem to hit equilibrium. Her mathematician's eye saw everything in terms of a graph, and she could plot the mood swings in almost regular intervals. She would feel calm and focused and resolved and determined, and something would throw her off... another period of calm and focus, then another upset. She couldn't control the triggers for these mood swings, because they all came from outside forces, almost always from people. This was not a situation in which a regimen of exercise and fresh air could set her on an even path.

She walked through the aisles of the small urban market, where she loved looking at the displays of foods she never saw in the suburban grocery store where she shopped when she worked at LGC. Her neighborhood included immigrants from more than a dozen countries and three continents, and the market stocked items such as packaged chicken feet, star fruit, and jars of intensely flavored condiments. She never hurried in this market if she could help it; she loved the fall scents of apples and spices and root vegetables that hit her the moment she entered. She loved strolling around and it was a good place to be lost in her thoughts. She certainly felt lost in her thoughts this day.

She turned a corner to go up another aisle and she saw a man a few feet ahead of her who, from the back, looked so much like Michael that Davie stopped walking and just stared at him. Michael's height and build, wearing chinos and an Oxford-cloth cotton shirt with the sleeves rolled up, as

Michael did. The man stopped, turned to look at something on a shelf, and his face was Michael's face, so much so that Davie stepped back and put her hand out, reaching for the edge of a shelf so that she could touch something and know that she was really there, really seeing this man. He looked so much like her dead husband that she wondered if she was actually in her neighborhood grocery store, or if she was slipping into an altered state.

The feeling that came over her was like the episode she experienced in her car the day she talked to the fire captain, but it was also just different enough that she knew this experience was really happening. She never seriously thought she physically left her car in the parking lot of Levellewyn, Grenoble and Carl to somehow be transported to the bluff overlooking Longnook Beach that morning. Even then, she realized that she just mentally left the present for that brief time because the conversation was so distressing, and summoned all of the trauma and terrible shock of the night Michael died. She knew that her mind took her to the only safe place she could imagine at that moment. This experience in the market was different; she knew where she was, but she was seeing a man who looked so much like Michael that it was jarring.

The man walked down the aisle, turned the corner, and Davie followed him. She could not fully see his face, but his walk, his general appearance, was eerily like Michael. She went down one more aisle, still following him, when he turned suddenly and faced her. Bearded, burly, Michael's glasses, but no recognition in his eyes behind them. Davie looked back at him steadily. It was as if they were the only two people in the store; no one else was in the aisle, and everything around her was quiet. He looked at her with an unreadable expression, and it occurred to Davie that most people would have said something like, "Sorry, do I know you?" Or, "I think you have me mistaken for someone else." For her part, Davie could not imagine saying to this stranger, "I'm sorry I was staring, but you bear an astonishing resemblance to my dead husband." Then she looked away, and when she turned back, he was gone.

She did not see him again in the small market as she finished picking up the few items she needed, and she did not see him in the checkout line or leaving the store. It was as if he had never been there at all, but she knew that he had been. Or at least, she knew she had seen him, and she realized that recognizing that fact didn't mean he had actually been there. The experience left her shaken. There was something haunting and otherworldly about the episode. She paid for her groceries and walked home, lost in the recollection of the man's resemblance to Michael, but also his unusual response to seeing her staring at him. Davie could not explain or understand what the experience meant. She didn't even know what to call it . . . a sighting? A hallucination?

She needed to talk to someone; she needed some help, and not from a friend, Davie realized. She didn't think the vision in the market was a product of her yearning and heightened thoughts about Michael because of the anniversary, and she was at last sleeping far better, so she could not blame sleep deprivation.

When Davie returned to work Monday morning, she closed her office door, called the statewide social workers' association and asked for a referral to someone who was experienced at working with trauma victims. She got the name of a woman in private practice as a licensed therapist very close, as it turned out, to where she worked in downtown Albany. She left a message and the therapist called her back. Davie told her the basics: that she was widowed a year before under terrible circumstances when her husband died saving her life on vacation—she did not elaborate—and that she was unexpectedly in need of some professional help, following a possible hallucination. She told the woman she also was having occasional episodes of what she thought was splitting, and that she'd thought she was over and done with these incidents, but now she was not so sure. The therapist scheduled an appointment for the following week and asked if Davie was in a crisis that day that required emergency intervention. No, Davie said, she was sitting in her office at her job, she didn't need emergency help; she just needed help, even though she thought she was past the worst of her recovery. She was functioning, and she was struggling.

On the appointed day, she walked to the therapist's office, wondering how wise it was to do this during a workday, but also realizing she had no other choice. Very few therapists offered evening hours, and of course none offered weekend appointments. Davie got there a few minutes early. On this day, she was in a pair of her dress hiking boots—not her real hiking boots—and a pair of her expanding collection of hiking pants, but with an acid-yellow-colored linen knit T-shirt under a gauzy linen-silk unlined blazer. This was part of her leftover summer wardrobe from LGC, and she topped everything off with a pearl choker that originally belonged to her mother, showing just above the V-neck of the T-shirt.

Davie knew the hiking boots and the pearls were an odd mix, but she was starting to have fun carving out her own look at this job, and that look got favorable reviews from colleagues. The fact that she was willing to go out in the field with the biologists a few times each season, where she did not wear any jewelry other than her wedding ring, and where she was willing to help carry gear, also got favorable reviews. She thought about the impression she would make on the therapist, and for reasons she could not explain, she felt it was very important to look sharp and pulled together. Maybe she wanted to belie how she felt, which was frustrated and confused. If she couldn't control her inner turmoil, she figured she could at least control how she presented herself to others.

Now, she sat in the waiting room of the therapist's office, mentally forming a list of what she hoped she could set for her goals in working with this woman. Less than ten minutes later, she was on her way out the door, never having gotten as far as the mental list. Two for two, Davie thought. If she kept walking out of therapists' offices in the first ten minutes, she would soon find that every therapist in the Capital Region was avoiding her like many of her acquaintances, friends and neighbors were now doing.

On her way back to the office, Davie thought over what happened, and was at least gratified to realize that she used that phrase to herself—*what happened*—instead of, *what went wrong*. Because "went wrong" implied personal blame or responsibility, and Davie was starting to think that she was so very done with feeling guilt, blame or responsibility. She was also coming to realize that the world around her was not equipped to deal with sudden, traumatic widowhood or grief, and inconsolable distress.

The therapist, recommended as an accomplished expert in trauma, sat on the edge of her chair during the brief introductory exchange, and Davie immediately noticed that. She looked stiffly prim. She was young, attractive and attentive, but her edge-of-the-seat pose suggested someone who was bracing herself for what would follow. Within the next two minutes, Davie thought that assessment was probably correct.

Davie expected the therapist would ask her why she was there, and she intended to give a brief but compelling account of Michael's death. Instead, the therapist cut in during a momentary pause in the story Davie had hardly started.

"I know enough of why you are here, and the experience is what we call a catastrophic episode. I don't think it's effective or useful for you to tell the full story in this first session. In fact, I don't allow clients to do that in the first session."

Several seconds of silence followed. Then Davie stood up and picked up her purse, both actions in one smooth motion. Her time at LGC taught her two valuable lessons: how not to treat someone who was in the grip of unimaginable anguish; and how to claim the upper hand in any conversation, by standing up while the other person was seated. Irina taught her both lessons, and while Davie never expected to feel gratitude to Irina for anything, ever, she mentally thanked her at that moment for teaching her the power of asserting control.

"How dare you say that to me," Davie said in a very calm tone to the still-seated therapist, who seemed stunned. Davie might have been delivering a report in a conference room at work. The fact that she was so calm, she realized, made her words all the more unexpected.

"The entire purpose of my being here is because my husband died, and especially because he died saving my life while we were on vacation," Davie continued. "So who the hell are you to tell me you won't *allow me* to tell you what happened?"

She spat out the words "allow me" with a particularly savage emphasis, the only strong emotion she injected into an otherwise dispassionate delivery, then she left the office. She did not slam the door, which would have been an unseemly display of anger; she just left. She made her point, of that she was sure. When she returned to her office fifteen minutes later and checked her phone messages, she found one from the therapist. Davie remembered giving the woman the number for her private line when she scheduled the appointment. Now the therapist, without identifying herself or her practice, very professionally and with an abjectly regretful tone said she understood Davie's concerns and that she should have handled their meeting better. She apologized. Anyone listening to the message would have thought it was someone from the state environmental agency calling to clear up a misunderstanding over a data analysis.

Davie listened to the message, deleted it, then leaned back in her chair and looked out the window at the Hudson River. What to do now, she wondered. It was more difficult to find a competent therapist who was also experienced at dealing with terrible loss than she could ever have imagined. Well, she realized, maybe she would just have to muddle through on her own. With that thought, and while running her fingers of her left hand absentmindedly over the pearl choker she remembered seeing her mother wear so many times, she tried to focus on her job. She put the thought of locating a good grief counselor somewhere in that box at the back of her mind where she put everything she could not resolve right now. Pretty soon, she thought, if she tried to push anything else into that box, she was going to have trouble getting the flaps to stay closed.

A few days later, at home in the evening, she got a text message from Ethan the Shuttle Driver, which was how Davie thought of him. She realized he was also Ethan the Physics Major and Ethan the Much-In-Demand Custom Woodworker and Ethan the Possibly Ex-Boyfriend of Andrea, but she only knew him in the context in which she met him.

How was your hike? she read.

Very good. I finished a day early.

That is wonderful. I would like to hear about it.

Would you like to hear about it over dinner?

Yes. When?

So with some disbelief—she last asked a man on a date about 20 years ago—Davie suggested they meet in Williamstown. She was far more willing to drive to Williamstown than she was to again encounter someone she knew while on a date in Albany. That was difficult to explain to herself; chances were, the people who were still speaking to her would be happy to see her out on a fun evening. But the memory of her date with Steve the DEC biologist came back to her, and if this was going to be a repeat of that evening, at least she wouldn't have to see Jay and Alanna on the other side of the room. Besides, she asked Ethan out, so it seemed that she should be the one to do the drive, and she could not think of any place in between Williamstown and Albany that qualified as fine dining.

She and Ethan spoke by phone to figure out the details. She told Ethan she would get a room at the Williamstown Inn the following Saturday, which she thought would be possible because it was after the start of the fall semester but too early for parents' weekend. The drive between Williamstown and Albany required back roads no matter what route you took, and she did not want to drive home at night. They set a time and Ethan suggested a Vietnamese restaurant down a side street in the center of town. Davie knew Williamstown; she knew she would have no trouble finding the place.

"Would you like me to pick you up?" Ethan asked in his courteous, old-fashioned way.

"No, thank you, I do not need a shuttle," Davie said, intending it as a joke. She nearly added, "Besides, I don't want to have to pay you for the ride," but she decided against it. Her sense of humor might be too edgy for him, she realized. This man sounded serious and thoughtful, but not humorous. OK, Davie thought, she would rather dine with someone who actually considered what he was saying. They set a time, and Ethan offered to make a reservation.

"This is my treat, you know, because I asked you to dinner," Davie said.

"Well, we'll see about that. For now, let's just plan on seeing each other there," Ethan said.

"Your friend Ethan got in touch with me and I asked him out for dinner," Davie told Andrea the next night, as they walked through Washington Park with cups of coffee after work. Her dinner with Ethan was a week from Saturday, because she could not get a room after all on short notice at the Williamstown Inn.

"You will have a lovely time," Andrea said. "He is a very intelligent, intellectually curious person, and a gentleman. He is also a long-ago boyfriend of mine, so long ago that it almost doesn't count. We were friends in college, we were not in touch for many years—we just went our separate ways—and then I learned that he lived in this area. I came across his name on a list of shuttle drivers the local AT trail club sent me, and I thought, 'Oh, my gosh . . . Ethan Van Meter—really? There could only be one in the United States.' So, we got back in touch, and we dated for a while, but we are friends, and believe me, you did not have to tell me you have a date with him."

"I wondered," Davie said. "I didn't really think you would mind, but I kind of wanted to check. I thought you two might have been a couple a while back."

"A couple . . ." Andrea frowned. Davie could tell Andrea's introspective expression from her tone of voice, and because she knew Andrea's inflections so well. They were walking side by side, sipping their coffees, and she could only see Andrea's face in profile.

"A couple . . ." Andrea said again, almost as though to herself. "I'm not sure we were ever a couple. I think we were two people who didn't exactly know what we were doing. We were dating, but I'm not sure we ever thought of ourselves as a couple. This is when my marriage had just broken up, and I had already moved over to Community Loan. I guess I knew you at that time—I must have, but I probably never mentioned him. I realize this sounds confusing."

"Has this guy ever been married?"

"Yes, he's divorced," Andrea said. "The divorce was a long time before our little situation so many years ago. Neither of us was talking marriage; it just was not an issue for either of us at that point in our lives. We hiked together, he'd just bought his place out on the Rensselaer Plateau . . . it was just a fun interlude, I think. And I think it is very nice that you will have dinner with him."

So, Davie drove to Williamstown on the appointed Saturday. There were a few ways to get there from Albany, but her favorite route was through the Petersburg Pass, an old road that cut through the Taconic Range from eastern Rensselaer County into Massachusetts. There was an ethereal quality to the color of the sky and the light falling on the hills in the Pass that explained why the Hudson River School artists didn't just paint rivers and lakes. The drive through the Pass also took you by a few astonishing overlooks, and more than one place where you could imagine but never clearly see the steep ravine that started just a few feet beyond the edge of the road. On the other side, the north side of the Pass, you saw sheer rock walls and steep paths heading up the slope. It was a bit like a homegrown Northeastern version of the Big Sur, with a forest at the bottom of the drop instead of the Pacific Ocean. Davie never drove through the Petersburg Pass in the winter, and preferred not to drive it at night, but on this September morning, she had one of Beethoven's late piano sonatas on the radio, clear skies and very little traffic in either direction.

She got to the inn hours before she was to meet Ethan. Feeling at loose ends, a bit keyed up about her dinner date, she walked into town. She wandered down Spring Street, looking in the shop windows. She bought an ice cream cone and sat on a bench to eat it, daydreaming and people-watching and idly noting what a rich little town this was, an impression she recalled having every time she was in Williamstown. Then she found herself remembering her first date with Michael, which was also at a Vietnamese restaurant. Davie didn't think about that when Ethan suggested their meeting place, but now she recalled that first date with Michael in detail. She lost track of time sitting on the bench, eating the cone as her mind went back over that night . . . fourteen years ago, Davie realized.

She picked Michael up in front of his apartment, she remembered, because his ancient Volvo sedan was getting a repair. She expected Michael to suggest burgers and beer at a pub, but he told her he'd made reservations at an elegant little restaurant Davie didn't know. That impressed Davie, that this burly, rough-hewn man—who was also brilliant, as she by then realized—demonstrated such refined taste and surprised her with his choice.

What she also remembered about that night was that he invited her into his apartment for a beer when she drove him home. He did not try to kiss her; he just asked if she wanted to come in for a little while. So, she did, contrary to her usual cautious nature. She thought, oh, what the hell, it's one beer, not the rest of the night, knowing that might well be a lie and recognizing a strong attraction she was sure he also felt. They ended up making out so passionately that they stopped one step shy of moving to his bed in the adjacent room. Davie had never done anything like that in all her years of dating; she was always careful, restrained. She also remembered feeling very strongly that everything about that first date seemed right. She went home certain that she and Michael connected that night emotionally and physically in a way that more or less sealed the deal for them. She thought then that he was the man she would marry.

Davie realized she'd been sitting on the bench next to the ice cream shop for more than an hour, but the elapsed time was not an episode of splitting. It was just a little mental trip back to a time when she could never have foreseen the turns her life would take because of that first date with Michael. That night was the first time in her life she gave over to an impulse instead of following her strongly ingrained sense of interior discipline. She wondered if she would ever feel that way again. Then she got up, brushed the chocolate sprinkles off her jeans and walked back to the inn.

❧

She entered the restaurant a few minutes before seven o'clock to find Ethan standing in the little vestibule outside of the dining room, looking at photographs on the wall that depicted a rural Vietnam from what looked like a very long time ago. He turned when he heard the door and Davie thought—for the second time, she realized—that he conveyed a smile without actually smiling . . . something about his eyes, and she wondered how he did that.

"Hello! I am looking forward to hearing all about everything that happened after I dropped you off in the parking lot five minutes from here," he said. He got back to that when they sat down and picked out what they wanted to eat. They each ordered a beer, and Davie was glad she was staying in Williamstown because she never would have had anything to drink if she faced a drive home that night on rural, winding roads.

"I'm not sure it will be so fascinating to someone who has thru-hiked the whole trail, but I'll give it my best shot," she said.

He listened, asked questions but otherwise talked very little. He just listened very closely, instead of looking like he wanted to jump in with something of his own to say. Davie could not remember ever talking to such a good listener, with the possible exception of Andrea. Michael listened best when they were alone, and she never doubted that she got his full attention every time she needed it, but in any setting that included other people, he went into what even he jokingly called "full Michael mode." That meant he commanded the conversation and the room just by the sheer force of his personality. Telling stories the way he did, relating anecdotes of the many political figures he dealt with in his work, made for great entertainment at a dinner party but was not conducive to anyone else getting a word in edgewise. Davie never minded this trait of Michael's, because she actually never tired of hearing his stories again, even several times. His delivery was so good, and she was so capable of holding her own against Michael's enjoyment of holding court, that Michael's public persona never bothered her. But Ethan just listened, and Davie still so keenly felt the lack of conversation in her ever-silent house that talking came very easily to her. The words seemed to pour out of her, in fact.

She told Ethan about how she briefly clutched when she left his car and heard him pulling out of the parking lot—which was walking distance from where they sat as she recounted the story. She told him about waking up to the sound of the bear clanging the chain on the box, and about her decision to hike beyond Greylock because she did not want to come out of the reflective silence of her first two days quite yet.

"You sound like you know how to listen to yourself and that you know how to recognize what you need," Ethan said.

"I don't always feel that way," she said. "This last year has been very difficult. All you have done so far this evening is listen to me. I'd like to hear about you now." She was very out of practice at being out on a date, if that was what this evening was, and she thought that it fairly could be called a date. A brief flash went through her mind: was she ready to have someone in her life? She wasn't sure. Maybe the best plan was to simply enjoy the evening, but aiming for simple often got very complicated for her in this life alone.

"We can talk about me later," he said. "Speaking of camping, I think the waitress is wondering if we are going to pitch a tent here at this table, so if you would like to go for a drink, if it's not too late for you, then let's do that and we can continue the conversation."

He picked up the check, which Davie didn't expect and thought she made clear that she intended to do.

"I will take care of this," Ethan said when she started to protest as he reached for the check. "You can take care of it next time."

So, she thought, there might be a next time. She was OK with that.

She didn't know significantly more about him now than the day she met him. He seemed like a person from a past century, with his old-fashioned manners and quiet way of speaking. Michael had indisputably been very much of the present: exuberant, brash, bold, a bit in your face, his mind moving faster than most people around him could follow. Ethan radiated the sense of someone who lived alone, and in an isolated situation—or maybe, Davie thought, a solitary situation was the better term—completely at ease with himself, but just more used to conversation as something to be savored. There was no comparison to Michael; they were completely different.

They found a tiny dark bar above Spring Street that also had an espresso machine. Davie supposed that if he was going to take her hand, the walk along the quiet street was the time to do that. He walked on the correct side—the street side, something she didn't think anyone under the age of seventy-five other than herself even realized was good etiquette—but he kept his hands in his jacket pocket. He was taller than Davie, about six feet to her five-feet-eight inches, but his bony shoulders were slightly stooped, a habit perhaps from his work, where she supposed he often bent over a project on a workbench. She was used to looking up at someone when she walked; Michael was more than six feet tall.

At the bar, Ethan ordered a scotch and Davie asked for a double espresso. That got the reaction it always did: Ethan looked at her as if he wondered whether she had vampires in her family background and did not need to sleep.

"It never keeps me awake," Davie explained. "I don't know why." She was sleeping better for most of the last six months and her blood pressure was back to normal. Her remark about the espresso reminded her of both medical issues in the terrible immediate aftermath of Michael's death, but she just did not want to recount the wild ups and downs of the first months alone, so she said nothing further. The topic of sleeping opened up too many difficult memories. Actually, Davie thought, the wild ups and downs still happened, only now they happened on the standard seven hours of sleep a night, so she could no longer blame sleep deprivation. The incident in the grocery store only two weeks earlier was still much on her mind.

"Tell me about your last day with Michael," Ethan said. Davie looked up at him across the little table, stirring her espresso and wondering what prompted the question. This was not a klutzy opening line to dinner, right up there with, *"I never knew how your husband died."* He knew how Michael died, but even if he didn't, he wasn't asking that question. He sounded like he genuinely wanted to know what they had done together, what parts of that day she carried as sweet and special, around the terrible ending, and he sounded far more interested in the beginning of the day than the nightmarish time in the hospital. Davie almost laughed, realizing that if she answered his question honestly, she would start with the high school quickie, the wildly fun and spontaneous lovemaking that began with Michael's hand caressing her naked ass.

"It's not an easy story to hear," she said. "The ending is pretty bad."

"Then skip the ending and tell me the best parts you remember."

"Well, my husband was the most amazing man I have ever known," Davie said, still stirring her espresso. She sent a rueful half-smile across the table. "You suggested I tell you the best parts I remember. I remember that about Michael all the time, not just that last day. He was a passionate, brilliant man, we got along extremely well, and he made me feel completely, unconditionally loved. And all of that was threaded through our last day together, which included a little bit of everything we loved so much about being at that particular place. You know . . . the Outer Cape. It looks a little like another planet—all dunes and sky and endless horizon."

She told him about going to the bay beach, and then up to Provincetown, and about eating dinner on the wharf.

"You said that Andrea told you what happened after that?"

"Yes, she did." As he said that, a thought flitted through Davie's mind: Did Ethan know about Andrea's cancer? She had no idea, and Andrea was often extremely private. Davie would never have disclosed that without being very sure that Andrea would be unruffled by Ethan knowing of her illness.

"I don't know how I got back to our cottage that night," Davie said, continuing her narrative. "I don't know how I got home. Sometimes—and I realize that this sounds crazy—I wonder, still, if I'm going to wake up and realize that I've just had an incredibly detailed nightmare that has spanned a year in my dream state, but was just that: a nightmare. Although I realize that's not going to happen."

Ethan took a sip of his scotch. Everything about him was measured, thoughtful, carefully considered. He had an interesting, handsome face, dark-brown hair sprinkled with gray, and blue eyes so dark they looked almost black. His features were bony and angular but made for an arresting look that she found herself studying as she waited for him to respond.

"I think it sounds like you have done an amazing job of rebuilding your life," he said. "I'm sure that it does seem like it's been a very long nightmare. You have very bravely moved forward, and you have not let anything deter you. I admired this about you even before I met you, based on what Andrea described about what happened to you."

"Thank you for that," Davie said.

He offered to escort her back to her inn, by following in his car, and as he noted, he would head back in that general direction anyhow to get home, so it was not far out of his way. She pulled into the parking lot at the inn, wondering what would be the best and least awkward thing to do—get out and wave her thanks and walk up the steps to the front door? Walk over to his car and thank him and shake his hand through the open driver's side window? How did people figure out what to do in her situation? Ending a first date after so many years was awkward as hell.

Ethan solved this problem almost as though he'd read her mind, by getting out of his car, which was parked next to hers, and walking over to her door, which he reached for just as she opened it and emerged. He walked her to the front door of the inn and just as she thought, *Oh, what the hell,* and reached toward him to give him a kiss good-night on the cheek, he kissed her quickly, lightly, on the mouth and then put his arms around her in the kind of genuine warm hug he gave Andrea at the trail head parking area. This was not an invitation to be asked up to her room, and she would have been astonished if she sensed that it was. She was relieved that she was not facing yet another difficult situation that made her feel uncertain at best or rattled at worst.

"I had a really nice time talking to you. I will see you again," he said, and then he was gone. Well, Davie thought, as she went inside, that was fine with her. She wanted to see him again; she was not sure she was ready for more than that. She decided to just wait and let whatever was meant to happen next unfold. She'd endured so much shock and uncertainty, so many abrupt upheavals, that the idea of just waiting to see what followed with this obviously intelligent, extremely kind and interesting man seemed, for a change, like a kind of peaceful decision to put into that overpacked box in her mind.

chapter 12

Davie's dinner with Ethan marked the beginning of what was, hands down, the most unusual relationship of her life. She drove home the morning after their date—she still didn't know what else to call it—without any clear idea of when she would hear from him again, if ever, but with a fairly strong feeling that she would. A week later, he popped up in her email . . . at first, she didn't remember giving it to him . . . but then she recalled that she sent it to him in a text message as their dinner date drew closer, in case he was a person who preferred email.

I think we should be in general contact, his note stated, *because it seems to me that at this point in your life, with so many changes, you would benefit from having someone as a sounding board. I would like to be that person. I am on deadline for two large commissions right now and I don't have a lot of spare time, which means that I don't know when I would be able to suggest another dinner, but if you feel that you could use good contact with a friend, then yes, I would like to hear from you when you feel like being in touch.*

Davie considered this note, which read like a piece of Victorian correspondence between cousins, and that evening she replied, telling him that she enjoyed her time with him, that she thought, yes, it would be good to stay in contact, that writing back and forth would be fine and actually a good way to communicate. She didn't get a response to that, but she didn't really expect one. She took this to mean that the next move could be up to either of them. She remembered Andrea's comment that Ethan could be a lot of work.

He didn't seem like a lot of work so far, but he did seem like someone transported from the nineteenth century—actually, she thought, make that the eighteenth century. He had internet and cell service, which she presumed were necessary if he was running a business that required him to communicate with clients all over the country, but in every other regard, he seemed quaintly unlike anyone she had ever known.

It felt very peculiar to be pondering her reaction to another man other than Michael, but she was going so slowly in this situation—if there was even a situation in which to be going, and she wasn't yet sure there was— that she reminded herself of her documented tendency to overthink new experiences. This was certainly a new experience. She was lonely, she realized; that accounted for her unsettled state. Thanksgiving was fast approaching, and Davie planned to spend it at home, by herself.

She barely remembered her first Thanksgiving after Michael's death; she remembered that she ate some leftovers at home after brushing off tentative inquiries from Andrea and Jay about the holiday. It was too painful to contemplate spending the day with someone, and she was afraid she would wreck the holiday for anyone who included her in their family dinner, because she felt so raw. Halfway through a plate of warmed-up Thai takeout, she dropped her fork, put her head down and held her hands against her face, trying to shut out a series of painful scenes. Her memories of Thanksgivings in the house with Michael were unbearable. She and Michael often hosted ten or twelve of their friends for dinner, and it was not unusual for Michael to call her once or twice at the last minute and ask if they could fit another person at the table, because he'd just found out so-and-so was going to be alone that day.

This year was not much better; she just did a better job of deflecting the inquiries. Andrea was traveling to Connecticut to visit her parents for Thanksgiving, and Davie pre-empted Andrea's question about her own plans by telling her she might go into New York City and see some friends from graduate school. Jay and Alanna were going skiing in Colorado and Davie told Jay the same lie about a trip to New York City. It was easier to lie than to make other people feel responsible for her.

Now, as Davie contemplated another round of year-end holidays by herself in the house, she realized that she faced a long time—maybe decades—in the expansive space Michael loved so much. She thought she'd better start getting more used to that.

⚓

"Andrea, we're not going *here*, are we?" Davie pointed to the elevation map of the White Mountains that she spread open on Andrea's dining room table. The lines went up and down and up again, and Davie could not believe that anyone could hike this at all, any time of the year. It was early

December, which made the prospect even more daunting. The sideways view of the mountains looked like a seismograph chart during an aftershock, or a medieval town seen on the horizon, all steeples and turrets and domes: a series of jagged, incredibly steep climbs and descents. Davie calculated the elevation gain for some of the ascents, and she found the results scary. One of the peaks was more than six thousand feet high.

Andrea threw a glance back at Davie. She was rooting through a drawer under the built-in sideboard in the dining room, which in any other home would have held tablecloths and napkins hauled out for Thanksgiving, Christmas and Easter, but in Andrea's home held backpacking gear.

"Huh?" Andrea said. "Let me see what you're looking at. It's impossible for me to see what you're pointing to upside down." She came over to Davie's side of the table.

"Oh, no, not anywhere near there," she said. "You've got the wrong map open. Those are the Prezies . . . the Presidential Range," she added, at Davie's puzzled expression. "We are not doing those, believe me. That's a summertime hike. I mean, yes, there are people who hike that section in the winter, but I'm not one of them. And I would not take you up there now even if I was. It's a difficult section." She folded the map Davie had opened, selected another on the table and opened that out and ran her hand over it, as though she loved the feel of the paper and all the promise it held. The maps folded like an accordion, but they always stayed flat when you opened them, and they were printed on durable, water-resistant paper. Andrea pointed at the section that occupied most of the map. It looked like a page out of a road atlas and showed the geographical features as well as the Appalachian Trail, the side trails and the highways and secondary roads and parking areas.

"See, we're going to park here, and hike up a side trail that starts here . . ." Andrea circled her finger on a point on the map and drew it up to their destination. "And this is a nice, gradual ascent. We'll go about five, five and a half miles, and then hook into the AT for the last half-mile, and then we're at the hut. There's no climbing up any steep parts. You will love the hut. It's a lot of fun to talk to the other backpackers."

"Just like that?" asked Davie, still looking at the elevation map. "You're sure about this? You've done this before?" She cared far less about the social scene at their destination—the backpacker's version of happy hour, although no one would have any alcohol, which was prohibited at the huts—than she cared about not ending up as a news story. She had a recurring image of a blinding snowstorm descending on them halfway up the side trail, with both of them battling to get their tents open in the kind of wind that snapped lines and carried gear off the slope as if by an airborne avalanche. Davie had done a little research, and she had read one too many accounts of disastrous hikes in the White Mountains.

"Yes, take my word for it, Davie, this is safe. We would not be going if I thought it was not safe," Andrea said in a display of great patience, because Davie had asked her this more than once. "You have your snowshoes?"

"Yes."

Davie rented snowshoes because Andrea thought it was wise to have them in the late fall in the White Mountains, but there happened to be very little snow on the ground so far from Albany to New Hampshire, so Davie never practiced with them. Andrea said they would carry them lashed to their backpacks, and Davie found herself fervently hoping she would not need to use them. Although, it might be easier to wear them than to carry them, because Davie was a convert to the "ounces become pounds" mantra, and a winter pack was automatically heavy. You needed more gear, and cold-weather gear weighed considerably more than summer gear.

Davie also now owned lined winter hiking pants and a pair of MICROspikes, a scaled-back version of crampons you stretched around your hiking boots on a flexible plastic web that went onto the boot sole like a fitted sheet. Davie could not believe how much gear she now owned. Even if she hated backpacking, which she most definitely did not, she would have continued doing it to justify how much she spent buying everything. She supposed she could have unloaded it all on a used-gear site or eBay, but that would have been a lot of work. She was glad she was using it, glad that she had gotten hooked on this unusual pastime. She was not sure it could be called a sport.

They would be gone for two nights. Davie took a personal day to get Friday off, so they could drive up the day before to a motel in New Hampshire close to the parking area for the side trail. Davie privately had very mixed feelings about doing this hike; she just felt it would be an entirely different and possibly much more difficult experience than their summer hike through Shenandoah National Park. Andrea, however, was completely matter of fact. She told Davie that she would check the weather forecast several times in the days leading up to their departure, through a couple of different sources in the area. Davie gathered that if you liked weather forecasts, the White Mountains were your dream destination. She found Andrea's promise to keep checking the forecast only slightly reassuring.

She got her first glimpse of the mountains when they drove up early Saturday, and fell silent in the car as she took in the view. The sky was so clear, so pale blue, the mountains so sharply defined, that they looked artificial, as if they had been made out of plastic, skillfully painted and then backlit in a museum diorama. An analogy came to her as they got closer: these mountains were to the Berkshires what Longnook Beach was to the kettle pond on the Cape. Vast, majestic, endless, versus intimate and secluded. There was nothing secluded or intimate about the White Mountains. Davie wondered how she could have lived in the Northeast all her life and never seen them. They were completely different from the Adirondacks, which spoke of wildly remote and undiscovered places, but lacked the grandeur and scale of what Davie looked at now. She found it difficult to believe she could hike into such a place; it looked impenetrable.

When she started up the trail with Andrea the next morning, she got yet another sense of the White Mountains. She thought of it as the difference between looking at a photograph of Earth taken from a satellite or space station, and being on Earth in one specific place, where all the details that were reduced to just continents and oceans in the space photograph suddenly surrounded you.

That first glimpse of the mountains on the drive up to New Hampshire the day before obscured the fact that when you were in their midst you would see old forests and small areas of wetlands and trickling little waterways that were sometimes not much wider than a ditch. Sunlight filtered down through branches, and although it was cold, it was not bitter. Davie realized that this might be a very different scene in just a week or so, dangerously cold for anyone who didn't know what they were doing as soon as the fine weather broke and the snow started. But on this day, she found the hiking easier than she expected. The sheer rock faces above tree line that Andrea described climbing up and down in this state on her section-hiking quest were further north. Davie thought that in her own progress with backpacking she had come a long way in a short time in terms of how she viewed a hike like this. She had done well just to start this hike, and while she still saw the White Mountains as formidable and unapproachable in sections, she found herself enjoying this day, this brief introduction to the region.

As with the summer hike through Shenandoah National Park, their hike was also a chance to blend thinking time with talking time. She and Andrea held most of their conversations on water breaks, standing up with their hiking poles leaned against a tree so they didn't need to remove their packs.

"So is Ethan still a part of your life?" Andrea asked as she unscrewed the cap on her Nalgene bottle.

"He is still writing to me like clockwork. I don't know if he would consider himself part of my life," Davie said. "We have had a steady exchange, back and forth, and this is how we are getting to know each other better. I am not sure we would be accomplishing the same thing in phone conversations, and it doesn't strike me as odd that this is what we are doing, because his cell reception really is not great, and his internet connection is a lot better—I have no idea why—but that's how most of our conversations unfold. It's a little like playing long-distance chess a century ago through letters . . . he sends a note, I write back, he writes back to that . . . and it takes six months to a year to play a game. I have no idea what we're doing, or where this is going to go."

"I suspect you don't have to worry about that right now," Andrea said. "He's a good person. He's a good person to have in your life."

"You said he had been married?" Davie asked.

"Yes, he married a classmate of ours, two weeks after we graduated," Andrea said. "He married the first person he was ever in love with, and the marriage lasted less than a year. Far less than that, if you count the time—just a few months—that they actually lived together as a married couple. I think the rest of the next couple of years was spent in undoing the marriage."

"He's never mentioned that," Davie said. "If I hadn't known he was married, I would have just assumed he'd been living this solitary life forever."

"He would not have mentioned it, I'm very sure," Andrea said. "But yes, I have a feeling that accounts for his leading the life he does now. He took the breakup of the marriage very hard. I guess some people make these early marriages—you know, what a sociologist calls a 'starter marriage,' and when it falls apart, they just file it under 'Life Lessons' and move on to their next thing. Not Ethan. He got burned badly, I think, and it made an impression on him. Because his divorce was a couple of years after we graduated, and mine was . . . six or seven years after his. Six or seven years can make a lot of difference in how you handle something like that."

"Do you know what happened?" Davie asked. "What went wrong?"

"I'm sure they were just too young and dumb to know what they were doing, but the specific cause was his wife falling in love with another man, a guy who was quite a bit older than she was. Last I knew, she was still with him, they got married, and it lasted." Andrea shot Davie one of her unreadable expressions—perfectly balanced and neutral. "So when I first learned that Ethan was living back in the area, my marriage had already ended for the exact same reason, of course, with the exception that my husband was screwing someone almost ten years younger than him, and Ethan's ex-wife had been screwing someone probably fifteen years older than her. And I do mean the word 'screwing.' Both Ethan and I were done wrong. If you want out of a marriage, get out of the marriage, but it's bad form to do to your spouse what was done to him and to me. And that, of course, explains the brief romance that Ethan and I had. You know, I looked him up, one thing led to another . . ."

Andrea seemed momentarily lost in her recollection.

"This was . . . well, I guess I already told you that this was probably a dozen or more years ago. Well, when did you and I meet? About fifteen years ago, right? My divorce was probably a year later. I'd already done Massachusetts, and I was going to start Vermont, so I was looking through the list of shuttle drivers in the Berkshires. You know, because a lot of times it's easier to have someone who lives close to a state line if you're doing the southern part of the state first, and that's when I learned that Ethan lived in Massachusetts and was doing shuttling on the side. That's how I knew how to contact him. Plus, we were two very upset people who needed some comfort. He was still that upset about his divorce, those many years later."

Andrea put the cap back on her water bottle and handed it to Davie so Davie could put it back into the difficult-to-reach bottle pocket on the side of Andrea's backpack.

"It didn't last very long, and we parted friends. In fact, it was so brief that I never mentioned it to anyone in Albany. I didn't really know what I was doing, and it just seemed easier to say nothing. We aren't in touch very often now. The funny thing is, I never did end up using him as a shuttle driver until you and I went out." A wry little grin came and went. "If I had used him all those years ago, I might have learned earlier that he would charge me, his former lover and longtime friend, the same rate he charged anyone."

Andrea cinched her hip belt a little tighter and picked up her hiking poles.

"You know, Davie, if you can have some fun, please do. You know what I've learned since I had cancer?" Davie shook her head, astonished that Andrea mentioned her cancer.

"I've learned what I think of as the secret to life," Andrea said. "And that secret goes like this: the greatest joy comes in the smallest packages, in more ways than one. A little tiny package can hold a diamond ring, and it can also hold a memory of a moment you will never forget. Those moments end up being as important as the big celebrations of life. I have a few memories of moments like that with Ethan, and lot of moments like that from backpacking. Your wedding day is another of those moments for me. Not a small moment for you, I realize, but the memories of parts of that day are little snapshots that I just love to recall. Remember when the manager pulled out that bottle of scotch and we all had a toast? I was so happy for you. You never know when it will happen." Davie was reminded of one of Michael's favorite expressions about the imponderables of life, the chance circumstances that Michael, who found more joy in life than anyone she had ever known, always saw as so enthralling: *You just never know now, do you?*

"I mean, I went through a rough time with my divorce, but now?" Andrea said rhetorically, looking around at the serene late-fall forest. "After surviving cancer? I have a whole different way of seeing things. My priorities have changed. It's as though I gained insight into something that a lot of people never figure out. Unfortunately, tragically, you and I have that bond now; we both learned this the hard way, you a lot harder than me. The admission price for all this wisdom was a little steep, but I believe that both of us will have this insight for the rest of our lives. And if you can have some fun with Ethan, go for it. He's a nice man. Now let's get moving."

They got to the hut, a very large building connected to an adjacent smaller building by a covered walkway. That second building held the privy and a sink. The hut was divided into two sections: the front room was a large common area with a kitchen at one end, tables and chairs at the other, and a wood stove in the center. The back section was a bunk room that could sleep more than two dozen people.

"Let's grab a bunk first," Andrea said when they entered. "We're early, but I think more people will show up." She led Davie past the wood stove, where a few backpackers were arranging wet boots in the circle of heat. "And don't ever do that with your boots; you'll ruin them," Andrea added in a quiet aside to Davie as they entered the bunk room. "They'll shrink, and it's a good way to dry out the Vibram soles and they'll just fall apart, just peel off from the uppers."

Davie unclipped her pack, sat down on a bottom bunk, shrugged out of the pack and let it tip over behind her onto the bed. She unrolled her sleeping bag and looked around the bunk room. It was a little strange to think of sleeping with so many other people in one room, sort of a high-altitude military barracks, but she also found the whole adventure intriguing. Andrea was in her element; she had done this before, she loved it, and she knew that Davie didn't need her to hover. The caretaker, a college graduate on a year off before starting a Ph.D. program, showed Davie where the pots and pans were if she wanted to use the huge gas stove. Someone was baking cookies, and they set a plate of them on the counter for everyone to share. Davie hardly talked to Andrea the rest of the evening; instead, she found herself in a lengthy discussion with a couple from Sweden traveling around the United States for six months. They were accustomed to hiking around mountainous regions in Europe in the winter.

The weather stayed clear, and it got very cold that night, but the wood stove and the growing number of backpackers in the hut kept it warm. Davie went to bed early. She found the sensation of being in her sleeping bag in such a remote place, so high up, incredibly cozy. She went to sleep in her puffy down jacket, a wool cap, and thick socks. She knew the room would cool down later, even with all the people in it, and she also knew she almost certainly would have to get up during the night. Using a bottle the way she did in her tent was not an option here; she would have to go out of the hut, follow the covered walkway to the privy some seventy-five feet from the front door, and try not to wake the whole place up with her headlamp in the pitch black. The absence of light in the nighttime was one of the most pronounced impressions Davie held so far of backpacking. Nothing was darker than a forest at night, and all the more so at such a high altitude, where you felt you were in a separate world above the clouds.

When she did wake up a little before midnight, the hut was dark and still. Everyone in the bunkroom was asleep. Davie got up, slowly unzipping her sleeping bag and grateful she was in a bottom bunk. She could see well enough to get out of the hut without turning on her headlamp or accidentally knocking over a chair. The wood stove was still throwing off heat, and that felt wonderful. She knew the front door to the hut would not be locked, but she turned the knob anyhow to make sure, imagining how dreadful it would be if she really did have to awaken a building full of exhausted people.

The outside was nowhere near as cold as Davie expected, despite the fact that the large thermometer on one of the posts of the front porch registered nine degrees Fahrenheit. Maybe it didn't feel that cold because the night was so still, Davie thought. On her way back into the hut, she stopped at the porch railing, struck by the quiet and the sense of the mountain forest just beyond her reach that fanned out below her. She leaned over the railing and looked up, and she saw a night sky she had never seen before in her life. The dome of the sky was the deepest black imaginable, but radiating with the light of a vast, dense display of stars. The sky seemed to pulse with their glittering frozen light, as though they were slowly turning on a wire that suspended them overhead, against a great, curved backdrop of polished onyx throwing off reflections as you angled it this way and that.

This was one of those moments Andrea tried to describe that afternoon, Davie thought, something you caught by chance and were fortunate enough to stop, take in and stamp into your memory. This would be difficult to describe even to Andrea; it was stunning and humbling to see. She stayed there until she finally did start to feel the cold, and then silently made her way back to her bunk, the vast span of the night sky imprinted in her mind. When she got back into her sleeping bag and closed her eyes, she still saw those millions upon millions of stars.

Their hike out the next morning was easier for Davie than the hike in, undoubtedly because she now recognized landmarks by which she could gauge the distance, and they were hiking downhill. The temperature had dropped overnight, but the sky remained clear and Davie knew that within minutes of leaving the hut she would be warmed by just moving. Fueled by a desire to be back in the car and heading home, she and Andrea talked very little. Davie was still struck by the sky the night before, which she mentioned in passing to Andrea when they first got started, but without feeling that she could convey its effect on her. She didn't even try.

They got back to Andrea's car by mid-afternoon, loaded their packs into the wayback, and had just gotten into their seats when Andrea touched Davie's arm and pointed.

"Look over there," she said. At first, Davie didn't see what Andrea was indicating, then she caught a movement as a bobcat came all the way out of the woods at the edge of the parking area, maybe thirty feet away. Davie had never seen one before, but she instantly knew it was a bobcat. Davie saw it very clearly as it paused and looked directly at the car. Neither she nor Andrea moved. The bobcat stayed like that for several more moments, assessing the open space where theirs was the only car, and then it seemed to just disappear. It went back into the woods without turning; it seemed to have just stepped back and vanished into the brush as they watched.

"Will you go back to Virginia with me this summer maybe, and we could finish the Shenandoah Park?" Andrea asked, as she turned on the engine.

"Yes," Davie said. "You can plan for us to do more than sixty-two miles. Let's go out for two full weeks."

Jay and Alanna held a Christmas party the weekend after the New Hampshire trip. Jay had long since moved out of the top-floor apartment in the Mansion Neighborhood where Michael and Davie met, and now he and Alanna rented the first floor of a sprawling Victorian house off Western Avenue. It was the perfect place for a large party, with a huge old kitchen and a dining room connected to the kitchen through a pantry with glass-fronted cabinets and built-in shelves and drawers. At the front of the apartment was a living room, a side parlor used for receiving visitors in a more formal era and a second smaller room which had been a library. Davie was surprised at how many people were there when she arrived, but she didn't see anyone from work, nor did she see anyone else that she knew. The guests were probably neighbors and friends from Alanna's department at the university, she surmised. She didn't feel like joining the conversations going on in the clusters of people all around her, and she always felt conspicuous showing up by herself. She very rarely drank alcohol, but she felt like having one glass of wine, so she made her way over to the table set up as a bar at the end of the living room.

"Hey, Davie!" Jay called from the front hall, where someone else had just arrived. She turned and Jay walked over to her and leaned forward to hug her.

"I'm glad you came," he said. Some people from their office were there earlier, he said, but they already left. He offered to introduce her to some of their friends, but she told him she was fine, she was going to get a glass of wine and walk around a little. She privately cringed at the thought of being taken over to a group of people who all knew each other, in a well-intended gesture that would send a signal that she was alone and should be included. How different this was from going to a party with Michael! She had gone to a lot of parties over the years with Michael: fundraisers, legislative gatherings, neighborhood association holiday parties, political meet-and-greets for prospective candidates in the backyards of well-connected Albany residents who were promoting an insurgent against the still very-much-alive Democratic machine, birthday parties for friends . . . and their own New Year's Day open house, held every year they had owned their home. It did no good to go over all of that now, Davie realized, but it was impossible to not remember.

"Jay!" someone called from the kitchen. "Do you have any more ice stashed anywhere? I'm going to restock your beer supply for you."

"I guess I'm being paged," Jay said. "Hey, I'm glad you're here, and I'll catch up with you more in a little while, OK?" He leaned forward and gave her a quick kiss on the cheek and disappeared into the kitchen.

She had just picked up an open bottle of Riesling and was reaching for a wine glass when a man came over to the bar. He must have been part of a group of people in the living room.

"So your name is Davie?"

Davie looked at him and in two seconds assessed him as quite drunk, based on the way he was standing and the unfocused look on his face.

"Yup," she said, looking back to her wine glass so she could pour her drink and get away from him. Her brisk tone would have signaled to anyone even slightly more sober that she was not interested in a conversation, but he stood there and watched as she poured her wine and set the bottle back on the table.

"So, I bet you've been mistaken for a guy all your life with that name," he asked. "Although I don't think anyone would ever mistake you for a guy once they saw you. Your parents must have been fans of that TV show from the sixties, I bet? You know . . . 'Davy, Davy Crockett . . . king of the wild frontier?'"

Davie picked up her wineglass.

"I'm not at all interested in talking to you," she said, and turned from him. She did not say "excuse me," and she didn't smile. She saw no reason why she should be polite to a sloppy drunk who was hitting on her. She had that streak in her, she knew, the ability to just go hard and cold and to skip the social conventions, for all that she looked the part of the perfectly mannered person. It was this streak in her personality that led to her parting shot to Irina, on a day when she was pushed beyond the limits of human endurance. She was nowhere near that point in this situation, but she was also a lot less likely to endure a man's unwelcome attention after fourteen months of being subjected to behavior ranging from frightening and threatening to pathetically inept. So now she turned away, her wine glass in her right hand, and then felt the man's hand on her left arm. It was not a light touch; he gripped her arm just above her elbow and his clenched hand was up against her breast as he held her.

"Don't walk away, honey," she heard him say. Without thinking, Davie let go of her wine glass—it shattered on the wood parquet floor—then she spun around, easily wrenched free of the man's hold and punched him hard on the jaw. She did this so quickly that he did not see it coming, and he was so drunk that he keeled over backwards, crashed into the bar and tipped the table on its side. The wine glasses shattered and the bottles and two ice buckets spilled their contents a good radius beyond where Davie stood.

In seconds, the little groups of people in conversation all around her in two rooms froze, Jay was suddenly there, and someone else pulled the man to his feet and hustled him to the door. Davie stood in the middle of the spilled wine and ice and broken glass, infuriated and expecting an apology from Jay for his guest's bad behavior. Instead, Jay seemed angry with her.

"What the hell happened, Davie?" he demanded.

"He was drunk, and he put his hand on me. I wish I'd hit him harder," Davie said, quite calmly under the circumstances.

"Why the fuck didn't you come get me if he was bothering you?" Jay sounded angrier than she thought he should.

"Oh, you think I should have said to him, 'Please wait here, Mr. Drunken Groping Slob, so that I can fetch the host and ask him to scold you for being so obnoxious?' *He put his hand on me,* he was trying to pull me back to him, he was restraining me when I was trying to walk away from him, and if he'd done this to your girlfriend, you would have cold-cocked him too." Davie's voice now pitched up beyond her calm tone of moments ago.

"Well, Jesus, Davie, there had to be a better way to handle it. I've never seen you do something like this," Jay replied. He looked up at the group near the door, several guys who were searching for the man's coat while two others held him up by the arms. "Hey, fellows, don't let him drive home!" Jay called. "Get his keys, OK?"

"Don't worry, Jay, we've got this," one of the men called back as they half-lifted the man out the door without bothering to put his coat on him. The front door slammed on a now very silent party, with people still standing in clusters as Jay and Davie confronted each other.

"*A better way to handle it?*" Davie said. "You wouldn't have said that to Michael. How dare you say that to me! And you've never seen me like this? Well, where the fuck have you been for the last fourteen months? You want to know what I've been dealing with, with all the men who have hit on me because they think I'm easy pickings, Jay? You want to know about the guy I thought was going to try to rape me in his store, a couple of weeks after Michael's death? And you dare to stand there and tell me there had to be a better way to handle this? To handle the fact that someone at your party was so drunk that he could barely stand up? And you're blaming me? You are unbelievable."

Jay actually flinched at the tone of her voice, the hissing intensity of her pent-up anger spewing out at him. He started to reach for Davie's arm, as if to steady her—or steady himself—and at the look on her face, he dropped his hand.

"Don't you put your hand on me," Davie said. She realized she was chopping up a friendship of some thirty years as if with an axe, but she didn't care. "Don't you dare touch me."

"Davie, I don't know what to say to you anymore. I don't know what to do to help you. You've changed so much, and you're so angry all the time."

"You want to know what to do to help me, Jay?" Davie said. "Then try understanding this. I've been in and out of contemplating suicide. I miss Michael so much that I think about driving into the Hudson River sometimes. I've had hallucinations and nightmares. I've had every man in my social circle try his luck with me. I've been trying for a year now to get the man who stopped to help Michael to talk to me, just so I could have a better idea of whether my husband's death was as agonizing as I think it was. You want to know what I think about every single day? That scene in the hospital, when I had to tell them to stop trying to get Michael's heart started. I hope you never know what this feels like, but you could do a lot better job of trying to understand how I feel. Go to hell."

She turned and walked to the front entrance hall, found her coat, picked up her boots without bothering to change out of her dressy shoes and went to the door. Then she hesitated and looked at the cleanup now going on in the room behind her. Several people were helping Jay turn the table upright, someone was picking up broken glass and two people were wiping the floor with bathroom towels. Davie put her coat and shoes down, walked back to the gathering—ignoring the looks of several of Jay's friends—and lightly touched Jay's shoulder. He turned and for a moment she thought he was going to tell her to get away from him.

"Jay, I'm sorry about the mess. I'm sorry for how we just spoke to each other. But he had his hand up against my bra, and he would not let go of me."

"Yeah, I know he was way out of line, Davie, but I wish you'd come and gotten me before you clocked him," Jay said. Davie realized they were going in circles.

"Jay, you aren't listening to me," she said, very quietly. They were talking in such low voices that no one else could hear them now. It was the most intimate conversation Davie could remember having since Michael's death; a bystander seeing the two of them without knowing the context of the conversation would have guessed they were in a flirtation, a precursor to leaving the party together, with their heads tipped toward each other and their faces averted from people standing near them.

"He was restraining me," Davie said. "I couldn't have gotten your attention even if I'd had time to think about it. I couldn't move."

"I know, Davie. I'm just . . . I don't know. It's not just this. It's . . . a lot of stuff. You seem in such bad shape that I don't know what to suggest to you."

Davie suddenly thought, she was in bad shape; she didn't need Jay to tell her that. But he was in bad shape, too, and it was probably easier for him to lay the blame for how he felt on her, she realized. Jay looked tired and sad. Davie lost her husband; Jay lost one of his best friends. The enormity of Michael's death went beyond his widow's anguish, but there was no mechanism for secondary mourners like Jay to express or even confront their loss. Even as this thought struck her, Davie knew she could not possibly take on Jay's unresolved, possibly unrecognized, issues about Michael's death. People might react to her grief with shock, they might recoil from it, but they also at least expected her to feel the way she did.

"You don't have to suggest anything," Davie said, still very calmly. "Jay, we both feel terrible. We are both torn apart. We can't do anything but get through this. I would rather we got through it as friends. I will always talk to you about Michael, if you want to talk to me about him. I am pretty blown apart, and I think you are, too, but we both loved him. You've been very careful about what you've asked me and what you've discussed with me, but this has been hell, and I think it would be better if we could talk more easily about his death. Take care of yourself."

Then she went back to the front hall, picked up her coat again and let herself onto the porch, into a night so cold and so still that she heard the latch click in the lock behind her as she pulled the door closed.

That was Saturday night. Davie did not hear from Jay the next day, nor did she expect to hear from him. Davie felt he owed her an apology, and a part of her that was now a lot tougher since Michael's death also told her that she'd better get used to navigating the loss and upheaval of her friendships.

She didn't contact Jay and suggest they talk again about what happened, because she saw no need to apologize, and she also felt that this was an irreparable split. She could not go back now and undo this; she had breached the bond of a longtime friendship, or, more correctly, he was unable to respond in the way that she needed him to respond. He probably never would, Davie realized, as she recalled how he made light of her being fired from LGC. Yes, he was the reason she landed the job she now held, a job she loved, but he never grasped the magnitude of the situation when she was fired, and now he didn't understand how or why she could pull up such anger over a situation he didn't think warranted that reaction.

As Davie thought over these conclusions, she also thought how very awkward it would be for her to work with Jay if their friendship was finished. There was nothing she could do about that, either, but she assumed they could both be professional enough to deal with each other. She did not really want to repair this rift despite the fact that it was the first since Michael's death with someone she genuinely did not want to lose as a friend.

The neighbors she had baffled with her cold anger; her colleagues at LGC, not one of whom ever contacted her to ask how she was; the couples she and Michael used to socialize with—none of them mattered. Jay mattered. Maybe that was why she didn't want to try with him, Davie realized; if even he could turn on her, then his action marked a final and very rude awakening about traumatic widowhood—you lost more than your husband; you lost the whole life you used to have. Davie wondered if men went through this after the death of a wife, or if gay and lesbian couples went through this in the same way. She couldn't begin to guess; she only knew how it was for her.

The widows' group site warned that shattered friendships were often the collateral damage of widowhood, and now Davie understood why. Not even your closest friends could grasp the anger, the pain, the punch-through-a-brick-wall desire to take no prisoners as you got backed into a corner with loss after loss after loss coming at you, and you decided to go down fighting. No wonder Jay told her she was so changed, that she seemed angry all the time. Davie knew she felt that way; what she didn't realize was that she radiated that anger all around her even when she thought she kept a lid on it most days. Jay just handed her a wakeup call.

She wished that she could talk to someone about this incident; for all that she did not want to try to fix this breach, her split with Jay was still a significant loss. Jay was the best man at their wedding, the person who represented a connection to Michael, who hoped that she and Michael would hit it off at that long-ago other party on a very hot July night.

Davie didn't want to bother Andrea with this upset, when Andrea seemed to be doing well and was at the one-year mark of her treatment with every indication that the cancer was still in remission. Davie didn't know at what point Andrea would be considered cured, but she also didn't want to cause Andrea any distress about her own problems.

She barely knew Ethan, although he seemed capable of displaying empathy toward her situation. She thought that trying to bring him up to speed on the past fourteen months or turn to him in such a time of need—he didn't even know Jay—was more than she wanted to take on with someone she had seen only three times. Still, she thought it was interesting that she even considered Ethan as someone to whom she could talk. She could not account for this, but he just gave her the sense of someone who would listen closely and would give a considered response.

She managed to avoid encountering Jay in the office that first week after his party by dodging the most common places where they would have run into each other: the coffee maker in the break room and the cold-water tap in the wall dispenser down the hall. They regularly filled water bottles to keep at their desks and used that time to chat. Now, she brought an extra water bottle to the office and made fewer trips down the hall for refills to reduce the risk of running into Jay. She would have to see him again, she realized; she could hardly avoid him forever, even in this expansive office, but she was in no hurry to have an encounter. Nor had he responded to her expressed hope that they could get past this, the last words she said to him at the party.

For the rest of that week, Davie managed a skillful show of doing two things at once. She concentrated very hard on her work, and for a reason she could not figure out, she kept thinking about the mechanic out on the Cape, the man in Hyannis who helped Michael but never contacted her. Maybe she wanted to get everything awful out of the way in one fell swoop—gee, lose a friendship and get blown off again by a Good Samaritan who refused to deal with her, both in the same week, she thought with some bitterness. Or maybe she knew that unless she tried one more time, she would be haunted by his lack of response, because this unresolved situation was always there for her, just under the surface of her thoughts every day. Either way, she decided to call him that Saturday, a week after the fiasco at Jay's party. She could not make such a call at work; that really might be catastrophic for her job, but she would do it Saturday, she decided. And she did, at ten o'clock in the morning.

"J.D. Autobody," a man's voice said. There was no sound of machinery in the background, and the line was a lot clearer than the last time Davie called. She thought this was the same man she spoke with the previous winter. That was not long after Andrea's surgery . . . that would have been late February. It was almost Christmas now, so almost ten months after her earlier call. She suspected this second call would be futile, but she also felt that she had to make it. She certainly did not expect that she was going to get any answers from this man at this late stage; clearly, he didn't want to talk to her. She was almost at the point where she felt like pushing his buttons because he never responded, and she knew she never made her best decisions when her frame of mind could best be described as, "I'm going to get in your face and I don't care." No one did.

"Good morning. I think you and I have spoken before. This is Mrs. Devlin from Albany, and I called about ten months ago, trying to speak with the owner. This is about my husband . . ."

"Yeah, I remember," the man said, cutting her off mid-sentence. "Look, I talked to my boss. I gave him your message, and he doesn't remember this incident you're calling about. He doesn't remember stopping to help someone near the hospital."

The response was so unexpected, so far from the explanation she thought he would offer—that the guy just didn't want to talk to her—that Davie had trouble speaking. She also sensed the man's impatience, so she said the first thing that came to mind.

"That's not possible!" she said, her voice rising. "His name is in the police report. He was *there*. How could he say he doesn't remember?"

"Miss, I can't answer that. I'm sorry. But he does not remember this incident. You know, he's at a lot of accidents, a lot of calls . . ."

"This wasn't an accident, and he was not on duty when this happened," Davie said, feeling as though she had just been punched in the stomach. *"He stopped to help my husband,"* she said, her voice rising with the realization that she was past the point of caring how she sounded. *"He tried to save my husband's life. He was there."*

"I'm really sorry, but I can't tell you any more than what I have just told you. He does not remember it."

Later, Davie would not recall if she disconnected the call or if he did, or if they said anything else to each other. The call ended, but she didn't know how. She was left holding her phone, standing by the bay window at the front of the house, and then she threw her phone across the room and screamed. The phone hit the SOC, and that was a lucky landing, because Davie hadn't been trying to hit something that would cushion the phone. She didn't care if she shattered it, but it bounced off the SOC and landed on the sheepskin rug under the coffee table. She doubled over, clutching her stomach and genuinely feeling like she was about to be very sick. Of all the scenarios she envisioned, this was one she never anticipated. She could hardly stand, her abdomen felt like an auger was drilling into it, an immediate sharp cramp keeping her doubled over and unable to move.

Finally, she was able to stand up long enough to get to the SOC. She stepped around her phone on the edge of the sheepskin rug and lay down, huddling under the oversized plaid wool throw that used to be in her parents' Riverside Drive home. Two thoughts occurred to her as she waited for the pain in her stomach to subside. She was overwhelmingly glad that she hadn't made this call during her lunch hour at work—something she hadn't done precisely out of a fear that she would end up feeling the way she did now. And she suddenly realized she had almost certainly just talked to the man she was trying to reach. She had also very likely talked to him the first time she called, almost a year earlier. He had very smoothly pretended to be his own employee, but now, Davie thought, this must have been him. No one would expect their employee to lie for them like that, or to pull it off even if the employee was willing to try.

Davie didn't know why she didn't think of this before now, but she supposed it was because the first time she called, almost six months after Michael's death, she still held onto a remnant of the trusting person she used to be, the good girl to whom Michael was drawn by her serious, thoughtful take on the world and her conviction that people generally did the right thing. That was one of their eternal differences, Davie thought: Michael knew that people often did the wrong thing; throughout his career, he saw politicians and the directors of other agencies with whom he regularly clashed amply demonstrate their ability to lie, cheat, break promises and undercut the competition. Davie knew that she needed to stop trying to get the man on the Cape to talk to her, that her quest would never yield any answers, she would never know why he refused to talk to her, and that this last attempt went exactly as she feared it would.

chapter 13

In mid-February, Andrea found a lump on her neck, and another one just below her collarbone. She didn't remember them being there the previous day. The cancer was back, and it had spread silently, insidiously, despite all the scans and the many follow-up visits to her oncologist. A scan done less than two weeks earlier didn't detect it. Her oncologist sent the new image and four previous images to Sloan Kettering for review, and everyone agreed: the cancer had been in remission, or so it seemed, less than two weeks earlier, and now it was growing like a vine trying to climb a fence, crowding out the slower plants in its effort to get to the sunlight. It spread without ever revealing itself. Davie didn't even question how this could happen. The answer, she knew by now, was that there was no answer. This was how Michael died of sudden cardiac arrest without a single warning sign. This was how her parents died on an absolutely clear, calm day, even though they approached every flight as though they were about to argue a landmark case before the Supreme Court. Tragedies rarely bothered to explain themselves.

Andrea's doctor sent her back to Sloan Kettering, to see if she could get into a new drug trial. Bern and Susan, her brother and sister-in-law, went with her. Davie didn't ask to go because she knew that Andrea didn't want her there. Andrea was too upset, too scared, too afraid of letting go of the rigid control she had over herself now. Bern called Davie that night. Andrea was asleep, he said. She asked him to call Davie. The doctor at Sloan Kettering told them that Andrea could not get into a clinical trial; the cancer was too advanced and there was nothing more that could be done for it. He told Andrea to go home and get her affairs in order; he told Bern to get hospice into the house. Davie could not bear to imagine what the drive home from New York City had been like for Andrea, after having just been told that she probably had only a few weeks to live.

Andrea never really roused after that night; she never got up again and she drifted into a half-awake, half-asleep state and stayed that way. She was without hope; she probably just wanted the endless waiting to end.

Davie struggled with whether to call Ethan and tell him that Andrea was dying, because she had never discussed Andrea's cancer with him. To do so now seemed a betrayal of Andrea's intensely private approach to her personal life, and it was also an admission for Davie—not that she needed any more proof—that Andrea was not going to survive. This was as difficult for Davie to acknowledge as it was for her to make sense of any of the other inexplicable events that had come at her in the nearly year and a half since Michael's death. She found it truly unbelievable that her husband and her closest friend could die so closely together. She wasn't even sure if Ethan knew that Andrea had cancer in the first place. She also didn't know Ethan that well . . . she had seen him three times in the last eight months. Andrea was the most private person Davie knew, and she was beginning to think that Ethan was the runner-up in that category. For all that they were in fairly regular contact, and he knew so much about her, he revealed so little about himself she could not guess how he would respond. Oh, screw it, she finally thought; he would want to know, and she thought the only way he would know would be if she told him.

She left Ethan a message the day after Andrea got back from Sloan-Kettering, just saying she needed to discuss something with him. She didn't know what hours he kept, whether he was a person who worked late at night, or followed a standard daytime schedule, but she thought he probably did not follow a nine-to-five workday. She knew that when he was finishing a commission he was sometimes in his workshop at unusual hours—very late at night, but also sometimes at daybreak. He returned her call a few hours later, about nine o'clock that night.

"You sounded like something is not good," he said, without bothering to say hello or go through any preliminaries.

"You have that right," Davie said. "I don't even know how to start here . . . I feel like I'm just teetering on the edge of an unreal situation, that it's difficult to believe this is happening." She paused and took a breath, steeling herself. "Has Andrea ever told you that she was diagnosed with ovarian cancer, a year ago in August?"

"Well, yes, actually, she did." Davie felt relief at that, although there was very little in this conversation that could be called reassuring.

"She probably also told you that the cancer was caught early, and that she underwent treatment for it? And that everything looked good, she thought she would be OK?"

"She wanted me to know that, yes. I haven't gotten a call from her since then, and that was quite a while ago. Before the hike she took with you up to October Mountain. We are not in touch very often."

"Ethan, Andrea just got home from Sloan Kettering in New York City. The cancer came back, this all happened very fast, and I didn't want to talk to you about it until I had a better idea of what to say. To be honest, I didn't want to talk to you about it until I thought I was past the point of Andrea knowing, because she is so private. I just did not want her to know I talked to you. Maybe that was cowardly of me, but I was afraid she'd be very upset with me, that she would think I betrayed her trust. But we're past that point, because she's just been told she's got maybe two or three weeks to live, and she got home from that appointment yesterday and just . . . she just checked out . . . her brother said it's as if she just was holding herself together until she got home, and she's just . . . she's not really awake now, not really alert. She pretty much never talked about the cancer after her first conversation with me; all I knew was that she thought she was way past the danger point with it." Davie was struck by her own delivery, how preternaturally calm she sounded; it reminded her of her conversations with the doctor, the nurse, the police officer in the ER, the cab driver, the night Michael died.

"So this has been pretty brutally hard on you, for more than one reason," Ethan said.

"Yes."

"I am glad you told me this, but I am very concerned about you. You need to really take care of yourself, because this is a terrible burden for you."

"Well, it must be terrible for you to hear," Davie said, her voice finally wavering. "You were her boyfriend a long time ago. I hated to tell you."

"No, I am glad you told me, although 'glad' is not really the right word to use here," Ethan said. "I appreciate that you told me. I don't know how to reach her brother anymore, and I don't want to know, because there is nothing he needs to hear from me."

"Can I let you know . . . if there's a change? You would want to know that she has died?"

"Yes, please, I would want to know that. I want to know how you are." He did not offer to come see her, and she understood why . . . because there was so much uncertainty about what they were doing, and the situation was complex right now.

There was no reason that she and Ethan could not be in contact as often as they were; Andrea knew they were in steady contact, and Andrea made it abundantly clear that Ethan was a friend, nothing more, and not a friend she was regularly in contact with now. Still, there was something there that made the connection to Ethan especially tightly wired right now for Davie. She was actually glad that he did not offer to drive out and be with her.

"I will let you know," she promised.

Hospice came to Andrea's house the next morning, took charge and moved her to a hospital bed set up in the alcove of the sitting room on the first floor of her house, overlooking the snowbound bare garden. The hospice nurse was there for several hours every day. Bern and Susan moved into Andrea's house to care for her, because they didn't want to be away from her now and leave her at night to the care of friends or a nurse. Davie offered to stay over a few nights to spell them, but Bern said he wanted to do this, that he could handle it.

But ten days into the vigil, he did ask Davie if she could come over for one night, on a Friday. He realized that he and his wife needed a break to go back to their home and make sure no pipes were freezing. Bern was a decent, kind man who did not show his emotions easily but was clearly distraught that Andrea had seemed to be doing so well, and now was so suddenly near death.

He could not arrange for their parents to come to Albany to see her. They were too old, too frail, and he didn't want to prevail upon a cousin in Connecticut to drive them up; they couldn't have gotten up the front steps of Andrea's home. He also couldn't have provided Andrea the help she needed now every day, while simultaneously handling even a short visit from their parents. He was also not sure they would have fully grasped the situation. He was quietly beside himself at how the last days of his vibrant sister's life were rapidly unfurling in one room of her house, when just a few weeks earlier, she was at her job and planning her next section of the Appalachian Trail.

He left a pile of phone numbers for hospice and instructions on what to do in every imaginable scenario, and reluctantly explained to Davie that she might have to check the diapers Andrea now wore. That didn't even faze Davie, but Andrea was taking in so little food and water by then that she suspected all she really needed to do was sit by Andrea's bed and

silently say goodbye to her friend by just being there. She didn't intend to
try to sleep, not even in the chair at the foot of Andrea's bed. She hoped
that Andrea would somehow sense her presence. She understood the disbelief Bern clearly felt, because Davie could not believe this was happening,
either, for all that she feared almost eighteen months ago that this might be
the way Andrea's life ended. She knew she needed to keep her grief tightly
controlled, because she didn't have the mental reserves to let herself grieve
a second time the way she grieved for Michael. The way she still grieved
for Michael, she told herself. She thought that Andrea would understand.

"I'm sorry to have asked you to do this," Bern said when Davie let
herself into the house. He came to the front hallway and spoke quietly,
because he didn't know how much Andrea could still hear and understand;
she was barely lucid. Davie, who rarely touched anyone uninvited, put her
hand on his arm.

"Don't apologize," she said. "I would do anything for Andrea." She
meant that. Andrea was the best friend she ever had. Davie had never
thought of Michael as a friend, for all that he referred to her as his best
buddy; he was in a category all his own. Husband, lover, confidant, the person who delivered totally unconditional love to her mental doorstep like a
subscription to the Dessert of the Month Club, so regularly, so predictably,
that Michael's love for her was the one true thing she had known she could
count on: indissoluble, irrevocable, forever. Andrea was her truest friend,
the friend who never pushed the wrong button, never said the wrong thing
to her after Michael's death. Even more so than Ethan, Davie realized in
surprise, because Ethan always maintained that careful wall around himself,
and Andrea always gave of her heart and soul without reservation. Andrea
expressed her compassion and empathy in the simplest way possible—*My
heart breaks for you*—and she was entirely comfortable with Davie's grief
and trauma, while also offering Davie the hope that recovery was possible,
that Davie would rebuild her life.

Had she done the same for Andrea? Davie asked herself that as she sat
in the dimly lit room in the utterly silent house. The curtains were drawn
over the double windows overlooking the garden because it was so cold.
Andrea wouldn't live to see the garden in the spring, and Davie was glad
she would not, because Davie knew, and Andrea must have known for far
longer, that there would be no good ending to this ordeal. Andrea likely
had known how this was going to end for quite a while now. She just never
talked about how long the remission might last. Davie sat there and wondered: did she ever give Andrea sincere, wholehearted hope through these

seventeen months since Andrea told her about the cancer? No, she realized, she never did, because she knew it would be a useless platitude, of the kind that people first offered her as a new young widow when they didn't know what else to do. They just reached for something to say, to cover their own discomfort. Davie thought that Andrea must have always displayed more hope than she felt, and she also realized that the optimistic prognosis that Andrea described the day that she told Davie about the cancer probably was a stretch.

Davie silenced her phone and put it in her purse and sat in the chair, watching Andrea as she lay so quietly that Davie checked once to see if she was breathing. She was, but with long intervals between each shallow intake. After remaining so far in the background for so long, the cancer had swiftly ravaged her, left her looking gaunt and drawn, but now she looked beautiful because she looked so peaceful. She did not need oxygen, and she was, miraculously, spared any pain. She was not on morphine; she was just not really there. Maybe not medically in a coma, but just no longer there. Her face was completely relaxed; she had let go of the rigid effort she had kept up throughout the course of waiting to see which way the illness would go. Davie thought about the tremendous effort Andrea made to help her through Michael's sudden, traumatic death. It was a gift of friendship from the deepest part of Andrea's loving personality, something that Davie knew she would carry for the rest of her life.

It's going to be a perfectly fucking awful year, but we'll get through it. Davie remembered what Andrea said in the coffee shop right after Michael's memorial service, the day Andrea told Davie about the cancer. The time spanned by Andrea's prediction turned out to be longer than a year, more like seventeen months, and it was not an awful time, Davie realized in astonishment. In some ways, if you could get around the two terrible events in their lives that pushed the starting button on those seventeen months, that time was one of the best periods of Davie's life. Very few people would understand how she could say that, but it was true. She'd gone forth unafraid, she was faithful to Michael's vision of how she should live, and she discovered a lot about being honest and expecting the same from the people in her life.

She thought that Andrea would also have felt this way, had she ever talked about how she approached her cancer diagnosis, especially because she did exactly as Davie did: she faced everything that came at her without fear. If she felt more fear than she ever displayed, well, then, concealing her demons took a lot of courage. Davie couldn't have said this to Andrea, who would have diverted the conversation to a different topic—probably backpacking—the second she figured out where Davie was going with this, but Davie understood Andrea's coping mechanisms.

Davie wanted to tell her friend everything she was thinking, but she doubted that Andrea was really conscious now and Davie thought it was wrong to use the silence to spill out her thoughts when Andrea could not respond. If Andrea was not in a coma, she was somewhere very far from the back sitting room in her house, of that much Davie was sure. Instead, Davie pulled out her phone and searched until she found a long recording of a whip-poor-will singing. She played that over and over, sitting in the chair at the end of the bed and remembering their backpacking trip through Virginia. That trip marked the first time Davie felt really good for more than just a few hours a day since Michael's death, and Andrea seemed so strong and healthy. She wondered if Andrea could hear the sound, if it would also transport her back to that amazing hike through the Shens.

Davie remembered how hard they laughed together, and how astonished she felt to discover she could laugh again. She remembered feeling a first stirring of interest in Ethan on that trip . . . so much seemed possible then, and she believed, at least for those two weeks, that Andrea would stay in remission and live a long life. Davie listened to the wild, haunting notes of the whip-poor-will, a bird permanently captured on the Cornell bird lab's *All About Birds* site some long-ago time and now memorialized in this random recording of its three-note song playing over and again, a song that still sounded hopeful. Davie thought it was as though the whip-poor-will was asking, *Are you there? Are you there?* which was what Davie called out into the dark of her bedroom the night she awakened with such a strong sense of Michael's presence. *Yes, I am, I am here for you, my friend*, Davie said to Andrea without speaking, as tears rolled down her face and she shook with silent sobs when she put her phone back into her purse.

A couple of hours later, she checked her phone and saw a message from Bern telling her that they would be back very early, before seven o'clock in the morning. She also saw that Ethan called close to midnight, but he left no message. When she heard a car pull up a few minutes before seven, she stood and picked up her bag. Andrea never stirred. As Davie left the room, but before she heard the front door opening—and with an unavoidable memory of looking at Michael's still face one last time coming over her— she bent down and kissed Andrea's forehead and held her hand.

"I love you," she whispered.

"Love . . . you," Andrea murmured. Davie heard her only because she was so close. She tightened her hold on Andrea's hand, and then gently released it and left the room without looking back at Andrea. Andrea never moved or opened her eyes, but she must have known it was Davie there with her.

Twenty minutes later, Davie walked around the corner from where she parked her car and headed to her house. She was glad for the freezing, clear morning air, glad for the silence around her. It was almost seven-thirty in the morning, a Saturday, and the neighborhood was very still. When she turned onto her street, she saw Ethan's old Volvo parked in front of her house. Astonished, she walked over to the driver's side as he opened the door.

"What are you doing here?" she asked, swaying with exhaustion.

"I tried to call you and when you didn't call back, I figured you were with Andrea," he said. He turned and closed the door and locked it and then wrapped his arms around Davie.

"I was," Davie said. "I saw that you called but it was just not a good time to call you back. She is slipping. I don't think . . . there's a lot of time left now."

"I just feel awful," Ethan said. "I'm sure you do, too."

"I sure do," Davie said. "I don't believe I will see Andrea again. But she knew I was there."

Davie stepped back and looked up at Ethan. Unexpectedly, she remembered Michael's arms around her in just this way on the last day of his life, when he hugged her and told her that marrying her was the best thing he ever did. Now, looking up at Ethan, she wondered if he ever talked to Andrea once he knew the cancer returned, but she didn't ask him that. He probably didn't, she thought, because there was no chance for him to talk to her, no way for him to go see her.

"You should come inside," Davie said. "You must be freezing. How long were you sitting out there in your car?"

"Well . . . a little while," Ethan said. "I was fine."

They went up the stoop and up to the third floor where Davie spent most of her time in the house. Davie and Michael called this the "Sort-of-Couch Floor," or, more often, simply the "SOC Floor." This was Ethan's first time in the house.

"Sit there, over on the SOC," Davie said, pointing Ethan to the Sort-of-Couch. "I'll make us some coffee."

"Sit on the what?" Ethan asked.

"Oh, sorry . . . Michael and I called that platform bed frame with the futon"—she pointed again—"the 'Sort-of-Couch,' or 'SOC' for short. It's a habit I can't seem to break."

"That seems like a habit you should not have to break," Ethan said. He did as she instructed, only the way he sat down could have been called collapsing, not sitting. He looked done in, Davie thought.

"So, some coffee?" she asked, thinking that if she didn't get some into her own system soon, she might start to have trouble focusing.

"That would be nice. Don't you have to go to work?"

"It's Saturday, Ethan, unless I've really screwed things up. A good thing, too. I'm wiped out."

"Me, too," Ethan said. He slumped against the pillows piled against the wall, his long legs stretched out beyond the sheepskin rug.

"I can fix us some breakfast, if you want," Davie said. Despite the perfectly horrible circumstances of this visit, she was very comfortable having Ethan in the house, even though photographs of her past life were everywhere. She was actually glad he was there; she felt pulled apart inside and she didn't think Ethan expected her to focus on him. Many of the men she knew over the years would have asked her to show them the rest of the house and acted as though everything was normal. Ethan wasn't talking about Andrea, but nor was he even trying to fake acting normal, which was fine with her. He did not seem to need much from her; he seemed to be just benefiting from her presence. She thought that he also must feel comfortable with her.

"Just some coffee, please, if you don't mind," Ethan said. "Thank you so much."

Davie made coffee, and when she carried the two mugs back through the open archway of the kitchen into the sitting room, she found Ethan asleep on the SOC, stretched out the full length of the futon, his boots upright on the floor at one end and one of the pillows under his head. Davie took this in for a moment, almost wobbling on her feet from exhaustion, then set the two mugs on the table and also lay down on the SOC, so that she was spooned against Ethan. She was very sure that even if he woke up, he would not take the gesture as a hint for anything more than the arm he put around her—whether he woke up for a moment, she could not tell—and she intended her action to be nothing more than what it was: a need for shared comfort. She detached Ethan's arm enough to reach down to the end of the SOC for the blanket-sized plaid wool throw, the same one she'd huddled under the day she called the garage in Hyannis. She pulled it over them and then settled back down, in desperate need of the temporary escape that a little sleep would offer her. Ethan never stirred.

As tired as Davie was, as distraught as she was, she could not fall asleep. She kept thinking of her wedding day—the one day someone would expect to see captured in a photograph in her home, the photo she of course did not have, never had—but it was the one day for which she also did not need a photograph. She could very clearly still remember the five of them—Michael and her, Andrea, and Jay and Alanna—spilling out through the heavy doors of City Hall and standing on the stairs, as she and Michael collected themselves. They were lightheaded with excitement and wondrous disbelief that they were newlyweds. She thought of how a photographer would have captured that moment, the little cluster of people that comprised the wedding party and the guest list, all in one easy package, with Michael and her standing on one step, and Andrea, Jay and Alanna on the step behind them.

Now everything was blown to hell, Davie thought, her inner turmoil completely hidden as she lay on the SOC listening to Ethan's quiet breathing. Michael was dead, Andrea was dying and Jay and Alanna were as effectively out of her life as if they too were dead. Davie took a long, hard look at that mental photograph, with a bereft feeling that sent a chill down her back, a bitterly poignant wish that she could be back in that moment, back when she could not possibly have foreseen how her all-too-brief marriage to Michael would end. The sudden intense feeling surpassed the present, despite the warmth of Ethan's lean frame snugged up against her spine.

She couldn't believe that everyone in that photo was gone, lost to her one way or another, and she was glad she did not have a real photo of that moment to display in her home, because she would have found it too painful. No other physical reminder of Michael could have hurt as much as a photograph of that particular moment in her life with her husband. She knew that didn't make sense, she knew that a photograph of their wedding day should have been a reminder of the love and joy and promise of that day, but she couldn't help how she felt.

Ethan left around four o'clock in the afternoon. They both stirred at almost the same time, Davie first, because she had not turned over for several hours and her right arm was starting to go to sleep, and then Ethan, who sat up with a momentary look of confusion as he took in the two mugs of cold coffee on the table. Davie stood, feeling stiff, went into the bathroom, washed her face, found an old toothbrush in the drawer and brushed her teeth with just water because the toothpaste was in the upstairs bathroom in her bedroom. She desperately needed a hot bath. She had no idea what time it was, but she could tell that it was getting on toward late afternoon, the start of the winter sunset visible from the bathroom window. She looked at the long streaks of pink and orange that should have suggested warmth and comfort, a February sunset of tulip colors that should have made you remember that winter would not last forever, even as it still felt good to be inside a cozy house. Instead, the sunset managed to just look cold in the bleak light, almost otherworldly, like a sunset on Mars.

When she went back into the sitting room, Ethan was sitting on the SOC, tying his boot laces.

"I want to apologize for showing up out of the blue this morning," he said, looking up at her.

Davie sat down next to him and regarded the cold coffee.

"Would you like a fresh cup of coffee for the road? I can unearth a travel mug somewhere," she said.

"Yes, please, if you don't mind," Ethan said. He stood up and hunched his shoulders, trying to loosen the muscles. "This is not the only way I want to spend time with you, you know. But I was not in a good frame of mind last night."

"I understand. Neither was I," Davie said.

Ethan went back through the kitchen and into the bathroom, and when he came out, he walked not back into the kitchen but turned into the little room at the back of the house, on the other side of the bathroom wall. When he did not reappear, she found him in the small back room she used as a home office. He was poking the spongy wood at the bottom of one of the window frames.

"I just wanted to see if the windows in both rooms at the back of the house were in the same condition," he said. "The front window frames are fine, but they are more protected. These windows must absorb a lot more weather. And they're not original to the house, although the glass looks original. Someone must have put a new frame around the original glass. These can be repaired."

"Repaired?" Davie asked. "I was going to scrap them. I thought they were beyond repair. I just haven't gotten around to it . . . or, at least, I had this project on next year's house list, date to be determined." They were talking about everything except Andrea, she realized.

"No, I could repair them, and save you a lot of money," Ethan said. "Let's put that on the house list. In the spring. Not now."

Davie shook her head slightly.

"Ethan, you're very busy with your work. You don't have to take on home repairs here."

"I'm not taking on anything. This is what I do. Or, what I used to do . . . now I do mostly commission woodworking, but I've done a lot of window repairs. These will hold up until I get to them in the spring. Especially now that I see that you plugged the rotten spots with Durham's Water Putty."

"Don't look too much more closely," Davie said. "I don't want you to see the cotton balls under the Durham's."

"I already did," Ethan said. Ten minutes later, he was gone, with another long hug at the door and a kiss that was not meant to be romantic, but was the kind of kiss she needed on that particular day.

Bern called at five o'clock, just minutes after Ethan left. Andrea had died a half-hour earlier, so quietly and peacefully that it happened when Bern left her bedside just to make a cup of coffee in the adjacent kitchen. Andrea's sister-in-law, Susan, was upstairs in the guest bedroom hanging up the clothes she brought back from their West Stockbridge home, because she expected it to be another week at least before they could go back to check their house. Andrea died exactly the way that Davie thought she would have chosen: on her own, in privacy. There was no struggle, no long, drawn-out process that alerted her family. The hospice nurse had been there that afternoon, and she left for the day because she did not think that the end was so close. Andrea simply drifted deeper into the sleep she had been in for almost two weeks, and stopped breathing.

Davie returned to her job Monday, because she didn't know what else she could do and she thought that sitting in the house and taking in her loss would be the start of a slide back to where she had been for most of the time since Michael's death. She'd thought she was prepared two weeks ago for Andrea's death. She thought she was prepared for most of the last seventeen months for the possibility that the cancer would come back, but now she realized there was no way to prepare for this. Hell, Andrea didn't have time to prepare for this. Davie hoped she would not encounter Jay at work, because she wasn't sure she could resist the impulse to tell him how much she appreciated his bailing on her for no reason at all, but she also knew that this would be a futile gesture and was certainly not one that should take place in the office. She was as done with Jay as he apparently was done with her. He would learn about Andrea's death, she assumed, but she did not intend to inform him. She kept her office door closed and just tried to focus on her work. The memorial service for Andrea would be very small and would be held in Connecticut the following week, so that Andrea's parents could be there.

Davie planned to go to the service, but by Friday, six days after Andrea's death, she was so exhausted and felt so ill that she could not get moving that morning to go to work. Her throat felt hot, more than sore; she didn't know how else to describe the sensation. She took her temperature soon after she got out of bed, feeling too queasy for coffee, and she was more than a little surprised to get a reading of one hundred and two degrees. An hour later, it was one hundred and three degrees. She called her doctor's office as soon as it opened, got an appointment with a nurse practitioner for eleven o'clock that morning, and left a phone message for her manager at work telling him she was sick. She had bronchitis, she learned. The nurse practitioner advised her to go to bed for the next several days and to finish the course of antibiotics that he was about to prescribe.

Davie was not at all baffled that she was so sick, and she was also relieved that at least for the next few days, she could stop trying to force herself to act normal and could also stop pushing herself into a return to her everyday life. She was strung out with grief and sorrow from waiting for the end of Andrea's life for the past two weeks; no wonder she was sick. She was stretched to her limit with loss and the inescapable fact that the one person in her life who seemed to totally get what Michael's death did to her was also now dead. She didn't know how she was going to manage without Andrea. She kept thinking of their last hike, how they talked of going back to Virginia in June. Davie didn't even care if it was selfish to think this way. She was incapable of feeling selfless; she could not contemplate how she would get through the next weeks, much less the rest of the year, without Andrea's steadfast love and understanding.

She also realized that between how wrecked she was after Michael's death, and how much she depended on Andrea, she had cultivated pretty much no other support system. She didn't think she could pull one together now. She had lost so many other friends since Michael's death that she could hardly contact people she hadn't spoken to for a year and expect to hit them up for help.

So for the first time in a very long time, as the magnitude of her loss hit her, she felt a little flicker of the long-ago backup plan shoot through her thoughts. She had not felt this way in so many months now that it scared her, how fast it all came back. The first time she struggled with thoughts of suicide, in the weeks after Michael's death, she never told Andrea how she felt. But just knowing that Andrea was there, that Andrea needed her as much as Davie needed Andrea, was one tactic Davie used to quell that feeling. Until now. Now Andrea was dead, and Davie sat on the SOC, wrapped in her wool throw and freezing despite the high setting on the thermostat, as the enormity of Andrea's death came over her in a way that it never did the day Andrea died.

That was easy to figure out; Davie shut down that day in much the same way she mechanically went into efficient mode at the Cape after her first outburst in the cottage the night she returned from the hospital. Then, there were tasks she needed to face, tasks she needed to steel herself for; now, she needed to face Ethan—for all that he was more worried about her—and she kept a tight control on her reactions so she would not fall apart in front of Andrea's family. With all of that behind her, she really did want to fall apart, and she was worried at the depth of her despair.

She made a mug of tea, dumped honey and lemon into it, and went into her little back office, the room where Ethan examined the window frames. She got on the widows' group and wrote a message that would go out to the members at large.

My husband died saving my life while we were on vacation almost 18 months ago. My best friend, who stood up for me at our wedding, died of cancer a week ago. I am rapidly sending my head right back to where it was when my husband died. I've tried two grief therapists in the last year who were trying to outmatch each other for ineptitude. I need help. Is there anyone reading this who knows of a competent grief counselor in Albany, New York? Thank you all.

An hour later, Davie got a response. None of them shared their names, so she never knew who wrote it.

Hi there, the note read. *I'm in Indiana, so I'd like to know how you and I ended up with the same two grief counselors?* ☺ *No, seriously, a lot of people in the grief therapy business should instead be working at McDonald's. At least they would be serving the greater good by asking, "Would you like fries with that?" Please know that my heart goes out to you. You need to stay strong, even though that's probably impossible to contemplate right now. And you are correct: You need someone trained and dispassionate to help you navigate this.*

A friend of mine who used to live in Latham, which I think is just outside of Albany, used this woman (contact information below) after my friend's husband and two children were killed in their car at a railroad crossing in Connecticut where the lights and gate failed. It was impossible to see the oncoming train because of the way the track was situated, and a witness saw the car stop, presumably so that the husband could look both ways, and the gate was up and the lights were not flashing, so he drove through the crossing at the exact moment the train showed up. I offer this awful story not to make you think someone has it worse than you, but so that you will know that you are not alone. Awful, unendurable stuff happens. Most people will never experience it at the level you have, or my friend did. Or I did, for that matter, but my widowhood has been a trip to Paris compared to what you have described; my husband died peacefully in his sleep and never knew what hit him.

Try this therapist. My friend thinks this woman saved her life. And please know that all of us are here for you, because we know that you have been handed more than anyone should be handed. I will be thinking of you. Please survive this.

A woman's name and telephone number followed. Davie left a message for the therapist, and then went back to the SOC and fell asleep under her wool throw.

chapter 14

The therapist's name was Sofia Tremblay, but Davie would always think of her as Dr. Tremblay. It was not Davie's nature to feel comfortable on a first-name basis with a clinical psychologist who was also her therapist. Dr. Tremblay was born in Montreal but grew up in California before moving to Upstate New York a decade earlier, so her accent contained almost no hint of her having been raised by French-speaking parents. Davie never learned much else about her personal life.

They spoke briefly by phone after Davie left the message. The therapist could see Davie very soon, but only in a daytime appointment. Davie debated the wisdom of doing this during a work day the first time, and then going back to work, but Dr. Tremblay did not have evening hours. So Davie took the latest appointment she could get, for four o'clock one after-noon, so that she could go straight home afterword. The therapist's office, as it turned out, was quite close to Davie's home, in an old brownstone on a side street.

Davie was the only person in the small waiting room, and she sat there hoping that this woman could help her, because she absolutely could not lose another job. She knew this was what Andrea would tell her, but know-ing that and trying to prevent it from happening were two entirely different things. Davie missed Andrea terribly; she was having a difficult time grasp-ing that Andrea was dead, because she was so very alive one week, getting ready to plan her Shenandoah trip with Davie, and then dying the next. In a way, it was even more cruel than Michael's death, because Davie was afraid of losing Andrea, and then allowed herself to believe she would not lose her, and then she lost her anyway. The feeling of being jerked back and forth, like being worried by a predator playing with its prey, and then being torn apart at the end kept coming over Davie. It was a terrible mental image, but it accurately summarized how she felt.

"What did the other two counselors do wrong, so I will know not to repeat their mistakes?"

Davie felt as though time slipped as the therapist asked that question. Davie remembered being in the waiting room, and now she was in Dr. Tremblay's adjacent room where she conducted a session—it looked like it must have been a parlor in the building's past life as a private residence in the 1890s, with an elegant marble mantle over the fireplace. Davie could not remember moving from the other room to this one, or any of the preliminary chat that they exchanged as she got settled. That worried her greatly, because she recognized the warning signals of her mental state for months at a stretch after Michael's death. She leaned forward and thrust her hands in her hair as she thought back to the first two fiascos.

"Well, the first one didn't listen to what I said, and the second one wouldn't allow me to say anything. I mean, I told the first one when I set up the appointmen that I have no religious beliefs at all, and when I got there, he barely waited until I was in the chair before he wanted to know if I believed in angels. The second one told me she would not allow me to talk about how my husband died. My God, I'm glad I got her out of my life before my best friend died of cancer—she really would have had a hard time shutting me up at that point."

"A lot of people in this work actually have trouble talking about death," the therapist said.

Davie looked up at her.

"No shit. Most people in this *culture* have trouble talking about death, I'm beginning to think. Sorry for swearing." The therapist waved her hand in a way that conveyed, *No problem.*

"I don't have trouble talking about death," the therapist continued. "I was part of the crisis team of trauma counselors who went down to the World Trade Center after the September 11 attacks. The statewide social workers' association worked on pulling that group together in conjunction with the state health department. No one who had trouble talking about death would have lasted twenty minutes there. So let me ask you, because you have just told me you are teetering: are you thinking of suicide?"

"You know, you are the first person to ask me that," Davie said. "I thought about it a lot when Michael first died, and I thought I got myself past that point. But I'm having some of the same things happen now, with Andrea's death, that happened after Michael died. I'm starting to blank out on stuff. I'm very concerned about my job, because if I lose another job, I will be totally at a loss for what to do next. I mean, I think I'm starting to have what I would call, for lack of a better term, mini-blackouts. After Michael, I sometimes just took myself to another place in my head to escape the stress. That happened when I was waiting to go into the memorial service with Michael's family, and it happened the day I was talking to the guy at the fire station about whether Michael knew he had saved my life."

Davie looked down at her hands in her lap, where she seemed to be tying her fingers into knots. She knew she had answered the question about suicide without actually answering it.

"I just feel like I'm starting to slip," she said, still looking down and speaking very quietly. "Michael's death blew me apart, and now Andrea's death . . . I don't even feel like I'm here. I feel like I'm . . . I've never known how to describe it. I feel like I'm somewhere else. I don't want to go on medication, I want to get through this. My husband never would have wanted me to end up like this, and my dear friend would never have wanted this for me." She finally looked up at the therapist. "But I do find myself wondering, how do I get better? Or, maybe it's more like, will I get better?"

"You will get better," the therapist said. "You have already done more than you realize. You know, many people would have just backed away from even their best friend the minute they realized that this was going to be round two of grief and loss. I don't even mean at the end, when Andrea knew she was going to die. I mean right at the beginning, when she told you she had cancer. You stayed there for her. That was much more difficult than you realize. I think you have a beautiful spirit, a beautiful space inside of you, to have given your friend that gift."

A couple of years earlier, if anyone ever talked to Davie like that, she would have dismissed it as New Age babbling. Now, it was exactly what she needed to hear. She needed to hear that she was doing better than she thought she was doing. Even if it wasn't entirely true, she needed to hear that. At the end of the session, she made another appointment with Dr. Tremblay for the next week.

They agreed that weekly appointments for the first few weeks would be wise, while she sought to regain her balance. Later, Davie would look back at that day and think that getting to Sofia Tremblay might very possibly have saved her life.

✑

Davie heard from Ethan steadily after Andrea's death, or, more exactly, she steadily read Ethan's notes to her by email, which she responded to in kind.

217

He called her the evening of the day that Andrea died, after he got the phone message Davie left for him. She didn't remember much of what he said that night, because she was so upset, but Ethan was extremely concerned about her and distressed that he left when he did. Davie assured him that he could not possibly have known that Andrea would die that day; no one thought that, even though everyone realized it would be soon.

Davie was actually surprised that he called her instead of composing a concerned, carefully written email. She didn't mind that most times, Ethan wrote to her instead of calling her. She now understood that writing seemed to be an easier medium than phone conversations for him, and that he was a wonderful conversationalist but also very unaccustomed to daily conversation in his life. She was fine with that, being in somewhat the same situation in her life. There was something sweetly old-fashioned about his notes, and she found herself drawn to responding. Slowly, they learned more about each other. He remained the reserved, courteous, thoughtful person of her early impression, even in writing. He asked her questions about herself, he asked her about Michael, and he reiterated his intention to help her with some of the work on her house come spring.

That was all that Davie needed right then, as she focused on just trying to get through each day. For months after Michael's death, she used to start to dial his phone number at work—they often called back and forth three, four times a day—and now she found herself wanting to see if Andrea was up for a walk around Washington Park before she shook her head and remembered. She was glad that Andrea's house was outside of the downtown historic district, where Davie lived, because that meant Davie would not have to see the "For Sale" sign that she was sure would soon be posted on the front porch of Andrea's bungalow.

Davie decided to go for an overnight backpacking trip in Massachusetts in April. An unexpectedly cold start to the spring kept the ground frozen in Albany, and Ethan told her there was still quite a bit of snow in the forest at the higher elevation where he lived. Davie did not want to pitch her tent on snow, so she waited. But she thought she would still get out in April, and she thought that this was important to do. The idea of planning a much more extensive trip back to Shenandoah National Park was more than she was ready to undertake for the summer. Maybe, she thought, she would just begin exploring the Appalachian Trail closer to her home. She was beginning to think about how much of the trail she could do, and she knew that the next step would be to wonder if she could section-hike the whole trail, as Andrea planned to do.

One morning in early April, Davie opened her email in her office and saw a note from the executive director to the staff. The header read, "A farewell to Jay Baldwin." The note read: *Please join us Wednesday at 3 p.m. in the conference room so that we can bid farewell to Jay Baldwin and his fiancée, Alanna Smythe, before they head to California and a whole new life. Jay will be starting in May as the conservation director at the privately owned Howell Preserve, a 10,000-acre mix of coastal and inland ecosystems in Sonoma County which has been managed by a board of directors for the same family for the past eighty years. This is a great move for Jay. We want to wish him well and thank him for his service here. Jay's last day will be Friday."*

Davie did not know any of this—the engagement, the job, the move—but then, she also had done a remarkable job of managing to avoid Jay in the sprawling office since his Christmas party, simply by staying in her own space and not mingling in the break room. She got along very well with her colleagues, she knew they thought well of her work, but she was just far enough removed from the full-time field staff to be a bit out of the mix on office politics and news. She did not plan to see Jay before he left. His actions around his party still hurt, and she not only did not consider it her responsibility to try to restore their friendship, but she strongly suspected that Jay would not respond to any attempt to do so. Around that realization, Davie just did not want to try. A year ago, she might have made the effort.

"He failed me," she said to Dr. Tremblay when she next saw her for an appointment. Davie was about to scale back to one session every two weeks, instead of every week.

"How has that made you feel?" the therapist asked.

"It makes me feel like I've gotten a lot tougher," Davie said. "He was best man at our wedding. I met my husband at a party at Jay's apartment, a million years ago. And Jay couldn't handle how my grief unfolded. I'm very angry at him, and I don't want to fix the friendship. I guess the biggest difference between me now and me even a year ago is that my feeling now is, if you can't handle this, if you can't handle what happened to me and how difficult it's been for me, then fine. Have a nice life. I'm less inclined to apologize and keep trying and selling my soul to keep people in my life who don't get it. Maybe I need new people."

"You are a lot stronger now, not just a lot tougher," Dr. Tremblay suggested. It was a statement and a question.

"Yes," Davie said. "And I'm finding out that no one can do this for me. I have had to find my own strength. I think at first, I was very afraid of anything getting upended in my life, on top of what had already happened with Michael's death. I mean, getting fired, or trying to get myself fired, from my previous job was an early lesson in how frightening it could be if I allowed one little thing to tip out of balance. So I got the new job, and my main goal was, don't have anything else happen."

"And now?"

"Now, I'm a lot less afraid than I used to be," Davie said. She paused, and gave a little laugh, shaking her head. "Probably no less angry. Sometimes, I think the anger kept me going, like an adrenaline high. The anger kept me from thinking about how awful I felt. And Jesus, for most of this time, I've been angry at everyone and everything that crossed my path. But Jay? That really hurt me. He just walked on me. But I can't control everything that happens. I just think I am starting to get better tools to handle the stuff I can't control. And now I'm starting to think, if something else happens that I can't control, I'll deal with it. I don't think I give myself enough credit for how hard it has been to work in the same office with Jay and never once confront him, never once let him know how much he hurt me."

"You are a lot stronger than you used to be," the therapist repeated. "You are making a whole new life, and I love how you are setting the terms for yourself that will make that new life a good one." She had a warm smile that lit up her face, as though she was imparting secret wisdom. That expression came over her face now and reinforced her optimistic words. How did anyone do this, day after day, Davie wondered. Dr. Tremblay was a trauma specialist—she dealt with people in situations like Davie's all day, five days a week. Davie knew she could never have done this work.

"You are generous and loving to people who deserve that from you," the therapist continued. "That's how you were to Andrea. Learning to accept that not everyone deserves that from you is such a valuable lesson, and you figured that out by yourself. It's just very impressive to see how you are building a beautiful new life for yourself, and how much you care about yourself, and how much love you have to give to the right people. It's very exciting."

As usual, Davie left the therapist's office in the brownstone on the quiet side street feeling like someone had just handed her a big fat raise. On the surface, there was very little that Dr. Tremblay said to her that Davie didn't already know, or that any trusted friend could not have said, but Davie realized the therapy was more complicated than that.

Behind the calmly pronounced assurances that still struck Davie as heavily steeped in New Age philosophy—but which she found herself enjoying, nonetheless—she knew that Dr. Tremblay possessed extensive clinical training and years of experience grounded in research to back up the talk. No trusted friend would have given Davie the safe space in which to talk about how often she thought of suicide. Being able to talk about that without seeing the other person flinch allowed her to bring that most frightening part of her widowhood into the open. As she brought it into the open, she was able to look at that hidden part of her life without Michael in a more objective way. She always knew she didn't want to be dead. She knew with equal certainty that she wanted to stop feeling so awful. She never knew how to reconcile the two conflicting facts.

Now she felt there was a path to feeling better that didn't involve harming herself, and even if she didn't entirely know what lay on that path, the important part was that she sensed it was there for her. It was as if that door in her mind that she closed in the ER that night reopened, and she knew now that she was no longer trapped, that there was a way through this situation she once visualized as trying to get out of a burning building. She began to believe that she would not feel this terrible forever. The graphic mental images, the endless loop tape of the scene in the hospital, the uncontrollable frightening thoughts and the sensation of dissociating from the present all began to recede.

On the day of the office party for Jay, Davie was working at her desk when a colleague who knew her from the whip-poor-will project stuck his head in the door. Davie had considered three options for the day: faking an appointment that would take her out of the office; showing up at the party, standing on the sidelines and sending a message to Jay intended to make him feel uncomfortable by her silent presence; or doing nothing and just working through the party. She decided to do nothing. She needed to balance thirty years of friendship, all that Jay did for her in the first year after Michael's death, against his inability to handle her grief and anger. Unlike Irina, he never deliberately harmed her. She actually found herself feeling sorry for him. She saw that he was ill-equipped to handle a tragedy of his own, should one come looking for him down the road—and given what Davie now knew about life, one probably would.

"We're all gathering in the conference room," her colleague said. "You going to join us?"

"No, thank you," Davie said, looking up and putting her whole heart into her smile. It felt better for once to not be spewing vitriol. "I've got a deadline here and I think if I get up now, this will all vaporize from my brain. I know Jay will understand. And I've already said good-bye to him."

❧

She hadn't seen Ethan since the day Andrea died, but they talked a number of times, at first because he was very concerned about her. Then slowly their conversations took a different turn; they grew closer. He seemed more at ease now in talking with her. The distance between their homes was just far enough, more than ninety minutes on not-great back roads, that getting together was complicated. Davie wondered what they would do when he came to Albany to help her with the house, as she planned to do as soon as he could. She could not see him doing that long drive home at night after dinner, if he came out to spend a Saturday. It was also way too early to raise this point.

This was the kind of low-level debacle she supposed Dr. Tremblay should help her navigate, but for reasons Davie could not entirely understand, she was reluctant to open the topic. Probably because explaining Ethan was complicated. She found him fascinating, if a bit eccentric or at least unusual. She knew he cared for her. She also never forgot that he was a forty-five-year-old single man who lived in a very remote area, heated his house with wood he cut on his own property and appeared to need none of the accoutrements of Davie's city life: nearby stores, parks and gardens, public transportation or the close proximity of other people. His life was so far removed from hers, he was so astonishingly different from Michael, that Davie could not fathom how there could be anything more than friendship between them.

Yet every time she got to this point in her musings, she also realized that she cared for him as more than a friend. Or at least she cared for him as much as it was possible to care for someone under these unusual circumstances. She wondered if her feelings stemmed from their mutual connection to Andrea, but she thought the attraction went beyond that.

Occasionally, Davie joined colleagues from her job for a drink after work at a pub on Broadway. These gatherings involved a mixed group of married people or dating couples; some of them were from the state or federal wildlife agency offices in downtown Albany. Davie was the only unattached person, but she felt less out of place than she ever did while trying to force the social life she'd shared with Michael to fit into her life as a young widow. The talk at these gatherings with the biologists and ecologists was field work, birds, and survey projects of endangered species, not neighborhood gossip. No one from her job knew Michael, now that Jay was gone, so there was no unspoken reminder of his absence. Davie's colleagues realized by now she was widowed, but no one ever asked her about Michael's death, and that was fine with her.

She also noticed that no one hit on her or asked leading questions about her personal life. She suspected the lack of inappropriate conduct from the men at these gatherings was because she worked with them, so they were mindful of propriety and office policies governing harassment. Everyone went their separate ways at the end of the day. Davie's co-workers were not city people; they mostly lived in the more rural parts of Albany County or nearby Rensselaer County, so Davie never ran into them at a backyard party or her grocery store. None of them knew her the way the couples in her social circle with Michael knew her. She was close to none of these people, outside of their shared interest in their work, but she also fit in better at this job than she ever did in her brief tenure at LGC.

At home, at night, she knew that Ethan would check in with her by phone or more often by email a couple of times a week. They always talked later at night—long, wide-ranging conversations that were a source of both great pleasure and some confusion for Davie. What they were doing was not a romance, which was not possible under such limited terms, or at least not possible by Davie's standard of how such things would normally go. She would not have called him a boyfriend, but nor was he simply a friend. She didn't know what he was to her, but he was *something*, a part of her life that she very cautiously allowed herself to count on as a steady presence. Whether that was wise or not, she could not say.

She was surprised at the depth of his conversations, how much he revealed to her about himself. He knew he led a solitary life, but he was very accustomed to it. He grew up in Chicago, where his parents and two brothers still lived. He came East for the first time to go to Williams and fell in love with the area. A period of moving around the country followed college—and must have also followed his divorce, Davie realized, but he never mentioned his marriage or its breakup. As he lived a nomadic life, he realized how much he did not want to be a physicist and how much he loved working with wood. He stumbled into his career when he took a job as an apprentice to a furniture maker in Georgia, and then it became his passion. He wanted to show her his land; he said they could hike on the trails he had cut through it.

"So would you be willing to shuttle me later this month if I did an overnight in Massachusetts?" Davie asked one night on the phone. It occurred to her that she would know how Ethan felt about her if he didn't expect her to pay for the shuttle. She smiled; she could not believe that she was navigating this unusual situation, but Ethan seemed to generate unusual situations and special consideration. Andrea warned her that he did.

"Of course I would," he said.

❧

Davie spread the Berkshires part of her two-section Massachusetts-Connecticut Appalachian Trail map on her kitchen table and considered her options. It was mid-April, but in the Berkshires, the month printed on the calendar bore very little relation to the arrival of spring. The season on the trail would still be winter. For this first solo hike of the year, her first since Andrea's death, Davie wanted to keep the plan simple. She was not yet ready to push herself; the associations with Andrea were vivid and painful. She decided to hike only a few miles in and out on this overnight trip, and she wanted each end of the hike to be on a road that would regularly have traffic, not a remote dirt road in the middle of truly nowhere. If the weather changed, and she was not yet at the shelter and decided to turn back, she wanted to make sure she could drive out without getting stuck. Or, if she got to her car the next day and it wouldn't start, she wanted a way to hitchhike into the closest town if she couldn't get a cell signal to call Ethan. She was always very careful and prepared; that was the mathematician part of her personality that liked precise endings and neat solutions. She just assumed she would have no cell reception on the trail, because she by now knew that reception was very spotty in many sections. So yes, she wanted a real road at each end of her hike, not a dirt road no one could find.

She settled on the Kay Wood Shelter, very close to the town of Dalton, Massachusetts, east of Pittsfield. The drive through Dalton was the route she and Andrea traveled on their first backpacking trip. That was the day Davie met Ethan. On this trip, Davie would park at a different trailhead on the outskirts of the town, and Ethan would drop her off where the trail crossed a road a few miles south. Both trailheads were almost walking distance from Dalton, but the roads got very wooded and rural not far beyond the suburban sprawl, as Davie remembered from her first trip to the area. She would have almost four miles to hike north to the shelter, and then a half-mile hike north back to her car the next morning.

She asked Ethan to meet her at that endpoint, a turnoff along a back road, on a Saturday morning. She was waiting outside of her car, her pack on the ground beside her, when his Volvo pulled into the turnoff. The ride to her starting point was no more than twenty minutes. Davie thought about Andrea during the drive, thinking Andrea would be very proud of her for getting back out on the trail. Ethan said very little on the short trip, but Davie knew by now that casual conversation did not come easily to him.

Ethan pulled into the small parking area where she would start. This road was farther outside of Dalton than where she left her car—hilly, heavily wooded and more remote. Davie was about to open the door when Ethan reached over to her and very gently ran the back of his hand down her cheekbone, so that she turned to him. He leaned over from his seat and began to kiss her, and then pulled back.

"This is OK to be doing?" he asked.

"Yes." She always thought he was very mindful of the fact that she was a widow, a widow who had been through sheer unadulterated hell.

They sat in the car kissing for what seemed a long time. Cars occasionally came over the hill on the road just behind them and sped past, but it was doubtful that anyone realized two people were sitting in the Volvo making out in silent passion, and they had as much privacy as if they had been in a field in the middle of nowhere. The physical contact, the allure of mutual attraction, felt absolutely terrific to Davie.

She'd hardly touched another human being in more than eighteen months, unless you counted the several hundred hugs she endured at the memorial service for Michael—the reason she now couldn't stand to be hugged by people she did not know well—and then knocking the obnoxious drunk at Jay's party clean off his feet with her well-placed punch, coupled with his assault that led to her clocking him. Her farewell to Andrea, then greeting Ethan outside of her house and later falling asleep with him on the SOC that same morning. The assault in the salon on Lark Street soon after Michael's death. But no touch, no gesture of comfort or attraction, had been offered to her with the sole intention of making her feel as wonderful as she felt now.

She could have stayed in the car for quite a while, kissing him and allowing him to start exploring her body with his hands through her many layers of warm clothing, even though she realized they were in full view of the road—albeit in a car that was difficult to see into, but still, someone else could have pulled into the turnoff for the trail. Davie didn't care. She was, she realized, starved for affection, for contact that was not connected to sadness, grief or anger. She did not necessarily want more than what he was offering right then, and even if she wanted more, their options were pretty limited. This was all they could have at that time, unless they ended up in the roomy back seat, but she could hardly imagine them doing that at their age. She very briefly thought of ditching her backpacking trip and asking him to drive her back to his home, which was closer than Albany, and she would pick up her car the next morning. But she did not dare suggest this; she thought that doing so would break the spell and he would get out of the car and offer to help her with her pack.

Instead, when they drew back from each other, she said, "I should probably get going."

He did not, as she half expected, nod and say in his very Ethan-like way, "Yes, that sounds like a good idea." Instead, he looked at her as though some of the same thoughts she was pondering were going through his mind. Then he sat up straighter and picked up his car keys from the cup holder.

"Let me help you get your pack out of the car." The words were so comically close to what she imagined him saying that she burst out laughing, suddenly buoyed by the realization that she felt good, this had been bound to happen, and she was not only fine with it, but she wanted it to happen again. Preferably when they were not sitting in a car with the engine off, in early spring in a forest. The car was getting cold.

"Uhhh . . . do I owe you anything for the shuttle?" Davie asked. She thought if he told her that she did, she might not be responsible for what she said next, but she could still see Andrea counting out bills in the front seat the day Davie first met Ethan.

"What? Oh, no, you do not. What made you think I would charge you for the shuttle?"

"Because I have never forgotten Andrea paying you for the shuttle you gave us," Davie said, a little more directly than she intended. "And I paid you the last time."

"Oh. Yes, I see. That." Ethan thought for a moment. "Well, I had not seen Andrea in a long time, and I . . . this doesn't make sense, I realize, but I thought if I told her it was a favor, she would think . . . and with you and me, now . . . I just would never accept payment."

"I see," Davie replied. "You were afraid that Andrea would think you were in the early stages of an opening move with her? And with us now, we're kind of past the payment stage?"

Ethan looked straight ahead, and Davie knew she had correctly guessed both answers.

"Ethan, I am going to tell you something that my husband used to tell me sometimes, always with the greatest affection. Sometimes you think too much. I assure you that Andrea did not think you were making a move on her. She thought very highly of you. She said only good things about you to me."

"I'm glad to know that," Ethan said. Then he really did get out of the car and reach into the back seat to pull her pack toward him. He turned it so that she could get it on more easily by sitting sideways on the edge of the seat with her feet on the ground while she pulled on the shoulder straps before she stood.

"So, will you catch my message that I'm off the trail?" she asked as she shrugged the pack a little more comfortably on her hips and clipped the belts.

"Yes. And I will talk to you about starting the work on your house. I'm in a bit of a lull right now, in between big projects. It's a good time to help you."

"OK." She turned to him, not sure what kind of parting they would have, but he put his arms around her—as much as that was possible to do with someone wearing a backpack—and then kissed her again.

"Have a good hike." Ethan got back into his car but waited to start the engine until Davie was almost out of sight. As she left the road behind, she could see green shoots and a few early spring flowers poking through patches of snow on the damp ground. She could hear the Volvo engine idling, and she realized that Ethan was watching her hike up the trail at a good pace. She turned, waved with one of her hiking poles, and couldn't see whether he waved back to her. The car started to back out and turn onto the road. Davie watched until it was out of sight.

She stayed another few moments, taking in the silence of the forest around her with the impression she remembered from her first solo hike over Mount Greylock: a feeling of being utterly alone with no choice but to go forward and follow her plan. She saw the high snow bank on the opposite side of the road where the trail continued south, but no boot tracks or pole marks breaking that snow. She thought she must have made the right decision in heading north. She supposed the sun didn't hit that side of the road as much; the trees were denser there because there was no parking area across the road. She turned, looking around at the bare tree limbs, the patchy snow but also the splashes of fresh, bright green here and there on the ground. She could tell that other hikers braving the early spring on the trail were going her direction—north—and she could see snowshoe tracks and boot tread marks in the thinning snow on the trail in front of her. She thought of Andrea's garden in Albany and wondered if shoots were also pushing up through the wet, cold soil there. Then she thought about how cozy it would be in her tent that night. She felt good, and she felt very much alive.

❧

"So, there's this guy who is kind of in my life now," Davie told Dr. Tremblay. "It's . . . I don't know . . . it's not easy to explain." She then proceeded to try to explain it.

"He's very nice. I'm very attracted to him," Davie said five minutes later.

"This is the first man you have felt interested in since your husband's death?" Dr. Tremblay managed to simultaneously have the kind of interested excitement you'd expect from a girlfriend you were telling this to over coffee or a glass of wine during happy hour, and a professional tone in her voice that indicated the coming shift into therapist mode soon to follow the friendly confidante part of the discussion.

"Yes, he is. We had one date, back in the fall. That was really nice. That was . . . oh, late September, early October . . . we went out for dinner, and it was lovely, but I have not really seen him in that context since then. I mean, I've seen him, but not for a date. I met him through my friend Andrea, my friend who just died." Dr. Tremblay nodded. Davie realized that her therapist would of course remember very well who Andrea was, and Davie again wondered, how did anyone keep track of each person's complex life story in this business?

"Andrea went to college with this man, they were briefly a couple a long time ago—and I do not think that enters into this situation, really, at all—but that's how I met him," Davie said. "He is as different from my husband as you could imagine. Michael was . . . he just filled every room he entered, he was always the center of attention, not because he was trying to show off or dominate the conversation, but just because he had so much command in his personality, his bearing. This man—his name is Ethan—he's very quiet, very thoughtful, very . . . to himself, but not in a bad way. He's not a loner, he just lives on his own in a remote area, up in the northeastern corner of Rensselaer County, almost up into Vermont. He's very intellectual, extremely intelligent. Andrea told me he went through a divorce that kind of blew him out of the water, but he's never mentioned that." She stopped, considered all that she had poured out, and looked up at Dr. Tremblay.

"Whatever it is that we're doing, it's not unfolding in a way that's even easy to explain."

"Maybe you don't have to explain it. You certainly do not have to explain it to me," the therapist said. "I just think it's wonderful that you are exploring your new life, all that it can offer you, and that you are opening yourself up to people who make you feel good and can offer you love. Do you realize how much you have accomplished in just the past few months?"

"I never dream about Michael," Davie said, plunging right along on her own train of thought. "Why don't I ever dream about him? I think about him all the time. He's just threaded through every day for me."

"Maybe he knows you are not ready to dream about him," Dr. Tremblay said.

"You don't really believe he's somewhere else . . . you do not believe his soul or his spirit is somewhere, and that I can have an awareness of that?"

Dr. Tremblay leaned forward.

"I know how you feel about religious beliefs," she said. "This is not a religious belief. I am telling you that this is not all there is. No, your husband is not somewhere else, watching your every daily move. But his spirit, his soul, call it what you will . . . that is not gone. It's just elsewhere. He will come to you when you are ready for that to happen. If you find it curious that you have not been dreaming about him, then you must also realize that there are many ways to receive a good, affirming message that someone who loved you so much, who would so very willingly have traded his life for yours, wanted nothing but the best for you. You do not have to believe what I am saying. But you have already sensed that he is very much with you."

"OK, so I'll believe that for now, with some reservations," Davie said. "But I don't have a strong sense of him. Right now, I feel he is very far away from me. I didn't used to feel that way. But of course, my life has expanded beyond where it was at first, after he died. I hardly left the house in those first weeks, really the first few months. Now . . . "

"Now you are in the world, and you are loving and exploring and making a new life for yourself. You are doing so very well. You are sharing so much of yourself with the world. This is what your husband would want for you, and it's so beautiful to see."

"So I don't have to figure out everything right now, you mean? Just go with it, and see what happens?" Davie asked.

"Yes, that is exactly what I mean," Dr. Tremblay said.

The whip-poor-will group got ready to go back out in May as part of its long-term effort to survey the population in southern Albany County, and the group invited Davie to accompany them. Davie decided to go on the first chance the group offered her, because she now knew that she had a very narrow window for doing this, and she wasn't sure what she would be doing in June on the next full moon, the last chance for the season. The group would go out two or three times in May and a couple more times in June, even though the June sessions were getting toward the end of the nesting season. The birds that had not connected with a mate right away could still have young for the next full moon, Davie learned. She decided to devote one May night to this effort, and she watched the forecast with as much interest as she did before a backpacking trip.

Steve of the disastrous date almost a year ago no longer worked at the state environmental agency, so she didn't have to worry about that awkward encounter. And of course, Jay was gone. But the state biologist who talked to Davie the previous year about how to interpret the whip-poor-will's song was there the night Davie went out, and Davie gravitated to her as a familiar and friendly face in the group.

"How have you been?" the biologist asked as they headed toward the sloping meadow from the road where everyone parked their cars.

"I had a rough winter. My best friend died of cancer in February."

The biologist shook her head as they walked in the fading light.

"I'm sorry. That is rough. Didn't I hear Jay say last year that your husband also just died?"

"Yes, my husband died almost two years ago. My friend who just died was my maid of honor at our wedding."

"I'm really sorry," the biologist said. "You and Jay were friends a long time, weren't you?"

"Yes, we were. We met in high school, and then he and my husband became good friends. He was best man at our wedding."

"Do you think you might go out and visit him in California when he gets settled? Sounds like you could use a vacation."

"I'd love to get out to California, and you are correct, I could use a vacation," Davie said. Then she surprised herself by adding, "But I'm going to be pretty busy the next couple of summers, because I'm going to section-hike the Appalachian Trail. I'm starting that this summer. I'm going to see how much of Vermont, Massachusetts and Connecticut I can do. Those are the states easiest to get to from here."

"Wow," the biologist said. "Then you have a plan. That's great. Good luck with that. Well, if you keep going out with us, you can update me this time next year. Unless you're doing a section on your AT hike when we're back on the whip-poor-will quest, that is."

They did not capture a whip-poor-will that night, and they didn't even hear one singing.

The only whip-poor-will song that Davie heard was from the recording set up near the nets as the biologist's played the male's song over and again, with no sounds of a live whip-poor-will anywhere in the meadow. Davie was less frustrated about this than she thought she might be. Instead, she thought about the idea she just seized upon, as they waited quietly and listened for a song. Yes, she had kicked around the idea of doing the whole trail, very casually, but she never told anyone that she wanted to do it before now. She just jumped from considering the idea to committing to it in her mind, and this suddenly seemed like an inspiration.

She was already thinking of what state she would focus on first while she helped the biologists roll up the mist nets ninety minutes later. The full moon cast a glow over the meadow, but for this task, when rolling the nets without twisting them was so important, everyone turned on their headlamps and left them on as they packed the gear. The headlamps were an admission that they were done for the night, with no intention of setting the nets up in a different location in the huge meadow, because they usually switched their headlamps off as they approached the site where they wanted to set the nets, so as to not spook the birds. They didn't hear a single note from a whip-poor-will as they worked.

"It happens sometimes," the biologist said to Davie. "I hope you're not too disappointed."

"No, I'm fine. I'll try another time," Davie said. She didn't know when that would be, or what she would be doing this time next year, but as she had just told Dr. Tremblay, she now knew that she—the world's most dedicated advance planner, who liked to crunch numbers and solve the problem—didn't have to figure everything out right now.

chapter 15

Ethan tipped the upper sash out of the window frame in the small office in Davie's house and set it very slowly, gently, on the floor against the lower sash he had already removed and leaned against the wall. He pushed the nineteenth century granite paving stone Davie used as a doorstopper against the badly rotted upper sash like a bookend, to keep both parts of the window steady for the time being. The windows contained original glass that was far more valuable than the frames. Then Davie held a sheet of plywood for Ethan while he tapped the edges into place with the smallest nails he thought would hold it, so that he didn't make larger marks than necessary in the original molding around the window frame.

"I'll have the windows for this room back in a week," he said. "The plywood should hold up fine for that short time." He paused and looked around at the door leading to the kitchen. "You probably would never use this room as a fire escape, but it's right behind the kitchen and you never know. So, in the remote possibility that you have to make a fast getaway, use this," and he held up a crowbar, then set it on the floor under the window, "and just pry off the plywood. It will pop right off." He stopped and considered. "That's a long drop to the ground. You don't have one of those fire escape ladders in here, do you? You know, one of those emergency ladders you hook over the window sill?"

"No, but I will put it on my shopping list," Davie said. "The house has been here for going on 125 years and it hasn't burned down yet. I'm not surprised you brought a crowbar to cover all possibilities. But seriously, Ethan, this seems like a lot of work. Not to mention a lot of expensive work. You sure I can't pay you for at least the materials?"

"Absolutely not. I've got the wood on hand already," Ethan said. "I know what I'm going to use. Just let me do this. If we get into larger projects, we can figure something out, OK?"

"OK. Look, I need to clean up before we go out for dinner," Davie said. "You probably want to, also. Do you want to use the shower?"

"No, I just need to wash up and change. I don't need a shower," Ethan said.

They had a reservation at a neighborhood restaurant, a bistro with a courtyard garden for outdoor dining that Davie loved. She supposed this was a date. Ethan was staying at her home that night because it was late for him to load the heavy windows into his pickup truck, drive back to his place and unload them into his workshop in the dark.

He didn't want to leave the windows in the bed of his pickup truck overnight, even covered with a tarp. He remembered a stained-glass panel in an old door getting broken that way when a branch fell on the truck. Davie couldn't remember ever knowing such a thorough, careful, detail-oriented person. He put her own well-documented propensity for planning to shame. She wouldn't have called this part of Ethan's personality rigidity so much as an unusual ability to consider every angle. She thought about his leaving a crowbar for her to pry off the temporary window covering in the impossibly remote chance that she needed to escape from the second floor. She wondered if he was always this way, or if this trait was the outgrowth of some past event he was unable to control, such as his divorce. The divorce that he still never mentioned and might not even realize she knew about, she thought. Davie didn't dare raise the topic.

He planned to repair these two windows, then the bathroom window. The work was an enormous gift of his artistry, time and materials, but threaded through it was a slowly dawning sense for Davie that he was doing this as a gesture of friendship, yes, but friendship completely devoid of any likelihood that the friendship would evolve into a romance. Davie could not avoid the feeling that he would have done this window project for anyone he considered a good friend. He was generous and he loved helping friends, that much she now knew about him. She almost thought sometimes that he derived a sense of personal satisfaction or well-being from helping friends, based on his accounts of other such projects. He had a small circle of people he seemed close to scattered around the country; he'd once mentioned the six weeks he spent somewhere in the Midwest a few years ago helping a couple of good friends renovate an old farmhouse.

Davie was beginning to think this was how Ethan thought of her—as a good friend. She didn't think he was doing this project for her as a gesture of gallantry or a signal of intent toward a woman he felt romantically interested in, and although Davie could not quite put her finger on what constituted the difference between a gesture of friendship and a gesture of romantic intent at such an early stage, she knew the difference existed.

Maybe Ethan was very mindful of her status as a widow, was being very careful with her, Davie mused. He knew the circumstances of Michael's death; he knew how fraught her recovery was, and he knew how Andrea's death four months ago sent her into a desperate downward spiral. Around the time that Davie got this far in her examination of her very unusual relationship with this fascinating, kind, brainy but self-contained man, she reminded herself of her remark to Dr. Tremblay—that she didn't have to figure out everything right now—and she also reminded herself of Andrea's admonition to simply have some fun with Ethan if she could.

All well and good, Davie thought, but she didn't know what the sleeping arrangements would be that night. She had a guest bedroom, and the SOC served as an additional sleeping place for company. Maybe they should just get through dinner. She was extremely reluctant to confront anything with Ethan, and not just because he was about to take her windows to the state line.

The dinner in the white-painted brick courtyard in back of the bistro was lovely. They ordered a bottle of wine, with Ethan telling Davie, "We will get vastly better service if the waiter knows that's going on the tab." They took their time over a four-course meal at a table in a back corner. It was early June, a mild night, and Davie was thoroughly enjoying herself. She was a bit dressed up and felt good about herself. Her earlier ruminations about the indecipherable situation with Ethan receded in the face of a delightful night out for dinner. She knew this was not the first time she felt confusion and a little twinge of uncertainty about Ethan, and she thought it probably would not be the last, but right now, at this moment, she wanted to very much do as she kept telling herself she should do: simply try to have fun.

"Davida? How are you?" A woman's voice, with a slightly hesitant intonation, interrupted the story Davie was telling Ethan about the night of the whip-poor-wills in Shenandoah National Park. Davie looked up and saw Irina, her former manager who fired her, standing by the table.

"Irina, hello," Davie said, careful to sound neutral and cordial. "I'm well, thank you." Well, some things really never changed: she was sitting down and Irina was standing over her. But Irina looked . . . contrite. There was no other word for it. She also looked a little cautious. Maybe she thought Davie was going to tell her to do something obscene with herself again.

"Uh . . . Irina, this is Ethan Van Meter."

Ethan stood up, as Davie thought he would, and he shook Irina's hand with a courteous gravity that Davie could see immediately left Irina taken aback. She also saw Irina do a split-second assessment of Ethan. His arresting, dark good looks, coupled with his slender but athletic frame, made a handsome presentation, and he could not have been more different from Michael's burly, strapping Irish-fisherman-Vermont-farmer appearance. That alone was enough to make people who remembered Davie and Michael together take a second look. Then she saw Irina's eyes pivot at lightning speed to Davie's left hand, where Davie still wore her wedding ring. She was looking for a diamond, Davie realized. Irina and Michael met once, at the holiday party for LGC. Michael wasted little time in letting Irina know—without being anything but his slightly edgy, charming self— that he pegged her in no time flat as an imperious, self-impressed climber who got where she was through family connections. Irina, climber that she might be, was also more than smart enough to have figured out Michael's take on her.

Then Ethan sat down, and Davie saw a small cluster of people standing by the door that led back into the restaurant from the courtyard—probably Irina's husband and friends they met for dinner. Remembering all the times Irina was so impatient to wrap up a conversation, Davie wondered why she lingered by the table.

"I . . . heard about Andrea's death," Irina said. "I didn't know Andrea well at all, but I knew about her work at the Community Loan Foundation, and I knew Bern and Susan years ago. I'm sorry for the loss of your friend."

Davie was not surprised that Irina knew about Andrea through the grapevine in the small, clubby world of financial services in Albany. What did surprise her was that Irina even mentioned Andrea's death, when Irina treated Davie as though Michael's death was an inconvenience.

Davie pulled out her game face: the smile that served her so well when she explained to her colleague why she was not going to Jay's farewell party in the office.

"Thank you," she said to Irina. "Andrea's death was very difficult for me. She was my best friend, and it's been very rough. So thank you for your condolences. It's nice to see you, Irina. Around the setback of Andrea's death, I'm doing very well."

"Yes. You . . . look like you are," Irina said. "Good night."

"Wow," Davie said as they walked back to her house. Ethan paid for dinner, over her protests and with her insistence that next time she would either fix him a fabulous meal at home, or she would pick up the check. "It's very affirming to learn that people are capable of remorse and mea culpas. Although, as I noticed, she still didn't say she was also sorry that my husband died. On the other hand, I didn't ever apologize for telling her to fuck herself."

"She was your boss?" Ethan asked. He walked very briskly, taking long strides with his long legs, and Davie was glad she never wore heels or she would have been asking him to slow down. As it was, she was nearly ready to suggest just that, even in the ballet flats she wore. She wondered if his pace was set to preclude a slower walk, one that would have made it easy for him to take her hand and stroll back to her house in a more measured way, while also allowing them to enjoy the late spring evening.

"She certainly was my boss," Davie said. "And after how I left that job, I'm amazed she came up to talk to me. That constitutes the closest thing I will ever get to an apology from her for how she treated me after Michael's death."

"Well," Ethan said. "It seems that if you thought it was necessary to tell her where to get off, you must have had a very good reason."

"I did. I wanted out of that job on my own terms, and I hit my limit."

"And she calls you Davida, which I assume is your actual name?"

"Yes," Davie said, with a flicker of the old exasperation that particular habit of Irina's always caused in her. "I kept telling her I didn't use it, never used it, but she just kept using it. I finally gave up trying to change that. You, however, do not ever have to use it."

They got back to her house and sat up for a while talking and sitting at opposite ends of the SOC, with Davie curled up against the pillows facing Ethan. He sat with his legs stretched out as he had before, and they never touched. Davie finally felt tired. She sat up and swung her legs over the edge and turned and regarded Ethan.

"Well, I am ready to go to bed." She stood up at the same time Ethan did.

"If you give me some sheets, I'll make this up," he said.

Davie went to her linen closet downstairs; it was the only closet with shelves in her old house. The few minutes she spent picking out some bedding and walking two flights back up to the SOC room gave her time to clear what she was sure was a tight, baffled expression from her face. She wasn't sure what she was ready for, she realized, but she would have preferred to have some say in the matter. Was this unreasonable, Davie wondered? Maybe Ethan thought she wasn't as ready as she thought she was for anything more than the cordial but constrained situation they were in right now. If he was going to come back several times over the summer to help her with the house, Davie would want to have a talk with him about what the parameters were. She still thought it was possible that he was being careful with her. Maybe he was waiting for her to say or signal what she would be comfortable with, but Davie was starting to think that if that was the case, Ethan would have by now broached the topic, explained how he felt . . . because she had no idea how he felt.

Jeeez, she thought, balancing a set of sheets, a blanket and a pillow on one arm and holding the railing with the other hand as she started back upstairs. She tried to remember if dating was like this before she was married. Probably not, because she didn't think that this situation could be categorized as dating. She remembered dating as occasionally fraught, often frustrating, but always evolving . . . the situation was either moving forward or backward with a guy, as she recalled, but it rarely stayed the same. With Michael, dating and then courtship were in a class all their own. He made his feelings for her known from the start, he took it as a given early on that they would get married, and if she made him feel that she took his breath away, as he once told her, he made her feel swept her off her feet. Those old-fashioned, time-honored expressions still held value, they still rang true in the right time and place, Davie realized, because they accurately described infatuation as it turned into real love.

It was entirely possible, Davie thought as she went up the final two steps into the SOC room, that this was all Ethan wanted, all that there would ever be with him. But she ran out of time to continue her conversation with herself; she was now setting the bedding on the glass coffee table in front of the SOC. Ethan stood in front of the shelf on the other side of the room, studying her photographs.

"Well, Michael was a very handsome man," he said without turning. "No wedding pictures?"

"We got married in City Hall and didn't tell anyone ahead of time. I guess that qualifies as an elopement, except we never left town. And no one thought about bringing a camera." She did not tell Ethan that her wedding anniversary was in four days. She couldn't do anything to top how she marked it last year on the Cape, and she wanted to have the time with Ethan without mentioning her anniversary. If he asked when she got married, she would tell him, but she didn't want to volunteer it.

"And these are . . . your parents?" He pointed to the picture she brought home from LGC the day she was fired, the photo of her parents standing in front of their Cessna.

"Yes. They both had their pilot's license, and that was their plane. They died when it went down in the Mount Washington State Forest just north of Salisbury"—she didn't elaborate, because Ethan certainly knew that the Appalachian Trail ran through that area—"and the cause of the crash was never determined. They were pretty amazing people."

"How old were you when that happened?

"Twenty-eight."

"So they never knew Michael, or knew you got married."

"No. I was living in Albany when they died, and I met Michael . . . about three years later, got married almost two years after that. I knew Andrea longer than I knew Michael. I met her at the Community Loan Foundation when we both worked there."

"You have had an astonishing amount of loss for so early in your life," Ethan said. He turned and faced her from across the room. "I admire you greatly for many reasons, but especially for how you have managed loss, and how you have rebuilt your life. And that was before I knew about your parents."

"I've had a terrible time after Michael's death. It's a work in progress. But one thing I have decided is that I want to live the best life I can, as my husband would have wanted for me. I don't want to stay stuck in that terrible grief forever." She intended this statement as a signal to him, an opening line, should he need one.

"I don't think that you will," he said. He crossed the room, hugged her and kissed the top of her head. "Good night."

That weekend marked the beginning of an unusual summer. Davie planned to start her section hike of the Appalachian Trail later in June, and decided that she would give three weekends a month for the next six months to backpacking and helping Ethan with his work on her house. She needed one weekend a month with nothing planned. Ethan's organized approach to the repairs he wanted to do on the house impressed and surprised her a bit. It seemed like a lot of work, but he had a list of projects to work on and he was intent on starting. The effort that started with her rotting windows expanded to numerous other ideas, and he was going to come to Albany once or twice a month through the summer. Davie wished she could have talked to Andrea about Ethan; Andrea would have offered some insights, of that Davie was sure. Davie deeply missed Andrea, and because she and Andrea never knew many of the same people, she didn't have any mutual friends to talk with about Andrea. Instead, she talked to Dr. Tremblay.

"What do you think she would tell you about your friend?" Dr. Tremblay asked Davie, who was still scheduling sessions every other week with the thought that she might cut them back to once a month in the fall. But for now, she found it extremely beneficial to spend that hour in the therapist's serene room, with its old marble fireplace, comfortable seats, and pillows thrown on the antique couch. She realized that the decor was all very artfully done for a purpose; every color was calming, all the furnishings looked inviting, but Davie was willing to admit that approach bestowed exactly the intended effect.

"I think she would, at this point, be a little more forthcoming than she ever was back when neither she nor I would have ever guessed that Ethan would be spending every other weekend at my home without laying a hand on me, other than to give me a hug," Davie said. "I'm sure that he thinks everything is fine. I think if some neutral party were to ask him to describe his relationship with me, he would say I'm a dear friend. That does not explain that time in his car when we were making out like two people stranded on a desert island."

"He's never made any other advances to you after that?"

"Oh, he will hug me when he arrives at the house, and he hugs me goodnight and he'll give me a completely unromantic kiss, but no, nothing that even begins to approach the feeling of passion he demonstrated that morning. My neighbors probably think I've got a hot romance going on. I wouldn't even have to draw the blinds at night when he's there; believe me, there is nothing going on. It's a given that he will sleep on the SOC . . . sorry, that is my abbreviation for what Michael and I called our not-quite-couch in our living room. It's a twin-sized Japanese futon on a steel platform bed frame, so it's like a daybed, and Michael and I called it the sort-of-couch, or SOC for short." Davie made a dismissive gesture that apologized for the long sidebar.

"I should just call it the couch, but I can't seem to let go of what Michael and I called it," she said. "But that's not the problem here. Ethan is too intelligent to expect that I would make a dozen years of my life with my husband just disappear. Michael, and Michael's death, are not standing in the way here. Something else is, and maybe it's not any more complicated than what Andrea told me . . . this man was badly burned by his divorce. He might be averse to ever risking his heart again."

"And you are not?"

Davie thought about that.

"It's very complicated to imagine a life with someone else. You know, I have never even really examined if I am in love with this man. I must be, if I'm spending all this time and money talking to you about him. I'm talking about him more than I'm talking about my dead husband."

"That's because you're secure in your feelings about your husband," the therapist replied. "Your grief is very separate from how secure you feel about your memories of him. He gave you unconditional love and passion; he expressed how he felt about you. You have that part of your life with your husband completely figured out. I have had people sit in this room, where you are sitting now, and tear themselves apart because their last memory of their dead spouse was an argument, a slammed door. Your last memory of your husband is of him very calmly doing what he needed to do to save your life."

"So it's not as strange as I have worried it might sound to you that I'm talking about this complex, brilliant, handsome man who is spending two weekends a month at my house working on home improvement projects, more than I'm talking about Michael?" Davie asked.

"It doesn't even surprise me," Dr. Tremblay said. "It indicates to me that you're embracing what life is handing you, that you are rebuilding your life, examining what you want from your life and your future, and you are doing an amazing job at this. You don't realize how beautiful this is for someone to see."

"Well, then, we can save for a fuller discussion next time about the complications that would come into my life if Ethan suddenly pronounced himself passionately in love with me. I really know how to pick 'em. He owns fifty acres of heavily forested land in the most remote part of Rensselaer County, where he harvests his own wood, has a workshop the size of a two-car garage for his business, and a house he designed that he seems to love. I have a job that I am enjoying very much, a house that my husband and I bought together, and all the benefits of a great small city. It would be very difficult to blend our two lives."

Davie paused for several moments.

"But that's not the problem here, either," she said very quietly, almost as though to herself. She was looking at the brass and glass coffee table in front of her, a fine example of designer-quality '70s home décor, and she was thinking out loud. Davie often found it easier to talk in this setting if she thought of the session as a conversation with herself, so she rarely looked directly at Dr. Tremblay. And the good Lord only knew that she'd gotten quite a bit of practice in the last twenty-two months at having conversations with herself.

"If we really wanted to work this out, we would find a way," Davie said. Now she did look directly at the therapist. "I'd be willing. There are more ways to make a relationship work than to just live in the same city as the person you love. And he's not exactly on the other side of the country. He and I have both been married. I'm not trying to duplicate what I had with Michael. The commitment, the feeling two people have for each other, is what matters to me. When you know you have that, you can figure out the details." She paused for a moment, thinking of the many details that trying to figure out anything with Ethan would bring into her life. Still, she felt she was willing.

"But if he never feels that he wants more than this, if there's never any way to move this forward . . . well, it may just be that for whatever reason, he just does not feel anything for me other than friendship," Davie said. "That may never change. I mean, it was just so easy with Michael. No one writes about this part of widowhood—that you find yourself feeling like you are starting all over. Maybe that's why some people can't let go of their grief. It drops into your life like a cargo container, it crushes everything else that was going on, you get used to it being there, taking up all the room, and it's not subtle. It dominates your life, and it makes it difficult to deal with the lesser stuff. Or maybe easy to *avoid* dealing with the lesser stuff. Michael's death did a lot of terrible things to me, but this situation with Ethan is one of those incalculable effects of his death that kind of creeps up on you," and here Davie smiled but did not bother to explain her amusement that she could fit a reference to calculations even into this outpouring— "You deal with the catastrophic, traumatic loss, and if you survive that, then you deal with all of . . ." she swung her arm out around her, ". . . all this uncertainty."

Davie started her section hike at the Connecticut-New York border, at a tiny Appalachian Trail parking area known as Hoyt Road. Connecticut was around the corner. She was doing the hike in the last few days of June.

Her two beautifully repaired windows were now in place in her home office. On the weekend Ethan brought the windows back to her, she cooked dinner for him, he slept on the SOC and Davie avoided thinking of everything she recently discussed with Dr. Tremblay. The push-pull she felt toward Ethan reminded her of the early period after Michael's death, back when she felt that her moods swung up and down and sideways. She loved spending time with Ethan. She loved it more than she suspected he ever realized. She looked forward to that return trip when he planned to bring the windows back with an intensity that she almost forgot existed: the excitement of spending time with someone with whom you were very likely falling in love.

At such times, Davie would think, he has to feel something of the same . . . no one would do the amount of work he was doing for her without some strong attachment beyond friendship. At other times, she would take a long, hard look at the situation, as though from outside of the participant's arena, and would remind herself to just enjoy each visit with Ethan, because she suspected that the disconnect, the lack of any apparent romantic feelings on his part, would simmer slowly until her mixed-up emotions suddenly boiled over into a discussion she really did not want to have. Just get through the summer, she thought to herself.

Davie also realized she could not possibly be the first widow to go through this, but she had no notes for comparison, and she was very hesitant to throw this situation into the anonymous network of the widows' group. She never knew the ages of the few hundred women who belonged to the group, but based on the questions they asked about helping young children adjust to life without daddy, or what to do about in-laws who proved to be no help at all, she thought most of the members were in their 30s or 40s. Chances were excellent that she'd find an empathetic response if she floated a question about unrequited feelings for a man. She hesitated to do so, because the forum was supposed to be a support group for serious problems and a resource for finding competent estate attorneys, financial planners, grief counselors. It was not supposed to be an online advice column for widows bumbling their way through something that Davie feared would come off sounding like an unrequited middle-school crush, instead of the very real confusion of a highly educated going-on-forty-five-year-old professional.

Then she started her section hike, and that helped her set aside her internal turmoil and simply go with the upward shift of her mood. Because Davie knew it didn't matter in what order backpackers did a section hike or a thru-hike of the Appalachian Trail, and because she thought Connecticut would be an easier way to start than Vermont, she decided to hike north from the New York-Connecticut line. Connecticut contained 50.1 miles of the Appalachian Trail, running between the lower Hudson Valley into a region of the state known as the Northwest Hills, at the Massachusetts state line. Davie knew that region all too well from her long wait in Salisbury, Connecticut, while rescuers searched for the wreckage of her parents' plane, then got her parents' bodies out of the remote crash site in the Massachusetts forest. How the Appalachian Trail Conservancy could so precisely know that the trail included an extra tenth of a mile in Connecticut escaped Davie.

Ethan was true to his word to be her shuttle driver on this adventure. For this first hike, Davie left her car on Schaghticoke Road in the town of Kent, and Ethan met her and drove her south to her starting point. She was only going ten and a half miles in two days, which she knew full well that Ethan would have knocked off in less than a morning's hike, but she saw no reason to push herself. She planned overnight sections between June and Columbus Day weekend, and she thought if she finished Connecticut this first summer, she would have accomplished quite a bit.

"Good luck," Ethan said as she stood up from the Volvo's back seat and cinched her backpack tighter. "Don't forget your poles." He reached into the back of the car and picked them up from the floor.

"Someday I'm going to really forget them, and then I will never do it again," Davie said. "That was Andrea's mantra about forgetting something you needed: 'You do it once, you never do it again.' OK, wish me luck!"

Ethan gave her the long, hard hug and the quick, friendly kiss that she expected.

"I do wish you luck. You will do great. You'll let me know when you are off the trail?"

"Of course I will," Davie said. "Don't worry. I know what I'm doing by now, but yes, I will send you a message. And . . . I'll see you soon?"

"Yes, you will."

Having finished the windows, Ethan planned to next tackle the rotting boards in the front stoop of her house. If he could replace only the boards that appeared deteriorated without tearing apart the whole stoop, he could get that done in one weekend. He always showed up with all the tools and materials he needed, and Davie stopped asking him if she could pay him. He seemed to want to do this, she realized, and she also knew by now that Ethan's income was considerably higher than hers was ever likely to be, ever again. So, she just let him do the work, and she planned to lavish her excellent cooking on him on the nights they did not go out for dinner.

The projects on the house seemed likely to become an easy routine, every couple of weekends. The weekend that Ethan came to get the third window out of her house, they again ran into someone Davie knew while they were out for dinner. It would be no time at all before word got around that she was steadily dating someone, Davie realized. Davie never introduced Ethan as her friend; she just introduced him without assigning him a label.

Now, working on the first mile of what Davie thought of as a momentous project, she was glad for the early summer day and the feeling of solitude. Andrea once told her that one of the benefits of backpacking was you would see places and artifacts you would never have seen any other way, sights that were not accessible from a road. The trail held many such places hidden from everyday view: remnants of nineteenth century settlements originally built on cleared land and now deep in the forest, tiny cemeteries with no carving on the crude stone markers, stone walls, stone foundations of homes and root cellars where the buildings were long disintegrated, natural scenes you would never forget—rivers, overlooks, glades, and meadows at the summits of mountains.

Anyone could hike the short distance from the nearest road crossing to the convergence of the Ten Mile River and the Housatonic River, which Davie came upon a few miles into her hike, but she grew up fairly close to this area and she was only seeing this astonishing sight now, for the first time. She supposed there were other such junctions of rivers around the country, but it was a novelty to stand on the footbridge at the merger and see the swiftly moving current as the two rivers rushed together and the current churned and then straightened itself out and poured on downstream.

She got to the side trail that led to the Schaghticoke Mountain Campsite a little before six o'clock, with plenty of daylight left to set up her tent. The side trail went uphill along a wide stream that rushed over rocks and really looked more like a small river than a stream. Large boulders at the base of the stream in a calmer section formed a natural footbridge she would use to cross the water in the morning. This campsite was the most remote, primitive place she had ever stayed on the Appalachian Trail, even more than any place she had been with Andrea. Shenandoah National Park didn't hold such a wild, lonely feeling, nor did the hut in the White Mountains, which, for all its far more remote location, offered many conveniences and contained many people. The Schaghticoke Mountain campsite was so isolated that it could have felt spooky, but just felt . . . special, Davie thought. That was the word. She was a bit surprised at her lack of fear at being in this place all by herself. She felt fine.

Her hike to her car the next morning was uneventful until Davie got down to a road near her parking place. She had to walk along the road a short distance. As she walked, she heard a car coming toward her, but she didn't pay it much attention until it came into sight and she saw that it held a group of young men, visible through the open windows. The car slowed as it passed, and Davie thought for a moment that she might have to think fast. She was on the road alone. There was no place to go if she was about to be the object of attention she really did not want and felt ill-prepared to face. As she watched, the car turned in at a small pull-off, backed out, came back toward her—then passed her, roaring up the road and kicking up a cloud of dust from the dirt surface. OK, Davie thought, her heart pounding, sometimes people are just turning around, but she also realized that she felt safer in that isolated campsite the night before than she did just now.

She got back to her car and pulled out her phone and sent Ethan a text message.

"I'm at my car, and I had a great hike. Thank you for catching my message. Talk to you soon."

When Ethan called her that night to ask how her first section went, she told him about the car and her momentary worry. When he arrived at her house the following weekend to start working on her stoop, he handed her something in a leather case with a snap closure.

"This is for you. Put it on the loop of your hip belt," he said. She opened what she now saw was a knife in a sheath, a fixed-blade knife with a handle made from what she guessed was antler, and a blade that looked about five inches long.

"This looks pretty serious," Davie said. "You want me to have this? This looks old, like it's something you've had for a long time. I guess you think I need an upgrade from the pocketknife?"

"Yes, I do, and I want you to carry this," he said. "I carried it on my thru-hike."

As a present from an uncertain not-quite-suitor went, this was a most unusual gift, Davie thought. She thanked him and attached the knife to the hip belt of her backpack through a little tab on the back of the sheath. It wasn't jewelry, and it was not exactly a romantic gesture, but it was a gift that spoke volumes about Ethan's confidence in her ability to take care of herself. Many men might have wondered if this section hike was even a safe thing to do, Davie realized, but Ethan just thought she needed this added level of protection. Would she ever entirely figure out Ethan's sometimes difficult but always surprising mind, Davie wondered? After all this time, she still didn't feel that she knew him at all well.

chapter 16

Davie stuck to her schedule for the summer. Ethan still came out to see her and to work on the house one or two weekends a month. She knocked off one section of her Connecticut hike after another, including the extremely difficult St. Johns Ledges, a surprise if there ever was one in an otherwise unassuming state. She didn't pay much attention to the casual mention in the Appalachian Trail guidebook that rock climbers used this area for training, and then she found herself standing at the top of a steeply pitched boulder wall, with none of the boulders spaced far enough so that she could step in between them. She would have to climb down, she realized; she didn't dare try to go from one boulder to another standing upright. Maybe a more experienced backpacker would feel more confident, but this looked to her like a great place to break an ankle. She worked her map out of her hip-belt pocket and found the place on the elevation grid. The descent of the boulder wall was at least five hundred feet down to a long, level stretch of the trail that ran along the Housatonic River and looked like you could play soccer on it.

She remained amazed at the varied features the trail contained—gently rolling meadows one day and then a boulder wall the next. She reminded herself that if she thought this was difficult, she would never get through New Hampshire. She wondered at Andrea's entirely self-effacing accomplishments in her section hike, when Andrea did the most difficult parts of the trail first in Maine and New Hampshire as a south-bound hiker, and never boasted about them. Davie very clearly remembered asking Andrea many times, when Andrea was back from one of her then-mysterious two-week Appalachian Trail trips, *How was your hike?* Andrea always simply replied that it was great, she'd had a lot of fun.

Well then, my friend, you probably would have just blown through this, Davie thought, and if you found it as tough as I think I'm about to, you would never have admitted that.

Davie shrugged her pack back on, studied the way down one more time, then started the descent. It took her an hour, while a few other backpackers went by her at a much faster pace, but Davie ignored them and stayed in a zone of concentration, as though this was one big water crossing with the current tugging her ankles over the rocks. She barely stood upright, she just moved from one boulder to the next, carefully easing herself over the edges. When she got to the bottom and allowed herself to take a sweeping look back up at the wall, she felt very good.

Davie turned forty-five in late August. She didn't tell Ethan the date, and she realized she did not know his birthday. She said nothing to him about her birthday being the next day, Sunday, when they went out for dinner in Albany that weekend. She didn't have any particular plans for marking the rapidly approaching anniversary of Michael's death, partly because of her backpacking schedule and all the work that Ethan was trying to do on the house for her before the fall, and partly because she felt very uncertain, still, about what she was doing in her personal life. Her professional life was fine. Her job was going extremely well, and she had just gotten a promotion and a huge raise. Davie now supervised an intern and a staff member newly hired to help with Davie's workload. That new staff member, just a few years out of graduate school, took on Davie's less-complex projects. This change freed up Davie to do long, in-depth analyses and reports that she found fascinating. She saw Dr. Tremblay once a month now, with a very tentative plan to continue until early in the new year.

The Friday night of her birthday weekend, she dreamt about Michael. She realized that was hardly a coincidence, with her birthday and the anniversary of his death so near, but it was the first time she dreamed about him since the night before her drive home from the Cape after he died. It was, as dreams often are, a bizarre mix of reality and fantasy, but it was just real enough to make her stay in bed for a little while when she awoke at daybreak, remembering the details. Ethan would be on his way soon; he would arrive around eleven o'clock that morning.

Instead of getting up and taking care of last night's dishes in the sink, Davie thought over the dream, which started with a real incident involving her irreverent husband. Michael often masked deep affection behind a lot of teasing, and the dream started with the night before her birthday probably three or four years earlier. How did she ever remember this, Davie wondered as she lay in bed. The dream was based on such an inconsequential memory. In real life, Michael stood in the kitchen as he scanned the wall calendar with a pen in one hand, circling upcoming dates they wanted to note. Then he looked at Davie across the room and said, "You have a birthday coming up. Gosh, you're getting old." He actually said that, in his affectionately annoying way, and she flung a pillow at him in response. She then got up and crossed the room to put her arms around him. They walked to the SOC, holding each other, and then they lay down on the SOC and stretched out, and she remembered how Michael slipped his hand down her jeans to very gently caress her lower back and then moved it under her panties.

That was the part of the dream that actually happened. But then in the dream, Davie thought, "I'm not going to tell him that he's not going to get old." She woke up at that point, and found herself remembering the vivid detail, the sense of her husband, and the longing the dream pulled up in her that she could still feel.

☙

Davie came to her last hike of her summer schedule. She planned this final section for Columbus Day weekend, so that she could do seventeen miles in three days and cross into Massachusetts. There was no road that hooked directly into the Appalachian Trail at the state line, where the trail crossed from the Northwest Hills of Connecticut into the southern Berkshire Mountains—or at least none that she could figure out how to easily access—so she would need to go at least go six miles into Massachusetts to the first possible parking area to leave her car. That particular parking place was also on a truly remote road, and after talking it over with Ethan, Davie decided to leave her car at the next parking area north and meet Ethan there. That would add four miles to her hike, but it would be a lot easier to get to by car, and easier to get out of on her way home, especially if it was late in the day. She did not want to risk rambling around on poorly marked dirt roads at dusk.

So she studied her map and decided she would do almost seven miles the first day. Ethan would drop her off in Salisbury, Connecticut, and she would cross over Bear Mountain on the state line and camp at Sages Ravine just into Massachusetts. Sages Ravine was supposed to be especially beautiful, with a fast-moving stream and a tenting area that stretched back into the forest. It was also just east of the steeply sloped, almost impenetrable forest where her parents' plane crashed. Davie could not help but

248

remember her 28-year-old self, when she waited through those long days in Salisbury for what she knew would be a terrible outcome once the state police showed her a map of the search area. It was inconceivable that this remote area would twice end up figuring so importantly in her life. The day she watched the ambulances carrying her parents' bodies finally arrive in Salisbury, she thought she could not get away from the town fast enough, and she certainly never expected to return.

After Sages Ravine, she would go as far as she could on the second day, with the knowledge that she would have two choices for that second day. There were two shelters about a quarter-mile apart on that second stretch, and she was confident she could reach the first one, at least. It was an odd quirk of the Appalachian Trail that there would be two shelters so close together and then stretches with no shelters or campsites for ten or more miles.

"You have some extra layers in there, I presume?" Ethan asked as he turned her backpack so that she could get the shoulder straps on from the edge of the Volvo seat.

"I am, if anything, overpacked," Davie said. She stood up and put her arms around him, thinking, as she always did, that if such a thing as a chastity belt ever really existed, it must have evolved into the sixty-liter backpack. She remembered reading that if a backpacker was ever attacked by a grizzly bear—something Davie didn't have to worry about, unless she hiked in the West—that the person should keep their backpack on and try to stay face down, because the backpack would make it more difficult for the bear to maul them. Davie found this entirely believable; her backpack seemed so well constructed, so durable, that she thought she could drop it from a thousand-foot ledge and the clips that held the top flap in place wouldn't spring open. Ethan, however, got his hands under the pack and held her to him and kissed her, as he always did, and then stepped back.

"So, your last section," he said. "You should be very proud of yourself. This is quite an accomplishment. Let me know when you are off the trail, OK?"

"Of course," Davie said. "You're my best message catcher."

"I think I have been your only message catcher," Ethan said, with that serious expression that somehow conveyed a smile—the expression she noticed right from the beginning.

Actually, Andrea was her first message catcher, Davie thought, but to say that would have been demeaning when Ethan was clearly so happy to help her. He just didn't remember that it was Andrea who caught her off-the-trail message on that first solo hike Davie did more than a year ago over Mount Greylock, to mark the first anniversary of Michael's death. And now Andrea was dead eight months.

Davie got to Sages Ravine in good time, even allowing for the steep but manageable descent down the north side of Bear Mountain. She lowered her pack in a few places on a strap she now carried for just this purpose, ever since the St. Johns Ledges, and she took her time. The campsite was empty, the seasonal caretaker long gone by now until next year, but Davie was completely comfortable camping by herself.

The air was sharply colder the next morning. The tree canopy was still thick, even with the leaves starting to fall, and Davie couldn't see the sky clearly, but the swirling breeze and lower temperature hinted at a storm brewing. She checked the weather forecast on her phone and was a little startled to see that the temperature might drop another ten degrees by afternoon, and that it would very likely start to rain then, also. She knew that forecasts swiveled in both directions, and she was not concerned about hiking in rain, but she faced two fairly steep climbs. She felt a little nagging worry about the combination of rain and the dropping temperature, but she also could see no choice but to try to get to the first shelter.

The rain started two hours later as she approached Race Mountain. She dug out her rain gear, pulled the rain pants on right over her boots, and kept going. Hiking in rain was part of backpacking. The climb up was not too difficult, but the descent was much steeper—much steeper in real life than it looked on the map, as she now knew to expect. The trail dropped about five hundred feet in a little more than a mile, which didn't sound too bad, but the wet trail slowed her pace. Then the rain started to freeze on the rocks.

Davie stopped again and pulled out her map. There was a campsite a half-mile east of the trail at the bottom of this descent. If she stayed on the trail and continued north, she would soon come to a steep climb of at least seven hundred feet, much of it on exposed rock. She didn't have her boot spikes, because they were heavy to carry and she never, ever expected to need them in mid-October. Where the hell did this storm come from, she wondered. Always, on the morning she left for a backpacking trip, she checked the weather forecast. She also realized she was hiking through a very unpredictable weather belt, and that less than two miles to the east, along Route 41, it might be a lot warmer and just raining. Well, Davie thought, she was here, not two miles east, and it seemed way too dangerous to try to do the next climb in what was shaping up to be an ice storm. If she slipped and got injured, she would be very exposed.

So she finished her descent, found the sign for the side trail to the campsite, and made her way carefully down to the tenting area. That half-mile hike seemed to take forever, even though she was no longer on rock. The bear box was at the entrance to the campsite—Davie noted the location for later reference—then she saw a tent platform about a hundred feet farther into the clearing. She pitched her tent on the wet wooden platform, threw the rain cover over the tent and clipped the cover into place.

Chilled and damp despite her rain gear, Davie realized she needed to eat something. Without the protective overhang of a shelter, she had no option but to eat in the cramped space of the tent vestibule, the area created by pulling the extension of the tent's rain cover taut and staking it into the ground just beyond the edge of the platform to create a small enclosed sitting area just outside of the tent's zippered door. Eating so close to her tent—practically inside of it—went against everything she knew about bear precautions, but she had no other choice. The bears were probably all denned up, nice and cozy and oblivious to the scent of her food at the entrance to her tent. Hell, they probably were more comfortable than she would be tonight. She tried not to think about a hot bath and the down quilt on her bed at home.

How many times did Andrea and Ethan get caught in situations like this, Davie mused. Probably so many times they would have considered it routine, but Davie worried how she would get anywhere the next day if the trail was covered in ice. The closest road likely to have any traffic was Route 41, at the base of the side trail she took to the campsite, but getting the rest of the way down to the road could take her a long time. The idea of hitchhiking back to her car, even if she got that far and felt safe accepting a ride from someone, did not appeal to her. She might reach her car and still be stuck if the storm continued, afraid to drive home on back roads and secondary state routes that could be all but impassable. Besides, if the storm went into tomorrow, there would be almost no traffic on Route 41 and therefore very little chance of hitching to her car or anywhere else. So now she faced a situation she always knew was possible: she was alone, the weather was dangerous and she did not know how she would get off the trail.

The rain struck the trees now with a clattering sound, and Davie wondered how much she had to worry about trees coming down around her.

She didn't have any large limbs hanging directly overhead, but she couldn't imagine what kind of advance notice she'd get if any of the nearby large trees started to uproot and keel over while she was asleep.

Her food bag contained enough snacks to pass for a meal: crackers, potato chips, trail mix, a chocolate bar, dried apple slices and cheese. Quite a tribute to Andrea's advice to always carry something that didn't need cooking, Davie thought with a smile and a little shake of her head—advice Davie never imagined she would put to use when Andrea first taught her about backpacking some eighteen months ago.

"I wish you were here now, so I'd have someone who knew what they were doing." Davie spoke aloud to her dead friend, surprising herself but also glad to hear a voice, even if it was her own. She felt a little less alone after that.

Sitting at the edge of the wooden tent platform on her foam sleeping pad, hunched over in the scant shelter of the vestibule as she ate, Davie considered making a hot drink but realized all she wanted was to crawl into her sleeping bag. Wearing her headlamp, she inched her way back to the bear box in the rapidly falling dusk, feeling with every step that her feet were about to go out from under her, even with her hiking poles for support. A half-inch metal point on the end of each pole was not enough for secure footing, and her unsteady progress just reinforced her worry about the next morning. She was safe enough for now; it was getting out altogether that seemed her biggest problem. She hated to call Ethan, because she was afraid that he would feel compelled to come get her, but she was in enough of a predicament that calling Ethan suddenly sounded like a wonderful idea. So she took her phone out, with no idea if she would have any service, and found a text message from Ethan.

Where R U now? she read.

Race Brook Falls Campsite, she wrote back. *In tent, safe, not cold, but iced in. No spikes, trail solid ice.*

He must have been watching for her response, because seconds later she read his reply.

R U OK there 2nite? The abbreviated text language was so unlike Ethan that had the situation been any less worrisome, Davie would have cracked up laughing.

Yes.

Stay there. I'll leave 1st lite come get U. Storm may last 36 hrs. Trees down. Can't go north. Solid ice. Side trail only way out. Will come 4 U. Stay warm. U not just saying OK? U R OK?

Yes. Not under tree. Plenty food water. She didn't even try to persuade him not to drive in the morning; she knew that his mind was made up and he would be there even if she insisted that he not do this. Well, Davie thought, if he was ever going to tell her that he loved her, now might be a good time.

She then read: *OK. Stay safe. Night.*

She wrote back: *Night. Thank you. I love you.*

The clattering sound went on all night. Davie slept fitfully, but she was warm in her sleeping bag. She turned her phone off and put it into her sleeping bag to keep it warm and conserve the battery. She never took off any of her clothing, just her boots. Daybreak was indeterminate, the dark just gradually faded. She pulled her tent apart, cracked off the coating of ice, shook it hard and didn't even try to put it back into the stuff sack; she just bunched up the tent and the ground cloth and pushed everything down into her backpack. She thought she could get down the trail a short distance and make Ethan's hike up the slope briefer. The ground was almost too slippery to even move; well, she would take it easy. She turned her phone back on, plugged it into her external battery, and saw a message from Ethan come up on the screen.

Almost there. C U soon.

It was six-thirty. He must have left around three-thirty in the morning, she calculated, because his place was probably close to two hours away, and much longer in these conditions on the mostly secondary roads. She felt overwhelming relief, coupled with a sense of gratitude that he would do this for her. She thought that she should at least try to get as far down the trail as possible, but without any way to grip the ice, she fell once and nearly fell a second time. It would do Ethan no good if she hurt herself and couldn't walk out, she realized, but she wondered how he was going to get her down the trail unless he could maintain a good hold on her arm. He would have boot spikes on, but that wouldn't do much good if she could barely move.

Davie sat on an ice-coated log and decided to wait, but she also realized she couldn't sit like that for long because she would get very cold. It was still raining, not as heavily as last night, more a freezing mist than a freezing rain. Maybe she should have stayed in her tent, but it was not her nature to sit and wait for rescue. She wore every extra piece of clothing she carried in her pack. Most backpackers, she knew, counted on two situations to stay warm in weather like this: hiking, which warmed you up faster than sitting in a sauna, as long as you could move at a brisk pace; or being nicely tucked into a down sleeping bag in the small, cozy interior of your tent. No one just sat as she was doing now, unless they were about to have a hot drink and dinner and then retreat into the warmth of their sleeping bag.

She thought that she should perhaps put her tent back together, but that seemed like more work than she had the energy for at the moment. She checked her phone again; no more messages. OK, Davie thought: What to do now? She never used her stove the night before; she didn't want to sit outside of her tent long enough to heat water. But she could do that now, if she could just get a little more motivated. The thought occurred to her that Ethan might be trying to get his truck out of a ditch, despite his earlier message that he was well on his way. And he might not be able to call or even text her; cell reception skipped in and out all through the area.

What would Andrea do in a situation like this? Well, Davie thought, she most definitely would not sit still and get even colder. Davie stood up, dug out a Snickers Bar, bit off a mouthful, unzipped her pack and pulled out the crumpled tent and ground cloth. She spread out the ground cloth, hoping she had enough coordination between her brain and her hands to assemble the tent. She desperately needed the warmth of her sleeping bag. She was just starting to connect the sections of the two poles that formed the tent frame when she heard a sound on the trail below her, and then Ethan came into view. He was using hiking poles, which she knew most guys hated for some reason she never understood. Probably because men felt an unrecognized desire to look rugged and not hike like a girl, and most women used them.

Ethan reached her, leaned his hiking poles against the log and held her to him, rubbing her back briskly. That felt good; Davie was beginning to get very cold.

"Why are you not in your tent waiting for me?" he asked.

"Well, I thought if you were nice enough to come out in this to fetch me, the least I could do would be to try to meet you halfway. As I now realize, that wasn't a great idea, and I was about to put my tent back together."

"We have to get you out of here," Ethan said. "You look way too cold." He looked worried. He wore a daypack, which he set down and unzipped to pull out a pair of boot spikes and a fleece warmup jacket. He helped her put the jacket on, and then had her sit down again on the log, with her wadded-up ground cloth as a makeshift seat cushion on the ice-coated surface.

"Like most backpackers, I have duplicates of a lot of gear," Ethan said, holding up the spikes. "Let me put these on your boots for you. These should be close enough to fitting your boots, and if they aren't, I'll jerry-rig them so they stay on. Then why don't you put my pack on, and I'll wear yours."

Davie was glad he put the boot spikes on for her, because her hands were so cold she didn't think she could manage on her own. Her gloves were wet and her fingers were numb, but she knew they would feel better once she started moving. She stood up once Ethan finished, and found that she could walk. The spikes were like little serrated knife blades that fit over the boot sole on a stretchy rubberized web. You just pulled the webs onto the bottom of the boots so they snapped tightly into place and came up over the heel and toe.

She also knew that sitting for so long was really dangerous, that hypothermia could creep up on you, so that by the time you realized you were in trouble, you were also impaired enough to make it all that more difficult to do anything about it. That probably started to happen to her around the time she thought about making a hot drink but then decided it was too much effort, Davie realized. She doubted she would have finished putting up her tent if Ethan hadn't arrived when he did. This was how people died, she knew—very subtly and also very quickly, without any panic and also with plenty of inertia. She would never again get herself into a situation where she couldn't either keep moving or stay warm if she could not move. She could hear Andrea saying, "You do that once, you never do it again."

Ethan let out the shoulder straps on her pack, swung it on easily and clipped the hip belt. He pulled a wool balaclava out of his inner jacket pocket before he clipped the chest strap, and helped her put it on under her hat so that more of her face was covered. He asked her to hold out her hands so that he could pull off her gloves, and then he replaced her wet, cold gloves with an extra pair of gloves he pulled out of another pocket in his jacket. They were warm from being in his jacket and felt wonderful.

"Let's get going," he said.

They hiked a mile and a quarter back to his truck. The trail was dirt and leaves, not bare rock, and also not very steep, but it was heavily coated with ice. Their trek down the trail took them ninety minutes. Davie knew that Ethan was worried about how cold she was. She felt warmer now, but he made her stop once to drink some water and eat a peanut butter sandwich he pulled out of his pack. He also carried extra socks and a dry rain jacket stuffed into the daypack.

"You really came prepared," she said as they started hiking again.

"I was very worried about you," he said. "I appreciate that you were trying to help me by trying to hike out of there, but I never thought you would do that. That is how people become hypothermic."

"Note to self: If you're hiking between October and May, take your spikes, even if you don't want to carry the weight," Davie said. She hoped he wouldn't lecture her any further about all her mistakes of the last eighteen hours.

"I am taking you back to my place," he said when they got into his truck and he got the heat going. "Even if I thought you were well enough to drive home by yourself right now, which you are not, you'd never make it on these roads. I would never let you do that. Don't worry about your car. It's fine where it is. I've got studded snow tires, and my truck is a lot heavier than your car. I'll get you back to your car tomorrow."

"OK. Thank you," she said. She was ready for someone to take care of her, and she also doubted that she could have gotten back to Albany. She was beginning to feel sleepy in the warmth of the truck cab. "What are you going to do if there's a downed tree in the road?"

"I have a chainsaw. It's on the floor behind your seat."

Davie thought he was joking. Then she realized, of course he would have a chainsaw if he harvested his own wood on his property. She wanted to say that she was really glad this wasn't their first date, because she would have gotten out of his truck at the word "chainsaw," but she wasn't sure Ethan considered anything they had ever done together a date, including their dinner in Williamstown. Ethan also did not respond well to humor when he was stressed, she knew; actually, he didn't respond much to humor at any time. Davie realized she couldn't ever remember him laughing, nor could she remember him ever making her laugh. Despite her exhaustion, all of this zipped through her mind in a moment, in the same way she did rapid mathematical calculations in her head.

"You brought a chainsaw?" she asked. "Oh, my gosh, Ethan, you certainly thought of everything."

"I also thought to bring some tow lines in case I had to haul a tree trunk out of the road after I cut it up," he said. "Yes, I thought of everything."

Ethan didn't look at her as he talked; he concentrated on his driving.

"I was very worried about you," he said. That was second time this morning he said that, she thought, as she started to fall asleep. He didn't say anything about her message in which she told him she loved him, and she wondered if that just went right past him in his worry about trying to reach her, and then his relief at knowing she was in a safe situation for the night.

She drifted to sleep and didn't awaken until Ethan pulled up in front of his house, at the end of a long, rough dirt road. It was an old logging road, he told her. The property was heavily logged in the 1800s, so that much of the regrowth matured decades ago, and many of those trees were in advanced old age now. He got her into the house, a large open room on the main floor with a wood stove and fireplace below a loft bedroom reached not by stairs but by a library ladder on casters. He lit a fire and added wood to the stove, then went up the ladder to the bedroom while she sat on a bench by the door and took off her boots. Everything took Davie longer to do than usual. She hung her rain jacket on a peg, and saw Ethan come back down the ladder with an armful of clothing.

"Here you are," he said, handing her a pair of merino leggings, thick rag wool socks, a merino T-shirt and a flannel shirt. "You can use the bedroom that way to get out of your hiking clothes"—he pointed to a hall—"and I will fix you something to eat."

He made her coffee, and reached under the counter and held up a bottle of brandy, asking by the gesture if she wanted a shot in her coffee. When she nodded, he poured some into the mug.

"I know you are not supposed to drink alcohol when you've been nearly hypothermic, but I think you are recovered enough that this might make you feel great," he said, handing her the mug.

"I have never seen anyone but my parents ever do that," Davie said, after she took a sip. "This is just what I needed. My parents used to drink coffee with brandy in it when they came in from the outdoors at their place in the Adirondacks in the winter."

"Do you still own that property?" Ethan asked.

Davie shook her head.

"Long gone. I sold that and the apartment on Riverside Drive fifteen years ago, after their rather complex estate was settled. My parents set up a trust fund for me, and they had multiple investments, so it took a while. I never thought I'd go back to New York City to live, and that apartment was beautiful but huge." She shook her head, briefly laughing. "Of course, I have ended up right back in the same situation. Owner of an oversized piece of real estate because of an untimely death. And if I'd known I was going to be on my own and earning half of what I used to, I wouldn't have locked up the money from those sales into the trust fund."

Ethan made them a cheese omelette with home fries and toast. It was just past noon, the freezing rain had stopped but everything outside was coated with ice. The maple table at which they ate was a spare design with a high polish. The table was one of his early efforts, Ethan told her, as was much of the furniture in the house.

"Thank you for this," Davie said between bites. She was famished and the hot food made her sleepy again. "I suppose I made some mistakes, and I obviously would not have gone out if I'd known this storm was coming, but it came out of nowhere."

"It wasn't predicted," Ethan said. "People forget that as exact as weather forecasting seems to be, you can still get surprised. That's happened to me. You did the best you could. You had all the gear that any prudent person would have taken this time of year. I wouldn't have taken my spikes on this trip, either. You got stuck in a bad situation, and you got yourself to a safe place and waited for help. You could not possibly have gone back the way you came to get back to a major road crossing. There was nothing between you and Salisbury if you'd tried to go back, and that was miles back in the opposite direction. You could never have gone up Bear Mountain in this. You got yourself to a place where there was a side trail, so that I could get to you. That was the right thing to do. The only thing I would have done differently would have been to have stayed in your tent, and I sure do understand that you thought you could cut off a little bit of my hike up from the truck."

"And if there hadn't been a side trail there?" Davie asked.

"I would have gotten to you anyway," Ethan said.

"Well, I am very glad I didn't try to summon search and rescue," Davie said. "I am not sure they would have been as kindly in their evaluation of my decisions."

"You didn't need search and rescue," Ethan said. The unspoken follow-up was a silent exchange as they looked at each other across the table: *You just needed me,* she saw in his expression, and her own coda, also unspoken, crossed with his: *I just needed you.*

✍

Twenty-four hours later Davie was home, having spent the previous night in Ethan's bed, with Ethan asleep in the guest bed downstairs. She remembered lying in his bed, burying her face into his pillow and breathing in his familiar scent. This was unfathomable, Davie thought as she lay there—this unusual, solitary and yet deeply caring man to whom she was so attracted was nearby, yet completely unapproachable. No one she knew would have believed they slept separately in his home that night, especially after the events of the day. Davie held absolutely no illusion about what Ethan's response would be if she slipped out of bed, went downstairs and asked if she could get into bed with him. He would be very polite, but the answer would be no. She thought the physical closeness, the warmth of his body next to hers, would matter more to her than passion.

Yet he seemed oblivious to Davie's feelings—feelings she was sure must have been obvious even before she wrote the message to him that she loved him. He was not Michael; there was no comparison, but she did not expect him to be Michael. Michael was dead, and right now he felt very far away to Davie. She faced many decades yet to go in this life, which she was living—with all its complications and confusion—because her husband got her to emergency medical help in time. Regarding Ethan, Davie wondered what Michael would have told her to do, as an imaginary and completely dispassionate observer of the quandary in which she now found herself. Davie thought that Michael would tell her to cut her losses and run.

Ethan was intelligent and interesting, she loved talking to him and she felt both extremely comfortable and extremely safe around him. She also thought that her unrequited feelings for him eventually would lead to a discussion she really didn't want to have. That discussion might not even be necessary, because Ethan always spelled out what he wanted without ever putting his intentions into words. He wanted friendship. She now felt that the moment he finished kissing her in the car at the trail head that morning back in April, he regretted it, although she never understood that at the time. She did understand that now, six months later with not the slightest indication of physical desire on his part. She was no longer trying to figure out the situation. She didn't know what she wanted to do, but she thought if she did nothing, her relationship with Ethan would continue just as it was.

You are expecting him to be something he either cannot be, or doesn't want to be, she thought. If she never opened this discussion with him, she would very likely have a loyal, special friend for as far into the future as she could see. Whether that would be enough for her, and what she would do if she met a man who responded differently to her, to whom she might feel attracted, she couldn't tell right now. She didn't see how she could have Ethan in her life as a friend, as a man she loved, and someone else in her life as a partner.

Ethan possessed a good heart, a true heart. He did not have a passionate heart, or at least not as far as she was concerned. Michael was passionate, and Davie knew that beneath her mathematical, analytical exterior, so was she.

None of these thoughts showed the next morning when Ethan drove her back to her car on roads that were now just wet, no longer icy. He helped her get her gear out of his truck, handed over her hiking poles—she would as usual have forgotten them—and hoisted her pack into the back seat of her Subaru. Then he turned and held out his arms to her. Davie let him wrap his arms around her, but when she lifted her face to kiss him, he hesitated for a second before quickly kissing her. OK, she thought, so he did indeed read that text message, and now he would deal with it by not dealing with it. The question was whether she could do the same, but there was no way to address that standing here, on an isolated back road, with both of them needing to get back to their own lives at home.

"I will see you soon," he said. Then they went their separate ways.

Davie did not expect to see Ethan at Christmas or New Year's. He was in New Mexico visiting longtime friends from high school. Instead, her sister-in-law Moira O'Connor in Boston, who as the oldest Devlin sister was in charge of the clan's plans and parties, invited her to spend Christmas with Michael's family. Davie was quite surprised. She did not think her in-laws had ever invited Michael and her to Boston . . . oh, yes, maybe once, she remembered, but so long ago she barely recalled the reason . . . perhaps a graduation party? They went to Boston many times during their courtship and marriage, but they were never invited to family gatherings or to stay at anyone's home in Michael's family. If they saw any of the other Devlins on those trips, it was always a hastily arranged get-together at a pub or a youth soccer game for one of the nieces or nephews in Michael's old neighborhood of Brighton.

Davie never really minded this, because Michael's family was a sprawling group of people with children and grandchildren and nieces and nephews all clustered in one fairly contained part of Boston. Davie reasonably assumed that Michael's siblings could barely remember what day of the week it was, their lives were so busy and so crowded with other Devlins. It was unrealistic to expect them to be in steady contact with their much-younger brother and his wife—whom they didn't really know—who lived in Albany, a city they never visited.

A friendly if not frequent correspondence by email defined her relationship with the Devlin clan, but Davie hadn't seen any of Michael's relatives since they pulled away from the curb in front of her house after the memorial service more than two years earlier. Even so, she decided to accept this invitation.

The Mass Pike contained almost no traffic on the drive to Boston the morning of Christmas Eve. For her hosts, Davie packed a bottle of very good bourbon from an Upstate New York distillery and a second bottle of wine from the Finger Lakes region. From the Italian market on Delaware Avenue, she brought a bright-red tin of paper-wrapped amaretti cookies and a panettone. For the assorted nieces and nephews, who ranged in age from three to thirty, she bought books. On this point of gift-giving, Davie was old-fashioned; she refused to give cash or gift cards to recipients whose taste in clothing or music she did not know. Instead, she gave books, and based on her success with the children of friends, she was confident about her selections.

The Devlin gathering was the kind of loud, long and raucous family Christmas that Davie last knew in childhood and young adulthood, when her parents hosted a steady stream of their interesting, often-famous friends at their Riverside Drive home. Those celebrations started on Christmas Eve and extended through the week, up to New Year's Day. The visitors were authors, artists and activists; judges and politicians and renowned defense attorneys whose names were taught in history classes. The conversations were intense, sometimes heated and always inspirational, fueled by generous amounts of smoked salmon, caviar and the excellent single-malt scotch Davie's father so loved.

For the Devlin celebration, Michael's family opened their home to friends of their late parents; the people who grew up with them in their cul-de-sac in Brighton; and the families on the short, narrow side street in Dorchester where Moira and her husband, Rob, lived. The beverage of choice was a local India pale ale; the snacks were chips and crackers and WisPride port wine cheese spread. The collective siblings, adult children and grandchildren piled into the enormous old three-story house and Davie never did get everyone's name, but it never seemed to matter. Michael's family took her into this warm, noisy atmosphere as one of their own, a part of the clan by virtue of having married Michael, and she had a wonderful time—far better than she expected to have.

In conversation, she glossed over the difficulties of the past two years and talked about her job, backpacking and looking for whip-poor-wills. These activities were as foreign to Michael's family as if she described collecting rocks on the surface of the moon.

She did not mention Ethan, because she didn't feel like trying to explain that part of her widowhood. Her in-laws saw that she still wore her wedding ring, but they were not intrusive people. Nor did she tell the Devlins that her best friend died less than eighteen months after Michael. The holiday gathering did not lend itself to that kind of deeply personal revelation, when conversations abruptly ended because the other party needed to settle a squabble between two toddlers across the room.

She certainly did not mention hallucinations, being assaulted by her hairstylist or getting fired for telling her boss to go fuck herself. Although, Davie realized, these educated, intelligent, no-nonsense Irish-American lapsed Catholics would likely have understood that part of her narrative, given that more than a few of their ancestors headed for the United States after having done something similar with the British authorities in their homeland. On the drive back to Albany the day after Christmas, she thought Michael would have told her she acquitted herself well.

In late January, Davie met with Dr. Tremblay for the last time. Davie felt ready to navigate life without the help of a therapist, and she knew she could go back for a tune-up, should she need one. She never mentioned Ethan in this final conversation. She would be seeing him soon, when he came to Albany to start helping her again with some of the projects on her house. They were in regular contact, with no discussion of any deeply personal topics. Davie still felt that she was in suspended animation on the situation with Ethan, with no clearer idea of what turn it might take, no less uncertainty, than she felt the last time she saw him, standing on a back road in Connecticut in the aftermath of the October ice storm.

Instead, she talked about Michael.

"I have had only three dreams about him, and I never saw his face in any of them," she said. "He is in my mind every day, even if I'm not directly thinking about him. I don't know why I have never seen his face. This bothers me."

"You will see him when you are ready," the therapist said.

Davie looked out the window at the back of the room, which she could see from the couch where she sat. She saw just sky in the general direction of the Hudson River.

"You know, I still have a hard time believing that Michael is gone, that I will never see him again," she said. She might have been talking to herself; this was a thought she had carried for a very long time and always felt was just below the surface of her everyday emotions.

"I mean, I know Michael is dead, I'm certainly not denying that or thinking this has all been one prolonged nightmare. But I still yearn to see him so badly that it's a physical longing. You know, the other day I pulled out the one old T-shirt of his that I still have and just buried my face into it. I can't even tell if it has his scent anymore, but I always think this will help me pull up some of the memories I've probably already lost. Time passes, and you don't realize all the thousands of little day-to-day moments that have receded. I worry that they're gone forever. But the memory of the trauma is still there. I just don't focus on it every waking minute, like I did in the first months. I don't think I will ever get over the loss, not entirely, not even if I end up with someone else. And I know I'm never going to get the answer I wanted." Dr. Tremblay knew about Davie's long, futile effort to talk to the man who stopped to help Michael.

"I think if I could have gotten that man to talk to me, then I might know if Michael knew that he saved my life," Davie said now. "Maybe Michael said something before he died . . . for all I know, Michael might have said, 'Get me to the hospital. My wife is there. I have to get to her.' And that might have just indicated that he expected me to be there; he might still not have known *for sure*. But I would at least have more to go on . . . and letting go of that effort is so difficult. You have no idea how much I wanted to talk to that man. So, no, I don't think I will ever get over the loss. And I will never know everything that happened that night. I never had another allergic reaction, and I'll never know what caused that one. So how can I get over this, *really* get over it, with so many unanswered questions?"

"You don't have to get over it," Dr. Tremblay said. She never failed to surprise Davie, because she never offered standard platitudes. "We talk a lot about getting over loss, about moving on, and achieving closure and healing in this culture. We talk far less about how to hold onto what we've lost."

"Maybe because people think holding on shows a lack of recovery," Davie said.

The therapist emphatically shook her head.

"No, holding on is not a lack of recovery. Holding onto memories and thoughts honors the life of the person who has died. The things you think you have lost? They are still there for you. They will come to you when you need them. You *have* significantly healed from the part of the trauma that you knew was doing you harm. You could not have sustained that level of trauma without doing terrible damage to your mind and your body. You realized that, and that's why you kept trying to get help. But the memories of your husband, the parts of him that you carry every day, the love you still feel for him—that's a healthy path to healing. Even the memories you think you have lost—they are there, and you will carry them with you forever."

"Well, I will try to remember that," Davie said. "I still feel like . . . it's always been difficult to describe . . . maybe Andrea said it best. I feel like I learned the secret of life because of Michael's death . . . you know, I feel like I live differently now, see the world differently now, from people who have never been through this. Although God knows that I would have sold my soul to have not had this happen to Michael and me. But it happened, and I can't go back to the way I was. I've learned something that most people just chase after, but my God, at a cost no one would want to pay.

"Andrea described it as realizing that joy comes in fleeting moments, and she said the trick was in learning to recognize those moments," Davie continued. "She was talking about how she got through her cancer, but she was directing that at me when she said it, not just talking about herself. I know what she meant. And if she could find joy in that last year and a half of her life, knowing that she was on very shaky ground with the cancer— she knew that before I did, I realize now—then anyone should be able to find joy in their life. I remember my wedding day, of course, but if you asked me on the count of three to name a special moment with Michael, I'd have a very long list, and none of those memories would be around my wedding or any other notable event. They are just little snapshots of what it was like to be married to him."

Dr. Tremblay listened, nodding, and she had a little smile now, as though she was thinking, *Go on, keep going . . . you've got this . . .*

"So now that I have all this wisdom, courtesy of my husband, I guess the assignment, such as it is, is to figure out how to use it in the best way possible," Davie said. "For myself, but maybe also in ways I have not even yet imagined, for someone else. Maybe for quite a few someone else-es."

"I think you will do that," the therapist said.

Davie looked at her watch. It was almost time to go.

"You know, I think you saved my life," she said to Dr. Tremblay.

Dr. Tremblay shook her head, still smiling.

"Your husband saved your life," she said. "All I did was listen while you figured out how to accept that gift and validate it by not just staying alive, but by really living."

chapter 17

A series of bad storms that winter, coupled with a busy period in Ethan's work, made it impossible for Ethan to get to Albany. He was in regular, almost daily contact with Davie, but she hadn't seen him since his trip to rescue her from the trail in the ice storm. He planned to come back to Albany in the spring to help her with some of the final projects he wanted to do in the house.

When he first suggested helping her, Davie saw it as a sign that he cared for her in a way that would allow their feelings to grow, and she thought this extremely unusual way of spending time together would draw them closer. She often served as his assistant during his work on her house, handing him tools, holding something in place as he drove in a nail, and always watching how meticulously he did everything. She was amazed at his level of concentration and his knowledge of the nineteenth century craftsmanship of the original construction. He talked about wood as though it was a precious metal that he could melt and then forge. She loved watching him fit a section of precisely cut lumber into place, so totally absorbed in his task that she often thought he forgot she was there. Among the projects he finished for her was a set of wall shelves he placed in an alcove in the SOC room, held up by wooden wall pegs he whittled. On top of everything else, he had given tremendously of his skill and his time. In her more irreverent moments, Davie wondered what the bill would have been for all this work, had he shown up one day and handed her an invoice the way he told Andrea, so long ago, what the shuttle fee would be for the October Mountain trip.

Sitting in the SOC room on an afternoon in late April, having just finished talking to Ethan about his plan to resume the work on her house in a week or two, Davie thought through the chronology of her relationship with him. Was she too impatient, she wondered?

She had met Ethan Memorial Day weekend the year after Michael died, the day she and Andrea started their overnight practice hike to the October Mountain Shelter. Ethan shuttled her when she did her solo hike over Mount Greylock that September, to mark the first anniversary of Michael's death. The dinner in Williamstown with Ethan was a few weeks later. Ethan had been a steady part of her life for a year after that dinner date, when Davie went on the nearly disastrous Columbus Day weekend hike in northern Connecticut. So that was last fall, she thought as she sat on the SOC, her phone still in her hand, and now it was April. Ethan had been part of her life for eighteen months, and although she knew him a great deal better now, the emotional and physical levels of their relationship remained unchanged. They had a friendship, Davie knew, and friendship often evolved into romance, but Ethan gave no indication that he wanted that to happen. Davie wanted that to happen; Ethan never seemed to consider it.

Davie also wondered about the inevitable conclusion of the work on the house; eventually, Ethan would have no more steps to repair or windows and railings to replace. The house projects were an easy way for them to see each other, but the effort never went beyond the carefully defined routine that started a year ago, as Davie knew full well. Ethan came out a couple times a month to work on the house. They almost always went out for dinner, he always picked up the check—and quelled her protests by reminding her that he earned about four times her salary—then they would come back and sit up and talk. Their conversations, as always, touched on many different topics: their respective careers, backpacking, his vast knowledge of birds—although her own knowledge was rapidly catching up with his because of her job—places they had traveled to and seen, childhood experiences . . . it was a level of conversation that made Davie feel she knew him very intimately, at least in that regard.

In addition to the weekends he had come to her house the previous summer, he shuttled her through Connecticut on her section hike—another huge effort, one that saved Davie a lot of money. She was about to resume her hike of the Appalachian Trail through Massachusetts from where she left off with the ice storm. The summer routine with Ethan would be the same this year, she thought, alternating between his work on the house and his shuttling her along the trail.

In all that time, there was the unspoken assumption that Ethan would always sleep separately from her on his weekends in Albany. There was never even a hint that there would ever be a repeat of the sweet, spontaneous time in his car the very first time he shuttled her, when they kissed as though nothing else mattered, as though they each were quenching the other's thirst. Davie likened that memory to one she had of filling her water bottle in a remote stream on the Shenandoah hike with Andrea, and then just chugging down half a liter because it tasted so good, and she so badly needed the drink, even though she knew she would have to refill the bottle as soon as she finished.

Since then, their physical contact remained nothing more than hugging and the quick, friendly kiss Ethan always gave her when he arrived and left. Ethan seemed perfectly fine with this, and Davie knew she was not sending him any signals she thought kept them stuck in one place—although she doubted that Ethan thought they were stuck. Davie realized a long time ago that he was not at this point being careful because of her widowed status. Rather, he did not think of her as a girlfriend, and if, for example, she were to email him to suggest that they plan a weekend away somewhere, he most likely would not respond. He would be back in Albany in a week as though she had never deviated from the set pattern and expectations. They had been on this plateau for a long time.

Davie still wore her wedding ring, and she wondered what Ethan's reaction would be if she removed it. Probably no reaction at all, she realized. If she'd thought that gesture would send Ethan a signal, she would have taken off her ring months ago. Certainly, she would have removed it at any indication that he felt desire for her, the way he did just once, and never again. Now, she doubted that he would even notice if she stopped wearing her ring.

Davie understood that this situation could not continue, not if one of them felt pure, uncomplicated friendship, and the other wanted that to change. What she didn't know was how to open the discussion. She knew how much she depended on Ethan. She was in love with him, but she also knew that around her love for him, he filled a huge empty spot in her life that was unrelated to romance. She also knew that if she needed help, if she was ever in a jam, he would drop what he was doing and he would be there for her, as he had already amply demonstrated. Davie did not take that part of Ethan's character lightly. She was painfully aware that such people in her life were in short supply, if not nonexistent. The prospect of losing Ethan's companionship, coupled with a genuine fear of finding herself completely alone, made her evaluate the situation carefully. She felt like she was running numbers in her head, doing a data analysis of her feelings, and every time she did this, she came up short no matter which way she went.

She was fairly certain that bringing this topic out into the open might mean the end of their indecipherable relationship of now a year and a half. A year and a half that included the terminal illness and death of her dearest friend, Davie reminded herself, thinking, not for the first time in her widowhood, that anyone who thought life would ever, just for once, remain static for even a year needed a reality check. There was nothing funny about this situation, but she had absorbed just enough of Michael's dark sense of humor to also think, well, if she ever did open up this topic with Ethan, at least she would be doing so after he installed the beautiful maple wall shelves in the SOC room. She hoped he would not take them with him on his way out the door.

On the first warm weekend in May, Ethan arrived with the intention of rebuilding the steps from the back porch into her garden. He had taken measurements the previous year, had cut the boards and risers, and thought that if he got up early on Sunday, he could finish the project in one weekend. He was removing one of the wood railings when Davie went upstairs to get him a glass of ice water. He was just about to start removing the second railing when she handed him the glass and said, "Ethan, what are we doing?"

Their hands met around the glass and he stopped and looked at her. Then he took the glass from her and drank most of it down right away. Davie sat down and waited for him to say something. He could not ignore her question, she thought. Ethan set the glass on the bottom step and climbed up the next three steps to sit down beside her on the little landing outside of the door to the porch. Davie turned to look at him and she could tell from just his profile that he wore a carefully controlled, tightly set but completely neutral expression on his face. He seemed to be considering a response, gathering his words.

Davie thought, in the stretching silence, that she must have come a long way in getting past her fear of what the neighbors would think. This might not be a discussion in front of her house in full public view, but the family two houses over with three little boys and the dog was in their backyard, and the six-year-old yelled across two fences, "Hi Davie and Davie's friend!" That was how the kids knew Ethan, as "Davie's friend." She saw the mother sweep an appraising glance at the steps where Davie and Ethan sat—the kind of look by which one woman sends another woman a beam of empathy without saying a word—and then Davie saw her draw her little boy out of sight and heard her say, "I think Davie and her friend are busy right now, honey."

"Ethan, you must have realized that this discussion would eventually happen," Davie said, when the silence continued.

"Well, I see us as very good friends," he replied. "You are very important to me, and you are a good friend. How do you see us?"

"Ethan, for a long time, I didn't want to upset my very carefully balanced recovery, and so—also for a very long time—what we were doing was just right for me."

"And it's not just right any longer?"

"Not anymore," Davie said. Another long silence followed. It was very difficult to gauge his reaction, but if she were to guess, he was not surprised that they were having this discussion but somewhat surprised it took this long to happen.

"You know, I didn't expect to feel this way," Davie said. "I thought you were interesting, and extremely nice, and very good to be around, but I was such a wreck when we first met, the last thing I was thinking about was falling in love with you. Andrea told me to just have some fun with you if I could. I think she genuinely thought it was good for me to have you in my life, and that I should just enjoy myself. She said you were a very good person and she thought it was good for me that you and I were in contact."

"She said that?"

"Yes. Why are you so surprised?"

"Oh, my God..." Ethan still wasn't looking at her. "If that's really what Andrea said about me, then I'm very grateful. We had a bad breakup, and I hurt her very badly."

OK, now I'm starting to get this, Davie thought. Andrea concealed that well.

"Ethan, Andrea told me you and she had a brief fling after her marriage broke up, and that it didn't last any time at all. I certainly would never have known about it unless she mentioned it. She knew I cared about you, and I believe she was genuinely happy for me about that. She said you were both in pretty bad shape from your divorces, that it didn't last very long between you two, and that you parted friends."

"Well, again, that was extremely good of her," Ethan said. He didn't express any surprise that Davie knew about his divorce, so she wondered if he had been waiting for her to mention it. "She had the 'pretty bad shape' part correct. But she didn't tell you a very accurate narrative about the rest.

She was really in love with me, in a way that she told me she never was with her husband. You never knew him, did you?"

"I met him once or twice, but I never really got to know him," Davie said.

"He was a difficult person, just very stern, very demanding," Ethan said.

"Were you in love with her?" Davie asked.

"I thought I was, but I had been living alone for a long time by then, and my own divorce left me very cautious," he said. "I wasn't sure of what I wanted. If we didn't exactly part friends, we were at least able to salvage a friendship out of the love affair with the passage of time. It was a long time ago."

Listening to this, Davie thought, everyone faced heartbreak eventually, but hers was a special form of devastation. Maybe precisely because of what she endured, she was more inclined to give this situation everything she could. Her standard for what constituted heartbreak was a little different from that of the average person.

"OK, so because you have had two bad experiences, you are determined to never let that happen again, is what you are telling me?" she asked. Davie thought it was better to not raise the time in his car when he dropped her off for her hike to the Kay Wood Shelter. There was no accounting for human impulses, and it was clear that he checked himself after that and determined that such an episode would not happen again. He possessed more self-control than most people; she realized that about him a long time ago, and she also felt now, listening to him, that nothing would change his mind about letting love back into his life.

"I am offering you friendship," Ethan said, slowly, patiently, but with a faint tone of exasperation. "I thought that was enough. I thought you understood this. I thought you wanted my friendship, and that you were happy with the way I was in your life."

"I have been happy, but my feelings changed," Davie said. "I got better, and then I felt ready for more than you seem capable of giving me." Ouch, she thought . . . she did not want to make him feel like he lacked something in his life or personality.

"Well, you are wrong about that," Ethan said, and he did sound hurt and a bit defensive. "It's not what I'm capable of giving you; it is a matter of what I want with you."

Davie remembered the day she stood at Irina's office door at LGC— the day she was fired. She felt then and she felt now that no matter what she said or did, irrevocable damage had already occurred, there was no going back, and she might as well speak her mind.

"Ethan, there's an enormous disparity, or inequality, in our situation," she said. "You have been affectionate and even passionate with me, on at least one occasion, and you express physical affection to me entirely on your terms. You hug me, you kiss me, but I know it will never go beyond that, because you will not allow it to. I was married to someone who expressed how he felt about me, physically and emotionally. I know what's missing here. You have been spending weekends at my home for a year, and I know, without you having to tell me, that if I were to ever extend that same attention or behavior toward you, that you have done with me—when you wanted to—you would shut me down in no time. I can't continue this. I've known this for a while now, but all the impediments that kept me from ever having this discussion with you . . . well, all I can say is that I want us to change, or I want this to end."

And that was, indeed, how everything ended: the conversation, their relationship and the work on the back steps. Davie told Ethan she would wait for him out front. Ethan replaced the detached railing for the stairs, securing it so that it could be safely used until it was repaired. He packed up his tools and carried them through the lower floor of the house out to his truck while Davie remained outside on the front stoop—the front stoop Ethan rebuilt the previous summer. Reminders of Ethan and their unusual, constrained relationship would be everywhere she turned in the house, Davie realized as she waited for him. She didn't have a single photo of them together, or a photo of Ethan alone, but he was leaving her with more than enough bittersweet souvenirs of how everything just fell apart.

Ethan neatly stacked the new stair treads and risers for the unfinished back steps in the guest room that led to the garden. When he finished packing his truck, he came over to the stoop where Davie sat.

"I am sorry about this," he said. He looked very upset; he looked like he had just had a rug pulled out from under him. He looked the way Davie felt when she realized she needed to get off the trail in the ice storm—as if one little misstep would send her flying on the hazardous footing.

"So am I," Davie said. But she couldn't tell him she had changed her mind, and she noticed he didn't ask her to change her mind. She knew as surely as she was sitting there that they were at an impasse and the impasse was longstanding and unfixable. Neither of them was at fault; they just could not find a way to feel differently, and she didn't want to have this conversation with him again. She did not want to make him feel this was his problem to fix, plus, she felt better prepared to handle loss and isolation than she suspected he might be. For that, she felt tremendous compassion and tenderness toward him. But, as Davie reminded herself, he suffered a nasty divorce, not a death. He didn't know how it felt to stand in a hospital ER and hold the hand of someone he loved, realizing that person was already dead, that their skin was already cool and hardening. She might be the tougher of the two of them.

Davie stood up, and without asking Ethan's permission by a look or a pause, she put her arms around him, and he immediately wrapped his arms around her. Davie remembered standing in front of her house the day Andrea died, and feeling Ethan holding her like this. She remembered him holding her like this the morning he hiked up to her on that almost impassable trail. He always made her feel good this way. But she also knew that this was as far as it would ever go with him.

"Please take care of yourself," she said. "Thank you for all that you have done for me."

Ethan nodded and walked around to the driver's side door of his truck, got in, turned on the engine and pulled out without another word or glance in her direction.

In the weeks that followed, Davie thought about Ethan a great deal. Every day, in fact. His departure left a sinkhole in her life, an image that Davie considered very apt, as a large sinkhole once opened up in her backyard when twenty feet of dirt over an air pocket formed by the disintegration of a long-forgotten nineteenth century wooden septic tank finally gave way. The column of impacted soil collapsed into the hole at the bottom in a heavy rain, one of a myriad of expensive mishaps with her old house that occurred at regular intervals. What Davie remembered best about the sinkhole was that it started out small, about the size of a large round tray, and how it rapidly expanded. The edges seemed to keep collapsing over and again for forty-eight hours, until the sinkhole's surface was the diameter of a dining room table that could have seated fifteen people. This happened as Davie frantically called contractors until she found someone willing to come over and tell her what was going on out there. The analogy matched her mood now, about Ethan. She needed to be careful, she thought, not to let Ethan's absence crumble around the edges so that it started expanding until it overwhelmed the rest of her life.

She remembered her very early feeling after Michael died, the feeling that one horrible event begat others, until everything started to slide downhill. She could not afford to let that happen now, even though her parting with Ethan was every bit as difficult as she suspected it would be. Even so, she felt no desire to contact him, ask if they could talk things over and try to resolve their differences. She did not think that was possible. If she tried again, all she would end up doing would be to settle for less than she thought she deserved. She could not change how Ethan felt, or, rather, how he did not feel. But she also could not help thinking of all the people lost to her in less than three years, starting with Michael, and then Andrea, and all the attendant friends who cut her off, or she had cut off, or who faded away as part of the collateral damage of traumatic widowhood.

She didn't feel the need to contact Dr. Tremblay; she didn't need expert advice to navigate the breakup. She knew by now that unless someone had died or gotten seriously injured, she would find a way to handle it, and in fact, she had handled the past thirty-three months after the deaths of two irreplaceable people in her life. But Ethan's departure from her life was extremely difficult.

Davie thought about her courtship with Michael. She was impressed from the get-go that no one in his immediate family was divorced, and that from the way he described his siblings, they were actually happy with their spouses, not just putting in time. Davie thought then, years ago and without any certainty of a scientific basis for her hunch, that the collective one hundred marital years of Michael's four older siblings suggested something positive and affirming about Michael's DNA. The Devlins married for life, and Davie thought that boded well for her prospects if she married Michael.

Nor did she and Michael experience a pattern of breaking up and getting back together during their dating and courtship. Davie always considered that a serious warning sign for a couple. She could cite examples aplenty of friends over the years who went ahead and married the boyfriend with whom they had serial breakups and reconciliations during their dating and courtship. Inevitably, that led to the final and vastly more destructive, expensive split of a divorce. And those incidents involved people who really thought they were in love with each other, who wanted to try to make things work. Ethan seemed very certain he was not in love with her, that he never would be. Every time Davie got back to that realization, she knew what would happen if she contacted Ethan and tried to change a situation that she did not think could be changed.

On top of everything else that Ethan's absence from her life meant to her, Davie now had to find a new shuttle driver.

She wanted to go back to the place where she left the trail in the ice storm and she wanted to resume her hike north through Massachusetts from that point. She worked out a plan that would let her finish the approximately ninety miles of Massachusetts by Labor Day weekend. On the morning she calculated her hiking trips for the summer, she stopped and looked back at the calendar. Labor Day weekend. Well, the third anniversary of Michael's death would fall on a Sunday this year, and she would of course have the following day off because of Labor Day. She hadn't really planned to wrap up Massachusetts that weekend, so she thought maybe she would see how her hiking went, and not focus too much on how and when she finished Michael's home state. She knew all too well now how plans got nudged off the trail in backpacking as in life, but she was also leery of getting caught again in an early storm. Northern Massachusetts was a much higher elevation and more rugged terrain than northern Connecticut.

However, Davie couldn't resist planning. She figured that if she did two trips each month from June through August, she would be able to hike over Mount Greylock on Labor Day weekend, and that maybe there would be something special about that this year. The previous year, she was so caught up in Ethan's weekends at her house, her sections through Connecticut, her sorrow and grief over Andrea's death just a few months earlier, that she never thought about doing anything on the anniversary of Michael's death. She didn't know if this would be a pattern for the anniversary every year for the rest of her life, that she would want to do something special to mark that date in some personal way, but she did this year.

She resumed her hike through Massachusetts in early June, on a weekend that happened to coincide with her wedding anniversary. She hiked back up the side trail that Ethan used to get to her, and she picked up where she left off in October. She found not just one shuttle driver to fill in for Ethan; she found a slew of them, all through the listings maintained by the Appalachian Mountain Club's Berkshire Chapter. She soon learned what Ethan spared her by shuttling her the previous summer; he knew all about the quirky world of backpacking shuttle drivers. The ones Davie used now were all good people, but they were also extremely memorable individuals—characters—every one of them. Davie supposed that Ethan fell into that category as well, but he was her memorable character, so she never minded his eccentricities.

Now, as she quickly discovered, she never knew what she would find when she climbed into her shuttle driver's car, because she ended up using different shuttle drivers for each section. Once, she shoved her pack into the back seat of a driver's small Honda because he told her the trunk was filled with thirty-pound sacks of dry dog food and there was no room there. She saw why he needed so much dog food when she followed her backpack into the car; his two malamutes were in the back seat. They were very friendly dogs, but Davie could hardly fit her pack first and then herself next to their combined heavily panting bulk, and she was reluctant to try to shove the nearest dog farther away from her. Her pack was covered with dog hair when she got to her trail head.

Another driver stowed several cases of homemade apple liquor on the floor behind the small back seat of his vintage pickup truck, which Davie discovered when she pushed the passenger seat forward to put her pack in that space. Hooch, the driver called it. He never explained what he was doing with it, but it seemed he had fit in her shuttle as part of his regular hooch delivery route, like a milkman on his morning run. Davie was sure he must be supplying every family in the Berkshires with the stuff, and she also suspected it was not legal, but she figured her chances of being charged as an accomplice moonshine runner were very slim. She never saw a local cop car in her ramblings around the Berkshires. When she got out of the truck at the trail head, the driver offered to fill one of her water bottles with hooch. Davie thought a couple of swallows would probably knock her out of commission for the day, but she still carried the extra water bottle Ethan gave her, so she let the man pour about a cupful of hooch into that. And then, because she was very curious, she sampled it before he drove off, and signaled her enthusiasm with a raised thumb because she didn't want to ruin the sensation of the mellow, liquid-amber apple liquor expanding in her mouth. She had prepared herself for apple-scented lighter fluid, but in the bottle the hooch looked like the afternoon sunshine of late summer, a faintly cloudy pale yellow, and it smelled the way an orchard in September smells when the fruit has fallen to the ground—earthy and sweet.

Just as Davie started her summer of backpacking, she learned she could go out again with the whip-poor-will group. The full moon in June was Monday, June twentieth. The whip-poor-will group decided to go out Friday the seventeenth, when the moon was, as Davie learned, in a waxing gibbous stage. That meant the moon was about three-quarters full, and the biologists who made the decision apologized for wrecking everyone's Friday night. The consensus was that because the weather forecast was good for Friday, and Monday might be cloudy and rainy, it was best to go out on a clear night. They caught two males and a female in May on two nights of setting out the nets, banded all three birds and attached tracking devices to them. Everyone was in high spirits about their success. Davie didn't go on either of those trips; she hadn't been in a good mood because those trips fell just after Ethan and she parted ways. Now, she hoped the group's luck would hold.

They went back to the same large, gently sloping meadow sparsely dotted with trees of the first two times Davie joined the group. Davie counted back while walking up the road from the cars with her colleagues, and thought with astonishment that yes, it was two years ago that she first went out with the whip-poor-will group. Two years ago, Michael had already been dead nine months, Andrea had finished her cancer treatment, and she had just met Ethan. She and Andrea were getting ready to go to Shenandoah National Park.

They heard whip-poor-wills singing almost as soon as they started to set up the nets. Two, three . . . then a fourth. The biologists knew they were different birds; the songs came from different areas of the meadow, with such brief interludes between the ending of one song and the start of another that the birds could not have flown such a distance so quickly.

A whip-poor-will flew into one of the nets almost as soon as the biologists stepped back after turning on the recorded call. There was nothing for Davie to do after that except watch. She stood as close as possible without getting in the way as one biologist gently held the bird and another banded it, attached a tiny tracking device to its back and took some measurements.

"Davie, would you like to be the one to let it go?" she heard a biologist say. It was the biologist who chatted with her both previous times—first about the meaning of the bird's song, and then last year about Jay.

"Me?" Davie was surprised. She did not feel qualified to hold this bird.

"You have honorary biologist status now with us, you've come out three times and you're finally seeing a whip-poor-will. You should be the one to let it go," the biologist said.

The others in the group laughed and urged Davie to step forward. She had never held a bird before and she was afraid of hurting it. The whip-poor-will was absolutely still in the biologist's gentle grasp, and Davie wondered what was going through its mind, in whatever way birds processed reactions. She looked at it closely as the biologist explained how to hold it.

The bird looked like a clump of leaves, with a bewhiskered face and a ridiculously wide beak. Then the biologist transferred the whip-poor-will to Davie's hands, saying as she did so, "Don't worry, you won't hurt him, and you have good hands for this—a very light touch." The bird's feathers felt like silk in Davie's hands, and that wasn't even an accurate description; it was just the closest comparison that came to her mind. She had never felt anything as smooth, as though a sheen had been converted to a physical sensation that the nerve endings in her fingers could detect. The biologist told Davie to walk a few steps forward and hold out her arms and gently open her hands. She didn't have to give the bird any momentum; she just needed to open her hands and it would take flight.

As Davie walked forward, the whip-poor-will remained completely still. Davie could not feel it moving at all. If the biologists had not reassured her that it was fine, she would have thought it had died of fright in her hands. Then she held her arms out and opened her hands, just as the biologist told her to do, and the bird came alive—gone in a split second, darting out of sight into the dark.

Davie found the experience thrilling and also deeply moving. With all the problems in the world, and everything that all of these people probably also were dealing with in their lives outside of work, they were trying to change one small aspect of nature, to help this species make a comeback. This mattered to them.

Davie hugged her arms against herself and looked up at the night sky, where the nearly full moon was so bright she could hardly see anything else up there. She thought of the whip-poor-wills in Shenandoah National Park, and how proud Andrea was of her then. Davie was grateful to Andrea for pushing her to go backpacking, because she knew that Davie needed to do something bold and adventurous. And backpacking proved to be a gift, Andrea's great and lasting gift to Davie.

Davie tipped her head way back and turned all the way around, slowly, taking in the moonlit sky, the meadow and the feeling of being very far away from her everyday life, but also very close to Andrea. This was one of those moments of joy, Davie realized, one of those moments Andrea talked about: an experience she would remember for the rest of her life.

Davie continued backpacking through Massachusetts and followed her section-hiking plan. She could get to any place in Massachusetts early enough in the morning to meet a shuttle driver and still do an overnight hike. She plotted her hikes so that she always got to a shelter. Other backpackers were usually at the shelters at this time of year, but on one of her hikes, in July, she went down a long side trail to a shelter that seemed isolated and a little spooky when she finally got there. No one else was at the shelter, and she saw no tents anywhere in the surrounding area. The side trail seemed to go on forever, and she suspected that other backpackers probably stayed at the last shelter she passed almost two miles south and much closer to the trail. She couldn't put her finger on what it was about this place, but she just did not want to stay there. She pulled out her map and studied it. The next campsite was four miles north, and she would never get there before dark.

She folded her map and hiked to the next road crossing, less than a mile north. It had rained hard that morning, and she would have loved to have hung up her rain gear in the shelter to dry, but she now realized she was going to stealth camp. There was supposed to be a stream somewhere beyond the road crossing, but Davie needed water, and she now knew that features along the trail changed with the passage of time. Andrea taught her that when you needed water, you filled your bottles at the first available opportunity.

She ended up filling her bottles from what was really runoff from the rainfall: a narrow trickle of water flowing downhill and pooling along the edge of the road, a trickle running over leaf mulch and sticks and soil, not the rocks and gravel of a true stream bed. The runoff would dry up and disappear by the next morning, but it was still deep enough in a few level spots before it reached the road that she could draw water from it. She pulled out her pump, connected one hose to the top of the filter and dropped the weighted end of the intake hose into the deepest place in the runoff she could find. She needed only a couple of inches of water to be able to draw the runoff up into the hose and through the filter, and she had that much. She still carried three bottles, instead of the two that most backpackers carried, and she filled all three now, including what she called the Ethan bottle.

She smiled at the memory of how she acquired that bottle as she pulled it out of her pack, and she found it pretty funny that she was now pumping water out of a rain ditch, she who used to be mildly disgusted at the thought of drinking water from a nice, clear stream. She had come quite a long way in her approach to backpacking to be doing this, but the water pump she used was so good that the water went into the bottle looking like the water that flowed out of her kitchen tap. She filled the Ethan bottle last, and when she took the cap off, it still had the apple scent of the hooch the shuttle driver poured into it at the beginning of the summer.

The scent and the bottle led her to wonder how Ethan was, and what he was doing. Probably what he usually did, Davie thought: working on furniture commissions, tending his property and living his interesting life all by himself. She never heard from him again, not that she expected to, but she often found herself lost in thought on these hikes about the three people—Michael, Andrea, Ethan—who had been so precious to her, and who all were gone from her life now in less than three years. She was amazed that she still did her hikes; two years ago, this amount of loss and upheaval would have flattened her. She missed Ethan every bit as much as she thought she would, but every time she got to thinking how much she missed him, she also thought that he never would have changed, he never would have told her he was in love with her. It was tough to be without the conversation and the good feeling he always gave her, but there was also a certain peace to living without the frustration, the endless internal conversation about how two people who seemed to do so well together could not feel the same about each other.

Davie put her water pump away, swung on her backpack—which she now did in an almost uninterrupted motion—and crossed the road. The area was so remote, so far off the beaten path that she doubted a car came this way from either direction more than a couple of times a week. Most backpackers did not like to stealth camp near a road where it was easy to spot a tent and could sometimes lead to problems, but Davie didn't worry about that here. She found a nice spot about one hundred yards beyond the road and set up her camp.

The following Monday, she was back at work, sitting down with her research assistant and the summer intern to go over a project. In keeping with the field-ready look of much of the rest of the staff, she still wore hiking pants to work, but with polished ankle boots of varying designs—of which she had quite a collection now—instead of traditional hiking boots. She saved her very well-worn hiking boots for the Appalachian Trail or her occasional forays with the biologists. The joke in the office—where Davie was well liked—was that she was Ralph Lauren's concept of what a field biologist should look like, straight out of an advertisement in Town and Country magazine. She was still getting good mileage out of her designer jackets and blouses from her past life.

Davie didn't mind the teasing; even she realized she projected a distinctive look in this unusual world where she worked, where people were ready to drop what they were doing and head out the door in any conditions if they got a call that one of their GPS-tagged eagles was down and injured, or that one of their radio-collared coyotes, bobcats or fishers was dead on a roadside.

Her colleagues generally knew that she was a backpacker and that she was section-hiking the Appalachian Trail, but at work, Davie was all business. She didn't talk about her weekends very much. Even so, in the middle of explaining to her two staff members on Monday about how they would merge their data with the data coming in from two other states on breeding populations of the American woodcock, her thoughts flicked back to unscrewing the cap off the Ethan water bottle and inhaling the scent of the apple hooch. Once again, she wondered how Ethan was spending his summer.

In another change that summer, Davie started to rebuild her social life. She knew many of the friendships she lost after Michael's death were gone for good, and she actually did not want to restore them. Instead, she sought new connections. She invited the family that lived two doors over, the family with the three little boys, for dinner. She went away for two weekends when she was not backpacking. In mid-July, she went back to Boston to visit a classmate from graduate school, and met two of her sisters-in-law for breakfast the morning she drove back to Albany. In early August, she went into New York City for an alumni function for her graduate program, and stayed for the reception after the panel discussion. That led to dinner that night with a group of classmates she had not seen in years. Not all of them knew about Michael's death, and she told those who asked about him that he died of a heart condition almost three years earlier. The whole story, the story of her life since then, was too complex to tell in that setting, she thought; it was impossible to bring someone up to speed in a crowded restaurant. Her classmates were intrigued by her job, and Davie recounted to rapt attention how she held the whip-poor-will. Most of her classmates still pursued the route Davie used to follow: high-paying careers in private business and investment firms. Her classmates found Davie's work unusual and enthralling.

When she got home from that trip, she looked at her long-ago list of five goals, the list she posted on her refrigerator door when she came home from her first hike over Mount Greylock almost two years earlier. She had kind of forgotten about the list, and it was now covered by repair receipts for her car, a large post card of Longnook Beach she bought at the Cape, and a torn-out page from a magazine that had a paint color she loved. The list read:

> 1: *Honor Michael's life by the way that I live.*
> 2: *Replace the windows on the third floor.*
> 3: *Get the trim on the house painted.*
> 4: *See a whip-poor-will.*
> 5: *Start hiking the Appalachian Trail.*

She crossed off four of the five items. She took almost two years to get this far, not the year she proclaimed in the heading of the list, and the list was still unfinished—she'd have to find someone other than Ethan to paint the trim on the house. But four out of five, Davie thought. Not bad.

In Albany, a woman Davie knew only casually as a neighbor ran into Davie at the takeout counter in the coffee shop on Lark Street and mentioned she was having a small party at her home the following weekend. Would Davie be free to make that? So Davie went to that party on a Saturday afternoon, and although she knew very few people there, she enjoyed herself. The guests gathered in the tiny backyard garden of the woman's home, with little groups of people who all knew each other already there when Davie arrived, and all of them intent on their conversations. Davie never minded sitting on the sidelines and just enjoying the setting, which was what she was doing when the hostess came over to sit with her.

"I haven't seen you around much this summer," Davie's neighbor said.

Davie told her that she was backpacking the Appalachian Trail, a revelation that always led to questions by people who didn't backpack and didn't realize that the Appalachian Trail was a mere forty minutes east of Albany. There was a time not long ago when Davie couldn't have found the Appalachian Trail on one of the AT Conservancy's own maps, where the trail was marked in bright red.

"Wow, that's amazing," the woman said ten minutes later. "It must be wonderful for you, because you look really fit. You know, I saw you out a couple of times last summer with a nice-looking guy. Is he still in the picture?"

Without intending to say anything more complex than, "No, he's history," Davie found herself talking about Ethan to this comparative stranger. Starting with how she and Ethan met the year after Michael's death, she described how much he helped her and how much she had wanted to be with him, to build a new life with him. Even as she talked, she realized, that was what Ethan's time in her life came down to for her: she wanted to be with him, and although she knew there would be huge complications to work through—starting with how they could merge two such disparate lives—she always thought that if they ever felt the same about each other as a starting point, they would have made it work.

"So that's what pulled us apart," she told her neighbor. "I fell in love with him, and he wanted friendship only. If I could have lived with that— settled for less than I wanted—I guess he would still be in my life."

Her neighbor looked at her with great compassion.

"Maybe he was only meant to be in your life for the time that he was. I'm sorry. I know that must have been difficult for you. But you were brave to risk your heart, to simply try. You have a long way to go. It sounds like you are going to have a terrific life, if you keep going the way you are now. I think Michael would be very proud of you. I think that most people don't begin to understand what a loss like that must be like."

That brief conversation stayed with Davie, as she worked out the remainder of her summer's hike through Massachusetts. Davie had risked her heart, after surviving something that she now realized not everyone would have survived. Her neighbor hit the mark on one point: Ethan helped Davie realize that she could love again and imagine a life beyond her loss, and that was a very valuable lesson.

There was more than one way to survive the catastrophic, traumatic death of your husband, Davie thought. You could end up alive, but barely functioning, so diminished by grief and trauma and emotional pain that you technically survived but you never really recovered. Or you could end up with a drinking or drug problem, and Davie now understood far better how that could happen when you so craved escape that you would try anything to stop feeling the mental anguish, even if only for a little while.

Instead, Davie stayed on a sometimes uneven, sometimes impossibly difficult route to where she now stood: alive and gamely still trying to make her life as good as it could be without Michael. She did not just survive, she thought, she really rebuilt her life. She also gained greater insight into the choices people made after a traumatic loss or some other event so terrible that it counted as trauma.

She thought of the people she had known, or known of, since Michael's death who faced their own version of this difficult crossroads. Such people were all around, she now knew; it was just that until such loss happened to you, you rarely realized how often it happened to others. Her doctor, who continued helping people in a healing profession even after her daughter was killed. Her boss's wife, who very possibly made a calculated decision to spare her young children and her husband the agonizing ups and downs of a death by brain cancer. The anonymous woman she learned of through the widows' group, who apparently found a way to continue living after she lost her family in one unspeakable cataclysm at a railroad crossing. Andrea, of course, who almost certainly made that last trip to Sloan Kettering knowing that she would be told that nothing more could be done. She made that effort because she wanted to live, and she wanted to make sure she gave herself every possible chance to do so.

Davie was also beginning to think that luck played as great a role as anything else in determining the direction someone's life took after a traumatic event, and she thought that was very unfair, because luck was such a random quality. But it did seem to her that it was just plain luck that two people in her life cared so very much that she survived, one of whom—Andrea—drew on the strong foundation of their long friendship to help Davie, while the other—Ethan, of course—came into Dave's life in the aftermath.

All of these musings added up to Davie realizing that she would never understand all of the reasons why some people survived, and some did not. All she knew was that she now faced the third anniversary of Michael's death whole, and with the humbling gratitude that she was also a great deal stronger than once would have seemed possible.

chapter 18

Davie decided to not repeat two of the three sections of the Appalachian Trail in Massachusetts she had already hiked. She'd started her very first hike on the Appalachian Trail with Andrea in the Route 20 parking area, where Ethan dropped them off for their hike to the October Mountain Shelter. She didn't think she needed to do that section again. Nor would she repeat the section of her first solo hike after Andrea's death, the April hike of fifteen months earlier. That was the hike where she and Ethan so passionately kissed and held each other when he drove her to the trail head outside of Dalton. Davie was avoiding a repeat of these hikes to save time—both would already count in her eventual tally of the entire AT she would submit to the AT Conservancy to qualify as a section hiker—but she also thought that hiking Mount Greylock a second time, as she planned to do this season, would be all the recollection she needed for one summer. This time, she was going to stay overnight at the lodge on the Greylock summit.

As she studied her map one morning in mid-July during her lunch break at work, she realized she was down to only three more Massachusetts hikes where she would need a shuttle driver, and one little section that she could do as a day hike. She would need a shuttle driver for her final hike of the season, the hike to mark the third anniversary of Michael's death. She was doing the Mount Greylock hike in reverse from what she did for the first anniversary of Michael's death. This time, she would leave her car in Williamstown and get a shuttle to her starting point south of Mount Greylock in the town of Cheshire. Cheshire had been her end point the last time. From Cheshire, she would hike north over the summit and continue to Williamstown. Then, from the ridge where the Appalachian Trail ran above Williamstown, she would come down a two-mile side trail known as the Pine Cobble Trail to the parking place where she could leave her car. The Appalachian Trail continued on toward the Vermont state line, a few miles north. Next summer, she would start her Vermont hike from the Williamstown parking lot at the base of the Pine Cobble Trail.

Davie continued hiking through the rest of July and into August. She used vacation time to extend her weekends on a few of the sections. Her hikes were uneventful and satisfying and she felt strong and accomplished as she finished each one. She loved Massachusetts, where she saw no bears but heard coyotes howling one night, and barred owls and great horned owls calling on several other nights. By mid-August, she finished her next-to-last hike in Massachusetts, and all that remained was the Mount Greylock hike on Labor Day weekend. Long ago, Davie started the practice of never looking at her email or text messages on her phone until she returned home. She enjoyed prolonging the feeling of the hike, and she never used her phone on the trail. She kept it with her for emergencies and carried a charged external battery, but otherwise, she never pulled it out of her pack to check messages.

She opened her email when she got home that night to find a note from Ethan. He wrote the way he spoke, with very sparing use of contractions, a characteristic that always made him seem like someone transported from the eighteenth century—something Davie thought long ago, when she read his very first note to her after their dinner in Williamstown, the note in which he proposed that they start a correspondence.

Now she read: *I learned in an unexpected way about your progress in Massachusetts, and I hope you do not mind this. Please know that I was not deliberately trying to find out any information about you.*

You made arrangements with a shuttle driver to get you from Cheshire to Grange Hall Road this weekend, and you may not know that he briefly thought he would have a conflict. He's a good person and rather than just leave you in the lurch, he contacted me, because he knows me, and he did not know our connection. He said that if I could pick this shuttle up for him, that he would contact the backpacker and ask if it was OK to make this change. I was available to help him, so I of course asked for the name and contact information of the backpacker. And so in this way, I found out how far you had gotten in your Massachusetts quest.

I did not think it fair impose myself on you without your having any choice in the matter, or put you into an awkward situation, so when I realized that this was you, I told your driver that I just remembered that I also had a conflict.

I hope he was either able to help you, or that he found someone else trustworthy and good for you.

However, this was an unusual coincidence, because I have been thinking about you, and I would like to talk to you. I would rather speak with you in person. I have a feeling that you will intend to hike over Mount Greylock on Labor Day weekend, as I know that the anniversary of Michael's death falls during that weekend. If you would feel comfortable letting me see you and letting me tell you what I would like to say, then I would like to know if I could shuttle you on that last hike for you in Massachusetts—on the assumption, of course, that this is your plan.

Please consider this. I will understand if you do not want to see me. I hope you are well.

Davie read this several times, and with a feeling of elation that she tried to quell. She had worked so hard to accept that Ethan was out of her life. She wanted to hear what he had to say; clearly, he had been thinking about their time apart as well. She waited until just before she left for work the next morning to respond, so that she would not sound as overjoyed as she felt at having heard from him.

Ethan, hello—It's good to hear from you. The shuttle driver I had hired for that section did show up, and he must have resolved his conflict, because he never mentioned thinking that he might not have been able to make it, and he never mentioned you as his potential backup person. I hope you are well.

You're right: I do plan to go over Mount Greylock Labor Day weekend, and I would appreciate a shuttle, so I'll accept your offer. I would like to hear what you want to talk to me about. If you can do this, I'd like to meet you in Williamstown at the AT trail head at the base of the Pine Cobble Trail Saturday of that weekend, at 7:30 a.m., if that's not too early for you. I need a shuttle to Cheshire. I can make this a little earlier or a little later, and later is fine, because I am not trying to get to the summit of Greylock until the next afternoon, on Sunday. I've got a reservation at Bascom Lodge for Sunday night. Let me know if this would work for you, and the best time for you to meet me. Thank you.—Davie

He was leaning up against the door of his Volvo when she pulled into the parking area in Williamstown, with his hands in his windbreaker pockets—the morning was cool—and his head tipped up looking at the sky. Davie remembered that this was how she first saw Ethan, standing just like that the morning she and Andrea hiked to the October Mountain Shelter in preparation for their section through Shenandoah National Park. He straightened up and walked over to her car as she got out, and he seemed hesitant to put his arms around her until she closed the door and held her arms out to him and then he wrapped her in a long hug, which felt so good to Davie.

"I need to make sure I have everything. Give me a few minutes," she said.

"May I help you move your pack?" Ethan asked. "And do you have your poles?"

"Oh, my gosh . . . yes, here they are." Davie reached into her car and handed them to Ethan. "I probably would have forgotten them. Please put them in your car before I leave them on the ground. You know, I have only ever forgotten my hiking poles when you were shuttling me, starting with the day I met you. I have no idea why."

She ducked back into her car.

"But yes, thank you, please do put my pack in your car while I finish up here," Davie said over her shoulder as she felt around in the passenger seat. "I'll take any help I can get. I'll be lifting it plenty for the next three days."

She made sure she had the external battery for her phone and that she hadn't left any candy wrappers on the floor, a sure way to lure a bear into breaking into her car. She stood up, locked the car, then zipped the keys into the pocket of her hiking pants. The keys would stay in that pocket through her hike, and she would either be wearing her hiking pants or have them a few inches away in her tent at night. If she became separated from her backpack—and she knew a true story of a bear carrying someone's pack off into the forest—she would at least be able to drive home. Ethan put her pack into the back seat of the Volvo.

"OK, I'm ready," Davie said. It was so good to see him, she thought.

Their conversation on the drive down to Cheshire was one-sided, with Davie talking excitedly about her hikes, about finally seeing a whip-poor-will and how her job was going. She realized she was talking in a gush of trying to catch up for the whole summer, so she asked Ethan how he was, how his work was going, what kinds of commissions he was getting. He responded with sparse detail, deflecting the conversation from himself, as he always did, and asking her more questions about herself. Then he turned into the parking area and shut off the engine. Neither of them spoke and Davie made no move to get out of the car. The last time they sat like this, she thought, Ethan very gently ran his hand down the side of her face so that she would turn to him. She did not think he was about to repeat that loving gesture now.

Ethan looked out the open window of the Volvo, then turned in his seat and looked directly at her.

"I have missed you," he said.

"Well, I've missed you also. This has been a good summer for me in terms of my work and my backpacking, but I have missed our contact and our conversations."

Davie looked down at her hands, as she did in her first sessions with Dr. Tremblay, when looking directly at someone while she opened up such pain had been just way too difficult.

"I've missed you more than I think you realize," she said. "I fell in love with you."

He looked like he was about to flinch but caught himself before the expression opened up on his face.

"You know, I never intended to mislead you," Ethan said. "I made a mistake very early on, I realize, in letting you think this would be a romance. I'm not even sure I knew what I was doing. I found you fascinating, I admired how you were handling an unimaginable loss, I care for you very deeply, and I would like to have you in my life. I would really like that. But I do not believe I can offer you anything but friendship. That is what I wanted to say to you. I just felt that I had to say this in person. You matter to me, I love you as a friend, but I don't ever want to get married again, and I do not want the kind of relationship that would let the question of getting married take over our lives. I don't want to live with you. But I can offer you a friendship that will last for as long as you want it to last."

When Davie didn't respond, he continued.

"If you could just take some time to think this over, Davie, I would be very grateful. I realize this is not what you want to hear me say, but it's the only thing I can say to you, and I do not believe I'm going to feel differently. That may seem selfish, but I just do not think I have in me the ability to love someone the way you need and deserve to be loved, which is the way that your husband loved you. Would you please consider what I have said, and would you consider letting me know if you can accept me as a friend?"

Davie listened to this, and all the effervescence she felt when she first got into his car evaporated.

"Well. You're right. This is not what I expected to hear." She looked at him directly, the kind of look Andrea used to give her when Andrea was about to deliver a blunt assessment of a situation. "I feel fairly foolish right now, because I didn't expect this to be why you wanted to talk to me. So, I hardly know what to say. I mean, Ethan, it's unrealistic. You think you will never fall in love with someone again, but you might. You can't know what's down the road. And how could I possibly ever try to make a life with someone else, if you were in my life in this capacity? Don't you have any idea how frustrating this could be for me? For both of us?"

"I think there is such a thing as trying to look too far down the road," Ethan said. "You are correct: neither of us can know what turns our lives will take. But . . ."

Davie cut him off, which was very unlike her.

"But have you considered how that will make either of us feel, or, more likely, how that would make me feel, if you found someone else?" she asked again. "The kind of relationship you are envisioning here is very, very difficult to pull off. I've been *married*. I know what it's like to have a whole, full life with someone."

Ethan used to be married as well, of course, but she doubted that his brief marriage so long ago had given him the same concept of a full life with a partner, of the kind her marriage to Michael gave her. What an astonishing start to a hike that was supposed to mark the anniversary of Michael's death, Davie thought. She wondered how she would ever clear her head enough to just focus on the next three days. And yet, Ethan had not said anything she didn't already know.

"I have had many guy friends through my life, but none of them were men I had fallen in love with, who ended up as friends because that was all I could get," Davie said, when he did not respond. "Look, Ethan, I can't give you an answer right now. I can't sit here and tell you yes or no."

"Would you at least think this over, and let me know if you think we could try to be back in each other's lives as friends?" he asked. "I loved helping you with your house. I loved our conversations. I just do not seem able to turn this into a love affair, and I don't think I ever will. But if you wanted my friendship, I would want yours. Would you at least think it over, and give me an answer when you have done that?"

"Yes, I will do that. I will give you an answer."

He opened his door, and Davie got out on her side and went around to where Ethan was turning her pack for her, as he always did. She reached in to pick up her hiking poles from the floor behind the front seats and propped them against the car while she put on her backpack. Finally, she'd remembered them. Then she stood up and clipped the pack in place and started to turn to pick up her poles when Ethan put his arms around her.

She suspected that she would never get another kiss from him, and indeed, he just held her. She remembered the wildly unrestrained feeling he demonstrated with her just once, almost eighteen months ago and never again, and she thought that she would rather have nothing from him than the always-careful affection he gave her after that one time.

Even so, it felt so good to be held, and in the few moments of his embrace, she thought of how difficult it would be to find someone else who *cared* so much. What she did not know was whether she could live with caring as a substitute for passion—the kind of passion that transcended aging, and which could take many different forms other than sexual expression as two people moved through their lives. But for passion, you needed one essential ingredient: you needed both people to be in love with each other.

"You will let me know when you're off the trail?" Ethan asked, stepping back and reaching around to hand her the hiking poles.

"Yes, I will," Davie said. She looked up at him, having given her hip belt one final tug. "You know, for the longest time, I thought you were being careful with me, because I was a widow who had been through a trauma that was one for the record books. I honestly thought that. It was only at the beginning of this summer that it finally dawned on brilliant me that maybe that was not the issue. But you never took advantage of me, and I do thank you for that." She smiled at him, although the smile was a bit unsteady. "You could have gotten me into bed any number of times, and it's good that you don't know how many times I wanted to get you into bed. Now, I'm going to get going. You will hear from me, and I will think about everything very carefully. And thank you for getting me here."

She did not say anything that hinted at finality, such as, "Take care of yourself," because she didn't know what she was going to do. She was surprised at how calmly she delivered all of this, because she felt quite capable of delivering some passion of her own right about then, in the form of distraught remarks and tears and bitter disappointment. But she didn't think Ethan deserved that from her. Ethan nodded, and got into the car as she crossed the road. There was no forest here yet; she was cutting through hay fields. She never heard the car start as she kept going without looking back, so she realized Ethan likely was watching her move farther away.

Davie quickly started to climb. She felt strong from her summer of backpacking, and she hiked the four-plus miles with little effort. It was far more difficult to turn off the replay in her mind of her conversation with Ethan. When she reached the side trail to the shelter, she stopped, leaned her hiking poles against a tree, put her face in her hands, and thought, what the hell was she going to do? Ethan offered her a situation she realized might be perfect for two people in their mid-forties who owned valuable property and had established lives and investment accounts. Ethan's request would give her much of what she missed in her life: companionship, the steady presence of a man who really cared for her, a man who already demonstrated that he knew what to do in an emergency and would actually do it. Davie had long thought that the difference between Michael and everyone else she dated before her marriage was that Michael knew the right thing to do—as did many people—but unlike so many other people, Michael actually did the right thing, once he discerned it. In that regard, Ethan was the same.

She continued this train of thought at the shelter, where she was the only hiker. She could remember sleeping in a shelter only once before, that time she set up her tent inside the shelter on the first night of her previous solo hike over Greylock. She decided to sleep in a bunk in the shelter that night, for simplicity. She was very distracted and didn't feel like setting up her tent; she felt like sitting still and thinking. She put her sleeping bag in one of the top bunks, found a small supply of wood stacked against the wall inside the shelter, and started a fire before she fixed her dinner. She had more than enough water to last until the summit of Greylock, only a little more than three miles north. Her thoughts went back to Ethan as she watched the fire.

Davie tended to make long-range projections in her life, as she so often did in her work. She was barely forty-six. She had hardly dated since Michael's death, but she suspected that the dating world was fraught with issues she didn't even know about yet. She knew how years added up, and she wondered: if she accepted Ethan's offer, how would she feel in five years? In ten, if they lasted that long? What implications would this have for many years down the road, if they assumed the responsibilities of a long-term relationship that would never be a marriage? What would they do if one became sick or disabled?

The financial end of this quandary was the least of Davie's concerns. She was not rich in her everyday life now—although she was doing a lot better than a couple of years ago—but she was the sole beneficiary of a sizeable trust fund, the trust fund her parents established for her retirement. She could not access that money until she was sixty-two years old, but she didn't even think Ethan had an inkling of what she would inherit, so she never for a moment thought he saw his connection to her as a financial prospect. If he felt that way, he would have married her. He was very well set himself, that much she knew, and whatever else she thought about Ethan's views on marriage and love, she was certain he was not mercenary.

Davie wondered if Andrea had wrestled with this issue with Ethan, but she strongly suspected she had not; Davie thought Andrea would have mentioned it in one of the few times she talked about Ethan. Also, Andrea's time with Ethan was years earlier. Ethan was at least fifteen years older now, old enough to know far better that friendship and companionship were very precious and difficult to attain.

Davie fell asleep wondering how Michael would have advised her in this situation. She realized it would have been very difficult to explain to anyone but Dr. Tremblay that she longed for advice from her dead husband about a very-much-alive other man, but Davie was not even surprised that she was thinking this way. She held out no mystical hope that she would find an answer to that question. In an odd way, although her conversation with Ethan was dominating a hike that was supposed to have been her special way of marking Michael's anniversary, she was actually glad she'd seen Ethan this morning, at the start of a long weekend, when she would at least not have this on her mind at her job.

She got to the lodge on Mount Greylock a little after noon the next day. The people there were almost entirely tourists or day hikers who just wanted to ramble around and see the views. The bunk room was empty when she dropped her pack on a lower bed before going out to explore the summit in a way that she never did during her previous hike. She sat for a while in the place where she and Michael encountered the young woman whom they realized was likely homeless, and she thought again of Michael's way of seeing the world, seeing the people around him, that almost everyone else never took the time to really notice. How lucky she was, how blessed, that Michael had come into her life.

She spent a long time sitting in the field where she sat the last time, that time when she decided that she did not want to talk to other people. Now, today, she did. She went back to the lodge, took a very long shower—thinking it was impossible to appreciate indoor plumbing more than during a backpacking trip—then put on the only clean shirt in her pack. She went into the dining room for dinner, interested in finding out more about the other people there.

She sat across from a couple a little younger than herself who said they were doing a long section of the Appalachian Trail as a vacation. Also sitting with them was a guy in his early twenties who had stopped his thru-hike of the Appalachian Trail for five weeks to recover from a badly sprained ankle.

Those weeks off the trail cost him miles he could never make up this season. He was back on the AT now, his ankle healed but still sore, and he was hiking slowly and carefully. He knew he would never get to the northern end of the trail at Mount Katahdin in Maine before the rangers closed the access to Katahdin for the winter. Nor could he travel to Katahdin now, do that climb and then hike south from there, out of order, because his ankle would not hold up under those more rugged conditions. He wouldn't qualify as a thru-hiker on this attempt, because he started in Georgia in mid-March. There was no way he could come back in a few months and finish the trail within the required year to meet the thru-hiker definition; it would be impossible to hike the mountains of Maine and New Hampshire in the winter. He was between college and graduate school, and he had enough money to hike farther north, so he planned to continue for about another month and try to get through Vermont before he hit severe weather. Davie admired his equanimity and lack of self-pity. He seemed to still be enjoying his hike.

As the diners went around the table and shared their stories, Davie realized she wanted to tell Michael's story. Her hike over Greylock was really Michael's hike, and the communal dining hall in a place he loved was a better setting in which to talk about him than the auditoriums where she had spoken out of a feeling of obligation to the United Way. So, she told the little group that she was hiking over Mount Greylock to mark the third anniversary of her husband's death. The summit was a special place for them, she said; she carried good memories of being here with her husband, and she was doing the hike in his memory for the second time. She told her rapt listeners how Michael died. Everyone was quiet when she finished, then the wife in the couple asked how she got through the three years.

"I was lucky that I had three people in my life who really cared, and helped me," Davie said. "I had two close friends at home who just stayed the course with me, and I had a grief counselor who was experienced in traumatic loss, who helped me figure out how to pull myself through the worst of it."

"I think we were all very lucky to have met you," the wife said. "I won't forget talking to you. Good luck with this hike, and with everything after this."

Davie filled her water bottles that night; the bottom bunk she'd taken would make it easy to slip out early the next morning. She might have been able to make it back to her car in Williamstown the next day, but she didn't feel like pushing herself. She knew she would be restless and ready to leave

in the morning. She also knew she would get to the next shelter well before
the end of the day, but she had a book on birds in her pack—she hoped
Andrea would have understood her decision to carry the extra weight—and
she thought if she got there early, she would just stretch her legs out to sit
and read with her back against the wall of the shelter. Maybe make a mug
of tea. That sounded good.

Davie came down the northern slope of Mount Greylock and got to
the Wilbur Clearing Shelter at the base of Mount Williams that afternoon.
She had taken a long, meandering route down to the shelter, detouring to
explore a couple of side trails and stopping for an hour for lunch. She was
having a wonderful time. After she set up her tent, she went to the spring
to get water. When she settled down on the rocks along the spring, she
looked up and around before she opened her water pump, as she always
did, as Andrea taught her to do. You never wanted to surprise—or be surprised by—a critter or fellow human also absorbed in getting water. The
feeling that backpacking always gave her, the feeling of having left everyday
urban life behind and having slipped through time to an earlier century,
came over her. This, despite the whining buzz of the pump as she pushed
the top lever in and out to create the vacuum that would draw water up
through the hose, then through the filter, and finally into her three bottles.

This was the shelter where she stayed for the first night of her three-
day southbound hike marking the first anniversary of Michael's death. She
sat on the edge of the shelter as she cooked her dinner and looked at the
forest that dropped away down the side of the mountain. She put her tent
inside the shelter on that anniversary trip, she remembered, and then it
came back to her that this was also where she heard the bear banging on
the chain of the bear box that first night. She remembered feeling afraid
but not panicked, and she remembered that she fell asleep waiting to hear
if the bear approached the shelter—probably because she had been so tired.
That had been a good trip, made all the better, she realized now, because
back then she thought that getting through the first year would set her on
a path to healing. She had just met Ethan, but she had no idea then of the
role he would have in her life. The one-year mark of Michael's death had
been a goal, a finish line with the prize of scoring well on the Good Girl
Grieving Widow Bar Chart of Recovery and telling everyone how well she
was doing.

What a fool she had been early on, what a joke that had been, she
thought, sitting in the late afternoon peace of the completely still forest. Later, she would listen for the whooping cackles of barred owls, but

now, while it was still light, she heard only her thoughts. She wasn't sure she enjoyed listening to herself, but she could not shut down the internal conversation.

Would she have had an easier time if Andrea hadn't died, she wondered? That was a lot to handle, to lose your husband and your best friend less than eighteen months apart. No one could answer that, Davie thought, not even Dr. Tremblay. She found herself thinking that three years ago, Michael had still been alive. They had twenty-four hours to go before they would be in Provincetown, walking on Commercial Street . . . and if they bought something in the market there that day for dinner to cook at the cottage, would Michael still be alive? *Can you please let me see the box? I know you said those weren't latex gloves, but I would like to see the box . . . thank you . . .* Those unanswered—hell, unanswerable—questions had set her on a path that landed her here, three years later almost to the day, forty-six years old and more alone than ever before in her life, but also finally more at peace than at any time since Michael died.

She idly wondered if other backpackers would show up, but didn't really expect to see anyone else. The thru-hikers had mostly been through here at least two months ago, and anyone who was still only a little past the halfway point of the ninety miles of Massachusetts in early September was going to need to push to get through Vermont, New Hampshire and Maine by mid-October, when the Katahdin trails closed. On paper, it was about six hundred miles with about forty days remaining to reach the northern end of the AT. You'd have to hike at least fifteen miles a day, as most thru-hikers aimed to do for minimum daily mileage. The guys in their early twenties considered twenty-five miles a typical day.

So, anyone who had gotten this far and could backpack fifteen miles a day would figure—despite everything they had read and heard to the contrary—that they could just keep marching on till they got to the summit of Katahdin, and fifteen miles a day would fool a thru-hiker into thinking they would wrap up with time to spare. In theory, getting to Katahdin from here by mid-October would seem entirely possible. In reality, as Davie now knew, paper calculations meant nothing in backpacking, even for someone like herself, with a career of plotting projections that made sense of a pile of data. By now, thru-hikers were tired, they'd lost weight and they had the toughest part of the trail ahead of them.

The realization would dawn on some of them around this point in the late summer that if they were going to finish the trail in one year, they'd need to go up to Katahdin soon and hike that out of order, then work their way south through Maine and New Hampshire. Easier said than done: parts of New Hampshire were twenty-foot descents down sheer rock walls at almost ninety degrees, with nothing more than tree roots to hang onto, Andrea told Davie. Parts of Maine were forest so dense you couldn't see more than ten feet on either side, along with some talus slopes Andrea considered too dangerous to be part of the AT. She did them anyway. Massachusetts was nothing by comparison to what lay ahead, Davie knew. She would remember that when she backpacked in the far northern part of the trail, she thought as she prepared to get into her tent. She expected to have the site to herself that night, and she did.

Until she woke up later. She didn't know how long she was asleep. The sky overhead was filled with stars, so clear, each one picked out in such surreal illumination, that she could see them through the ceiling of her tent. It was as if the tent had no ceiling; she had an unobstructed view of the night sky. Instead of being alarmed, instead of pushing the light button on her watch or reaching for her headlamp, she unzipped the tent and crawled out to see what caused this strange sensation, this amazing sight. She stood up, stiffly, and looked up at the sky she had seen through her tent ceiling. It was a late fall sky above a remote place, endless, an arch of hard, impenetrable obsidian black thickly dotted with stars. It was a sky that made you realize the infinity of the universe. This was the sky she had seen the night she stepped out on the porch of the hut on her December hike in New Hampshire with Andrea, almost two years earlier. The tree canopy of the Massachusetts forest was gone; she was on the north slope of Mount Williams in early September, but she was looking at the December night sky of the White Mountains. Somehow, this made perfect sense to Davie.

Michael stood about ten feet from the tent, waiting for her to notice him. He wore his backpack slung over his shoulder, the way she had seen him for the first time. This was not the terrifying first two dreams she remembered from the night before she left the Cape, and anyhow, she knew that this was not a dream. Nor was this moment anything like the frantic twists and turns through the aisles of the grocery store, where she had seen him but never quite seen him all the way. She was never sure if that man was a real person or a hallucination. She still was not sure. No, this was different. She was awake, but the sky was indeed the night sky of her trip with Andrea. Michael was really there; Davie could really see him. He looked at her with an expression of such compassion, such tenderness, such poignancy, that she could feel the tears running down her face. She thought that if she moved closer to him, he would disappear.

She didn't have to move; she could tell what he was saying to her from where she stood.

She heard every word, even though he never spoke. The path she needed to take was in front of her; she could sidestep it or she could start down it. She had come to a place where she had to make a decision. It was as if Michael was telling her that the decision was entirely up to her, that whatever choice she made need only be the choice she thought best for herself.

She could stay as she was, knowing that Ethan would never be in love with her but would offer her a lifetime of friendship—sometimes fraught, often never enough for her, with Ethan often unresponsive, often remote, and then without warning so emotionally responsive that it took her breath away in the gush of gratitude that he always caused in her. Always holding back just enough so that she never took him for granted, always just enough to occupy more of her time and thoughts than he had any right to do, because he never thought about her as much as she thought about him. He cared, he cared deeply, he probably really did love her as a friend, but he was not in love with her, he never would be, and he would always keep her at a distance and remind her that she was a friend. Nothing about her stirred his passion; the disconnect was an inexplicable fact. He would never tell her that seeing her was like seeing the ocean and the sky for the first time.

That would never change with Ethan, Davie realized as these thoughts ran through her mind and Michael still stood there, as though he could hear what she was thinking. Nothing would change with Ethan if she stayed in his life another three years, another five, another fifteen. That was her future if she took one direction at this fork in her mind.

If she did not go back to Ethan at the end of this trip and tell him she would accept what he offered—all he was able to offer, as she saw it; all that he wanted to offer, as he saw it—she might well end up facing the rest of her life alone. She could not let go of Michael in her heart, and that was why she had stayed with Ethan so long. Ethan kept her from living with her enormous loss. She did not think there would be anyone else in her life again like Michael. Michael had been the real deal, and not even Ethan had come close to filling that aching gap. She knew now that Ethan was indeed meant to come into her life, as her neighbor suggested a few weeks ago in that backyard party. Ethan had been set in her life for a reason, and instead of sidestepping him, she had gone toward him. But now she needed to leave him behind her. She was ready.

Suddenly, the memories, the blank spots from the night Michael died came back to Davie in a rush. She was still standing outside of her tent, and Michael was still standing there, looking at her and radiating a sense of peace and calm. There was no sign of the agony she always feared he suffered at the end. She remembered lying on the gurney just before they loaded her into the ambulance. She remembered being so woozy that she couldn't see anything clearly, but she could feel Michael's hand on her shoulder. "Ride with us. Hop in the ambulance," she heard one of the paramedics say to Michael from the other side of the gurney. She saw Michael look up and shake his head, even though at the time she was not alert enough to follow the conversation. No, Michael said, he was going to follow them in his car. He wanted to get his wife back to their cottage later. She never remembered hearing him say that, she was too far gone to remember it, but she heard it now, she knew now that he said those words. The crew chief told her months later what happened, but she heard Michael's exact words now, the way he had spoken them, and the crew chief had never told her exactly what he said.

Then she heard another voice say, "Sir, I need you to step back so we can get her going. Go around to the other side and hop in the back if you're coming with us." She felt Michael's hand grip her shoulder as she started to slip, as sound and the night air and everything just . . . pulled away. Her peripheral vision was closing. "You're going to be OK," Michael said to her. He was right by her side still, but his voice was also pulling away, fading with her vision. "*You're going to be OK!*" That was the last sound she heard. And she let go—it had been so easy to let go—because she thought Michael would be there with her. She should have been terrified, but instead, she just felt calm, and that was how she always knew she nearly died that night. At the end, it was just very soothing, like falling asleep. She didn't even want to stay. She was completely calm. Nothing mattered anymore.

She knew for a long time what had happened. She had known since she had called the fire station after Michael's death, and the fire captain called her back the day her job imploded. But hearing that account back then was one thing; remembering how it had been, that elusive memory she never regained until now—the exchange between Michael and the paramedics, which she heard but never could remember—and then Michael telling her she would be OK, which she did remember—that was very different from being told about that frantic scene. She hadn't told him to ride with them because she couldn't speak and even if she had been able to, she knew he was going to get into the ambulance, she'd heard one of the crew tell him to get into the ambulance, so she didn't have to ask him to go with them. She just never was able to remember that he said he was going to follow them.

Now, standing beneath that sky that looked like lake ice under a full moon, she saw that Michael understood all she had endured, and she also realized that he knew she survived. She just knew at last, with a profound conviction, that he was very sure she survived. That was his last thought, that she was alive, that he saved her life. She had sent him that message without realizing it because their connection was that strong, and so he died knowing she was going to survive. And because of that, he died with a final feeling of peace that overrode the terrible, panicked sensation she thought he endured—the sensation of drowning as his lungs filled with fluid—the imagining of which haunted Davie for three years. She knew this as strongly as though Michael spoke the words to her: his suffering had been over for a long time, and now hers was, too, because finally, she had the answer to that last question. He had known he'd saved her life.

"OK," she whispered. She meant, she was going to be OK, she was giving him back what he had given her, the promise that she would sur-vive . . . and she also meant she understood now, she accepted, that she must stay and finish out her life, however it unfolded.

Then Michael was no longer in front of her. It seemed that he stepped back and just disappeared, the way the bobcat did that day Andrea and she pulled out of the parking lot in New Hampshire. The sky was obscured by the tree canopy, the way it should have been, and she couldn't see the stars now. She was still standing outside of her tent, but now she felt the freezing night air of the high-altitude forest in September. She crawled back into her tent and zipped it closed. She was shivering; she could not warm up fast enough. She pulled on her thin down jacket and pulled up the hood and slid into her sleeping bag and wrapped it around her, and felt herself slowly warming as she fell asleep.

<hr>

You will see him when you are ready.

Davie awoke the next morning in her tent on the anniversary of Michael's death, thinking of Dr. Tremblay's promise. Three years ago, this was the day that turned into the night she never went to sleep, the day followed by a morning of standing on the porch of the cottage and watching the sun rise above the Outer Cape. That day marked the beginning of months of sleep deprivation. On this morning, three years later and in a very different place, the sun was fully up as she recalled the assurance Dr. Tremblay gave her in her last session seven months ago. At the time, Davie interpreted that to mean that she would have a dream about Michael when whatever process in the mind that dealt with dreams determined that she both needed to see her husband that way, and could handle doing so. In the three other dreams about Michael since his death, she had never seen his face.

Whatever happened last night, she had at least seen Michael's face. Davie could not begin to explain the experience. She thought it might possibly be attributed to a hallucination, or an astonishingly vivid dream, but it did not feel like either to her. It felt like Michael had been there for her, and instead of being frightened by the experience, Davie found it very comforting. She also realized she would be unlikely to share this experience with anyone. No one in her circle of acquaintances would understand it. To share it might really make them think she was losing her mind. Dr. Tremblay wouldn't think that; she would just smile at Davie and tell her, *I knew you didn't believe me, and I knew you would find this out on your own.* Davie was very sure that would be the response, so she didn't think she needed to run back to tell Dr. Tremblay that what she predicted had come to pass.

No one could really understand how the human mind worked, Davie thought as she packed her gear. She had known all along that her mind worked to protect her at certain times during her recovery, by allowing her a few times to more or less leave the present and go where she felt safe. She had long known that those episodes of splitting had been just that: a buffer against her anguish. She still could not explain the vision, or hallucination, or quite possibly the living person she had stared at so hard in the grocery store. By comparison, the experience of the previous night seemed a lot clearer to her.

But whatever had happened last night, Davie thought it was a gift. Maybe a psychiatrist would tell her that she thought she really saw her husband, out of bittersweet longing and post-traumatic symptoms made worse by the anniversary she was marking today, and the circumstances of the hike. Davie thought that might well be what someone would tell her, but she thought otherwise. She thought—no, she *knew*—she had seen Michael. She could not explain it to herself, but for once, she did not feel the need to solve the equation. She could not possibly be the only person to have had this kind of experience, and maybe this particular equation would never reveal its answer to anyone who tried to solve it.

❧

Davie hiked the six miles to her car, with a steep two-mile descent down Mount Prospect. She got back to the parking area at the base of the Pine

Cobble Trail in the late afternoon, took out her phone and plugged it into her external battery. No message from Ethan; she did not expect one.

No need to block his number; Davie knew he wouldn't contact her again once he got the answer she promised him, unless she issued a clear invitation that he was welcome to do so. She also knew she would never see him again. He would still be living about an hour and a half away from her, but he might as well be across the Atlantic Ocean, on the other side of that horizon she always loved to look at from Longnook Beach.

The prospect of solitude did not worry her the way it might have two and three years earlier. Ethan showed her that she could love again, and for that, she was grateful. Now the rest of her life lay ahead of her, a long stretch of years she strongly suspected would play out for her in unexpected but solitary ways. She would almost certainly live alone, that much she thought with conviction. She could hear Michael saying, *"You just never know now, do you?"* Yes, Michael, I do, she thought, and you would too, in my situation. You can't be duplicated, and fuck anyone who tries to tell me differently.

No more screwball first dates, no more getting her hopes up, or allowing herself to think that all the patience in the world, all the loving support, all the settling for less than she deserved with Ethan would make a difference. How did she delude herself for so long? The answer was simple, and she had known it even in the midst of the delusion: Ethan allowed her to avoid facing the prospect that Michael really was the one great love of her life, the man who had loved her unconditionally and passionately and forever. Now she was strong enough to accept that.

Michael had given her decades of time to use as she wanted, to spend as she wished. It was a fortune that surpassed the life insurance, the retirement account and the house combined, and it exceeded the memories she recalled when she was so lonely that she wondered how she would get through the rest of her life. The conviction that she would live a very good, rich, long rest of her life had never felt so strong as it did at that moment, as she sat in her car and pondered the decision she had just made. Indeed, as she was starting to realize, she no longer felt guilty about Michael's gift to her.

She held her phone while all of this ran through her mind, then she punched up the screen and hit the text button. To Ethan, she wrote, *I am off the trail and heading home. Thank you for catching my message. The answer to your question is No.*

She re-read what she had written, then she looked out the window and followed the little path out of the parking lot in her mind's eye, up to where it connected with the Pine Cobble Trail she had just descended. The Pine Cobble Trail climbed to the top of the ridge, and there lay the Appalachian Trail. Just a little farther north was the start of the Long Trail, which went end-to-end in Vermont and overlapped the Appalachian Trail for a good part of the way through the state. She imagined following both trails north, until the Appalachian Trail split off and continued to Maine, and the Long Trail headed to Canada. She would follow the Appalachian Trail when she hiked Vermont but she also wanted to hike the Long Trail. Someday, she thought. It would be wonderful, to do that. She thought about going back to the Cape again, maybe in the fall, and rambling around by herself and maybe once again turning down the road she and Michael took that night.

She already knew what she would see. She would see the perfectly ordinary-looking fire station, the sky arching over that far end of the Cape, and then the ocean, where a part of Michael was now part of the sand and the water. She would see the terrible scene in the car and then the one in the hospital flash through her mind—she knew now that those memories would be part of her last thoughts—but she would also see adventures yet to be undertaken, and endless possibilities.

What she would see would be the rest of her life.

She might know sorrow and grief again, but she would also know contentment and peace and joy—joy being the emotion Andrea described to Davie as so elusive, that Andrea had conferred on her as the province of a very special group of people who had survived something awful.

Davie brought the screen back up on her phone, read her message to Ethan again, and added, *Goodbye.* She never said goodbye to Michael that night at the fire station, but now she knew that she needed to write that to Ethan. She hit "send," waited to make sure the message had been delivered, then put her phone away and headed home.